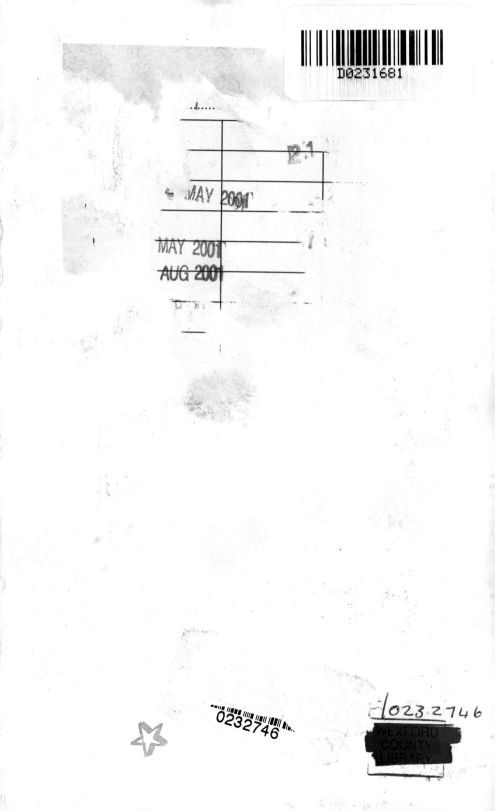

The Mermaid's Feast

Janet Laurence

The Mermaid's Feast

A Darina Lisle Mystery

MACMILLAN

First published 2000 by Macmillan
an imprint of Macmillan Publishers Ltd
25 Eccleston Place, London SW1W 9NF
Basingstoke and Oxford
Associated companies throughout the world
www.macmillan.co.uk

ISBN 0 333 90236 X

1 3 5 7 9 8 6 4 2

A CIP catalogue record for this book is available from
the British Library.

Typeset by SX Composing DTP, Rayleigh, Essex
Printed and bound in Great Britain by
Mackays of Chatham plc, Chatham, Kent

To my lovely niece, Julie,
with much love

Acknowledgements

Many thanks to P&O Cruises and particularly to Captain Chris Sample and Purser Zak Coombs and many of the staff of the *Victoria* for all their help with research for this book during a highly enjoyable cruise that Keith and I took to the Norwegian fjords. Also Alan Pitt, Margaret Murray and Peter Jetterson Smith for help, information and advice. Despite all the help I received, I have to say that the *Empress of India* is not intended to be the *Victoria* nor are any of the personnel or passengers on the *Empress* based on any living person. None of the incidents in this book has occurred on any P&O cruise – or any other come to that – except by coincidence.

Thanks also to The Group: Shelley, Maggie, Wendy, Sarah and Anna, for all their invaluable comments and help during the writing of this book and for their unfailing support whatever happens in life.

Also to my editor, Beverley Cousins, for her patience over the non-arrival of this manuscript at the time it was promised, and the considerable delay afterwards!

Finally, thanks, as always, to my dear husband, Keith, for all his patience, both during the cruise and the writing of this book, and for all his help in the background.

Chapter One

A claw of a hand reached across the table. 'Got any strawberry there, dear?' The hand scrambled around the little pots of jam and honey. 'Only strawberry will do for scones, don't you think?'

Bright eyes twinkled under an arch of pencilled eyebrow. The hair was a tasteful shade of purple arranged into stiff curls. Long earlobes supported massive fake diamond earrings. At least, thought Darina Lisle suddenly, they have to be fake, don't they?

'Sailed on the *Empress of India* before, have you?' The questing fingers found a pot of the desired jam. 'I think they do it deliberately, hide the strawberry ones, I mean. Just to test you. Alfredo!' The hand waved imperiously at a busy waiter. Not too busy, though, to stop him gliding up to the table almost immediately.

'Mrs Carter, madam?'

'Where are you keeping the strawberry ones, eh? You know I like strawberry.'

'You don't have some, madam?' The waiter looked pointedly at the container of jam on her plate.

'Of course I have, Alfredo, but the rest of the table don't. Bring more strawberry.'

A slight inclination of the head, a small smile as two pairs of brown eyes met with perfect understanding. A few minutes later a plate of pots of strawberry jam was placed with gracious ceremony in the centre of the table.

'Alfredo knows what I like,' the woman said complacently. She split her scone and applied generous portions of butter and jam.

'You've cruised on this ship before, then?' suggested William Pigram, Darina's husband, courteously.

'Eighth time.' The scone was vanishing with enormous rapidity, eaten with efficient little bites. 'As soon as George, that was my husband, retired, he said, "Enid, my girl, I've said goodbye to the business rat race, we're off cruising." And we were. Round the world first time, cost a packet it did,' she added.

'On this ship?' William asked.

'No, that was on the *Catriona*, much, much larger. We didn't try the *Empress* until just before George died three years ago. He loved her and I've sailed with her ever since.'

'We love the *Empress*, too,' volunteered a quiet woman sitting beside Enid. 'This is our fourth trip.' She smiled at the man she was with. They appeared to be at least seventy, an insignificant-looking couple, their clothes neat but not stylish.

'We're William and Darina Pigram,' said Darina's husband cheerfully to the five people around the table.

Enid Carter had introduced herself when they'd joined her. Now the insignificant couple confessed they were Mary and Jim French from the Midlands. 'Jim's in windows,' said Mary.

'French windows,' Jim agreed with a beaming smile that banished the impression of insignificance. 'I made that a bit of a slogan but we make any kind of windows.

2

Specialists, we are, for the building trade. Though I'm more or less retired now – the sons have taken over the business.' Leaving him ample leisure time, was the implication.

'Which ships have you cruised on?' Mary asked Darina.

'I'm afraid this is our first,' she said with a smile.

'You're very young,' the other woman said doubtfully. 'The northern ports don't often attract the young ones, they usually go for the Caribbean or Mediterranean. Like the sun, you see.'

'Aren't we going to get the midnight sun on this cruise?' asked William. 'That's what I'm interested in.'

'Depends on the weather,' Jim said jovially. 'But we've a good chance, a good chance.' The couple who'd arrived last at the table said nothing. They looked to be in their late fifties, maybe early sixties. Solidly built, they had the sort of faces that seemed born for cheerful smiles instead of their current gloomy expressions. If Mary and Jim's clothes lacked style, these looked as though they were from a charity shop – the man in a well-worn cardigan over a tieless shirt, the woman wearing a badly made sleeveless top that drew unkind attention to her sagging upper arms.

Darina Lisle told herself not to be catty. There were more important things in life than worrying about the leading edge of fashion. But why on earth had she agonized for so long over her cruise wardrobe? Looking around the room, how many passengers could feature on a fashion page? Where was the glitz and glamour she had imagined? Had her vision of cruising been a throwback to a golden age of luxury and leisure, when small numbers of passengers paying large sums of money were all smartly dressed and socially adept? Reality, as so often, didn't measure up to advance publicity. But anticipation bubbled inside her. Cruising was going to be a completely new experience.

She wanted to ask this couple why they looked so miserable at the start of what should be a fortnight of pleasure. Their weatherbeaten faces reminded her of the Somerset farmers she'd met so often when she was growing up not far from Taunton, and where she and William had lived in the cottage near his first police station a few miles from Frome.

Darina had by now completely forgotten that she'd wanted to explore the ship and that it had been William who'd said he was dying for a cuppa and couldn't they start their tour in the restaurant? A red-coated waiter had seated them at a large table with Enid Carter. The others had come along almost immediately but had not proved socially inclined.

'Why do you like this ship so much?' William asked as the conversation threatened to run aground.

'Oh, the *Empress* is beautiful!' exclaimed Enid. 'All this wood panelling and brass fittings. So traditional. And only seven hundred passengers, it's really cosy.'

'The ones they're building these days are monsters,' sighed Mary French while Jim nodded cheerfully. 'Miles from stem to stern and just so many decks and lounges. You can meet someone first day out and never see them again for the rest of the cruise.'

Darina looked around what she could see of the dining room from their slightly elevated position on a platform beside a line of portholes. Outside was a splendid view of Southampton docks, the ship wasn't due to sail for another hour or so yet. Yes, the ship was beautiful but would she care if she never saw any of these people again? Beside them, she and William, in their thirties, appeared impossibly young. But so often first impressions had to be corrected later. There were bound to be people on board they would enjoy spending some time with. And, after all, it was only for two weeks, and she had William with her.

When Darina had told her husband there was a free cruise on offer, he'd been unexpectedly hard to persuade to come along. Too many people, not his thing and, anyway, there was too much work on, he'd said.

'Who's always wanting to get away and relax and then says he's bored with beach holidays?' asked Darina. 'Who likes variety, visiting lots of places, and loves his food? Come on, you're owed all that holiday and you don't have to talk to people.'

Eventually he'd agreed and so far he'd shown no disinclination to communicate with his fellow passengers. Here they were, together on a luxury liner and for two weeks she could enjoy William's company without any danger of him being called away. Two weeks when he had nothing to do but enjoy himself. Two weeks of not being exhausted at the end of the day and able to talk to his wife without work coming between them. That is, unless the job that Darina had been hired for proved more time-consuming than had been described. She hoped fervently that it wasn't going to occupy too much time. William and she needed this space in their lives.

Enid was studying Mary French with open curiosity. 'Haven't we met before?' she said abruptly. 'Weren't you on the *Empress of China* about three years ago? The Treasures of the Mediterranean cruise?'

5

Mary looked startled. More, she looked nervous. 'I, I think we were,' she said.

Enid looked complacent. 'Thought so. Never forget a face. Wasn't that the cruise there was all that rumour we had a paedophile sailing with us?'

Mary now looked alarmed. 'I don't think so. I don't remember anything like that.' She glanced at her husband. He was drinking his tea and appeared to be oblivious of the conversation.

'It was just after that nasty court case. You remember, when a granddaughter accused her grandfather of interfering with her? Nothing was proved but it was all very upsetting. Then someone said he was sailing with us under a different name. Surely you remember?'

Mary shook her head firmly. 'It must have been another trip,' she said with finality.

'What do you like so much about cruising?' William asked her.

'What do we like about cruising?' Mary repeated. She looked around the table as though someone else could come up with a good answer.

'We came to get away from everything,' the woman who had said nothing so far suddenly declared. 'Isn't that what cruising's about? Being somewhere no one can get at you, being looked after every moment, never having to think? It's an escape.' Her voice shook slightly. Her husband looked even more morose.

She had a broad country accent that Darina thought came from the east Midlands, Cambridge or Norfolk. 'Are you farmers?' she asked gently.

'Yes,' the woman said, then appeared to realize they were the only ones who hadn't introduced themselves.

'Joyce and Michael Harwood,' she said. 'At least,' she added jerkily, looking at her husband, 'we *were* farmers.'

'We've been put out of business,' the man said harshly.

Faced with an intrusion of nasty reality, the table fell silent.

'I'm so sorry,' Darina said sympathetically. 'I know farming is very difficult at the moment. Were you in cattle? Was it BSE?'

At that moment the glass-paned door to the restaurant was flung open by a young man in his early twenties, dressed in jeans and a T-shirt with 'Set my Willie Free' emblazoned across it. Unsteady on his feet even while the ship was still in dock, he grabbed at the little rail at the head of a small flight of stairs leading down on to the main floor of the dining salon and surveyed the array of tables. 'They're still serving,' he sang out over his shoulder, maintaining his hold on the rail. He had a splendid head of black curls, dark eyes and lashes any girl would kill for together with a face that was an odd combination of the macho and the feminine with a strong nose and a mouth that was almost a cupid's bow. He looked very striking as he swung gently on the rail waiting for the rest of his party, silently whistling some tune.

Enid Carter looked at him and harsh reality flew out of the porthole. 'Oh, for my lost youth! To be twenty again and confined on a ship with that young man,' she said lasciviously. 'Shipboard romances – everyone should have one. What a dreamboat!' Her dark eyes flashed with fun.

Mary French looked deliciously scandalized. 'My granddaughter thinks Leonardo DiCaprio is wonderful but, really, are looks everything?' she asked virtuously and patted her dull-looking husband's hand.

The Harwoods said nothing.

William sighed. 'I think he's stoned,' he whispered to Darina.

'You're not on duty now,' she said in a meaningful sotto voce.

Behind the young man came what could only be his father – the same dark curls, the same dark eyes, his face stronger, without the feminine notes, but still very handsome. His mouth, though, was a thin line of disapproval. He caught his son under the armpit, brought his mouth close to his ear and gritted out words that had to be cautionary.

Ever watchful, the head waiter had them both seated at a convenient table before breath could be drawn or the rest of the party descend the short flight of stairs. First came a small, slim woman, middle-aged with a spare face and watchful eyes. Everything about her was contained; her clothes said that here was someone who was careful about everything, from the neat little scarf tied round the neck of her ordinary cream jumper to the well-cut but very basic navy-blue trouser suit. The only striking note about her was her hair. Prematurely silver and cut very short, it wisped around her well-shaped skull in a style both youthful and very becoming. She paused on the stairs and reached back to emphasize something she was saying to the woman behind her, laying a shapely hand on the other woman's arm. There was an easy familiarity about the gesture – *we are friends*, it promised.

Laughing at whatever it was that had been said, the last member of the party was shown at her best. Middle-aged also but polished and confident, she was strikingly attractive. Medium height, her waving blonde hair just above shoulder length framed a sexy face and her good figure was shown off by excellently cut jeans and a jumper in a matching blue embroidered with cream flowers.

The older man got up as they approached the table and held a chair out for the woman with the silver hair. She smiled at him, her face suddenly radiant. The other woman gave a discreet smile to the man and studiously ignored the youth. He slouched sulkily in his seat, head thrown back, one hand playing with a knife on the tablecloth.

'My God,' said Enid Carter in awed tones. 'It's the lottery winner!'

'Really? Which one?' asked Darina, always interested in such nuggets of information about people.

'The grey-haired woman. I read all about her. That's her husband and stepson. She's a scientist and she's going to give the entire seven million pounds to research!' Enid gave a grim chuckle. 'I wonder what her family thinks of that!'

Chapter Two

Phil Burrell, assistant purser and stores manager on the *Empress of India*, flopped into his swivel chair with a sigh of relief. He stretched out his arms and eased his shoulders. Supervising the loading and stowage of the catering supplies for a two-week cruise was the worst part of his job as assistant purser. Still, it was done now and they were out at sea. Already he could feel a slight swell moving the boat. But it wouldn't shift any of the vast amount of supplies he'd spent the day organizing. He gave a great yawn and mentally reviewed all they'd achieved. Below decks, in a series of huge lockers, were enough foodstuffs to keep a small town going through several months of siege. The passengers of the *Empress of India* would manage to consume most of it in two weeks.

It was a frightening prospect. At this stage of each cruise Phil couldn't help playing with visions of well-dressed pigs jostling at designer troughs, siphoning up endless streams of gourmet food with insatiable squeals of delight. Then he'd feel guilty. It had to be tiredness, he always told himself. Passengers were important. One of these days he would be the chief purser of a ship and have to host a table in the restaurant. And the passengers on that table would expect him to be suave, debonaire and charming.

The prospect was daunting. Phil knew he was good at his job. Provided he continued to work hard, and barring accidents, he should achieve his ambition. But social chit-chat was not his forte.

His ex-wife, Lizzie, had said that living with him was like living with a book written in a foreign language. You had to work extremely hard to extract any information and there was no entertainment in the process. Phil had found that rich, considering that her conversational powers wouldn't challenge a four-year-old. But at least, she'd said, she let him know what she was thinking. That she had indeed. Phil had often reeled from the force of her emotions.

They never should have married. Phil supposed it had been an office romance and all the more concentrated for being together on a ship, but all her attractions had vanished once they were locked into a formal relationship. It had been such a relief when the divorce had finally come through.

Was he about to make the same mistake again? No, definitely not! Karen was everything he wanted in a woman, lovely, warm, funny and full of common sense. She made him feel really good about himself. Later, when she'd finished her duties for the evening, he'd go and find her. Perhaps tonight would be the night their relationship would really start to go somewhere.

Eagerness immediately combined with stage fright. What if he'd misread all the signals? If only he could go to her now and find out. Waiting was hell. Biting one finger, Phil brought up FreeCell solitaire on his computer and tried to lose himself in the intricacies of moving the cards around to solve yet another deal of the patience that he strongly believed was the most satisfactory ever conceived. It depended so much on skill rather than the lie of the cards. Almost immediately, though, he could see that he'd made a wrong move. He gnawed again on his knuckle as he contemplated the screen, trying to work out if the game could be salvaged.

The door to his office opened. 'Got a minute?' his assistant, Roger Coutts, asked cheerfully.

'Sixty seconds, yes,' Phil said, waving Roger in and clicking the button that banished Freecell to an icon at the bottom of his screen. 'Any longer than that and I'll need a shot of something. In fact, that's not a bad idea.' He reached into the bottom drawer of his desk, pulled out a bottle of whisky and a couple of glasses. 'Want one?'

'Not half!' Roger flopped into the chair on the other side of the desk. 'I'm gutted!' He ran a hand through his short fair hair. Roger had a broad, open face that was always cheerful but Phil reckoned he was going to have to gain a little polish if he was to get on in his career. Phil poured a couple of stiff ones, added a splash of water and handed a glass over.

'Still, got everything packed away now,' Roger said, swallowing nearly half his drink in one.

'You can spend tomorrow morning on the computer bringing the inventory up to date,' Phil said with a slight smile.

Roger eyed the screen on Phil's desk and nodded gloomily. 'You joining us all for a drink tonight?'

Phil shook his head. 'Get my head down early, I thought,' he prevaricated.

'Oh, yes? That's what you call it, is it?'

Phil flushed slightly. If there was one thing that really got to him about shipboard life it was that everybody always seemed to know everything about everyone.

'Can't hide it, you know,' Roger added unnecessarily. 'But if Sky-high Harry gets to hear about it, you'll be for the drop, you know that?'

The first officer had been given his nickname long before Phil had joined the *Empress of India* from her sister ship the *Empress of China*. He'd never been able to find out where it came from but thought it just about summed up Harry Summers. Far too eager for the big time, he was.

Phil grunted something into his drink. Then decided he had nothing to hide. 'I might see if Karen is free a little later,' he admitted.

Roger gave him a big grin. 'That's the stuff,' he said encouragingly. 'Faint heart never won, and all that. Don't tag you with a faint heart, though, not after last trip.'

Phil topped up their glasses and said nothing. He had no wish to go over that little incident again. He'd suffered enough over the repercussions and there was no way he was going to get involved in a replay.

Roger raised his glass in acknowledgement. It suggested as much that he had done with teasing as thanks for the drink. More whisky disappeared down his capacious throat, then he reached behind the computer. 'Thought you'd be interested in this. My sister sent it, saved it for me specially.' He drew out a six-week-old copy of a tabloid newspaper. 'Mean old so and so, she is. Could have sent it out to one of our ports but she prefers to save on the postage. I just had time for a quick shufti after we got in this morning.' He folded the paper open to an inner page and handed it to Phil.

LOTTERY WINNER CHOOSES CRUISING, announced the headline.

Phil ran his eye down the story and whistled. 'So we've got a celebrity on board with us, have we? Don't envy them the hangers-on that will try and freewheel champagne once they realize they've got a millionaire amongst them.'

'Sounds as though any hangers-on will get pretty short shrift,' Roger said idly. He finished off his drink. 'Well, I'm off for a spot of relaxation before beddy-byes. Thanks for the grog.' He disappeared out of the door.

Phil hardly heard him go. His attention was riveted on the newspaper. He forgot entirely about turning off his computer as everything clicked into place and he realized just who the lottery winner was. Dismay flooded through him as he was engulfed by memories.

He sat and stared at the article. Had the past really caught up with him?

Chapter Three

William leant over the railing on one of the upper decks of the *Empress of India*. Wet air blew across his face and a long swell gave a slow, slight rolling motion to the ship. The engines throbbed deep within her. He watched the Isle of Wight disappear astern and felt something like contentment. For the next fourteen days he could forget about all the difficulties of life ashore, the tensions and rivalries amongst his staff, the difficulties of attempting to maintain law and order, and the evils man could do to man. For the next fourteen days nothing need disturb him and he had his wife all to himself. Along with seven hundred other passengers, that was.

On the horizon a large container ship steamed gently in another direction.

Is there any red port left? William muttered to himself. Red port left, green starboard right.

This seafaring wisdom had been taught him by his father. An army officer, William's father had not been a great sailing man. But the Pigram family had once spent a holiday sharing a house on the Isle of Wight with some friends, and dinghies had formed a major part of the activities. William had loved it. He'd hoped that they'd go there again but his father's next posting had been to Germany and his mother for some reason hadn't wanted to keep up the friendship with the sailing family.

Looking back now, William remembered a remark he'd overheard her make to his father. 'Andy Wright will never make partnership, not enough go. Not that a partnership in that piddling little country solicitor's would be anything much. Are none of your old school-friends making a mark in the world, John?'

William couldn't remember what his father had answered, if anything. John Pigram had been very good at ignoring what he didn't want to hear from his wife. He'd also been very good at not hearing what his children said. Very different from Darina's father; according to her, Dr Lisle had always had time to talk with his daughter. Oh, fatherhood! William both longed for the experience and feared he would be found want-ing. How good was he going to be at recognizing the needs of a child?

But that wasn't something he was going to have to grapple with in the near future. During countless dis-cussions on the subject, Darina had made it plain she wanted time to establish herself in her career first. He hoped she'd either get where she wanted soon or give up. Leaning on the rail now, watching the hypnotic way the sea surged around the ship, its glassy surface seeming to restrain a strength that was gathering its forces, William thought about careers. The demands of his own meant he was seldom home at a time when he could enjoy bathing babies or reading night-time stories. Even weekends could never be guaranteed free of sudden intrusions. But at least his work was important, necessary.

The ship rolled slightly, the power beneath that glassy surface seemed to be making itself felt.

Of course, William told himself, he wanted to see Darina achieve her ambitions. The days were long gone when a woman could be satisfied with looking after a husband and bringing up a family, making a home as his mother had done.

'You saying a last goodbye to land?' Jim French leant against the railing next to William and pulled on a pipe.

William looked out to sea, plenty of ships but precious little land now. And it was a composition in grey, no sunset tonight, too much cloud. The ship moved slowly under his feet. 'Think it's going to rain?' he asked.

Jim shrugged. 'Never been a weather man myself but I'd say more than like. Still, the *Empress* 'as got good stabilizers.'

William followed this elliptical statement without difficulty. 'That bad, eh?'

'They say it's going to give a bit of a blow tomorrow.' He puffed contentedly on his pipe.

William wondered how good a sailor Darina was. Then he wondered how good he was himself. 'Shouldn't be too bad in summer,' he volunteered.

Jim said nothing but the way he didn't say it disturbed William.

Jim pointed his pipe in the direction of a cross-Channel ferry just coming into sight. 'Remember the days when they were half the size, precious few comforts and full of lager louts making the most of the duty free? Used to grit your teeth before you went below deck then. Now they're all luxury, steady as anything and the crossing's all part of the holiday instead of something to forget about as soon as you get to the other side.' He paused, thinking, then added, 'No more duty free, though.'

'Doesn't seem to have made much difference,' William commented as they watched the huge ferry surge through the waters. As he followed the line of its passage, William caught sight of the ex-farmer, Michael Harwood, leaning on the rail further along the deck.

'Sad business, that,' volunteered Jim. 'Too many farmers on their uppers these days. Too much interference by governments, that's the trouble,' he added sagely. 'One of the reasons I handed over to the lads was all the paperwork you have to cope with nowadays.'

William thought despairingly of the bureaucracy that dogged his life.

'Now what's brought you and your lady wife on board with us this trip?'

'Darina's a cook,' said William. 'She's something of a specialist in Scandinavian food and the shipping line have asked her to help the chef devise a few national dishes.'

'Like a bit of steak myself,' said Jim. 'Not one for all that foreign muck. Though the curries they offer us at lunchtime aren't half bad,' he added thoughtfully. 'Mary gives them a go at home sometimes but they're never the same. She reckons they don't use the ready mixed powders. Many of the catering staff on board are Goanese so it's no wonder.'

'Darina's going to show passengers how to do open sandwiches,' said William.

'Open sandwiches, eh?' Jim said reflectively. 'No top, then?'

'No.'

'Difficult to eat, I should think.'

'You use a knife and fork.'

'Hardly a sandwich, is it?'

William thought he wouldn't report on this conversation to Darina.

'Still, something different, I suppose. That's what one likes, isn't it?' Jim sucked on the pipe, making strange little bubbling sounds. 'It sounds as though you're a lucky man, living with a food expert.'

William thought of the times he came home to a kitchen covered with cookery bits and pieces, dishes all over the place but nothing to eat, everything either not ready or destined for the deep freeze and Darina at her computer, cooking her words for an article or a book. When food was put before him, Darina always waiting anxiously for his comments, it was dishes with strange spices, odd pastry, even raw vegetables. Never, it seemed, sensible food such as shepherd's pie or roasts or even kedgeree.

William shifted uncomfortably at the rail. Of course, very often he enjoyed what Darina produced, however odd he thought it was; she was certainly a brilliant cook.

'You on first or second sitting?'

'Second.'

'That's what Mary has signed us up for,' Jim said gloomily. 'I likes my meal early, got the evening then, but she says second sitting's got more style. What do you do for a living, may I ask?'

'Civil servant,' said William promptly.

'Thought you weren't in industry,' said Jim with satisfaction.

'Why?' William was curious.

Jim looked him over carefully. 'Suppose it's something to do with how you look at people. Like you're assessing us, seeing how we tick. Bet you're a policeman.'

William laughed, Jim was more astute than he seemed at first glance. 'Rumbled!'

'Can understand why you don't want it known, mind you.'

'You can?'

'Of course; every time anyone sees a copper, they feel guilty.'

'I'm afraid that shows your age; these days precious few people regard us with any respect.'

'Makes your job difficult, that.'

'You can say that again!'

'Your secret's safe with me,' Jim said comfortably.

Michael Harwood was still looking disconsolately at the ocean, now beginning to develop a somewhat stronger swell.

'Reckon he looks as though he's thinking in the briny might be a better bet than on it.' Jim sounded uneasy. 'Think I'll say hello, like.'

William wondered for a moment whether he ought to extend the hand of friendship as well, then thought that the older man on his own had a better chance of making contact. As he turned to find his way below decks, he bumped into a large, uniformed man. Apologizing automatically, William suddenly realized it was someone he knew. 'Sergeant Dobson!'

The man took a step back and looked at him closely. 'Well, if it isn't Detective Sergeant Pigram. Except I don't suppose it's sergeant any longer, sir, is it?'

'Recently made chief inspector,' William acknowledged with a deprecating twist to his mouth. 'Been lucky.'

'Oh, aye, always were a lucky bastard, you. Amazing the way the harder you worked, the luckier you got.'

'Have you switched services now?' William asked, inspecting the gold braid on the dark navy uniform of his old desk sergeant. 'Thought you'd gone up to Liverpool to be with your wife's family.'

Sergeant Dobson moved to let a little group of passengers pass along the narrow piece of deck. 'Served my thirty years, sir. Then just as I retired, I heard there were opportunities for security officers on liners. The wife died a few years back and I always wanted to travel, so here I am. Nice to see you again, sir, glad you're doing so well.' The ex-sergeant obviously had duties to see to.

'Sorry about your wife. Hope we can get together sometime when you're not on duty and have a jar,' said William. 'It'd be good to catch up on old times.'

The big man's craggy face lit up. 'That it would, sir. Be seeing you around, then.' He almost saluted. William watched him move purposefully down the deck and thought ruefully that police work was something that never seemed possible to leave behind completely. Still, he'd always liked Stan Dobson and it would be pleasant to spend a little time with him. Could there be a criminal element to cruising?

Below decks Darina had unpacked. 'I've never seen such a neat use of space,' she exclaimed excitedly as William came in the cabin. 'I could have brought many more clothes.'

21

William thought of the length of time it had taken her to pack what had seemed the major part of her wardrobe and looked at the end of a case that was sticking out from underneath one of the beds. 'You wouldn't have been able to stow the luggage away if we'd had any more,' he said, then grabbed the edge of the dressing table as the ship rolled. 'Jim French says we're in for a bit of a blow,' he added and sat heavily on his bed.

Darina looked out at the grey sea, little white crests on the waves the only feature separating it from the equally grey sky. 'That's all right, I'm an excellent sailor,' she said cheerfully. 'I'm going to have a shower now and then change.'

'I thought one didn't for dinner the first night out.' William remembered various Hollywood films with embarrassed nouveau riche passengers arriving in the dining salon in full fig when everyone else was in day clothes.

'Not into anything formal but I thought I'd put on a different pair of trousers and that top you like me in.' Darina finished stripping off her jeans and sweatshirt and disappeared into the bathroom.

'Ah!' said William, picking up the ship's sheet of activities.

'Oh, and we've been invited to a cocktail party, by the cruise director,' Darina added, popping her head back into the cabin, shower cap in place. 'That'll be before dinner. Stick with me and you won't have to pay for drinks!'

Chapter Four

'You ready for a drink before dinner?' asked Paul Mallory, smoothing down his heavy knitted cardigan over moleskin trousers and suede shirt, all in shades of dark to light peacock blue. He looked in the mirror above his wife's head and ran a hand through his almost black curls, looking for the first hint of silver. He couldn't find one.

His brown eyes met his wife's amused hazel ones. 'I can't wait for you to start going grey,' she said. 'You'll look so distinguished.'

'I thought I did already.'

'Goes without saying, but I suppose you like to hear it anyway.'

'A man always likes to hear his wife admires him.'

'That's quite enough of that,' she said severely. 'You'll become swollen-headed.' But her voice was teasing.

He put his hands on her shoulders. 'Seriously, Shona, I'll always be amazed you chose me.' His eyes were serious, his mouth tender. Her gaze caught his in the mirror and her face softened. 'I mean, you're so intelligent, so clever, all your degrees and your job and everything. And I'm just an ordinary chap who runs an unsuccessful business.' He sat down abruptly on one of

23

the little sofas in their stateroom. 'I could never have afforded to bring you cruising in such luxury.' He waved a hand around the spacious cabin with its flowers, bottle of champagne, basket of fruit and panoramic windows – no one could call them portholes – now with the curtains drawn against the grey of the evening, its designer decor glowing with yellows, ambers and cream.

She gave him a warm smile through the mirror. 'I'm glad you're pleased. It seemed such a good idea. But don't get too used to it all, we won't be able to afford this sort of accommodation again.'

His mouth tightened but he said nothing.

'That's not to say we won't be able to go on another cruise, though. After all, we're not exactly on the breadline, are we?' she added lightly. She was turned on the stool towards him, her face anxious now, the smile gone.

He couldn't bring himself to acknowledge that the not inconsiderable income that sustained their present existence was hers. Not when she could transform all their lives so easily.

'You do understand why I'm doing this, don't you?' she pressed him.

He reached forward and poured out the last of the champagne. 'Look, you've told me and I've accepted it. I don't understand but don't bother to go through it again. I thought your family meant something to you, something more than a luxury cruise, that is.' He slouched down in the corner of the sofa and drank from the glass as though it was water.

She watched him for a moment then turned back and finished repairing her make-up, her mouth set in a thin line.

'Aren't you going to change?' he asked, suddenly realizing she was in the same trouser suit she'd worn all day. The only difference was she had put on the pearl necklace he'd given her instead of the little scarf that had been tied round her neck.

'No, it's first night out,' she replied, applying a coral lipstick. He thought the colour too bright, too obvious, but didn't comment.

'Even so, you could have put something else on.'

She said nothing.

He felt brought down, diminished, by her attitude. Why go through all the rigmarole of booking a state-room, doing the thing in style, the sort of style he'd been trying to educate her into ever since they married, then not bother to put on something different for dinner?

Was she pissed off at Julian's behaviour? Maybe he ought to say something about that. 'I'm sorry the boy's being such an ass,' he said awkwardly.

She gave him one of her level looks. 'I can understand why he does it even if I can't do anything about it. But he's heading for disaster, Paul.'

He hunched his shoulders. Why the hell did she have to make him feel guilty? None of it was his fault. 'If you could only see your way—' he started resentfully.

She stopped him, turning again, her lipstick upheld in one hand. 'Don't, Paul,' she said. 'Just don't. You know why.'

Frustration began to build in him but he knew he couldn't afford to let it take control. He came over and wrapped his arms around her. 'I know,' he said gently, allowing the increasing roll of the ship to sway them together. 'I know. It's just that I'm not such an altruist as you. I'm selfish, I admit it.' He kissed the top of her head and felt her relax against him. 'You're my great gift and you must teach me to be a better person.'

'What nonsense,' she said crisply. 'I'm no saint and you know that. But I'm doing the best I can, for us all.'

Even while she was leaning against him, Paul realized she hadn't relaxed completely, her shoulders were still taut, as though she couldn't or wouldn't allow herself to give way totally. He increased the pressure of his arms. 'I love you,' he murmured into her ear. 'Love you, love you, love you.'

He felt the tension go out of her and her limbs become soft against him. She reached up and twined her arms around his head, pulling it down into the curve of her neck. He could smell the faintest hint of the olive oil soap she always used. All of a sudden he felt a surge of sheer lust. He dragged her off the stool and over to the large double bed.

She laughed, for once an uninhibited laugh that gloried in the emotions she'd raised in him. Her hands reached for his shirt buttons while he grappled with the fastening of her trousers.

The telephone rang.

'Don't answer,' he ground out, finally managing to unfasten the navy-blue cloth round her waist.

'Don't be silly,' she said, twisting her body away from his grasp and reaching for the receiver.

It was no use, if Shona felt the telephone should be answered, answered it would be. Anyway, he realized, the urge had gone now.

Paul sat on the edge of the bed and did up his shirt buttons.

'Daphne! Yes, of course. Come round now and we can have a drink together before going into dinner. No, of course you won't be interrupting anything!' Shona laughed happily, that moment of joyous response obviously quite forgotten. She replaced the receiver and squirmed off the bed, fastening up her trousers, her movements efficient.

Paul rose as she twitched at the quilted bedcover. He shook the empty bottle in its cooler. 'Better order another from the steward if Daphne's coming over,' he said and pressed the button beside the bed.

'Ring Julian and see if he wants to join us.' Shona glanced around the stateroom. Surely she knew it was immaculate, Paul thought irritably as he dialled his son's cabin number. There was no answer.

The steward arrived. He'd already given them his card, Manuel was his name, a large, smiling, dark-skinned man who moved slowly but with purpose. By the time Daphne Rawlings arrived, he had produced another bottle of champagne and clean glasses.

'My, this is something,' Daphne said, looking at their surroundings as she came in. Shona's only greeting was a smile. It always amused Paul how his wife never indulged in the easy kissing most women seemed to think was a necessary part of friendship. Daphne had explained it to him once. 'It's all part of her fear of rejection. She's so used to being controlled, it's very hard for her to open up.' Paul supposed it made a certain sort of sense.

As Paul had known she would, Daphne had changed. Perfectly fitting light beige slacks with a matching knitted silk top, a beige and gold long silk

27

scarf casually knotted halfway down her chest, gold chains roped around her neck.

'How's your cabin?' Shona asked anxiously.

'Beautiful,' Daphne said reassuringly. 'It's over the other side of the ship, are we port side here or starboard? Anyway, whichever it is, I'm the other one. And towards the sharp end.'

'I hoped we'd be nearer each other,' Shona complained.

'We were late in line,' Paul explained, popping out the cork and neatly pouring the foaming champagne into glasses. 'Had to take what was going.' He carefully topped up the glasses and handed Daphne one. 'Julian is at the other end of the ship from you,' he added, 'one deck up but same side as us.'

Daphne helped herself to a small handful of the cocktail snacks that had been brought with the champagne. 'So, we're dotted around,' she said casually as she tossed the crisp little bits and pieces into her mouth.

'I'm afraid we are,' Paul agreed, sitting down beside Shona on one of the sofas. He raised his glass and smiled at his mistress.

Chapter Five

Karen Geary, cruise director, scrunched up her waterfall of red hair, then let it fly loose. Casual elegance was her style. She leaned forward towards the mirror and applied the grey eyeshadow that defined and enlarged her rather pale grey eyes and sighed.

Nearly time for her first-night party for all the performers. The party was important. The more the entertainers thought they were appreciated, the more effectively they would entertain the disparate collection of passengers embarked on the *Empress*. They were a varied collection themselves: comedians, a magician, dancers and singers, musicians of all sorts, even a cook for this cruise. A cook as performer, whatever next?

The party was also an opportunity for them all to meet each other, though not all were on long-term contracts, some were only engaged for this cruise. Karen liked to think she was enabling them to form friendships among colleagues instead of having to winkle them out as the cruise proceeded.

Get the party out of the way and Karen could concentrate on sorting out the passengers she was going to need to cultivate during the cruise. She was beginning to find this hard work. Selecting the right ones could be tricky and you always needed some in reserve in case the chosen ones proved difficult in the end. And available time seemed to get shorter and shorter.

Was she beginning to find it all too much?

Karen looked at her image in the mirror and adjusted the set of her waisted green brocade jacket with its peplum and diamanté buttons. Had they been lucky to get away with things thus far? Or was the system really foolproof?

Harry said it was. But it had been Harry who had lost his cool in Lisbon.

Harry had to be made to see sense. If he continued in this way, it could only mean disaster.

She picked up the phone and punched in a number. 'Could I speak to First Officer Summers, please?' While she waited, Karen worked her mouth, studying her reflection to check on the outline of her lipstick. 'Harry? It's me. We need to talk. Meet in our usual place, say half-past twelve? OK, see you then.' She rang off.

Harry hadn't been pleased to get a call while he was on duty. But he had to realize she was an equal partner. He couldn't call all the shots. If she refused to co-operate, where would he be then?

In any case, there wasn't too much time left to them now.

Phil had mentioned something about meeting her for a drink after she'd finished that evening. Karen smoothed her eyeshadow with a skilful finger. Phil was a sweetie in so many ways, quiet and high-principled. It was refreshing to be with a man who was so honest and up front. Who never hesitated to do his duty. It was a pity Harry had turned against him. But she wasn't going to let Harry rule her life or decide who she should or should not see.

Yes, if Phil asked her for a drink this evening, she'd have one with him and if Harry found them together, he could make of it what he would. Karen could manage without Harry Summers – in fact, she was going to have to. But not yet.

Lulu Prentice finished checking her equipment. Her little empire was deep on the lowest deck of the *Empress*. Exercise machines, massage facilities, body-building equipment, tiny swimming pool – should passengers feel guilty about all the food and alcohol they were enjoying, they could work off the ill-effects down here.

Lulu, christened Lucinda, a name that had been quickly shortened at school, picked up a couple of wet towels. She'd already had some of the new lot of passengers coming down for a dip. 'Thought we'd get up an appetite for dinner,' they'd said. Others had made welcome appointments for metabolic and fitness assessments. Odd how keen they could be to improve their health in certain ways and then do their damnedest to ruin it in others! Lulu wondered how many she'd get this trip for her eight o'clock mile walk round the decks.

Finally everything was pristine for the morning. Lulu looked at her watch and wondered what she should do with the rest of her evening. There were sure to be some amusing members of the crew in their mess but she knew she didn't feel like joining in whatever activity they had going there this evening. Everyone would be tired, anyway, changeover day from one cruise to the next was always exhausting.

Lulu was a small girl with a sturdy, compact body and short dark hair that made a loo brush look silky smooth. Femme fatale she was not. But she was extremely popular nevertheless. The good time everyone had with her, though, seemed to be confined to horseplay in the mess, or ragging around ports when they had free time. No one propositioned Lulu.

Which didn't worry her. Men were a whole heap of trouble, in her opinion. All except one.

What were the chances of her finding Phil Burrell and suggesting they went back to his cabin for the rest of the evening?

All right, so he had told her their good times together were over, that she was a great friend but not to count on him for anything more. And it had been she who had made all the running in their relationship – but if she hadn't, there wouldn't have been a relationship. Lulu really couldn't believe, though, that he actually meant everything between them was over. That business with Karen Geary couldn't be anything serious. The whole ship knew Karen had ambitions far beyond a humble stores manager. She was playing with him. It was up to Lulu to show Phil what in his heart of hearts he must know, that she was the girl for him, not Karen.

She closed and locked the door of the gym and took the lift to B Deck. Phil wasn't in his office. Lulu made an educated guess and headed for the main reception area. There she came across him, walking from the direction of the stores manager's office.

'Heavens, Phil, you look like you've seen a ghost,' she said.

'What?' he said and then seemed to come back from a great distance. 'Oh, Lulu, it's you.' He brushed aside her comment. 'Ghost, well, you could say that.'

'Hey, let's go somewhere quiet and you tell me about it.'

His face took on its pained expression. 'Lulu, I thought we'd sorted all that out.'

'Oh, I don't mean, you know – just thought we could talk and have a drink, relax, unwind, you know? Who's your best friend?' Lulu plunged her hands into her pockets and stood trying to look jaunty and as though nothing much mattered.

'Another time, Lulu, OK?'

She thought he looked very tired and worried. She wanted to stroke his forehead and snuggle into his arms, tell him she loved him and that everything would be all right. But she could see she wasn't going to get the opportunity. Not tonight, anyway.

'Hey, OK, no probs, see you around!' She turned on her heel and walked straight towards the lift, fighting tears. It was stupid to mind this much. Stupid, stupid, stupid. This was the last time, she told herself, absolutely the last time.

Staff Captain Alan Greenham tapped his pencil irritably on the chart table as his first officer took the call. It was personal, he could tell by the way Harry turned so that he presented his back to the main part of the bridge while he talked.

'Which of your lady loves will be waiting for you tonight?' he enquired, a raw edge to his voice, as Harry put down the phone.

Harry shrugged deprecatingly. 'Can one help it if one's irresistible?'

The officer of the watch sniggered as he checked the Decca radar.

'I wouldn't push it if I were you,' Alan said repressively, firmly directing his gaze to the busy shipping lanes of the English Channel. It was always pressured getting through to the North Sea. That on top of all the paperwork necessary at the end of the last voyage made sailing day a time to be got through as quickly and efficiently as possible.

The one advantage to all the endless business of getting the ship out to sea was that officers didn't have to sit with passengers at dinner.

Oh, what an effort it was to make amiable conversation and get people to talk to each other! Praying there would be some extrovert souls at the table – which there usually were, it tended to be the extroverts that asked to be put on an officer's table – then hoping that no one passenger would dominate, which was all too likely, and that the women would be attractive but not too flirtatious.

Hosting a table was all part of being a senior officer on a cruise ship. And in a couple of years' time, if he was lucky, Alan would be appointed captain. Which would bring a great deal more socializing. However, then he would have a staff captain under him who would assume the senior executive officer's task of running the operational side and sharing some of the captain's responsibilities for emergencies.

Alan prayed there would be no major problems on this trip. On the last one they'd left a passenger behind at one of the ports. Her fault, of course, but it had still entailed endless to-ing and fro-ing between the ship, head office, and the British consulate before the wretched woman could be organized to rejoin the *Empress of India* at another port. So many enquiries to be made to establish responsibility, so much form-filling.

Alan eyed the neat figure of his first officer. At least he wasn't going to have to be worried by Henry Summers for much longer, he was almost at the end of his two years with the ship. He was, of course, an efficient officer. He was also a great hit with the female passengers. Not to mention the ship's more attractive staff. Whilst he was married he had at least been discreet. Since he'd separated from his wife, however, discretion and Harry no longer seemed on speaking terms. It would be a pity if his appointment had to be terminated prematurely.

Chapter Six

The party given by the cruise director was in a small
lounge leading off a large bar and entertainment area
that included tables for gambling.

'Really glad to make your acquaintance,' a luscious-
looking redhead with tremendous verve said to Darina
as William escorted her into a room already humming
with people. *Karen Geary, Cruise Director,* said a badge
on the chic green two-piece. The redhead beckoned to
another bubbly dark-haired girl in a purser's uniform.
'My assistant will introduce you to some of your fellow
performers. You are all going to make this voyage very
special for us.' Another charming smile and they were
handed over to the other girl.

'Darina Lisle!' exclaimed the assistant with enthusiasm. 'You're the cooking lady, aren't you? I love cooking, not that I get much opportunity except when we're
on holiday. Spend my time trying not to eat,' she
giggled and gave an endearing wiggle of her minuscule
behind. 'Now, who would you like to meet? We've got a
great selection on board with us.' Rapidly she pointed
out various of the other entertainers: a tall, Latin-
looking magician with a very glamorous assistant; a
comedian, and a singer who in the old days Darina
reckoned would have been called a crooner – both had

faces she thought she recognized from television, with names that were also familiar. Then there was a group of much younger men and women who apparently were the ship's troupe. 'Lovely lot they are,' said the cruise director's assistant. 'So talented and they've some wonderful routines, you're in for a real treat this trip. That's our bridge lady, if you want to sharpen up your table technique.' She indicated an older woman in a smart suit talking to a man with a carefully composed face that Darina reckoned also made visits to their living room. Or maybe past tense would be correct here, surely she hadn't seen him recently? 'She's talking to our classical music specialist. You know this is a Classical Cruise?'

Darina didn't. She hadn't had time to do much more than check the ports they were going to visit in the glossy brochure that had been sent to her. She wondered just how much classical music they were going to be offered.

'Oh, there's our very special baritone, Mervyn Pryde, you must meet him.'

The singer was a large man with a shock of blond hair and a face that looked as though it had had an argument with a rugby scrum and lost. On being introduced he extended a hand as big as a table tennis bat. 'Pleased to meet you,' he said, displaying a dazzling set of white teeth.

'Mervyn Pryde, I can't believe it,' Darina said enthusiastically. 'I'm such a fan of yours. We saw your Figaro in a touring production at Yeovil a couple of years ago, you were wonderful!' She remembered the evening vividly. Mozart's wonderful music had come across with enticing freshness and all the singing had

37

been superb but this man had been particularly good, his voice a mixture of cream and silk with wonderful depth, his phrasing memorable.

'Are you really going to sing for us?'

The big man nodded, his smile revealing gleaming teeth. 'This is my third trip on the *Empress* and I really enjoy giving the passengers a bit of a treat.'

Standing a trifle disconsolately beside the singer and twirling an empty wineglass was a very bored-looking girl, her sexy little body displayed with panache in a strappy number made from a minimum amount of scarlet silk.

'Are you an entertainer as well, or a hanger-on like me?' asked William. 'My name's William Pigram and my wife's going to give a cookery demonstration.'

Amused, Darina watched the girl cheer up, opening her eyes wide as she looked at William with studied concentration. 'I'm Tara Greene. I'm with Merve. I'm a singer, too, but I'm not performing on the cruise,' she ended petulantly.

'That's very interesting. Do you sing opera as well?'

Darina didn't think so. It wasn't so much the minimal dress and impact-laden make-up as the lack of discipline in her manner that suggested here was no classically trained musician. Great skill, though, had gone into the presentation of her looks. Tara's slight figure, rounded face and unremarkable features had all been packaged brilliantly. The wide open eyes were a hesitant shade of blue that had been given emphasis with dramatic eyeshadow, the lack of cheekbones were compensated for with blusher and a too small mouth was enlarged with clever use of lipstick. Frizzy platinum-blonde hair was drawn back with the sort of hair clamp current fashion appeared to have borrowed from car maintenance.

While Darina listened to Mervyn Pryde giving her a foretaste of the treats he had in store for the passengers – mostly well-known arias, it appeared, together with some lieder – she watched William listening court- eously to the flirtatious Tara, who was obviously delighted to have an audience at last.

'Merve says I should do more with my voice. I sing with a backing group but I'm planning some solo sets. Merve says I've got star potential,' came shrilly through as Mervyn expounded with a dramatic gesture on his devotion to Mozart's *Don Giovanni*.

Darina tried to give him her whole attention. He was a rather overwhelming individual. If the little room hadn't been so crowded, she would have taken a step back. As it was, she felt her head leaning away from the powerful face that seemed almost threateningly near hers, the dark eyes shining with passion as his mellifluous voice articulated the nego- tiations that were presently going on for his first appearance in the role of the amorous Don. Articu- lated so well, in fact, that sibilants spurted spittle in her direction.

Trying to maintain a suitably entranced expression, Darina managed to squeeze a little more room between herself and the singer, lurching slightly as the ship moved in a threatening way beneath her feet. Per- forming a rapid dance step with her feet, she managed to keep her balance.

Tara grabbed at her partner's arm but it wasn't lack of balance that had prompted the move. 'Merve,' she said excitedly, 'I told you you should be doing more for me, this chap says I ought to have a spot, that it should be organized.'

Darina almost giggled as she caught sight of William's face as he realized the seriousness with which Tara was treating what must have been a light-hearted comment.

'Does he?' The singer turned towards William. They were much of a height, both well over six foot, but William lacked the other's sheer bulk. As Mervyn Pryde looked at him, Darina thought that maybe the rugby scrum had come off worse after all.

'Well,' Mervyn said smoothly, 'he'll have to see what he can do then, won't he?'

Just as William sketched a small, helpless gesture, there came the sound of a gong over the public broadcast system announcing second sitting for dinner. Just in case anyone didn't get the message, the sonorous notes were followed by verbal instructions.

'Ah,' William said with the air of a settler beset by Red Indians who sees the cavalry arrive. 'Food!'

Darina slipped her arm through his. 'I need some support,' she murmured as they moved with everyone else towards the exit. 'This ship is getting ideas above its station.' The rolling was becoming more pronounced. It must be the motion of the ship that was affecting her, there hadn't been time for more than a couple of not very large glasses of wine. But Darina enjoyed the feeling of her husband close beside her. Once again the glorious realization of the two weeks of almost total relaxation ahead of them filled her. Discussions with the chef and a demonstration couldn't be that taxing, surely?

Down in the restaurant, soft lights illuminated

beautifully laid tables, each decorated with a flower arrangement.

'Which is ours?' William asked, looking at the card with the table number on it that had awaited their arrival in the cabin.

'Over here,' Darina said, moving towards a table for eight at the side of the room. 'I noted the numbers when we left after tea.'

'Little Miss Efficiency!' William laughed.

Then he saw that Mervyn Pryde and Tara had followed them to the same table. 'Ah, how nice, we're table companions,' he said to the baritone, managing to sound as though he meant it.

Mervyn looked less than entranced.

Already seated at the table was the young man with dark curls who'd swung on the entrance railing at teatime. He'd changed into a dark red shirt with huge sleeves and braiding round the collar that made him look dashingly Byronic. How exciting, thought Darina, we're going to have the lottery winner and her family at our table!

Tara slipped into the seat on the young man's right and Mervyn sat next to her.

When William drew out the chair on the young man's other side for Darina, she hesitated. 'Is it all right if we sit here?' she asked.

Before he could reply, a girl in her late twenties or early thirties arrived. She looked at the other diners, checked the table number on the card she was carrying in her hand, then said, 'It seems I'm sitting with you.'

William drew out the chair next to the one he'd chosen. She smiled at him a little doubtfully but allowed him to seat her. She looked very pleasant with a neat figure, regular features and a well-organized head of tightly permed fair curls, but Darina thought her manner was rather – well, repressed was the word that came to mind. Perhaps she was shy.

'That place is free,' the Byronic youth said to Darina. She sat down beside him. There were only two places left at the table now, so the other three members of the lottery winner's party couldn't be joining them.

A moment later Enid Carter arrived, her face lighting up as she recognized Darina and William. 'Well, isn't this nice?' she said.

That left one last place. This remained empty as tables filled up all around them.

Darina introduced herself to the young man. Somewhat grudgingly, he told her that his name was Julian Mallory.

'You're with your parents, aren't you?' probed Darina without shame. 'We saw you at teatime.'

'My father and stepmother,' he corrected firmly. 'I said I'd only come if I didn't have to sit with them.'

'Bit old, are they?' suggested William teasingly.

Julian said nothing.

'And you are?' William turned towards the girl sitting beside him.

'Beth Cartwright,' she said, closing her mouth firmly after her name.

'And have you been cruising before?' he persevered.

'Well, yes, I suppose I have.'

'You suppose?' he prompted her with a smile.

'Well, I was sort of doing a job,' Beth explained in a quiet voice.

Further conversation was prevented by the arrival of the wine waiter.

42

'Shall we take it in turns to provide wine for everyone?' suggested William. 'I gather that is a usual
custom.'

'We'll do our own thing,' Mervyn said. 'Saves a lot of
trouble, doesn't it?'

'I like beer,' volunteered Julian. 'Got any Becks?' he
asked the waiter.

'Certainly, sir.' The order was scribbled down.

'Well, can I invite you both to share a bottle?'
William asked Beth and Enid.

'What a gentleman,' Enid responded expansively.

'Thank you, that sounds very nice,' Beth said
primly.

There followed a discussion on whether white or
red would be more appropriate.

'What are you choosing to eat?' asked Darina,
looking at the elaborate and beautifully set out menu
card.

'I'm just having the steak,' Beth said, closing the
menu firmly.

'Really?' William was astonished. 'No starter, no
soup?'

'No,' she said.

So that appeared to be that! While the rest of the
table worked their way through five courses, Beth
Cartwright sat and fiddled with her wineglass and took
little part in the conversation. She hardly needed to,
thought Darina, as she listened to tales of backstage
rivalry in the opera world told by Mervyn with panache
and excellent timing.

'Are you interested in opera?' she asked Julian
during a pause in the flow of stories as the baritone
addressed himself to his steak.

'Not really. But I am into music. I'm going to manage pop stars, I'm setting up my own company.' His eyes shone and for the first time he revealed a hint of a personality that could match up to his appearance.

'Really?' Tara chimed in. 'Then you'll want to manage me! I'm going all the way.'

He switched his attention to her. 'Tell me about yourself,' he invited with a charm he'd so far kept under wraps.

But Mervyn had fed his voice sufficiently for it to be aired once again and he launched into a tale of chicanery that held his listeners even though they seemed slightly less entranced than during his first session.

'We'll get together later,' Tara whispered to Julian.

Darina shut herself off from what Mervyn was saying and gave her attention to the food. The smoked salmon starter had been reliable, Darina had had better examples but not many. The soup, a borscht, had been brilliant, its deep colour a fitting companion to the depth of flavour given by a good meat stock. Whilst most of the table had gone for steak, she'd opted for sea bass and had not been disappointed. Perfectly cooked, the flavour of the tender, meaty flesh had been subtle and nicely accompanied by a wine and butter sauce. The kitchen knew its stuff, all right. She looked forward to meeting the chef.

Beth had said she preferred white wine, her quiet voice quite definite on the choice. William had discovered an excellent Sancerre that was being offered at a bargain price as an end of bin. 'Let's have that,' he'd suggested. And it was delicious, delicate but full of clean flavour with just a hint of sweetness. William had ordered himself and Enid a glass of the ship's house red to go with their steak and all of them were happy.

When it came to the final course, Darina said she would pass and so did Beth. 'Isn't it hell trying to keep one's weight down?' Darina said cheerfully to her in a pause while Mervyn was studying the menu for his choice of dessert. 'Though you hardly need to worry, I'd have thought,' she added, eyeing the other girl's neat figure with envy.

'It's all a matter of eating healthily,' Beth said in her prim little way.

It was the sort of statement that stopped conversation for Darina but William said heartily, 'My wife knows all about that. She's got me on a diet that avoids all sorts of things that were upsetting my metabolism.'

'Really?' Beth said politely.

'Oh, you're not one of those food maniacs?' Enid was astonished.

'Far from it, just avoiding things like wheat and dairy products,' said William, pouring cream over his profiteroles.

Enid looked pointedly at his plate.

'Well, most of the time. It's made a great difference to my energy levels,' he added hastily.

'George would never have agreed to anything so ridiculous,' Enid sounded completely positive. 'How on earth did you persuade your husband?' she asked Darina.

'Oh, my wife's a food expert,' William said blithely. 'Writes articles and things. Very well, too. If only she'd work at something important, she could be a bestseller, I'm sure of it.'

For Darina it seemed as though time stopped.

45

Conversation went on around her but she couldn't take in anything that was being said. William's comment had pierced through her. 'If only she'd work at something important,' he'd said. As though writing about food wasn't anything that mattered. She drank the rest of her wine and the waiter gave her the last of the bottle of Sancerre. William was leaning forward, saying something that made the table laugh. Darina had no idea what it was. She sat frozen. She couldn't have it out with him now. Obviously no one else thought there'd been anything odd about what he'd said.

In a move to distract herself, Darina looked around the dining room, and found herself looking straight at Julian's family. They were at a large table prominently placed near the centre of the room. That table, too, had an empty chair.

'We're missing a lot of passengers,' she said. To her surprise, her voice sounded normal.

'Only the officers,' boomed Mervyn. 'That'll be the captain's table,' he added as he saw where she was looking. 'The officers never sit with us on the first night. Too busy with getting us off in the right direction and making sure we don't bump into anybody, see?'

'Is that why we're missing someone at our table?'

'No.' He made a wry face. 'That chair will be for another passenger. Maybe they're too tired to join us tonight, or they could have switched to the first serving. We're not thought important enough to be awarded an officer at our table.'

'Nothing to do with that,' Enid said briskly. 'We just didn't ask to be placed on a table with a member of the crew. Last thing I want; poor things, always having to make conversation and trying to remember if they've met you before and where you come from. I'd rather take my chances with other passengers. And look how lucky I've been!' Her bright eyes surveyed the table. That set Mervyn off again with tables of passengers met on other cruises he'd sung on. Darina continued to study the captain's table. Mrs Mallory's husband was holding forth. As Darina watched, however, he skilfully brought other members of the table into the conversation. Good at socializing, she decided, and wished he could give some lessons to Mervyn. Mrs Mallory, the lottery winner, said little but she looked happy enough, her eyes watching her husband, her body relaxed. Every now and then she would exchange an amused glance with the other woman in their party.

As coffee was cleared away Mervyn said, 'Well, who's for the little entertainment show, then?'

'What sort of show?' asked William with a touch of suspicion. 'I thought we'd get an early night.'

'Oh, the director will introduce her team, they'll do a turn or two, she'll say a few words on the entertainment you all have to look forward to, we'll all take a bow then that'll be that.'

'I'm going,' said Tara meaningfully. 'I'll see if I can get together with her afterwards.'

'You do that, love,' Mervyn said cheerfully. 'I'll be flat on my back by then. Don't wake me up when you come in.'

Tara looked resentful. It was an expression that seemed to come easily to her. 'Let's go and have that chat about me,' she said to Julian, picking up her envelope bag and a wisp of stole.

'I'm for bed,' Enid announced cheerfully. 'See you all tomorrow.' She walked off, grabbing chair backs to

47

maintain her balance as the ship moved first one way then another.

'I think we'll sample the entertainment,' William said positively.

No chance, then, of bringing up his remark tonight. Darina realized she didn't want to, she'd handle herself better after a night's sleep. She turned to ask Beth if she wanted to join them, but the girl had left.

Karen was an accomplished performer and her team were talented. The little show provided a pleasant way to pass the time. 'Maybe I won't be spending the evenings with a good book after all,' William said as the applause finally died down and the band struck up a waltz. 'Shall we venture on the floor?'

'No,' said Darina decisively. 'I don't feel like dancing.'

'Oh? Well, let's have a nightcap instead. I know where there's a nice little bar.'

'I'm not the only one keeping their eyes open,' said Darina, following his lead. 'I wondered what you'd been up to.'

The bar he took her to led off another large lounge which had tables for gambling and a side room offering fruit machines. From there the sound of levers being pulled and the chink of coins carried through music and the hum of voices.

In the bar, though, things were quieter. As William and Darina entered, an officer rose from a little group of smartly uniformed colleagues. 'This has to be Darina Lisle,' he said, eyeing her height and long blonde hair. 'I once caught you on the television, great stuff! I'm Francis Sterling, the purser. Welcome aboard.' He was a small man with a beaming smile and easy social style. 'I was going to track you down tomorrow and make an appointment to introduce you to the chef. Can I offer you and your husband a drink?'

In a moment he had Darina and William seated at a small table. 'Now, what's your poison?'

'Do you have a Macallan?' Darina asked.

'The Macallan? Of course.' The waitress scribbled on her pad. William ordered one also.

'And I'll have another of my specials,' the purser said. 'Would you mind talking shop for a moment, Miss Lisle, or may I call you Darina?'

'Of course.'

'That's great, Darina. Now, do I understand you're willing to do a demonstration for the passengers?'

Darina nodded. 'I thought maybe a selection of open sandwiches? Very Scandinavian and it wouldn't require any cooking equipment. I can talk about other dishes during the demonstration and perhaps the chef will have some of them on the luncheon or dinner menus.'

The purser pulled a bit of a face. 'We'll have to see how they fit in with the corporation menus. Everything's dictated by Head Office these days. Your discussions with the chef are really meant to point the way for the future rather than this cruise. Still,' he cheered up a little, 'we have a bit of autonomy. Let's get together tomorrow and go through the possibilities. Shall we say two thirty in my office? Go to the Information Desk in the main hall and one of the girls will bring you up. Perhaps we'll leave introducing you to the chef until we reach the first port, things will be a little quieter in the kitchen then.'

That sounded fine to Darina.

'I expect you'd like to see something of how we organize the food and the cooking on board?'

'If it isn't too much trouble, I might be able to get an article out of it,' she suggested.

'Great stuff. The company likes a bit of publicity.' Francis beamed at her. He wore glasses but the eyes behind them were a bright blue and very keen. 'Over there is Phil Burrell, our stores manager.' He indicated a medium-sized man in his mid-thirties with an attractive face, called him over and introduced Darina and William.

'I thought it would be a good idea if you could show Darina your lockers, give her an idea of how our food is stored and handled,' Francis Sterling said. 'They're quite a sight,' he added to Darina.

'I'd be delighted.' Phil smiled at Darina, giving her the impression he was really pleased with the suggestion. 'Perhaps a little later on in our cruise? At the moment it's difficult to see anything properly, all the produce is piled so high.'

As he was talking, the cruise director came into the bar. If Phil Burrell had seemed pleased before, his face now looked as if interior lights to rival Blackpool had been switched on. 'I'll be in touch,' he said hurriedly and moved towards the newcomer. 'Karen,' he said joyfully. 'Come and have a drink, bet you need it after all your hard work.'

The cruise director looked at her watch and Darina, checking hers, was surprised to realize that it was almost midnight. Karen smiled at the stores manager. 'Why not?' she said graciously.

They went and sat in a far corner of the bar. Darina

saw that Francis Sterling was watching them out of the corner of his eye.

'This bar seems a popular one for your officers,' William suggested.

Francis nodded. 'We seem to find our way here when we've finished doing what we have to do.'

'Long day,' commented Darina.

'Sailing day always is. Lot to get organized. Tomorrow, too. After that things should settle down a little and we can start to enjoy you lovely passengers.' Then his attention was caught by the appearance of another officer entering the bar. Francis looked rapidly at Phil Burrell and Karen drinking in the corner and waved hurriedly at the newcomer, a tall man with wide shoulders, a strong face and a determined look in his eye.

Francis's signal was ignored. The officer saw the stores manager and the cruise director and headed straight for them.

'Oh, dear,' said Francis. 'That's Harry Summers, our first officer.' The information seemed irrelevant. William made some comment about the number of passengers who had cruised before. Francis explained that only ten per cent of passengers on any cruise were first-timers but his manner was abstracted. His attention seemed to be focused not on his guests but the group in the corner.

Afterwards Darina couldn't say exactly what happened, it was all too quick. Suddenly Phil Burrell rose and spat words at the first officer, gesturing wildly. Karen reached forward in a placatory gesture but one of Phil's flailing arms caught her face with the back of his hand. She reeled back. Then the stores manager was on the floor, felled by a quick blow from the other man.

Conversation in the bar stopped as abruptly as a car meeting a brick wall. A red mark appeared on Karen's face. She raised her hand to it, her expression dazed.

'Excuse me,' said Francis. In an instant he had Phil on his feet, spoke some stern words to the other officer and gestured to a woman in a purser's uniform to take care of Karen.

'I think we should leave,' said William quietly, polishing off his whisky. 'This is a ship's matter.'

Darina followed him out of the bar. But not before she'd seen Phil Burrell yank his arm free from Francis Sterling's grasp and turn to Karen Geary. He appeared to be pleading with her. But she turned angrily from him with a gesture of rejection. The officer who'd knocked Phil down put his arm around her and drew her close.

'Oh dear,' said Darina. 'This is not a good omen for our cruise.'

Chapter Seven

William woke early. The ship was still rolling but not quite as much as it had done the previous evening, and when he drew the curtain back from the porthole, the sun was breaking through grey-edged clouds, lighting the choppy sea with a mackerel shine.

He looked at his watch. It was an hour before the time they'd ordered tea to be brought.

Darina still seemed to be fast asleep. She'd seemed a bit out of sorts towards the end of the previous evening. She hadn't wanted to talk at all when they'd got back to their cabin after the fracas in the bar. He'd been really disappointed, he'd wanted to discuss what had happened. He hoped she wasn't being affected by the movement of the ship.

William snuggled down under the covers. How wonderful to know the phone couldn't possibly ring with some emergency to drag him away from enjoying himself. Several minutes later he realized sleep had fled. He placed his hands behind his head and lay examining the cabin fittings in the grey light that came through the porthole. The *Empress* was certainly an attractive ship, he decided.

He picked up the book he'd brought with him but after no more than half a page of its examination of the sociological implications of current criminal law, his mind wandered. The book was replaced beside the bed and William wondered if putting on the television would disturb Darina, then he recalled an item on the day's itinerary that had been delivered to the cabin the previous evening.

'I thought I'd do the mile deck walk,' he announced to the humped figure of his wife that was now beginning to stir. 'The exercise will be good after all that food and drink last night. You coming, too?'

Darina raised a bleary face. It was rather an odd colour, pale with a touch of green. 'I don't think so, I feel pretty dreadful,' she groaned. 'It must be the boat.' Then she made a quick dash for the bathroom.

William got up and hovered uncertainly outside. 'Anything I can do?' he called. Darina wasn't often ill and when she was didn't like him making a fuss but he felt helpless as the sound of her distress came clearly through the door.

After a few minutes there was the sound of the loo flushing, water being run and then Darina emerged, little beads of sweat on her brow. 'I think I'll just lie quietly,' she said, slipping back into bed. 'Could you bring me a drink of water, perhaps?'

William made her comfortable and asked if she would like him to stay. He was told she'd much prefer to be left on her own, so he pulled on pants and a tracksuit, found his trainers and then made his way up to the swimming pool at the stern of the ship. According to the ship's programme, this was where the mile walk round the deck was to start.

There was no sight of land, only white-capped waves and a blustery sky. The ship was moving, no doubt about that. William didn't think the sea could really be called rough, though. He was surprised that Darina seemed to be so badly affected. Other passengers were up and about, some even having their breakfast on the open upper deck where there were tables under bright umbrellas, the deck sides protected with glass screens, all too necessary against the stiff breeze. These brave passengers were warmly wrapped in sweaters and jackets. It seemed a triumph of determination over circumstances and William decided he would go downstairs to the restaurant for his breakfast.

Out on the deck, having battled with the door against the wind, William made his way to the rendez-vous point. No one seemed to be waiting for the walk. Was he the only brave one? He looked at his watch. Five minutes to go to eight o'clock; maybe passengers were leaving it to the last minute to turn up but surely the Keep Fit Instructor should be here to welcome her fellow walkers?

Then he realized that someone was tapping on the picture windows of the sun area overlooking the pool and that there was a group of people inside grinning at him.

'We felt like waiting to see how long you would hang around,' said a small, effervescent girl with a knitted cap pulled down over her hair. She wore leggings and a capacious navy blue sweatshirt with an *Empress of India* logo. 'But that wouldn't have been fair. I'm afraid we can't go outside today, too rough. Now, I wonder how many more hardy souls we're going to collect.'

There were half a dozen gathered around her. Two were obviously a couple but the other four looked as though they didn't know each other. Middle-aged was the best description for them.

'I'm Lulu Prentice,' said the girl in the knitted cap. 'I run the gym downstairs. If you haven't found it already, make it a stop this morning. We've got an indoor pool down there, all sorts of exercise machines, and I'm happy to check your general fitness and work out a routine for you. As you know since you are here, I organize a mile walk round the decks, showing you parts of the ship other walkers never reach. We need five circuits of the deck for one mile so you can all count each one off.' She looked at her watch. 'Just on eight, we'll wait a few minutes to see if anyone else is coming. Usually I set off on the dot but this is the first morning.'

Even as she said this, the door from the big stern lounge opened and through came Beth, the girl from the table last night. One of the benefits of his profession was that, amongst other details, William had been trained to remember names without difficulty. He gave her a welcoming smile. She looked at him doubtfully, as though her memory was not nearly as good as his and she doubted his intentions. Like William, she was dressed in a grey track suit with an efficient looking pair of trainers on her feet. She was also wearing a pair of knitted gloves and had a knitted sweatband round her head.

'Hi,' said Lulu, bouncing up and down on her feet. Then she jogged over to the outside door and had a look along the deck. 'No one there. I'll just check the lounge, hate to miss any eager beavers!'

William and the others exchanged nervous smiles while they waited. One or two people swung their arms in warm-up movements. After a moment or two Lulu was back. 'No, I don't think anyone else is going to make it, we've given them a good five minutes' grace, so we'll start. Remember, at the end of the walk, I'm going to hand out vouchers. Collect eight and you can have a free foot and ankle massage.' Everyone looked more cheerful at this. 'Now, follow me.' Off she set through the starboard side door into the large stern lounge where the gambling and dancing had been taking place the previous evening. In an untidy straggle, the little group followed, William bringing up the rear.

The lounge now looked rather forlorn with chairs upside down on tables while its carpet was being vacuum cleaned. Lulu led them through a narrow bit of passage, then out on to the sheltered Lido Deck where brave breakfasters were tackling bowls of fruit and cereal, plates of eggs and bacon and ample quantities of croissants, toast, Danish pastries and other delights. William's tummy began to rumble as he followed swiftly along.

The little trail of walkers raised considerable comment as they made their way round the ship. There were many doors to be opened, stairs to be negotiated, lounges to be circled. The pace was fast, too fast for comfortable conversation and William noted that not everyone was managing to keep up. Beth, though, certainly was. She swung easily along, hardly out of breath, whilst some of the others were beginning to pant and had to break into a run every now and then to catch up. Well, thought William, apart from Lulu, Beth and I have to be the youngest in the group, it would be a scandal if they weren't in reasonable shape.

As they started on the second circuit of the ship the

public address system asked if Philip Burrell could go to the purser's office. That probably meant the stores manager was going to be carpeted for his part in the fracas the previous evening. Belonging to a service himself, William didn't have much difficulty in imagining how severely such a lapse in discipline would be looked upon by senior officers. Then he forgot about the incident as he found it required concentration to keep up with the diminutive figure of the Keep Fit Instructor.

As they completed the fourth circuit of the ship, there came another call for the stores manager. Beth was beside him as it came and she made a small face. 'Wonder what he's up to,' she commented as William held a door open for her.

'What do you mean?'

'They're obviously having difficulty finding him,' she said, moving easily and directing her words over her shoulder.

'There was a bit of an incident last night,' he said, projecting his words so she could hear him. 'Perhaps he's sleeping things off.'

'No, they'll have checked his cabin,' Beth called back to him.

William remembered she said she had worked on a cruise ship. He almost suggested that perhaps the stores manager had been in someone else's cabin but not only did that seem out of place but he remembered the look on the cruise director's face. If she'd been prepared to make things up between them later that night, he'd take early retirement.

They passed doors to the companionway that ran round one of the decks. These were barred with a notice forbidding passengers to go out on the open deck but through them William saw his old friend, Sergeant Stan Dobson, striding along with a purposeful step. The ocean spray did not seem to trouble him.

Lulu was now moving even faster, she seemed intent on getting the walk over and done with as quickly as possible. Several of her team called out to her to slow down. She turned an apologetic face. 'I'm sorry, but you'll have to shape up, you're obviously out of condition. OK, one more circuit of the deck then we're done.'

That didn't, in fact, turn out to be the end, for after the last circuit there were stretching exercises for leg and thigh muscles.

'Same time tomorrow,' Lulu said after straightening up from the last stretch. She thrust a small voucher at each of them.

'She's in a rush,' commented one of the walkers.

William walked thoughtfully back to his cabin.

Chapter Eight

Lulu dashed straight from the mile walk down to one of the lower decks. 'Where's Phil?' she demanded, addressing the Goanese steward who hovered outside his cabin. She tried the door but it was locked.

The steward shook his head. 'Not sleep in bed last night,' he said.

'Show me!'

He hesitated a moment then produced a key, unlocked the cabin door and opened it for her. Lulu looked inside. The room was incredibly neat, as Phil always was. Not like her, she was always leaving clothes on the floor, newspapers strewn around, half drunk cups of coffee on any available surface. The bunk was pristine, the cover neatly arranged, the bed-clothes beneath obviously undisturbed. No nightcap stood on the little shelf the way Phil always put it as he prepared for bed.

Lulu made a small, despairing noise and tore out of the cabin in the same mad rush as had brought her down from the upper decks. Further along the corridor, was the cruise director's cabin. Careless of the steward, now relocking Phil's door, she banged on the polished wood.

Nothing happened. Panic, frustration and bitter

anger were all welling up inside her. She banged again.

A voice mumbled something. The door was slowly opened and there was Karen, pulling the belt of a silk robe around her. There was a bruise on her left cheekbone, a disfiguring darkness that would soon be purple. Lulu ignored this and pushed past the woman. 'He's in here, I know it.'

Inside was more neatness, the utilitarian cabin made feminine by silk cushions, an arrangement of flowers, a collection of photographs. There was no one else there.

Lulu yanked open the tiny shower room. That, too, was empty.

'What are you doing?' Karen said angrily, her voice hostile.

Lulu sank on to the rumpled bunk and put her head into her hands. 'I was sure he was here,' she mumbled.

'What the hell are you talking about?' Karen shut the shower door and came and stood in front of her.

'Phil!'

'He'd better not be anywhere near here! What on earth made you think he was?'

Lulu wasn't going to let her get away with that. 'You know why! He's been running round you for weeks, ever since that time you went off together in Athens. After that he went right off me.' She brushed angry tears away. 'We were an item before that.'

Karen found her a tissue. 'That was hardly my fault,' she said, her frostiness warming slightly. 'But you're wrong, there was never, I mean, there isn't any-thing between us. Oh, I liked him, he was, is a nice fellow, but, well, there's someone else, you see.' She glanced involuntarily at one of the photographs on the dressing table.

Following her gaze, Lulu recognized a snapshot of Harry Summers, the first officer. 'Go for the top brass, don't you,' she said spitefully, looking round the cabin again. The privileges of position! She had to share hers with one of the hairdressing girls and they didn't have a shower. The times she had to wait for one to be free!

Karen sat down in the sole chair the cabin offered and arranged one long and shapely leg over the other. She rearranged the silk robe then reached for a packet of cigarettes. With graceful gestures, she pulled one out, found a gold cigarette lighter and lit it. She took a deep drag, blew a long, cool spiral of smoke into the upper reaches of the cabin and said, 'I don't know why you thought you could barge your way in here and find Phil. What on earth brought that on?'

Lulu stared at her. 'You must have heard, there are messages out for him. He's missing!'

'Missing?' Karen gave her a level gaze. 'What on earth do you mean? We're at sea, how can he be missing? You're the sort who gets her exercise leaping to the wrong conclusions.'

Lulu let out a mew of distress. 'You bitch! As soon as I saw his bed hadn't been slept in, I knew where he'd spent the night. Why don't you just tell me?' By now she didn't care Phil had been unfaithful, after all, he'd dumped her days ago, she'd been through all that. She just wanted him safe.

Karen took another drag on her cigarette and sighed. 'You're hysterical. He's just checking the stores or whatever and is wanted urgently for something else.'

'But they've called his name twice. Something must have happened to him.'

Karen gave another impatient sigh, emitting yet more cigarette smoke. 'Honestly, Lulu, your imagination is working overtime. Get back to work and let me get up.' She looked at herself in the mirror and winced. 'My God, I've got a job in front of me before I can face anyone today.'

Now Lulu registered the bruise. 'What happened? Sky-high Harry go for you?' she needled.

'No! For heaven's sake!' Karen looked exasperated then gave a shrug of her shoulders. 'It'll be all round the ship before lunch, I expect. I'm surprised you haven't heard already. Harry and Phil had a bit of an altercation last night in the Oyster Bar. Phil waved his arms and my face was in the way. So Harry hit him.' It came out smoothly, as though she'd practised the explanation. 'That's all,' she ended firmly. 'So don't you go building it up into some great drama. It'll all be sorted out by the end of today.'

But Lulu stared at her. 'Harry Summers hit Phil? In the Oyster Bar?' she gasped. 'Over you? I don't believe it. A fight could mean instant dismissal.'

Karen bit her lip. 'It was a misunderstanding.'

'You two-timing bitch! You keep Phil dangling after you then ruin your other lover's career. Fine entertainment you provide!'

In one swift movement, she was off the bunk and out of the cabin, slamming the door behind her. The impetus carried her down the corridor for a little way, then she slowed down and started to think. Was Karen telling her the truth? Phil could be a moody bugger. If Sky-high Harry had actually knocked him down, he could easily have gone off somewhere for a real sulk. Maybe got hold of a bottle of whisky or something. Perhaps even now he was flat out on one of the upper decks, dead drunk. If Karen had given him the old heave-ho, it'd be what he'd do.

Lulu dug fists into the pockets of her sweat pants. What a stupid idiot Phil was! Why on earth did she care for him so much? Especially after he'd treated her so badly.

Suddenly she became aware of the time. She could have clients queuing up for the swimming pool and the gym! Sod Phil, she had a career after all! Lulu turned round and headed for her little domain.

Back in her cabin, Karen stubbed out her half-smoked cigarette with controlled violence. She picked up the telephone and punched in a number, drumming her fingers on the shelf as she waited for the ringing to be answered.

'For God's sake, Harry,' she said when at last it was. 'Did you take sleeping pills, or something? I've had that stupid little keep fit girl, Lulu, here. She says there's a call out for Phil. She thinks something's happened to him . . . What do you mean, keep calm? I am calm!' she shouted down the receiver. 'Only if she thinks that, what about the rest of the ship? And she didn't even know what happened in the Oyster Bar! Bugger you, Harry, why can't you keep your temper? And why can't you turn up when you say, not half an hour early!' She slammed down the receiver and fumbled for another cigarette, tears streaming down her face.

Chapter Nine

As William walked back to his cabin whistling 'Down among the dead men', he felt the ship change direction.

Surely, he thought, their route must lie in a more or less straight line? He stood still, tried to assess where they were going, then ran back upstairs.

Back on deck, he could see that the ship was swinging right round. It looked as though they were returning the way they'd come. He wasn't the only passenger to notice, either. People were starting to crowd the rails, pointing and talking amongst themselves. The words 'Man overboard!' floated towards him. Suddenly the suggestion that the call for the stores manager was being made because he'd gone missing began to acquire a sinister meaning.

He walked back to the cabin thinking deeply.

When he opened the door, Darina was sitting up in bed drinking a cup of tea and looking much better. 'Perhaps I'm getting my sea legs,' she said as William gave her a kiss. 'How was your walk?'

He sat on the bed and started stripping off his tracksuit as he gave her a boisterous account of their rapid circling of the deck, deliberately omitting any mention of the stores manager. 'You'd have thought she was aiming to make Olympic walkers of us,' he finished.

'Shall I organize breakfast in bed for you or do you feel up to the restaurant? There are lots of people on the Lido Deck but it's a bit blowy for me.'

Darina put her cup carefully on the bedside table. 'I think I could manage the restaurant,' she said cheerfully.

They found a table for two, William saying that he thought it was better if Darina didn't have to make the effort to talk to anybody else. While she had fruit and a yoghurt, he tucked into bacon and eggs followed by toast and marmalade. 'My, that makes a man of one,' he said at the end.

'I think you're going for this walk just so you can justify having a proper breakfast,' Darina laughed. 'What are you going to do to work up an appetite for lunch? Dash up and down the swimming pool?'

'In this weather, you've got to be joking! I thought we could have a nice quiet morning, I think you need it,' he added, looking at her closely. Darina had lost the greenish tinge she'd had earlier but she still looked pale.

'What about all those fantastic activities they're offering us? Bridge, line dancing and I don't know what else!'

'Look, as long as you don't have to be working, I'm happy to take a good book and find somewhere quiet to get away from everything.' William was determined to make the most of this comfortable, very attractive ship. It was like being in a grand, floating hotel, with all its conveniences but none of its bustle; there was nothing to worry about and people to look after you at every turn. It seemed a shame to start dashing around doing things when you could relax and forget all about the world back home. Pity about the weather but it was bound to improve soon.

'Ah, my work,' said Darina and he didn't like the note in her voice. 'Do you remember what you said last night?'

William didn't.

Darina told him.

He stared at her. 'But I didn't mean anything derogatory. I think you're fantastic, you know that.'

'You said my cookery writing wasn't important.'

'Is that what it sounded like?'

She nodded, looking at him with big, hurt eyes.

William sighed, heavily. 'I didn't mean it like that.' He flapped a frustrated hand in the air. 'It's just, well, sometimes . . .'

Darina said nothing, just waited.

William pulled himself together. If he wasn't careful, things could get very difficult here. 'Darling, you're the most wonderful cook, you write well, you come over a treat on television, you've making a marvellous career for yourself and I'm your most loyal fan.'

It wasn't enough.

'So, what did you mean about getting down to something important?' insisted Darina.

Then, as he tried to think what he could say that would convince her, she leaned towards him. 'What you mean is, food is something we all have to cook and eat so what's the big deal.' It was a statement, not a question. 'Despite the fact that you admitted last night you feel so much better cutting certain things out of your diet, you still can't see that winning the Booker Prize isn't any more important than persuading people that making food enjoyable and healthy can transform their lives.'

William shifted uncomfortably in his chair. 'I'm sure you're right, darling, and I'm backing you all the way. After all . . .' He hesitated – too long.

'After all, you put up with all my experiments and not wanting to start a family and not earning vast sums of money,' Darina finished for him, sounding, he realized with a sinking heart, more than a touch bitter.

'Money doesn't enter into it!' he said swiftly.

'Ah, so the other things do,' Darina said equally swiftly.

'Look,' William said with great emphasis. 'I do think what you do is important, really I do.' It sounded weak, even to his ears, but at the moment she seemed determined to turn everything he said the way she wanted. 'You'll just have to believe me.' He wondered what had got into Darina, she wasn't usually sensitive like this.

She looked down at her plate and he noticed that she hadn't added mascara to her pale lashes. That was unusual, too. He waited, knowing that he couldn't think of anything else to say that would help but dreading what she was going to come up with next.

At last she looked up at him with sad eyes. 'I suppose I've got to try and believe you,' she said.

'That's something,' he encouraged her. 'Now all I've got to do is prove it.' At least he wouldn't be foolish enough to speak without thinking again.

She gave him a weak smile.

William felt as though the ship had narrowly skirted a *Titanic*-sized iceberg. He cleared his throat. 'They've got some quite nice postcards of the ship. Think I'll write one to the parents. You sending one to your mother?'

'I'll wait until we reach a port,' Darina said. 'I'm going to look for a good book.'

The library led off a quiet lounge with comfortable settees and chairs and a piano that no one was playing at the moment. Outside was the grey sky and the white-capped waves. As Darina made for a pair of unoccupied chairs by the big picture windows, Enid Carter waved an excited arm at them. 'Have you noticed we're going backwards?'

'What do you mean?' asked Darina, glancing at the sea. 'Surely we're going straight ahead!'

'But we've turned round. It's all because one of the officers is missing. He's thrown himself overboard after a fight over a woman!'

'Good heavens!' Darina sat down with a thump beside Enid. 'Are you sure?' She looked at William, as though he must know the truth of the matter.

He wished he could be more reassuring. 'They do seem to be looking for him, and Enid's quite right, the ship does appear to be going back the way we've come.'

'He definitely had a fight with one of the other officers. Someone who was there told me.'

'We were there, too,' said Darina. 'What did you hear?'

'You were? Oh, well, then you'll know all about it.' Enid sounded disappointed.

'Tell us what you heard,' William said. No one knew better than a police officer how accounts of any incident got twisted in the telling. It would be interesting to see what had happened to this one.

'Well . . .' Enid recaptured her initial excitement

and leaned forward. She seemed unaware that her waistcoat, caught between the cushion and the side of the chair, was pulling off her back. 'Apparently,' she said in a confidential tone, 'Mr Burrell, that's the stores manager, caught his girlfriend, the cruise director, in such a smooch with one of the officers in the Oyster Bar, what was his name? Smith? Spring? No, Summers, that was it.' She gave a brief, dramatic pause. 'So Mr Burrell dragged the officer up, said he was a two-timing bastard and hit him.' Another pause. Neither William nor Darina interrupted. 'Then he hit Karen and the other officer hit him. There was such a fight! When it was stopped Mr Summers swore he was going to kill Mr Burrell and Karen said she'd never have anything to do with either of them again. What do you think of that?' Enid ended triumphantly.

Darina and William looked at each other. Then William said, 'I'm sorry but it really wasn't as dramatic as that.' In a few words he told Enid what they had seen.

'Well,' she said undaunted, 'it's still serious. He'll be due for hauling up in front of the captain – and as for the first officer, I can't imagine what will happen to him. Still, I can't quite see why they turned the ship around, I bet Mr Burrell just went and drowned his sorrows in alcohol and then passed out somewhere. They'll find him.'

'I hope so,' said William, thinking that she might well have the right explanation.

'Oh, look, there are Jim and Mary French,' Enid waved at them just as she had at Darina and William. 'I must go and see what they've heard. You don't mind if I leave you two young things?' Taking their permission for granted, she bounded up and went over to where the other couple had settled themselves in a quiet corner.

'Do you really think that's what's happened?' Darina asked William.

'You mean, is he lying in a drunken stupor in some dark corner? Heaven only knows.'

'He seemed so nice last night.' Darina's face creased in distress. 'I thought the fight was bad enough, that other officer seemed so, so overbearing. I'm sure what happened was because he lost his temper. I hope that Phil Burrell is found.'

William could only agree. He watched Darina open her book and gradually become absorbed in its recipes.

His own book was the autobiography of a stewardess who'd survived the *Titanic* disaster. It had looked more interesting than sociological implications of criminal law. He leafed through the first few pages then found himself thinking of the place work had in people's lives. Darina and he had nearly had a major row over his thoughtless words that had denigrated her career. Now here was the stores manager, whose working and private life were so bound together that it seemed a whole ship was in danger of being drawn into a personal drama. Then there was the ex-farmer, Michael Harwood, who, at an age most men were looking forward to retirement, was so obviously mourning the loss of his livelihood. Having worked in a country police force, William knew first hand how hard a farmer's life and how much more than a job it was to most of them. And what about the lottery winner, Shona Mallory, giving all her winnings to her profession? What area of scientific research had so claimed her loyalty that she would give it money most people would welcome as the chance to achieve the sort of lifestyle they could only dream about? And, yes, thinking back to Enid Carter's comment at tea yesterday, what indeed did her family think about this decision? Had they been consulted, had they encouraged her, or were there tensions building up between her and those she loved?

William looked at his wife, seemingly lost in the cookery book she had chosen from the library. She really was dedicated to her career.

What about himself? How dedicated was he to his? A couple of years ago, William would have said he was as ambitious as anyone. Now? He wondered. The coalface of police work interested him as much as ever, it was the endless bureaucracy that got him down. That and the difficulties of managing the men under his command. Half the time when he should be pursuing an investigation, he was having to do paperwork or sorting out personnel problems. The rigid hierarchy of officers and men was advantageous in some ways, extremely difficult in others. The police really was a service as much as the army or navy.

With the navy, he was back to the problem of the stores manager. William thought again about the calls for him to go to the purser's office. Was he really missing? Had he been unable to face the results of his altercation with the first officer and gone into hiding? More likely that Enid Carter was right and he'd taken refuge in drink. The first officer, though, would be in for an even worse time. Perhaps there'd be a call out for him shortly.

'I think I'll have to go and get a sweater, it's not as

warm as I thought it would be,' Darina rubbed at her bare arms. 'I should have worn long sleeves.'

William looked appreciatively at the short sleeved-shirt and jeans she was wearing. Too often she chose loose-fitting clothes that hid her long legs and lovely curves. 'You sit there, I'll go and get it,' he said.

'Thanks, darling.' Darina gave him instructions on how to find the sweater she wanted.

Leaving the lounge, William made his way to an upper deck. The sea looked a little calmer, fresh air was an attractive thought and maybe the doors to the deck would be open.

They were and a watery sun was breaking through the clouds as he made his way towards the stern of the ship, noting that it was still headed back towards Southampton. Then he realized that considerable activity was taking place all around him. Sailors were opening odd lockers and doors and moving deckchairs. If anyone had asked him what was going on, he'd have said it was a very thorough search of the ship.

Where was Phil Burrell? Still on board, or had he, so to speak, jumped ship?

Chapter Ten

People moved in a slow flood out of the ship's theatre. The first of the port lectures was over.

'Did that make you want to visit, what was the name of the place, Sandane?' asked Daphne Rawlings.

'I think you pronounce the final "e",' said Shona Mallory. 'And it's "ah" in the middle. Sandahnuh.'

'Have you been there before?' Daphne asked idly, pausing to look at the window of the shop displaying sequinned tops and sweatshirts with the ship's logo.

'No, but there's a Norwegian in our office and I went through the itinerary with him a few weeks ago and learned a few phrases.'

'Obviously more than our friend the port lecturer did,' Daphne murmured.

Shona wondered if Daphne wanted to go inside the shop, she was looking very intently at the displays. The last thing Shona wanted to do was idly scan mementos she had no intention of buying or look at clothes she'd never in a million years wear.

Numbers of passengers, though, saw browsing as a profitable way of passing time and pushed past them into the well-lit interior where enticing signs offered them camera bargains and porcelain mugs decorated with the ship's logo.

Daphne finished her inspection. 'Nothing to interest me there, I'm afraid. Shops always tell so much about their clients, don't you think?'

Shona, relieved as well as amused, laughed, 'You mean, you don't have a very high opinion of your fellow passengers' fashion instincts.'

'Do you?' Daphne's glance as she looked around at the thinning-out crowd around them was contemptuous. 'Now if we were sailing in the Mediterranean or the Caribbean, we'd see some really smart passengers.'

'You know I'm hopeless where clothes are concerned. If I didn't have you to guide me, I'd rival the worst Oxfam devotee. Let's go and find a quiet seat somewhere, this swell makes getting around quite tiring. A cup of coffee would be nice, too.'

'Will Paul be joining us?'

Shona made a moue, though if anyone had described the disappointed yet derisive movement of her lips as such, she'd have said she'd never heard of the word. 'I doubt it. He's gone to the bridge lecture, says it's an ideal opportunity to brush up on technique. I don't suppose we'll see him until lunchtime.'

They found two comfortable armchairs in a lounge where a waitress in a smart uniform offered to bring them coffee.

'The crew are better dressed than most of the passengers,' observed Daphne as the waitress left with their order.

'You should have brought some of your stock with you and set up in competition with the shop.'

'Yardarms and plank-walking would be considered too good for me if I tried anything like that!'

Shona looked at her friend. Daphne today was

casually elegant in navy slacks with a white sweatshirt decorated in slashes of navy blue and turquoise. Large enamel earrings in dark blue and gold added dazzle to her bronzed skin and blonde hair, cunningly cut so that it waved around her head in seemingly careless curls.

'How long does it take you to do your face and hair in the mornings?' Shona suddenly asked.

Daphne brought her attention back from studying the passengers. 'Good heavens, what a question! What on earth makes you ask that?'

'Oh, I don't know. Yes, I do,' Shona said honestly. 'I hope that looking wonderful the way you always do requires considerable effort. But I don't suppose it does,' she added mournfully. 'I mean, you still manage to look good even after a workout.'

Shona had met Daphne Rawlings at a health club near her home in Surrey. Conscious that as she reached the mid-forties, time was gradually eroding her physical energy, Shona had decided regular exercise was necessary. Golf took too long and tennis required other people, but an aerobics class at the local health club seemed the ideal answer. Paul spent Wednesday nights playing bridge with a male four and had long suggested she find something to do with herself that night.

Shona had signed up for an evening of strenuous activity; what hadn't occurred to her was that she might make friends with other women doing the same thing. Friendship wasn't something Shona really understood. But the first evening she'd gone to the class, she'd been swept up by Daphne.

'All virtuous from our exercise, we pop down to the local for a quick one before going home, how about joining us?' Daphne had suggested as they changed out of leotards and leggings in the well-appointed dressing room.

Shona's immediate reaction had been to recoil from the suggested intimacy. She started to say she had to get back. Then changed her mind. What had she to go back to? Paul wouldn't be home until late, the house was beautifully looked after by her daily, Mrs Warren, Julian no longer lived at home and the work she'd brought back from the office with her could wait. She was suddenly aware of the spartan isolation of much of her life. 'Why not?' she'd said with a smile that only later she'd realized was grateful.

Five of them had gone to the pub. There were two lawyers, an accountant and Daphne, who, Shona quickly learned, ran a classy dress shop just off the local high street. It seemed all the other women were her customers. At first Shona, cynically, thought that Daphne used the health club as a networking aid and that she'd been asked along with the others in order to attract her to Daphne's shop.

Even if that was so, though, Shona had enjoyed herself that first evening. Not since university had she mixed with intelligent women enjoying each other's company.

Against all the odds, for Shona had never been one for socializing and had always despised women who considered appearance was important, Daphne became a friend. For the first time, Shona had discovered the delights of confessing life's minor disasters and receiving reassurance on her conduct. No man had ever, in Shona's experience, understood this role.

Not even Paul. He was far too likely to take what

she told him at its face value and she would end up justifying her actions instead of being told not to doubt herself. So she'd stopped telling him about her day and learned to listen to his doings instead.

With Daphne she found she could rely on sympathy and a shared understanding of how stupid other people could be. After a few weeks, Daphne had suggested Shona have her page boy hairstyle cut short and then persuaded her into more flattering clothes than the severely plain chain-store suits she customarily wore. Soon they were talking on the telephone between Wednesday evenings, then playing golf on Sunday afternoons with Paul and whoever else was available at the club.

Once during a conversation on the shortcomings of men, Shona had asked Daphne about her ex-husband. But Daphne's usual stream of information had died. Instead she just said, 'Darling, he was horrendous. A common little man. It was the great mistake of my life. I can only say that at the time I thought marriage was better than being single and he seemed an eligible choice. *Grosse erreur!*' Daphne had a habit of peppering her conversation with odd French phrases. Shona first thought that she must have lived there.

'I wish!' Daphne had said in heartfelt tones when she suggested this. 'I think the only time I'm really happy is when I'm in France. The country, the food, the wine, the lifestyle, everything is *très très sympa*. But there's never been the opportunity to live there. More's the pity. I just go whenever I can.'

'I'm sorry we couldn't go to France,' Shona now said defensively to Daphne as their coffees arrived. 'It's Paul's fault. I thought he'd jump at the idea of a visit to the Côte d'Azur in a luxury hotel. But he said he'd always wanted to sample life on board ship and to see the Norwegian fjords. And he said the south of France was dreadful in the summer,' she added, even more defensively.

'Never dreadful,' murmured Daphne, sipping her coffee. Then looked up with a little, puzzled frown. 'Paul said he wanted to visit Norway? I thought he said it was you who wanted to go and he'd thought, what a good idea.'

Shona couldn't ever remember saying anything about Norway. Typical Paul, she thought, slightly exasperated, making it seem as though the gift she was giving him was something for her.

'And this is wonderful,' Daphne continued, looking around the panelled lounge, half filled with somnolent or reading passengers. 'Though I'm reminded of the time Dorothy Parker was told President Coolidge was dead and she said, "How can they tell?" Where are the young, or even the middle-aged? When I worked on a cruise ship, they were everywhere!' Then she looked as though she could have bitten out her tongue.

'You worked on a ship?' Shona picked up on the comment immediately. 'You never told me.'

'Not one of my more glorious episodes.' Daphne actually looked embarrassed. 'It was just after I'd separated from my husband. I needed a job, someone told me a ship's shop needed staff and it seemed a perfect solution.'

'Was it?' pressed Shona.

'Well, I enjoyed the ports, it was a world cruise, places I'd always wanted to visit, like Singapore and Hong Kong – the shopping, my dear! – and some of the passengers were fun. But when we got back home the divorce had come through, I'd got my settlement and could open my own shop so I said goodbye to ship life without regret.'

Shona wasn't bothered about the rest of the passengers. Their little party was a self-contained unit. Then, belatedly, she realized how it mightn't be so for Daphne. 'No doubt you probably hoped to meet some eligible single man or two,' she said, a trifle stiffly. She didn't like to think Daphne needed other company than theirs.

Daphne gave her the warm, open grin that lit up her face. 'They're only trouble, darling! Oh, I won't deny that if a really attractive, really wealthy man fell across my path, I wouldn't be grateful. In the meantime, though, I'm absolutely thrilled to be with you and Paul in this lovely ship with this fascinating sounding voyage ahead of us. If only the boat would stop moving about so much!' she added with a small grimace.

'You're not feeling seasick?' enquired Shona in some alarm, she wasn't good around any sort of illness.

'Nothing a brandy a little later won't settle.'

'Little later, nonsense, now!' Shona waved at the waitress and ordered a large vintage brandy.

'Wonderful to have one's lightest wish satisfied,' Daphne said in a wry tone.

'Oh dear, am I being patronizing?'

'You've got to stop apologizing. I didn't mean anything other than it's lovely to be so well looked after. You and Paul are just sweet to have me along with you.'

'We enjoy your company,' Shona assured her, softening her prickliness. 'But you mustn't feel you have to keep thanking me,' she added earnestly. Having you with us was something I really wanted. You've given me so much over the past three years, more than I can ever repay.'

Shona meant this. Making friends with Daphne had been as exciting and enjoyable as falling in love with Paul – though in a very different way, of course.

'Listen.' Daphne leaned forward and put a hand on Shona's knee. 'The way you've welcomed me into your family has been a real joy.'

Paul hadn't taken to Daphne initially. 'All gin and golf club,' he'd said after she'd had supper with them that first time. 'Can't think what you see in her.'

'That's because you've only seen her social side,' Shona had told him. She'd been very disappointed that the conversation had never got beyond the superficial chit-chat that had turned her off so much of the Surrey society Paul had introduced her to when they'd first got together. After the fourth dinner party they'd attended, she'd complained, 'What is the point of spending precious time discussing the state of the golf club greens and how the High Street has declined and what the price of houses is at the moment, versus what it will be next month? We would have been better off spending the evening at home with ourselves.' She'd stroked his arm as she said this, she who normally hated physical contact with others. That was how he had affected her.

'You would have had to cook,' Paul had teased.

Yes, indeed! Paul was the first to say that Shona's cooking was not what he had married her for. Shona wanted to know what it was about her that had attracted such a charismatic man? She who was plain and had few social graces.

81

'You give me gravitas,' he'd said the first time she'd asked him. 'You make it clear there's more to me than a slick public relations parasite.'

He'd smiled as he said it but for once Shona thought he might not be joking. It was this streak of honesty in him, this straightforwardness, that had made her accept his invitation out for dinner after they'd met at her cousin Natalie's second wedding.

She had wandered out on to the terrace, clutching her glass of champagne as though it might be snatched by terrorists. There she'd found Paul. Or he had found her.

'Of course he wants you,' Natalie, still besotted by her new husband all of three months later, had said. 'You're a director of research at one of the country's top scientific establishments. You are interviewed in serious newspapers. You belong to the intellectual establishment and they'd never give him a second look. You're much more of a trophy wife than some long-haired bimbo. The wonder of it is that you consider he's got something to interest *you*! Get a life, Shona, he'll bore you in ten months and this is from one who knows!'

But Paul had never bored her. Perhaps it was because at the end of the day what she wanted was to switch off rather than to indulge in deep, meaningful discussions (deep, meaningful discussions were not Paul's forte) and he made her laugh. Still, she enjoyed discussing life's issues with Daphne and her group, and it was a shame that Daphne hadn't shown any of that side of herself when she'd come round for supper.

Shona had persevered, though, and eventually Paul had admitted that there was more to Daphne than he'd first thought.

'Shona,' said Daphne abruptly after her brandy had arrived, 'are you still intending to give all your lottery winnings to research?'

'Oh, Daphne,' Shona sighed, 'we've been through all that.'

'I know you're terribly idealistic and that you said money was the root of all evil and it would ruin your relationship with Paul but isn't giving it away going to place a strain on it as well?'

'If it wasn't that I know the money will do so much good, I could wish I'd never bought the ticket!' Shona said violently. So violently, interested looks were thrown at the two of them, though nobody, surely, could have heard exactly what had been said.

'Why did you?' Daphne asked, warming the brandy glass in the hollow of her hand with as much care as though it were an egg and she the mother hen.

'Because I needed the money to set up my foundation. The lottery was my only hope; after all, where else could I get hold of such a large sum? I never expected to win so much but it meant I could dream. And I did explain it all to Paul. If I won a really huge amount, I said, we'd have a super holiday, but he wasn't to think it would revolutionize our lives. I've seen what money can do and I never want it to happen to us.'

'What have you seen?' Daphne tossed back the brandy and signalled to the waitress that she'd like another.

Shona wished she hadn't spoken so hastily. But it wasn't the bare facts that were important now. 'I knew someone once who was ruined by too much money,' she said after a pause.

A clear mental picture of Charlie rose before her. Lovely, charming Charlie, who had made life such fun; more, he'd made her feel she was somebody special. 'You're pure crystal,' he'd said. 'Much more precious than gold.' His collection of crystals was placed carefully on a long coffee table; he claimed they filtered life for him.

With all the innocence of nineteen years, Shona only gradually realized she was part of Charlie's rebellion against his rich family and their accepted social mores. After it was all over and she was very much wiser about people and the world, she'd seen herself for what she was: a repressed, shy, clever girl from a working-class family whose father used to beat her if her schoolwork fell below par.

And that was what had attracted Charlie. He'd said that his father had beaten him psychologically, placing his expectations on Charlie's shoulders. Shona, he'd said, was his refuge.

Fine refuge she'd turned out to be! But perhaps no one could have rescued him from the damage his retreat into drugs had caused. Towards the end he used to rail at her for not understanding, for being so righteous about his habits. 'You don't really love me at all,' he'd complained bitterly.

It had torn Shona apart. She'd fought so furiously to make him understand he had to give them up. His family had fought, too, but by hiring expensive lawyers to get him out of trouble. Such as when he'd tried to smuggle a huge amount of cannabis into the country from India. And then when he'd been arrested for stealing after they'd cut off his allowance. Even though he said he'd rejected all their middle-class values, he'd always known they were there for him, that they'd never let him go to prison.

All their money, though, hadn't helped in the end. Charlie was doomed. He knew it and took what he saw was the only way out.

Was that when Shona had refused to allow anyone else to come near her until she met Paul all those years later?

'Who was it?' Daphne asked eagerly. 'Who had his life ruined by money? He must have been important to you.'

Sometimes Daphne could be too intrusive. 'It was a long time ago,' Shona said dismissively. 'I only knew him for a short time.'

She'd been married to Paul for over four years and they had flown past. In contrast, the two years with Charlie seemed to have occupied decades. So much passion, disappointment, frustration, heartbreak and the final, numbing pain that threatened to destroy her totally.

Daphne looked sceptical but seemed to realize nothing would be gained by pressing for more information at this stage. 'So, just because you once knew a spoiled rich kid, you refuse to allow your family to benefit from your good fortune.'

Shona was suddenly alert. 'Has Paul put you up to this?' she asked Daphne.

The other woman was saved from an immediate answer by the arrival of the brandy.

After the girl had left, she said, 'You can't think that Paul would discuss something like that with me, can you? But I can see how it's eating away at him that you won't provide the capital he needs to rescue his business. And how Julian resents the fact that you could start him in his career but won't.'

Wow! Shona thought in dismay. Is that the way it appears?

'Look,' she said abruptly. 'It's our business, nobody else's.'

'I know,' said Daphne soothingly. 'But I'm your friend and I can't see you ruining your life without saying something.'

'That's what you think?' Shona stared at her. 'That I'm ruining my life?'

'All your lives,' Daphne urged.

'That's the trouble with money,' Shona said bitterly. 'The moment there's a lot of it around, people assume they have rights to it. And it poisons everything.'

'You're a hard woman, Shona,' Daphne said.

'If I am it's for the best. I'm not going to finance Julian into setting up a musical agency because if I did it would fail. He hasn't the experience or the contacts. This way, he has to work his way up and when he's a success, and I really do hope he will succeed, he will have done it all himself. As for Paul . . .' She hesitated a moment, but too much had been said for her not to continue. 'Would it be kind to enable him to make a second failure of things? His company is going under because he's a hopeless businessman. I've said I'll pay off his creditors but I won't give him the capital to start again because I know he'd make an even worse mess of things. I'm realistic, Daphne, and if that makes me hard, well, I'm sorry but that's the way things are. I'm not prepared to compromise. Putting large sums of money at Paul's and Julian's disposal would just ruin them.'

Daphne drew her breath in sharply. 'My God, did you really tell Paul that?'

For the first time Shona wondered whether she wouldn't have been wiser to wrap things up a bit when she'd had it out with Paul. Even to have given him, say, two hundred thousand pounds? But it wouldn't have been enough. It was taking a hundred thousand to buy out his creditors and she needed all her winnings if the foundation she was planning was to carry out its aims. 'Look,' she said to Daphne, 'I've told Paul he's a really good PR man and if he works for somebody else, he'll be brilliant. He's had job offers, well, one offer.'

'From a boy who doesn't know what time of day it is,' Daphne said bitterly.

'He told you?' Shona's voice was brittle. 'When was that?'

Daphne looked suddenly uncomfortable. 'Oh, I don't know. The other day when I came over for supper, you must have been out of the room.'

Shona hadn't realized Paul was on those sort of terms with Daphne.

'He was boasting, really,' Daphne hurried on. 'You know, saying how he was being head-hunted, you know the way Paul talks!'

That had the ring of truth all right. 'There you are, he's admitted it himself! That he has to find a job instead of trying to run his own company.'

Daphne looked at her friend in total astonishment. Could she really not see what her refusal to use this unexpected windfall to set Paul up properly was doing to him? Surely he could hire a real accountant who could keep him from making the same mistakes he had in the past?

How could Shona give all that money away? Especially to such a cause.

Shona had always been an enigma, it had been part of her attraction for Daphne. Mostly people were too easily manipulated. Shona had been a real challenge. How on earth had she managed to attract Paul? She was too sharp, too awkward for such a socially adept man. As Paul now realized.

Daphne was going to have to arrange matters. Somehow Shona had to be prevented from giving all that money to her stupid foundation. Not only was Daphne dead against its aims, she had to ensure that Paul – and Julian of course, she'd like to pull him into the circle of those who admired and loved her – received what was surely only his due, both their dues.

Daphne downed her second brandy in one decisive gulp.

Chapter Eleven

William made his way to the stern of the ship, noting still more signs of a painstaking search of the ship.

What a relief he was on holiday and no part of this investigation! He caught sight of the ex-policeman, Security Officer Stan Dobson. Almost he went and asked him what gave. But he controlled the impulse. Nothing would be gained from interrupting an obviously very busy man and, anyway, William repeated to himself, he was on holiday.

He looked over the side at the waves moving powerfully as the ship steamed through them. The sea couldn't be called really rough, it was as though the forces were playing, determined to demonstrate their strength whilst keeping it in check. The water looked very cold, the little white caps dancing like frosting edging December foliage. He imagined the effect of falling from one of these decks into its dark depths.

He looked at the speed the ship was going. How long could anyone survive in these chilly waters? And what were the chances of them being found? William was pretty sure the answers to both those questions would not be hopeful for any victim. And if the stores manager had fallen overboard, had it been an accident? Had he intended to jump? Or was he pushed?

Below decks there appeared to be an equally thorough search going through the cabins. Stewards were knocking on doors, then letting themselves in when no reply came.

When he got to his cabin, William found Manuel there. The bed had been made, the tea tray removed, he could just have finished doing all this but William didn't think so. 'Quite a job you've got on,' he said cheerfully, going to the cupboard where Darina had said she'd hung her sweater. The door wasn't quite closed. Had she left it like that or had the steward been looking inside?

The steward muttered something incomprehensible, opened the shower room door and glanced inside, then excused himself and left.

William grasped the sweater, locked the cabin door and hurried back to the upper decks. But Stan Dobson had disappeared, so had most of the sailors. It looked as through the search had been completed. Did that mean Phil Burrell been found?

Back in the lounge, Darina was still sitting where he had left her and Enid Carter was deep in conversation with Jim and Mary French. Several other couples had drifted in and seated at the piano was Julian Mallory, looking more alive than William had yet seen him, playing the hit song, 'Memory', from the musical *Cats*. Singing the words whilst leaning nonchalantly against the boudoir grand, holding Julian's gaze with hers and seemingly oblivious to any audience, was Tara.

'We're having a concert,' whispered Darina as he handed over the sweater.

'So I see,' he replied. He sat down beside her and tried to forget about the missing stores manager.

Tara had a sweet and true voice. In a larger setting, though, she would need amplification, the sound she made didn't carry far. But the wistfulness she conveyed was attractive and to William it sounded as though she'd been well trained.

Julian's skill at the piano matched her singing.

A couple of people broke into applause at the end.

Tara gave a delighted little bow, then waved a hand at her pianist and Julian grinned. Away from his family he seemed somehow older and more, well, responsible was the word that came to William.

'What would you like to sing now?' Julian asked, looking encouraging.

Tara thought for a moment, 'Can you play, "I Will Survive"?' she asked.

'Of course.' Without hesitation Julian went into a short introduction, gave her a nod of his head and plunged into the melody. William knew the song as a theme tune for gay men but Tara reclaimed it for her own. Totally different from the wistfulness she'd shown for 'Memory', she was raunchy and held nothing back.

With the song in full flood, William suddenly noticed Stan Dobson standing in the doorway trying with all the unobtrusiveness of a heavyweight fighter on his way to a title to attract his attention. Murmuring an apology to Darina, William quietly went to join the security officer.

Stan Dobson was apologetic. 'Sorry, sir, I know it's none of your business but there's something of a difficult situation and I'd welcome a word of advice, like.'

William took a deep breath as he felt adrenalin flood through him. Now he could admit, to himself at any rate, how deep his interest in the disappearance of the stores manager was. 'Do I gather you've got a case of a missing person on board – if that's not a contradiction in terms?' he asked as he was led down the stairs to B Deck.

'Well, sir, we hope that he is indeed on board because we don't want to consider the alternative,' Stan Dobson said heavily. 'However, it now looks as though Mr Burrell could have taken matters, as you might say, into his own hands.'

William's first frisson of excitement vanished. This was a man's life at stake.

'It looks, in fact,' Stan Dobson continued, 'as though we may have to call in the police but there's a bit of a complication come up and seeing as how we had a senior officer already on board, it seemed best if we could ask you to have a look at the evidence, such as it is.'

The security officer opened the door of what looked like an inside cabin. A discreet sign, though, announced that it was the stores manager's office. A very worried young officer in shirt-sleeves waited for them. Behind him was a desk with a computer. The computer was on and the screen displayed what looked at a quick glance to be a letter.

'This is Roger Coutts, assistant to the stores manager. Roger, Detective Chief Inspector William Pigram has very kindly agreed to look at what you've discovered.'

The worried look deepened. 'You don't believe me, do you, Sarge?'

'I believe what's on that screen, there.' Stan waved a hand towards the computer.

'But you don't see what the rest of it means!' Roger Coutts sounded exasperated.

William remembered back to the days when he worked with Stan Dobson. A reliable, hard-working officer who could be depended upon to do everything by the book and believed that painstaking police work solved any crime. Imagination, though, and grasping the importance of small details that didn't quite fit in to an overall picture were not his strengths.

'Not something that means anything,' Stan said stolidly now.

'Perhaps you could explain exactly what you've found,' suggested William, trying to see what was on the screen.

Stan squared his shoulders. 'What Mr Coutts means, sir, is that he switched on the computer this morning . . .'

'I didn't, that's the point,' the young man said quickly. 'That's what seemed all wrong.'

'And found that message on the screen,' continued Stan as though he hadn't spoken. It was obvious what he considered most important.

They all looked at the computer and now William could read what was displayed there. *Nothing's worth anything any more. I'm sorry but I have to end it. Goodbye.* At the end of the message were the initials PJB.

'Philip John Burrell,' said Stan, intoning the name as though tolling a bell. 'Seems clear enough to me.'

'But that doesn't take into account that the machine wasn't switched off.' Roger was getting more exasperated by the minute.

'Let's start at the beginning, shall we?' suggested William, his mind switching smoothly into the routine of assembling information. He patted his pockets automatically but of course he didn't have a notebook on him. 'Got some scrap paper and a pencil?' he asked Roger Coutts.

'No problem.' A notepad appeared in an instant from a drawer plus a sharp pencil. Matters seemed to be well organized in this office, thought William. Nothing was out of place, everything neat, no piles of paper, empty cups or any of the paraphernalia that so often cluttered offices, including his own.

'Shall we sit down?' he suggested, taking the swivel chair.

For a moment it seemed as though the security officer was going to object, then a lifetime's training in submitting to senior officers clicked in and he took the chair that sat beside the desk. There wasn't another but Roger darted into an interior room and brought one out. 'That's my office,' he said, as though an explanation was called for.

They all settled themselves. William, in the missing stores manager's chair, was definitely in control. 'Right,' he said, looking at Roger. 'Start at when you first realized something was wrong.'

'Well, Phil's usually here when I come in just before eight. Devil for work he is!' Roger gave an involuntary grimace. 'He wasn't this morning but I thought he was probably opening up a locker for food to be taken out to start the day's catering. The butchers require meat, the kitchen needs vegetables, fruit, stores, all that, you see,' he added quickly to William. 'But then the chap in charge of the meat locker arrived and asked if Phil

94

could come and open it. So I said wasn't he down there already, and Raj said no, he wasn't. I didn't have the keys to the lockers, Phil always keeps those, he has this ruddy great ring with a collection that could act as ballast.' He swallowed as the awkwardness of his simile struck home.

'Did he always keep the key ring with him?'

Roger nodded. 'Security,' he said with a glance at Stan. 'I rang his cabin in case he'd overslept but there wasn't any answer. So then I put out a call for him.'

William remembered hearing that first call just after the morning walk had started.

'I thought he'd appear in a moment. Phil's ever so conscientious. But nothing happened. So there we were with no Phil and no keys. I didn't know what to do,' Roger said miserably. He sat hunched over, his hands between his open knees working themselves together.

'And what time was it by then?'

'It was ten past eight. I know because I looked at my watch.'

'Not very late, was it?' asked William, making a note.

'No, but, it wasn't like him,' Roger sounded obstinate, as though he knew what the facts in this matter were. 'Anyway, we needed the keys to the lockers. There's a different man in charge of each store and Phil hands him his key at the start of each day, then takes it back in the evening. There's a hell of a lot to do on the butchery side, they were desperate to get hold of the meat and I knew the cooks'd be screaming for fruit and vegetables any minute.'

'So you sent out another call?'

'Yes. But the purser has duplicates of the locker keys so he gave me those and told me to get on with things.' Roger ran a hand through his short red hair. 'At least that meant the kitchen could get started.'

William turned to the security officer. 'When did you get involved, Stan?'

'After Mr Coutts had alerted him, the purser got the steward to open up his cabin and they found that the bed hadn't been slept in. So then I was called. I didn't think anything much about it to start with until Francis filled me in on the incident in the Oyster Bar last night.' Stan paused for a moment. 'It was hard to believe Mr Summers had lost his temper like that. He'll be up before the captain and I doubt he has much of a career left. Well, anyway, that was when we informed the captain, he turned the ship round and we instituted a proper search.'

'We opened all the lockers,' Roger interposed eagerly. 'Just in case, well . . .' he left the sentence unfinished.

'Were they all locked?' asked William.

Roger nodded.

'So if you had found Mr Burrell in any of them, someone else would have had to lock him inside?'

'Quite, sir,' said Stan. 'It wasn't something we expected but routine has to be followed.'

Of course it had.

'The entire stores area was thoroughly searched,' Stan said grimly. 'Quite a job, sir. Any number of places you can hide someone down there. Then we started on the rest of the ship.'

'It sounds as though you thought you were looking for a body,' William suggested, drawing a small doodle on his pad as he absorbed the implications of the situation. A missing person on land could mean a number of different things. A voluntary disappearance, amnesia, an accident, a misunderstanding. Only after all those eventualities had been explored was either foul play or suicide accepted as a strong possibility. A missing person at sea was different; provided that it could be proved the person was not actually on the ship, the number of options narrowed alarmingly.

Stan considered the question. 'A body? Well, there had been the incident in the Oyster Bar and if the two participants had met later and come to blows again – you see, a fall in a ship in the wrong place can produce a nasty result. We felt he mightn't be dead, though, just unconscious.'

William noted that the possibility the first officer had knocked out the stores manager and just left his body to be found had been considered to be real. It said a great deal about the character of the first officer. He pictured again the tall, vital figure of Harry Summers striding into the bar and the way Francis Sterling's eyes had kept nervously returning to him.

William said, 'So, the search for Mr Burrell's body, alive or dead, continued, and you,' he turned back to Roger, 'do what?'

'I came back here to get on with paperwork. Not that it's paper these days, more like computer work. Though I suppose the printouts could count as paperwork,' he added as though it was important to get such matters absolutely right.

Was that Phil Burrell's training? William wondered.

'But when I came to turn the computer on, I

realized that it hadn't been turned off, only put on standby.' Now he sounded excited. 'And when I woke it up, there was the message.'

They all looked again at the screen, Stan twisting round so that he could see it properly.

William read it again. *Nothing's worth anything any more. I'm sorry but I have to end it. Goodbye.*

'Roger called me in immediately,' said Stan. He sounded tired and defeated. 'We'll finish the search, of course, but it sounds as though the answer to everything is at the bottom of the sea.'

'But, sir,' said Roger obstinately, 'the thing is, the computer wasn't turned off. Phil always turned off the machine. Completely off. That's the way he got rid of the FreeCell programs he couldn't finish. He wanted a perfect score on the statistics.'

'I can't see how that means anything,' Stan protested. 'If a man's going to jump overboard, he's going to leave his message where everyone can see it.'

'But he didn't leave it displayed,' Roger was almost shouting now. 'That's what I mean! I had to wake the computer up. That's when the message came up on the screen. It was arranged to appear immediately.'

'Let's just see what you're suggesting,' William said calmly. 'If I have it correctly, you think that because the computer wasn't completely switched off, you believe the message wasn't left by Mr Burrell but by someone else?'

Roger leant back in his chair and looked relieved. He nodded. 'That's it, exactly.'

'It's ridiculous,' Stan said immediately. 'Who would want to do something like that?'

Someone who wanted to make it look as though the

stores manager had jumped into the ocean, thought William. But Stan was right; on the face of it, the whole thing looked distinctly unlikely.

'Who has keys to this office?' he asked in a neutral voice, making more notes. 'Presumably it's kept locked?'

Roger nodded. 'Phil insisted on security. As to keys, apart from Phil himself, I have one and so does the purser and the staff officer. Oh, and the steward, of course, has a master that will open the door.'

That made five keys right away, thought William. 'Tell me again why you don't think Mr Burrell left that message.'

'Phil always turned the computer off. Right off,' Roger said obstinately.

'And why did he do that?' asked William quickly as he could see Stan take a deep breath as though about to treat this statement with the scorn reserved by New Zealand for the England rugby team.

Roger paused awkwardly for a moment, as though realizing he needed the persuasive powers of a politician. Then he reached for the mouse and brought the curser down to the bottom of the screen, on to a playing card icon. He double clicked and the screen was filled with a game of patience. 'Phil was – is,' he corrected himself hurriedly, 'a FreeCell addict.'

William looked at the game, which was also on his home computer. He rarely had time to play it but every now and then it could provide a moment of relaxation. If the cards lay badly it required a testing ability to think ahead. In the game now revealed, the player had reached a point where it was clear that that particular one would not work out.

'One for the scrap heap. You said he worried about the statistics?'

For answer, Roger opened the relevant file. There was a perfect score showing over nine hundred games had been successfully played.

'That requires skill amounting to genius,' said William. 'But he couldn't have been that good, could he? And you're not suggesting that ruining his score by failing to work out one game made him suicidal?' He looked at Roger.

'No, sir. Look at all the other games!'

Now William saw that the bottom of the screen contained more playing card icons. Roger brought each of them up and it was obvious that the games had all reached impasse.

'I didn't realize you could put them on standby, so to speak,' William said, marvelling at the procedure and feeling a veritable tyro.

'Not only that,' said Roger, rapidly returning each patience to its icon stage by clicking on a tiny button in the top right-hand corner of the title bar. 'Now, if you turn the machine off—'

'Don't,' warned William. A belated but necessary precaution.

'No, sir, I won't. But if you did, all those games,' and he indicated the half a dozen or so icons at the bottom of the screen, 'all of them will be wiped out and you can start again when you next turn the computer on.'

'Good heavens,' said William, realizing that he might now be able to achieve his ambition of winning one hundred games in a row. Or of it looking as though he had! He returned to the matter in hand. 'And your suggestion is that because the computer hadn't been

100

turned off, Mr Burrell wasn't the one who left the message there?'

'It's not logical,' Stan said angrily. 'It can't mean a thing. Nobody would worry about a thing like that when he's intending to throw himself overboard.'

Roger looked even more obstinate. 'Yes, he would,' he said. 'Everything with Phil was habit. He placed everything on his desk exactly so.' He indicated the neat arrangement of pens, paperclips and other office bits and pieces. 'He was always ahead of time arriving for work, he's even made me punctual!' He gave a small shamefaced grin. 'That's why I knew something was wrong when he wasn't here this morning. He was obsessive about doing everything just right. I don't care what anyone says about the balance of mind being disturbed; even if he *was* meaning to throw himself overboard, he'd switch off the computer. I mean, particularly if he was planning to throw himself overboard, he wouldn't want anyone to discover those abandoned games,' he said fiercely.

The argument did have a certain logic.

Stan, though, exploded. 'It's ridiculous!'

William could see the security officer's point of view. A lovelorn stores manager flinging himself overboard was bad enough, but admit what Roger was suggesting could be true and matters became much more sinister and much less tidy. Then he felt the *Empress* change direction. There was no porthole in the office so it was impossible to check but the difference in the ship's steady progression was obvious. They were turning around. William saw Stan look at Roger and that they were all thinking the same thing. The search for Phil Burrell had been abandoned.

'If you are right,' he said gravely to Roger, 'you realize what it would mean, don't you?'

Roger gazed at him wretchedly. Yes, he'd obviously thought about the implications. 'It would be murder, wouldn't it, sir?'

Chapter Twelve

The sight of Sandane tucked neatly into the bottom folds of the mountains that surrounded this arm of the fjord was spectacular. Darina wrapped her jacket more warmly around her and leant against the ship's rail. The mountains weren't as stern as she'd imagined they'd be but the snow icing their tops looked permanent and the little town, huddled on the edge of the dark, dark waters, had the air of somewhere closed in on itself.

It was eight o'clock in the morning. The ship was anchored and already tenders were out, ready to ferry passengers ashore.

William had got up at five o'clock. 'I must see us cruising up the fjord,' he'd said.

Darina had felt so wretched when the alarm had gone off, she'd had to abandon the idea of watching the approach as well. Even now, safely at anchor, she felt as though the ship was still moving in that sickening way it had, like a bad joke she couldn't appreciate, though very few other passengers seemed bothered by it. Perhaps they had a better sense of humour.

There was always the possibility, though, that she wasn't suffering from seasickness. After all, she never had before. They'd been at sea two days and by the

afternoon each day, her nausea had completely disappeared and she'd felt fine, the swell hadn't bothered
her at all. Perhaps she'd caught some odd flu bug.
Whatever it was, she hoped that it would go away,
otherwise it was going to spoil the whole trip.

More and more passengers were crowding the
rails, exclaiming over the view. Then they all turned
as a troupe of people walking very fast came along
the narrow deck. The morning milers! William was
towards the end, talking to the girl who shared their
table, Beth something or other. She looked more
animated than Darina had seen her before. Perhaps she
was coming out of her shell.

Those two days at sea had acted like marinade on
meat, developing flavour, sometimes unsuspected.
Who would have supposed that Enid could have kept
the dining table entranced with an account of her time
as a wild young thing in the fifties? 'You should have
seen the skirts I had,' she exclaimed, her eyes bright
as new-minted pennies. 'So many petticoats I could
hardly get through doors, all stiff nylon and net. And
off-the-shoulder sweaters – oh, George's eyes popped
out all right! They talk about Carnaby Street in the
sixties but we knew all about having a good time in
Leeds before then. The moors were only a few miles
away and off we'd go on George's motorbike, me in
pedal pushers that he said did things to my figure that
sent him mad, my arms wrapped round his waist, the
wind in my hair – no helmets in those days, eh, we
were daft.' She'd smiled reminiscently, her face soft.

Perhaps it was because Mervyn hadn't been present
that she'd been able to talk without interruption. He
was between concerts, conserving his voice.

Darina and William had attended the one he'd given before dinner.

'No pandering to common tastes,' had been William's comment after several operatic arias and a couple of Schubert lieder. But he'd had to admit that, harnessed to the demands of introducing each item and linking it to the next, Mervyn's eloquence had been enjoyable. The fifty-minute concert had provided a wonderful before-dinner aperitif.

Darina looked up at the mountains. The air here was wonderful, clear and still, you only had to sniff at it to feel healthy. She took a deep breath, and immediately wished she hadn't as nausea threatened to overwhelm her.

Standing very still, she forced herself to think of other things. Down on the waterline, tenders were filling with passengers on their way to one of the many excursions offered at all their ports of call. Darina and William had studied the brochure giving all the details and had been tempted to book for a number of attractive sounding options, then had counted up the cost involved.

'We'll leave it until we get there,' William had said.

'Anyway, I could be working,' Darina had added.

What neither of them had foreseen was that it was William who might be too involved to consider an expedition ashore.

Darina could see Shona Marshall, the lottery winner, enter the tender with her husband and her friend, Daphne Rawlings. Darina had met Shona the previous afternoon, when they'd both attended a talk on Mozart given by the pianist who accompanied Mervyn Pryde in his recital. The talk had been illustrated on the piano.

The lottery winner had come into the ship's theatre on her own and found a seat beside Darina.

'That was so interesting,' Darina had said impulsively after the talk had finished. 'Mozart is one of my favourite composers.'

The other woman's severe face had lightened immediately. 'Mine, too. I wish my husband enjoyed music, but anything that's tagged "classical" he says is beyond him. Andrew Lloyd Webber is as far as he'll go. He actually thinks *Phantom* is an opera!'

They drifted out with the other passengers, then decided to have some tea and went down to the restaurant.

Darina had found Shona wasn't the easiest of people to talk to but she seemed happy to listen to Darina describing why she was on the cruise. 'I've brought a whole lot of recipes with me and the Purser thinks it may be possible to have a Norwegian lunch or a late evening supper.'

'A midnight sun supper,' mused Shona, her eyes lighting up.

'Hey, that's a good idea, I'll suggest it to the Chef.'

'And are you going to give us a talk? I'd love to hear about Norwegian food.' Shona unbent a little.

'I'm supposed to be giving a demonstration at some stage,' Darina said, sounding apologetic. 'Though with all the other attractions that are put on, I can't think many people will want to come.'

'I will,' Shona assured her. 'And I'll bring Daphne.'

'Doesn't she like Mozart either?'

'Said she was feeling a little seasick and thought it would be a good idea to lie down. But you're right, she's not a music buff either. We didn't see that this was billed as a classical cruise, we only looked at the itinerary!' Her dismay at the inappropriateness of the entertainment as far as her party was concerned was comical.

'What about your stepson? He's obviously musical, he was playing the piano beautifully yesterday.'

'He got that from his mother. He took music at university but now it's pop and light rather than classical that he's interested in.' Shona paused for a moment and fiddled with the piece of fruit cake she'd helped herself to.

'Is his mother still alive?'

'No, she died of cancer a year or so before I met Paul. Julian apparently was devastated. He never talks about her.' Shona considered this statement for a moment then added, 'He's quite a good pianist but he says he wants to manage others rather than perform himself.'

'He and Mervyn Pryde's girlfriend gave us an impromptu concert, she's very keen for him to manage her.'

'Ah, yes, Tara!' Shona's expression said she was less than ecstatic about this relationship.

'You don't like her?'

'Oh, I've hardly met her. I've got nothing to do with the matter.' Shona was dismissive. 'Julian wouldn't care one way or the other what I think, anyway. No . . .' She suddenly hesitated, as though she oughtn't to carry on.

Darina waited. She'd discovered early on that if you were a sympathetic listener and didn't press for details, people told you the most amazing things. Now, she said nothing but sat with what she hoped was an open expression on her face.

Except that Shona wasn't looking at her. A tiny hole in the tablecloth was receiving her full attention, and she was picking away at it as though if only she could make it large enough all her problems would vanish down it. Finally she said, 'Here I am, blethering on about nothing. Daphne would tell me to pull myself together.'

Darina thought it was interesting that it was Daphne's name that she invoked, not her husband's. 'She must be a very good friend of yours,' she suggested.

Shona's face lit up. 'Oh, yes. We met at a health club and she's been such a help to me, advises me on my clothes, listens to my problems at work, she's much more understanding than Paul as far as that's concerned, and is such fun.'

'No wonder you've brought her along with you,' Darina said.

'It was a way of thanking her for being my friend,' Shona said simply. She paused for a moment and Darina could see she was wondering how to put something.

Darina waited.

'Tell me,' Shona said abruptly. 'You're involved with food, you say?'

Darina nodded.

'Can you really tell the difference between organic and non-organic food?' There was a curl to her upper lip, as though she knew what the answer had to be and anyone who tried to assume differently would be subjected to an inquisition that would make *Newsnight's* Jeremy Paxman seem a pussy cat.

Darina felt a prickle of unease. 'I'd hate to have to

108

do a blind tasting,' she said slowly. 'What I can do is pick out well-produced fresh food from the intensively grown or reared stuff. I'm sure you know that vegetables grown with care in well manured ground and cooked almost as soon as picked are unbeatable. They mightn't meet Soil Association standards as organic, though.'

Shona mulled over this for a moment, her eyes frosty. In a matter of minutes she had changed from a sympathetic woman to a cold interrogator.

'What's your interest?' asked Darina. 'Are you worried about your palate or your diet? I'm a firm believer in producing food as naturally as possible. Our bodies are assaulted with enough toxins and pollutants these days without having more added by what we eat,' she ended with conviction.

'You don't believe in science interfering with agriculture, then?'

Just in time, Darina remembered Shona Mallory's profession. 'I'm sure science has a great deal to offer food production,' she said carefully. 'The trouble is we are all still suffering from the shock of having scientists exposed as less than godlike over the BSE scandal.' What would she make of that?

Before Shona could launch into a defence of the scientific profession, they were joined by her husband, Paul, and their friend, Daphne. Both fell on the remains of the tea with loud expressions of delight followed by questions on how the concert went.

'I had a wonderful rest,' said Daphne, stretching luxuriously. 'I feel so much better. I went in search of you,' she said to Shona, 'and ran into Paul. So we joined forces to track you down.'

'And here you are,' said Paul, bending to give his wife a kiss on her cheek.

There was no chance of further discussion on science and food. Instead, Darina watched with a certain amusement as Daphne and Paul seemed to vie with each other in offering diversions for Shona to enjoy that evening. They appeared to be a close-knit trio and Darina soon excused herself and left.

Now she saw the little group of three taking their seats in the tender for the excursion to the Briksdal glacier. Shona was certainly not skimping on any aspect of this cruise.

William came up, looking smug after his walk, and gave her a kiss. 'Feeling better?' he asked.

'Much,' Darina assured him, hoping that she might convince herself.

'When's your appointment with the chef?'

'This afternoon, I thought I might go ashore this morning, there's an open-air folk museum that ought to be interesting. Can you come?' she asked, knowing what the answer would be.

'Afraid not. Those police officers I told you about yesterday are supposed to be arriving this morning. Stan Dobson wants me to help report on the circumstances surrounding Phil Burrell's disappearance.'

Immediately Darina forgot all about herself. 'You mean . . . ?'

'Yes, I'm afraid it is not looking at all good. There are some serious decisions that will have to be made.'

An hour or so later, Darina went ashore in a tender that smelt almost unbearably of diesel fuel. By concentrating hard on something else she managed to reach the shore without consigning her breakfast to the waters of the fjord.

'You don't look very well, dear,' said Enid Carter as the passengers clambered on to the jetty. She looked very dashing in a scarlet anorak, the hood drawn up against the keen little wind that blew around the small harbour.

'I'm fine,' Darina assured her. 'Are you going to visit the open-air museum?'

'Thought I would, have you any idea which direction it's in?'

Darina consulted the map they'd been given. Sandane was really quite small. Behind the harbour was a collection of shops, the odd industrial site, some very nice looking wooden houses and a school. The route to the museum was quite easy to follow. They set off, Enid showing no difficulty in keeping up.

The folk museum was composed of eighteenth- and nineteenth-century farm buildings brought from all over the province and re-erected in a pleasant, grassy setting with woodland behind.

Enid proved a lively companion, commenting in a none too complimentary manner on the ancient Norwegian living conditions.

'My,' she said, looking at the simple wooden furniture in one of the houses. 'Not what you could call comfortable, is it? Give me a nice three-piece suite any day.'

Darina looked at the lamp hanging over the table and tried to imagine months of dark days with only a few hours of light. 'What sort of oil did they use?' she asked the tall, blond young curator.

'Cod-liver oil.'

Darina wrinkled her nose. 'Did it smell?'

'Of course,' he laughed at her.

'Good heavens,' exclaimed Enid. 'How could they stand it?'

'You get used to anything,' she was assured.

Darina and Enid exchanged a glance that said neither of them thought they could get used to living with the permanent smell of cod-liver oil.

Later they visited the museum building that offered displays that included folk costumes, musical instruments and models of water mills and boats. As they came round a corner and found a display of wedding regalia, Enid grabbed at Darina's arm. 'Look, there's the couple that were on our tea table the first afternoon. What were their names?'

'Joyce and Michael Harwood,' Darina whispered to her.

'They were so very gloomy. I wonder if they've cheered up at all.'

Enid marched up to the Harwoods as they studied a rowing boat. 'Having a nice time?' she enquired with the sort of good humour that Britain was supposed to have won the war on.

Joyce Harwood glanced from her to Darina, appeared to realize that they'd met somewhere and made an effort. 'What a life it must have been,' she said faintly. 'So isolated, so dark! Makes anything we suffer today seem nothing.'

'At least they didn't have governments and big companies interfering all the bloody time,' Michael Harwood said suddenly. His pleasant, ruddy face was contorted and his tightly held body displayed aggression in every line. 'People could do things the way they wanted then.'

'Now, dear, don't go on so.' Joyce put a hand on his arm.

He shook it off and turned on her, his face darkening, eyes bulging out of their sockets. 'Bloody hell, woman, don't keep flapping around me! For God's sake take a grip on yourself.' He strode off down the other end of the museum hall.

'Oh, dear,' Joyce bleated. 'He's just impossible! If I try to pretend nothing is wrong, he asks me what I'm so happy about. If I sympathize with him, he gets like that.' Her eyes filled with tears. 'I don't know what to do. I thought, we all thought, that this cruise would make all the difference, that getting away would mean he'd forget about the worst of what's happened, instead he just seems to be brooding all the more.' The tears spilled over. Joyce fumbled in her handbag, found a tissue and dabbed at her eyes. 'Oh, I'm so sorry, I'm making such a fool of myself.'

'Nonsense,' said Enid stoutly. 'Come and have a cup of coffee.' She took the woman by the arm and led her back into the main reception area of the museum, where there were tables and chairs and a counter serving refreshments.

Darina got them all coffee while Enid sat Joyce down at one of the pale wood tables.

'Is it the farming?' Darina asked after she'd supplied them all with cups.

Joyce wiped her eyes determinedly. Her face looked as scrubbed clean as an old-fashioned school- girl's. Just as well, if she'd been wearing mascara she'd now resemble a panda. She blinked rapidly, as though to clear her vision. Then she looked around. 'He's not coming to join us, is he?'

Darina was sitting opposite the entrance to the exhibit hall. She couldn't see Michael Harwood and said as much. 'He probably wants to be by himself for a little.'

'That's what he's always been like. Any trouble and he goes off and worries about it on his own. Never has been able to discuss things. When I had the children home, it didn't matter so much, I could talk things over with them, I never hid anything from them. They're good kids, they're the ones who paid for this trip.'

'How many children do you have?' Enid asked.

'Three, two boys and a girl.'

'Have they all gone into farming?'

Joyce shook her head vigorously. 'Thought it was too much like hard work! Of course, they helped out on the farm as they were growing up. But they saw what it did to their dad, and . . . and how it affected me, him being like that, and they couldn't get off quick enough.'

'So what are they doing?' Darina asked, hoping that continuing to talk about her children would calm Joyce.

The sodden tissue was squeezed into one hand now. 'Oh, they've all done so well! Martin, he's the oldest, he's a solicitor, joined our best local firm, we're ever so proud of him. John's in agriculture, but on the industrial side. Goes all over the country he does, selling milking machines. And Jan's a teacher. She's just been made headmistress of our local junior school.' Joyce finished triumphantly.

'Are they all married?' asked Darina.

Joyce nodded. 'Jan's husband is ever so nice and I

114

get on well with the daughters-in-law too. Kind girls they are. Got eight grandchildren now, Martin's got four, John three and Jan's just had a little girl. Patience they've called her because they had to wait such a time until she came along. Jan's thirty-five but they never gave up hoping. That's what Michael used to be like. Whatever came along, he'd bounce back sooner or later but now, well, it's all just been too much.'

'Do you want to tell us about it?' Darina enquired gently.

'It was those crops!' Joyce said indignantly. 'I told him not to get involved. Not natural, I said. Don't have anything to do with it. But he would! "What's left else?" he said. The beef business was all gone, that was BSE, the dairy side was packing up with the price of milk being so low. He'd gone into sheep in a big way and then the price of lamb collapsed and we weren't getting the wool cheque either, at least, not enough to make a difference. John told him to go organic. That's where the money is, he said. Supermarkets are crying out for organic produce, can't get enough of it. Most of it's imported from abroad, he said. Go in for organic and you'll be all right. But it takes so long for a farmer to switch over. And the government subsidy had all gone by the time we applied. Michael said disaster was staring us in the face. He couldn't sell the animals, couldn't afford to keep them. He said there wouldn't be more than ten pounds profit an acre for wheat, and that he'd be lucky to get that by the time it was harvested. Oh, he was in a right state.' Joyce stirred what was left of her coffee round and round with her spoon. The words that had spilled out so easily once she got going seemed to have dried up.

115

Darina and Enid waited.

'Then this company came along and persuaded him to plant crops for them. I knew it wouldn't come to no good!' Joyce's eyes filled with tears again.

'What sort of crop was it?' asked Enid, puzzled.

Joyce stirred some more. 'Not natural, that's what I said,' she muttered.

'It was a genetically modified one?' Darina asked, certain what the answer would be.

Joyce nodded. 'Right! Special rape seed it was. They said it was safe as safe, nothing for anyone to worry about. Then it all started.'

'What started?' Enid's eyes were gleaming, she seemed almost excited by what she was being told.

'The trouble!' Joyce removed the spoon from her cup and placed it in the saucer with a clatter. She looked both Enid and Darina in the eyes. 'You wouldn't believe what people can do. There were public meetings and people spitting at me in the supermarket. Other farmers wouldn't speak to Michael.' Her gaze dropped. 'He said he didn't care, he wasn't doing anything wrong and they could lump it. But I could see it was eating him up. If only he could have talked about it. But every time I tried to say something, he'd shut me up, tell me it was none of my business.'

'Were the crops attacked?'

Joyce looked at Darina. 'Oh, yes. There were all these protesters. Said it was their business to make sure the pollen didn't spread when it came into flower.'

'Isn't there a theory that it can contaminate other crops?' Darina asked. 'Especially organic ones?'

'There weren't any organic rape seed crops within miles of us,' protested Joyce. 'But they said that didn't

116

matter, the pollen could be borne on the wind much farther than anyone thought. Michael told them not to be ridiculous, of course it couldn't. So that got them into more of a lather. He had a real run-in with one of them in the Fox and Hounds, he gave him a black eye.'

'Good heavens!' Enid exclaimed excitedly. 'What happened then?'

'Michael was hauled up in front of the magistrates for causing a breach of the peace. That really got to him, said if it hadn't been for that other chap, there wouldn't have been no breach of the peace.' Joyce was talking faster and faster now, as though she had been storing everything inside her and it had been fermenting, like homemade beer, until now it was overflowing and nothing could hold it back.

'Michael brooded and brooded about what had been done to him. He knew the rape was ripening and that any time those chaps would be back to destroy it. And Michael couldn't bear it.' Joyce raised a hand to her mouth as though the very act of remembering what had happened was too much for her.

'What did he do?' Enid breathed.

'Only torched the chap's car!' Joyce blurted out, then she reached across and grabbed at Enid's hand. 'Only you're not ever to say that! There's no proof. When the police came for him, he said it was a case of give a dog a bad name and could they prove it? And they couldn't. And I said he'd been home all evening!' Her eyes were huge and round, panic stricken. 'And I thought he had been. I really did!'

'But do you know he wasn't?' Darina asked.

Joyce looked wretched. 'I don't know! I mean, I

117

didn't see him. He'd got one of his records on in his office. Beatles it was. He plays them all the time, says that's when pop music was really music. Loves them, he does. So I never thought he wasn't there. But I didn't see him!'

'So what happened next?' Darina was certain the story wasn't over yet.

'They came the next day. Hundreds of them, trampling over the fields, pulling up the crop, scything it, dancing on it. I never seen anything like it; they was so excited, as if it was some religious rite. And Michael was hopping mad. He rang the police and the NFU – what he thought they would do, I don't know!' Joyce's indignation was almost comical. 'And I was trying to calm him down. And we both went out to try and stop what was happening. Might as well have tried to stop Niagara flowing.' Her face suddenly crumpled. 'And then someone shouted, "Fire!" And everyone turned and our house was burning! And someone shouted, "Serve them right!" And the others chanted, "Burn, burn, burn." So nobody did anything except Michael and me. We couldn't get into the house to call the fire brigade; the police hadn't arrived and I reckoned they weren't getting a shift on because Michael had been so rude to them over that other business, and Michael didn't have a mobile on him because you can never get a signal where we are, so I had to get in the car and drive down to our neighbours to ring the fire brigade from there.' Joyce rubbed fierce tears away. 'When I got back someone had had a heart and got some of the protesters organized with a chain of buckets from the old milking parlour. But there weren't many of them and the fire had got a real hold by then. We lost everything,' she said bleakly. 'All the photos of the children when they were little, our wedding photos, Michael's mother's china, she had some lovely pieces, the cushions I'd embroidered and, well, everything! Two hundred years old that house was and I'd done ever such a lot to it over the years. Decorating and such like. The curtains I'd made!'

They were all silent for a moment, mourning the loss of Joyce's memories and the home she'd built over the years.

'So that was our life – all gone!'

'Dreadful,' said Enid, her face alive with the drama of it all. 'But surely you got compensation?'

'Oh, we got something from the company for the rape but nothing like what Michael had expected. And he'd let the insurance on the house lapse. Couldn't afford the premium, he said. Michael tried to get the GM company to pay him, said it was all their fault, that the protesters had burned it deliberately and they ought to stump up. The NFU helped us with lawyers but in the end they said that there wasn't anything they could do. We were given a few thousand which was sort of out of the kindness of the company's heart and didn't mean they accepted liability, like,' Joyce said bitterly. 'We had to go to Save the Children and places like that for clothes. Fancy coming on a holiday like this with a wardrobe from Oxfam! The kids wanted me to have some really nice things but I couldn't bear them to spend any more on us.'

'What a dreadful story,' Darina breathed. With a shudder she remembered wondering why they looked as though they'd been dressed from charity shops at that first tea. To think about the escalating series of events that had destroyed Joyce's life was too awful. 'What are you going to do now?'

Joyce pulled at the wadded tissue she was holding, shredding it. The tiny bits floated down like untidy snowflakes. 'I don't know. The children all clubbed together to give us this holiday. It's our fortieth wedding anniversary and they said we should celebrate it somehow. But Michael just buries himself in his misery. He's convinced it's all the GM company's fault and the fact that I was against him planting that wretched stuff in the first place just makes it worse.'

'Perhaps he should join the anti-GM food movement,' suggested Darina. 'There's a lot of activity going on and it would give him something to do.'

'He could start on the ship,' Enid said excitedly. 'That scientist, the one who won the lottery? Well, she's into GM foods, that's what all her winnings are going on!'

Joyce stared at her in horror. 'Never! That's dreadful! Don't tell Michael,' she grew agitated. 'I don't know what he would do. Please, promise me, you won't tell him!'

Chapter Thirteen

Detective Inspector Derek Rider removed his battered raincoat, rolled it up and stood in Roger Coutts's small office looking for somewhere to put it. He had the air of a deeply disappointed man and William knew for sure that life was about to get difficult.

Detective Sergeant Luther Conran exuded the energy his senior officer lacked. He placed his brief-case on the desk then stood flicking his fingers against each other, his gaze darting around the office, his eyes eager and interested, their whites very white against the smooth darkness of his skin.

'The missing man hasn't turned up, then?' Derek Rider said with a deep sigh.

He looked old enough for retirement to be advancing with the speed of a homing pigeon. William wondered where his career had taken the wrong turning that had anchored him in the rank of inspector. He'd met men like Derek Rider before, usually they were bitter at injustices they imagined that had advanced lesser men before themselves. Rarely were they resigned or able to acknowledge they were in some measure responsible for the way a fast track had ended in a cul de sac.

The officers had arrived from England at Sandane

the previous evening and had been waiting on the small jetty as the *Empress of India* anchored in the fjord.

The security officer had brought them down to the stores manager's office. 'No, sir,' he said now. 'Not a sign of him.'

William took the rolled-up raincoat and the other man's leather jacket and hung them on the back of the door.

The steward entered with a tray of coffee and biscuits. William poured and Stan Dobson handed around the cups. Soon the four men were settled.

'As I understand it,' Derek Rider said with heavy emphasis, 'Detective Chief Inspector Pigram just happened to be on board the ship when the missing man went, well, missing. And as security officer,' he addressed himself to Stan, 'you decided Detective Chief Inspector Pigram should be invited to form part of the investigation. I believe you worked together some years ago,' he ended, managing to convey the impression that some sort of conspiracy had taken place with the most sinister of motives.

Luther Conran put down his briefcase, opened it and took out papers that William recognized as copies of the report that had been sent through from the ship. One was given to Derek Rider and one put on Roger's desk. His computer and records had been removed and squeezed with Roger himself into another of the purser's offices. Roger's complaints at being put so far away from the stores and lockers had been vigorous but went unheeded.

Conran then produced a notebook from an inside pocket of his well-cut suit and a silver automatic pencil. His movements had the quietly efficient air of a

Treasury official and his manner the same self-confidence.

Stan Dobson gazed stolidly at Inspector Rider. 'Yes, Chief Inspector Pigram and I recognized each other shortly after the ship sailed. When Assistant Purser Coutts brought certain facts to my attention during our search for Mr Burrell, it seemed a sensible course of action to ask Mr Pigram to assist us in our investigation.'

William would have liked to congratulate Stan on the way he'd refused to be rattled by the inspector's attitude. He waited for his turn.

'Ah, yes, "certain facts", as you say!' Derek Rider turned to the copy of the report he'd been supplied with and turned the pages. 'Let's see now. Your message stated that because the missing man's computer had not been turned off, foul play was suspected, is that how we are to understand the situation?'

Put like that, the notion did indeed sound ridiculous. 'As the report states, it was not a factor we gave great weight to,' William said mildly. 'But it did seem something that should be noted, given the strong reaction it called forth from Mr Burrell's assistant. Nothing we could say would shake his insistence that Mr Burrell would have turned off his computer, even if his mind had been disturbed enough to place a suicide note there. Mr Burrell's computer remains next door, untouched, the way Mr Coutts found it.'

Derek Rider said nothing, merely looked contemptuous. He flipped over the pages of the report. Various passages had been highlighted with yellow marker pen. William didn't think Rider had done the marking.

'Mucky little story, isn't it?' Rider jeered at them. 'Eternal-triangle stuff. Lover gets the push-off and pops himself in despair. If the body could be found, it would probably be full of booze. After all, he'd been drinking heavily before the fracas in the bar.' He pronounced the 's' on the end of fracas.

'He wasn't known as a drinking man,' Stan said gloomily as though the fact had to be placed in some sort of divine balance against the evidence that was undoubtedly about to be brought out.

'Two whiskies in his office with his assistant, Roger Coutts, two with his colleagues in the Oyster Bar and another with Karen Geary, the last unfinished.' Luther Conran had picked up his copy of the report and read out the details in a deadpan voice that would have done credit to a stage performer.

'Mr Burrell's assistant left him in his office with a bottle of whisky that was more than half full,' Rider said in a colourless way that managed to sound insulting. 'I understand that an empty bottle was found in the wastepaper bin the next morning.' His eyes bored into the security officer's, then he switched his gaze to William. 'Not everyone, of course, would reckon that an extortionate amount of alcohol.'

William said nothing.

'He wasn't known as a drinking man,' Stan repeated quietly. 'And the officers drinking with him in the Oyster Bar said he showed no signs of over-indulgence.'

'No signs of overindulgence, not a drinking man,' repeated Rider in a colourless way. 'What does that suggest? Eh?' he suddenly shot at his sergeant.

'Victim returned to his office and drowned his

sorrows in drink,' Luther Conran said in the same deadpan voice he'd used before.

'Returned to his office and drowned his sorrows in drink.' Repetition seemed to be a Rider technique. 'Then reckoned a more permanent drowning was the answer to his troubles.' He shuffled through the pages of the report again.

William knew what he was going to refer to now.

'You will of course remember this piece of evidence: "About one o'clock in the morning I was half asleep. I never draw the curtain across the porthole, I like to see the sun in the morning. Well, I thought I saw something going past, like a sack of rubbish dropped from the deck above and I thought I heard a splash. I didn't really think much of it, other than it was a bit odd, I mean, you never see them throwing refuse overboard, do you? It was only when I heard that someone was missing I thought I should report it." Mrs Witchett, cabin A373, port side.' Rider looked up from the marked passage in the report. 'Seems pretty conclusive, wouldn't you say?'

'Mrs Witchett's cabin is amidships,' Stan said slowly. 'It's directly below a small upper deck that's sheltered and private. A member of the crew did see Mr Burrell heading in what could have been that direction just before one o'clock. That was the last time anyone saw him.'

'A sheltered upper deck, ideal for a jumping-off point, wouldn't you say?' Rider murmured.

'There are easier points to choose if you wanted to throw yourself off the ship,' Stan said, sounding like a man given a choice between a lifebelt that had lost its buoyancy and a rubber dinghy with holes.

'Having inspected the deck, I felt it was an excellent

choice as somewhere for a quiet chat,' said William, feeling it was time he added his pittance.

'Meaning you think Mr Burrell had an assignation there and was pushed overboard, maybe after a fight? Not a suggestion your report makes.' The inspector's tone said it was a suggestion to be placed in a box marked 'fantasy land'.

'We reported on such facts as had been established,' William said, trying to keep his voice expressionless. Why on earth had he got involved with this matter? It was worse than his early days with an inspector who thought sarcasm was the soul of wit. He eyed Luther curiously. He looked intelligent and ambitious, did he normally work with this man? Was he waiting for an opportunity to make his mark and move upwards? 'You will have read our account of the interview with Karen Geary,' he added, voice totally under control now.

Rider flicked back and forth in the report, then switched his copy for the one silently held out to him by his sergeant with the passage quickly marked in pencil. 'Yes,' he said after swiftly looking through it. 'Your point?'

William cursed the man for his attitude. 'No actual point, sir.' He outranked the older man but his presence wasn't official so the title seemed only courteous. 'Just that drowning his sorrows in drink seemed a somewhat extreme reaction to what actually happened.'

'You actually believe what you were told by Miss Geary and Mr Summers, Detective Chief Inspector?' jeered the inspector. 'Would it be impertinent to suggest a modicum of naivety?' Bitterness filled his voice. William's status obviously rankled.

'I think the report shows that nothing was taken at

face value,' William said, managing to keep his temper. 'Every statement made by Miss Geary and Mr Summers was checked with other members of the crew.'

The cruise director had arrived in a cloud of expensive perfume, her red hair severely held back from a face that looked strained and nervous. Through her thickly applied make-up, the bruise on her left cheekbone was clearly visible. She wore a snugly fitting jersey dress with a jaunty scarf at the neckline.

She'd played down an involvement with Phil Burrell. 'He was delightful, of course, but there was nothing serious there.' She stroked the jersey skirt, as though she'd wanted to pull it further down her shapely thigh, crossing and uncrossing her legs in a movement that only drove the material further up towards her crotch. Her use of the past tense did not escape William. Was that because she considered whatever their relationship had been was now over or because she believed Phil was dead?

When asked about the incident that had happened at the end of the previous cruise, she'd first flushed, then her face had gone very pale, the bruise standing out starkly beneath the pancake-thick foundation. William and Stan had noted the dismay on her face and waited for her to speak. She'd given a small shrug. 'It was nothing much. Phil and I had only met up for a drink a couple of times, once accidentally in Athens and then in Lisbon. I don't know why Harry got so upset. It's not as though he and I are an item.' She'd pouted prettily, then added. 'Harry's divorce isn't through yet.' By then she'd recovered her poise and there'd been nothing else interesting in her evidence.

'Real little cock-teaser,' said Stan after she'd left.

'I've watched her in action. "Leave them gasping" is her motto. Don't suppose poor Phil ever came near it.'

'Did she make him think he was in there with a chance?'

Stan nodded gloomily. 'He had all the signs. Don't know what went on in that Athens bar but afterwards he was after her like a puppy on to a bone. In Lisbon they came back to the ship together in a taxi. I was having a word with one of my assistants at the bottom of the gangway. Karen waltzed up it leaving Phil to pay the fare and carry all her high-class shopping bags on board. She waited for him at the top of the gangway, striking a pose like some sort of model.'

William could picture the scene.

'Something made me look up at the ship,' Stan continued. 'And there was Harry. His face was thunder. Later I heard there'd been a fight between decks.'

'Between decks?'

'Where the food lockers are. After Phil had secured everything for the night, Harry found him there. One of the coloured boys came back for something and found them hard at it. He came for me. But by the time I arrived, it was all over, nary a sign of either of them. Just as well, they'd both have been before the captain otherwise.'

'Useful man with his fists, is he, your first officer?'

Stan nodded grimly. 'He was a boxer in the navy. He blotted his copybook there somehow. Anyway, the story is that he reckoned he'd never make it to the top and thought he'd have a go at the merchant service instead.'

'So, he's got a temper but manages to keep it under control most of the time?'

'Things went swimmingly until his marriage broke up, he got together with Karen Geary and then Phil Burrell came along.'

'Did the cruise director figure in the marriage break-up?'

Stan shrugged his big shoulders. 'Who knows? It's difficult keeping a marriage going when you're serving in a ship like this. Wives get a number of opportunities to come along, it can mean they make friends with colleagues, understand what the life is all about. But it's difficult, if you've got kiddies going to school and all that. Harry's wife holds down a demanding job in the City. It seems to have suited her to have him away much of the time.'

William thought of the claustrophobic nature of life aboard this floating community and the tensions that must arise between colleagues working and living together at such close quarters. And of the dangerously incandescent quality of the cruise director.

After Karen Geary, they'd interviewed Henry Summers.

He'd walked into the small office as though it was the bridge and he was in charge of the ship. He could have stepped out of a thirties film, dressed in immaculately cut blazer and slacks and a very smart cream silk shirt, open at the neck. It was only as he sat down that the width of his shoulders and the power of his neck were evident. His feet, though, were quite small, shod in a brightly polished pair of black loafers complete with a pair of tassels on each shoe.

He crossed one leg over the other, adjusted the set of his trouser leg then sat back in the chair, arms resting lightly on the wooden arms, every inch of him poised.

Asked about the antagonism between Phil Burrell and himself, he was dismissive. 'As stores manager with the rank of assistant purser, he hardly registered with me,' he said dismissively. 'My only problem, if it was a problem, was making clear to him that Karen was out of his league.'

'Wasn't that her prerogative?' suggested William smoothly.

Harry Summers raised an eyebrow. 'You know what women are like, don't want to hurt a chap's feelings? He was pretty keen, can't think how he'd got the idea she could entertain any sort of relationship with him.' Again that contemptuous note in his voice. If Karen Geary had in any way encouraged Phil, he must have found Harry Summers's attitude intolerable.

'You don't think it was possible Miss Geary found Mr Burrell a pleasant companion, someone it was enjoyable to have an occasional drink with? After all, they were both single, unattached,' William suggested provocatively.

For a moment something flared at the back of Harry Summers's eyes – but it was only for a moment. 'Women – who can say what they find amusing? Especially Karen. But, no, there wasn't a chance she'd find him anything more than a passing amusement. He just couldn't understand she was out of his league. Take last night. We had a date. My watch finished at midnight, we'd arranged to meet in the Oyster Bar for a nightcap. I find her there with Burrell. I tell Burrell, in quite a friendly way, to hop it and he gets all excited. Before I knew what was happening, Karen had caught a blow meant for me.'

Disdain filled his oddly attractive face. It took a

while for William to realize that the oddity came from the fact that each profile was quite different from the other. One was sculptured with strong bones, the other was softer, had an almost feminine quality. It was unsettling; if someone had announced Harry Summers was a schizophrenic, William thought that he would accept it without question.

'Did you see him after he'd left the bar?'

Harry shook his head. 'No way I was going to have anything more to do with him, that evening or at any other time.' Again that disdain.

'So you didn't meet him on an upper deck later on?' Stan Dobson put in stolidly, as though he had to make the position quite clear.

'Absolutely not.' Harry recrossed his legs.

The interview failed to yield anything else significant.

After he'd left, William asked Stan, 'Do you trust a word he says?'

Stan shook his head. 'His only hope of keeping his job is to play down the whole incident.'

Yet when they'd interviewed the other members of the crew, to a man they'd supported what had been said by both Karen Geary and Harry Summers. Nobody believed Phil had made much progress in his pursuit of Karen and nobody believed he could have been made suicidal by the way she'd turned on him after he'd hit her in the bar.

'Phil was so level-headed,' Lulu Prentice said, wiping tears away with the heel of her hand. 'Oh, I know he got carried away by that bitch, thought he was in there with a chance. We'd had a bit of a row.' She took a deep breath, tried to get herself together. 'I

131

mean, I'd told him a girl doesn't want to hang around for ever. We'd had a thing going for months and nothing was happening. I said either we got engaged or he could find someone else. He said if I wasn't happy the way we were, that was that. He never wanted to be tied to another woman who made demands on him. As if I would! I just wanted him to be happy – and me to be happy. Was that so much? I never thought he'd go after Karen!' The words ended in a wail.

They'd talked to the ship's doctor. Ian Westlake was in his mid-forties, suave and attractive. He was six foot tall with broad shoulders, no sign of middle-aged spread, a strong face, a sweep of dark hair and eyes that sparkled. His manner was easy and open and he seemed to strive to be helpful. 'Of course I know Phil Burrell, but not well. He wasn't a very forthcoming chap.' Ian Westlake studied his nails for a moment then looked at Stan with frank openness. 'Did I ever tell you that I met him on a cruise I took on the *Empress of China* a couple of years ago, before she was decommissioned? The doc there was an old chum from medical school. He introduced me around and showed me what his job was all about, gave me the idea it might be something for me. He and Phil were quite friendly, Phil had come to his help when he'd been mugged ashore one time. Phil joined us for a drink one night, together with his wife. A very large and very dominating lady – I wasn't at all surprised to hear from Phil when he joined this ship that they'd divorced soon after.'

'Would you class him as a possible suicide?' William asked.

Ian Westlake stared at the bulkhead, thinking.

'Difficult one, that. Not all suicides cry for help, life just becomes not worth the effort and something snaps. I will say this, Burrell was the type to bottle things up. He might well have come to the end of his tether without anyone realizing.' Ian Westlake brushed an invisible piece of fluff off his knife-edged trousers. 'Sorry I can't be of more help.'

'What's your opinion of Karen Geary?' asked William, waiting for his response with deep interest.

'Ah, Karen!' The doctor sat immobile for a long moment. Then he sighed, 'A girl made for trouble. Needs constant male attention to maintain her self-image. On a ship like this, well . . .' He shrugged his elegant shoulders. To William the subtext of this was obvious. The doctor was far too much of a social animal to refuse a light flirtation with such an attractive offering. However, he imagined he would have extracted himself without too much difficulty.

'The doc's got quite a way with women but I think Miss Geary met her match there,' said Stan after Ian Westlake had left.

'How long's he been with you?'

'On the *Empress*?' Stan thought for a moment. 'About eighteen months. Joined us from Harley Street. Was a specialist of some sort, bones, I think, but couldn't take the pressure, he had some sort of breakdown and decided life at sea could be the answer.'

'Does he get much call for his services on board?'

'Depends. He's got a couple of nurses and I reckon they do most of the work. But some of our passengers aren't in too good shape, not to be wondered at when you look at the average age on a cruise like this, and he's kept reasonably busy. Has to keep the social side going, has a table in the restaurant, great favourite with the ladies, he is,' Stan added a trifle sourly.

There was little else that could be gleaned from any of the ship's staff and the report William and Stan had prepared concentrated on facts rather than theories.

Luther Conran shuffled the pages of the report, cleared his throat, caught everyone's eye, and got the attention he needed. 'The trouble we have with an alternative scenario to suicide,' he said in his deep, resonant voice, 'is that even if you accept that Mr Summers could have been jealous enough to arrange a rendezvous with Mr Burrell and push him overboard, he would then have had to come down to his office and leave the message on his computer. Did he have access to the keys? The report doesn't suggest he did.'

Derek Rider wiped his nose with a vast handkerchief taken out of his sleeve. 'There's the little matter of the computer password as well.'

William nodded, his expression kept deliberately pleasant. 'As we say in the report, various members of the ship's company have keys, including the steward, who has made a statement to the effect that he didn't let anyone into the office. At present there is no reason to disbelieve him. As for the computer password, Roger Coutts knew what it was. I believe Burrell had a fondness for bird watching and that's why he chose the word albatross. Coutts said it was a joke as well, as Burrell held that the computer was an albatross around his neck. Security does not seem to have been high on this point.'

Stan said, 'Detective Chief Inspector Pigram and I have formed no firm conclusions on the matter of Mr Burrell's disappearance. That is for you, sir.' He stood up. 'Captain Walters hopes you will have lunch with him in his day cabin. Until then, that telephone will connect you to the purser's office and he will arrange for anyone you want to interview to attend you here.' He paused a moment. 'Of course, ship's business has to continue so you will understand if sometimes it might not be convenient to see certain officers immediately?'

Outside the cabin he produced a handkerchief and wiped his brow. 'Bill, it's not often I say this, but I need a drink. Come to my cabin.'

Once he'd poured them both a beer from his private fridge, Stan Dobson said, 'I hope to hell they decide Mr Burrell did top himself. I mean, a murderer amongst us on this ship? It doesn't bear thinking about. What if a passenger was involved!'

Chapter Fourteen

Tara Greene poured suntan lotion into her hand and applied it slowly and sensuously to her left leg, then repeated the operation on her right. Julian watched her through half-closed eyes. She had long legs, long and shapely. There were no hairs on them, the skin was satin-smooth and a very pale gold. He reached across, took the lotion and started lightly stroking down first one leg, then the other.

Tara leaned back in her lounger and raised her face to the sun. 'Oooh,' she said, 'that's lovely, Jools.'

His hand reached the slim little ankle and folded around it, then slid over the heel. With a feather touch, he eased the lotion across the sensitive sole, looking back at the girl, at the half closed eyes, the little feline smile on her mouth. They'd found a small, upper deck that was nicely sheltered and private. So far, they had it to themselves. It was a suntrap, protected from the breeze that kept the temperature down elsewhere.

As he started on the other leg, Julian could feel the sun's warmth on his shoulders. With Tara's skin soft and alive beneath his hand he felt wonderful.

'My back as well,' she said, eyes closed, shifting herself so that she lay on her stomach.

Now he could massage right up to the small buns of

her buttocks. Above the bikini bottom, her hips were ever so slightly bulging – too much good food on the ship?

'Mmmm,' she said as he started on her back. 'Like that!' She reached behind and untied the bikini top so that he had unfettered access to all her skin.

'There,' said Julian after he'd covered the entire area of her well-muscled back. 'You're ready for the grill. Medium or well done, ma'mselle?' He drew his fingers gently along her right breast, a flattened, small pumpkin against the lounger.

'Later,' murmured Tara and swatted away his hand as she might have a fly.

Julian wanted to slip his hand all the way round that soft swelling but he never felt masterful with girls. Instead he registered the promise in her voice and decided he wouldn't push matters now. 'Want a spliff?' he asked, taking out his marijuana kit and starting to roll a reefer.

Tara refastened her top, got up in one easy movement, grabbed the kit and ran to the side of the boat.

'Hey!' said Julian angrily as he saw her chuck the whole lot overboard. 'What are you doing?'

'I told you, they're dead against that sort of thing on this ship. Merve explained it all to me.' She came back and sat down again. The sex-kitten image had vanished and she showed a determination that wasn't to be argued with. 'You'll get us thrown off, then where will we be?'

'Together somewhere we can have some fun,' Julian said sulkily.

Tara arranged the back of her lounger so that she could sit up, relaxed against it and sent him a sultry look from underneath her lashes. 'We've got so much time ahead of us,' she said huskily.

Julian's blood ran a little faster. There was no doubt but that Tara was the most exciting girl he'd met in a long while.

Julian's good looks were deceptive. He found it easy enough to attract girls but difficult to keep them. He lacked the fast backchat that seemed to get you anywhere you wanted. Take the matter of the spliff. He should have been able to snatch it back with a flippant remark that would have got Tara laughing and then they'd have smoked it together and she would have thought what a great guy he was. Was it always going to be like this? No, he decided, this was an opportunity he was not going to let slip. No matter what it took. He felt excitement building, this was his great chance and nothing was going to take it away from him.

He leant towards her, narrowed his eyes and dropped his voice. 'Isn't it about time we talked about you and your future and what I can do for you?'

'Yeah!' breathed Tara.

'But first there's a little matter to clear up,' Julian said sternly, pushing back his dark hair resolutely. 'Where, exactly, does Mervyn Pryde fit into your life?'

Tara opened her eyes wide. 'But I thought I'd explained. Mervyn is just a chum. As part of the deal on this cruise, he gets a double cabin and the freedom to bring whoever he likes with him. I just happened to be around when he was making the arrangements. That's all.'

'So he's not going to object if I sign you up?'

'Of course not, silly,' she giggled. 'Anyway, what's

he done for me apart from offer the freedom of his cabin? And he snores,' she added resentfully.

Julian wondered fleetingly if she'd occupied his cabin last night merely to get some quiet. Then dismissed the thought, she'd been far too enthusiastic, it had been a wonderful night. And how excited Tara had been about the size of his cabin. Something he should be grateful to his stepmother for, he supposed. But what was a luxury cabin when she had the power to make everything he'd ever wished for come true?

'Look,' he said decisively. 'What we need is to make a splash with you. Organize a gig that will show you off, with a good band, somewhere people will want to come. Then invite lots of producers and record company people and TV execs and, well, you know.' She was looking at him, her breath coming fast; it was just the way she had been last night. He plunged on. 'We'll get a top arranger to organize your programme and find a new song with number one potential that will be just you.' Julian could see it all. The prospect was so exciting it was practically orgasmic. He remembered his father once saying that a successful piece of business was as good as sex.

'Oh, yes!' breathed Tara. 'That sounds wonderful.'

'Of course, you'll need to sign a contract with me first.'

'Of course,' Tara agreed. She glanced down at her hand, the fingers splayed out against her upraised knee. 'I can use Merve's lawyer, he's first rate, Merve says.' Her hand still seemed to have all her attention. 'He knows all about all the little bits and pieces you have to be so careful about. You wouldn't believe how some singers get stitched up, especially by record companies.'

Some of Julian's excitement evaporated. Top-flight lawyers meant his operation would be put under severe scrutiny. His operation at the moment amounted to little more than a dream. However, surely now his stepmother would come to his aid? All that money, she wouldn't miss a few hundred thousand.

'I trust you, of course, Jools, don't think I don't but you can't be too careful, especially these days.' At last she looked at him, her eyes wide and innocent. Too innocent.

'Mind if I join you?' asked a girl's voice.

Tara gave a little pout. 'We thought no one else knew about this place.'

'It is out of the way, isn't it?' Beth Cartwright said. She drew out another lounger and positioned it to catch the sun. Too late Julian rose to help her.

'I can manage,' she said briefly, dropping a tapestry bag on the deck, taking out a large towel and arranging it to her satisfaction.

He sat down again, feeling he'd been found wanting.

'I just love the sun,' said Tara, leaning back and half closing her eyes but sending Julian a smouldering glance.

Julian felt a bit better.

Beth stepped out of a loose cotton dress, revealing a modestly cut one-piece swimsuit, neatly folded up the dress and put it in her bag, taking out a magazine as she did so. Her figure wasn't nearly as good as Tara's, Julian thought. It was almost too thin, the hip bones sticking through the black Lycra of her costume. And her skin had a sort of looseness about it, a lack of tone.

Beth looked up and Julian had a nasty feeling that she could read his mind. 'I hope I haven't interrupted anything,' she said, her voice as neat and precise as everything else about her.

'We were just discussing my career,' Tara said enthusiastically. 'Julian is going to manage me.'

Beth put down her magazine. 'Is he? Do you manage just singers or musicians as well?'

'It's just singers at the moment,' Julian said, delighted with how positive he sounded.

'How did you start? I would have thought you needed quite a bit of experience before you set up in that sort of business.'

Exactly the sort of thing his stepmother said. 'I may look young but I've been working in that field for quite a few years. When I was at university, my group did gigs everywhere. I met lots of people. Virgin signed us up,' he added proudly.

Beth considered this achievement for a moment. 'What happened?'

'Oh, I was with them for a couple of records but then I needed more time to study.' That sounded so much better than the truth, which was that he'd been thrown out of the group. He hadn't enough rhythm, they said, and he couldn't carry a tune. 'The rest have gone on to great things, you've probably heard of them, The Hole in the Wall Gang?' He'd watched their success with bitter envy. Now, though, he'd be able to show them a thing or two.

'I'm sorry, I don't follow pop music. So, you gave up fame and fortune to complete your degree, was that it?'

'I didn't feel my future lay in playing,' he said briefly.

'But he has all the contacts,' Tara put in, wriggling lower on the lounger in a way that emphasized the pertness of her little breasts. 'And personality counts for so much in our business. Jools knows just how to chat people up.' She gave him another smouldering glance.

Julian loved the way she made the two of them sound initiates in a life that Beth could know nothing about.

'Money helps too,' Beth said. 'Having lottery winnings behind you, I mean.' As she said this, she raised an eyebrow in an enquiring kind of way.

'Doesn't it just,' Tara agreed.

Julian said nothing.

'After all, your mother can't be giving *all* her winnings to whatever foundation it is she's setting up,' Beth continued. 'What exactly is it for, anyway?'

Julian should have known it wouldn't be long before someone brought this up. He hadn't somehow, though, expected it to be Beth, she sat so quietly at their table at dinner, hardly opening her mouth, except to consume minuscule amounts of food. Perhaps she, too, could be inhibited by paralysing feelings of inadequacy. The thought made him feel sympathetic towards her so, instead of clamming up, he gave her as much of an answer as he could manage.

'It's to do with GMOs. Don't ask me exactly what, I don't know, and when Shona tried to explain it gave me a headache.' He didn't even know exactly what Shona's job was. Giving him some background before introducing him to her for the first time, his father had said she was frightfully clever and was a scientist working for a large industrial company. Well, Julian had let all that wash over him, confident that the Shona woman would disappear from his father's life as quickly as all the other women he'd been introduced to since his mother had died.

'GMOs?' Tara asked. 'You mean genetically modified organisms?'

Every now and then Tara really surprised Julian. He was beginning to think she was a great deal more intelligent than she seemed most of the time. He hadn't known what the acronym stood for the first time he'd heard it.

'Shona works in biotechnology,' he explained. At least he'd learned that much. Not that he'd had much help from his stepmother.

'Honestly, Julian,' she'd said in that superior voice of hers. 'Didn't your school teach you any science at all? I really don't think there's much point in my trying to educate you in what are, even for scientists, quite involved issues.' And that had been that.

'You mean genetically engineered foods?' Beth asked.

Tara sat up with a screech. 'Not those nightmare things that can poison us and destroy natural foodstuffs?'

'I think that's putting it a little strongly,' Beth said with a small frown.

'I always look for packets that say organic and no GMs,' Tara said virtuously. 'I mean, you can't be too careful, can you?'

'But aren't there advantages to genetic engineering?' Beth asked in that precise little voice of hers. 'Like helping to feed the Third World and eliminating various diseases?'

Julian lost his brief sense of empathy and began to get irritated. 'The thing is, it's no use eliminating

143

genetic disease if the Third and every other world ends up poisoned. And, anyway, medical biotechnology is quite different from the food area. It's GM foods that Shona wants her foundation to research into,' he added in case there should be any misunderstanding about this.

Tara's eyes rounded in horror. 'Really? More and more of these food what-you-ma-call-its? Jools, that's awful! Can't you stop her?'

Stop Shona? As well try to stop the world turning. When Shona got an idea, nothing was allowed to stand in her way.

Chapter Fifteen

Enid and Darina left Joyce going after her husband in the museum and caught the next tender back to the ship. Also on the tender was Mary French, looking fresh-faced and happy.

'Weren't all those old houses fascinating?' she said, making room for Enid and Darina to sit next to her. 'Jim says the boat is so nice when most of the passengers are on shore that he wanted to stay aboard and have a quiet read but I really enjoyed myself. Nice to have some exercise too,' Mary added cheerfully. 'At home I'm always taking out the dogs.'

'William is doing the mile walk round the decks each morning,' said Darina.

'Aren't you doing it with him?' asked Mary. 'I'd have thought you were the sort of couple who did everything together.' She looked around as though expecting William to be lurking on the other side of the tender.

Darina shook her head. 'I haven't been able to face it, I've been suffering from a touch of seasickness,' she confessed. 'But I hope to get my sea legs any day now.'

Mary looked keenly at Darina. 'And your husband hasn't come with you this morning?' She sounded quite shocked.

'He's got involved with the investigation into the

missing stores manager,' Darina said. 'He's a police-man, a detective,' she added.

'He's on a busman's holiday, then,' said Enid, her face alight with interest. 'What a thing! And has he discovered what's happened to that poor man?'

'He's only been involved in a preliminary investigation. Two official policemen arrived this morning to take over.'

The tender had started its passage back to the ship and Darina waited for nausea to rise the way it had going ashore. Instead she just felt rather strange, distanced from her surroundings.

'I reckon that chap must have thrown himself overboard,' she heard Enid say with a certain ghoulish relish. 'Otherwise they would have found him by now, wouldn't they?' she said to Darina. 'That must be what your husband thinks, isn't it?'

'I don't know,' Darina said, finding that at this moment she didn't care one way or the other.

'Are you all right?' Mary asked anxiously. 'You've gone terribly pale.'

'I'm fine,' Darina asserted through gritted teeth. At least she wasn't feeling sick. But everything was moving around in a very odd way.

The tender came alongside the ship and passengers stood up to disembark. 'You sit still,' Mary said positively. 'Let everyone else off first.'

Darina was quite happy to do as she was told, sitting with eyes closed, trying to convince herself that nothing was the matter.

'Now,' said Mary after a few minutes. 'We can go aboard in comfort.'

Darina opened her eyes.

'Take my arm,' said Mary. 'Enid, you go on her other side.'

This was what it was going to be like when she was old, Darina thought, allowing herself to be guided off the tender and up the ramp.

'Can I see your ship's pass, please?' said the officer at the top of the ramp.

Enid started to expostulate but Darina fished out the little white card from her pocket and showed it. She was beginning to feel a little better.

'Let's go and find somewhere quiet to sit down,' Mary said once they were past the guard.

'I could do with a drink,' Enid said, pressing the button for the lift that went up to the public saloons.

How very strange, thought Darina. Here was she, nearly six foot tall, young, strong, being looked after by two elderly women, neither of whom came up to her chin. Something was very wrong. But she had lost any power to make decisions or take command and was very happy to be steered in the direction of one of the lounges.

Once there, Mary guided her into a comfortable chair and motioned to one of the waitresses. 'Not alcohol, I think,' she said decisively. 'Some sweet tea. For two,' she ordered. 'And what about you, Enid.'

'Brandy,' Enid said eagerly. 'And make it a double.'

Sitting down, Darina began to feel more like her old self.

'You're looking much better,' said Enid in a relieved voice. Then launched into a dramatic account of how Joyce and Michael Harwood had lost their home.

Mary tutted disapprovingly. 'What a dreadful thing! No wonder they look so unhappy. That poor woman.'

After she'd had a cup of hot and sweet tea Darina began to feel hungry and realized that she'd felt too awful earlier to eat any breakfast.

Mary looked at her approvingly. 'Much more the thing,' she said. 'Now, dear, do tell us, when is it due?'

'Due?'

'Well, you are pregnant, aren't you?'

Darina gazed at Mary, torn between denial and a realization that it was the perfect explanation for her ailments.

'Oh, no, don't tell me. You didn't know?'

'I can't be, I'm on the pill.'

Mary smiled in a kindly way. 'My dear, I've given birth to three sons, I've got three daughters-in-law and nine grandchildren. I know the signs. I'd place money on the fact that you are expecting.'

'Skipped any of your pills, have you?' enquired Enid, dark eyes glittering happily.

'No, it's routine, every morning,' Darina said. Then she remembered a bout of gastric flu some two months earlier. For two days she hadn't been able to keep anything down. That must have included the contraceptive pills she'd continued to take. And she remembered how well William had looked after her and the evening she'd felt so much better. She'd had a bath, William had remade the bed with clean sheets and brought her a piece of plain fish he'd cooked in the microwave to her instructions. It had tasted wonderful. Then he'd lain beside her and they'd watched television before William had clicked it off and turned to her. They'd made leisurely love in a way that had banished all memory of her stomach upset. The next day she had felt completely better.

Darina gazed stupefied at Mary. 'I suppose it makes sense,' she said slowly. 'I've never suffered from sea-sickness before, in fact, I've always been rather a good sailor. And the nausea has cleared up in the afternoons, only to return next morning. Do you really think I'm pregnant?'

Mary nodded firmly. 'It's something in the eyes, a sort of general bloom.'

It sounded anything but scientific to Darina. 'If only I could get hold of a pregnancy test kit.'

Enid got to her feet. 'I'll pop back to Sandane, I remember exactly where I saw a chemist.'

'I'm feeling much better now, I'll go,' said Darina.

'No, you don't,' said Mary putting out a hand to stop her. 'And there's no need for you to go either,' she told Enid. 'Jim likes doing things like that and there's plenty of time before lunch.' Mary looked delighted to have a mission.

'Well,' Darina acknowledged, 'it would be good to find out for certain.' The implications if she really was pregnant were so enormous, she could hardly think straight. Then she grabbed at Mary's arm. 'You won't, that is, can we keep this just between us and your husband? I'd hate William to hear about it from anyone but me.'

'Of course,' Mary beamed at her. 'We're the soul of discretion, that's us. Tell me your cabin number and the kit will be delivered as soon as Jim returns.'

A moment later she had gone.

'Well, dear,' said Enid, swallowing the last of her brandy. She waved at the waitress for another. 'What a thing, eh? How d'you feel about it?'

Darina felt those bright eyes looking right down

into her soul. Mary and Jim French might be souls of discretion but Enid Carter definitely wasn't. What was it that made her so dedicated to winkling out gossip and spreading it around? Darina was going to have to find William and tell him the news as soon as possible or the whole ship would know before he did. 'It's going to take a bit of getting used to,' she said slowly.

'I had a child,' Enid said abruptly. 'He died when he was four.'

'Oh, I'm so sorry,' Darina said. 'Was it an accident?'

'The Lord took him,' Enid said, her eyes glittering.

'I'm so sorry,' Darina repeated, 'it sounds terrible.'

'It was,' Enid said simply. 'We never had any more. Not for want of trying but it just didn't happen. So you enjoy this child. Babies are a gift and a blessing from God.'

Darina felt humble. How could she have guessed that Enid had had such a tragedy in her life? Was her curiosity about other people a way of burying her grief? Had her husband, George, been a support?

'Strange,' Enid mused, shooting a sidelong glance at Darina, 'I could have sworn that Mary and Jim were on that *Empress of China* cruise when we all got so excited about the paedophile. Dreadful that was,' she added with rich satisfaction. 'To look at the people around you and wonder if it could be this man or that. We never found anything out, just rumour it was but, my, it got us all going. Funny Mary not remembering anything about it.' Another sidelong glance at Darina.

'Exactly when was this cruise?' asked Darina.

Enid thought for a moment. 'Two and a half years ago. George died six months later. Phil Burrell, the officer that's disappeared, he was on that ship as well.'

Mary arrived back. 'All organized. Jim's just pleased as anything to be able to help.' She smiled at Darina. 'He thinks you and your husband are really special.' Behind her heavy lensed glasses, Mary's eyes shone with warmth. No longer did she look at all plain and unassuming.

Darina thanked her again and then said she ought to try to find her husband. 'I've got to tell him as soon as possible,' she said, and left the two women settling down to more brandy.

She found William at last with Stan Dobson in the latter's office off the main reception area. William gave her a big smile of welcome.

'Join us for a drink?' asked Stan, rising. 'We could do with a spot of cheering up.'

'Trouble with the investigating police?' asked Darina sympathetically.

'Only if you count bloody-mindedness trouble,' he replied.

Darina commiserated with him then said she was sorry, but she wanted a bit of a word with William.

'Of course you do,' Stan said immediately, his lugubrious face creasing into a warm smile. 'Take the lad away, I've taken up far too much of his time as it is, and him on holiday!'

'Let's go and find somewhere quiet,' Darina said when they were outside the office. 'I've got something to tell you.'

'I know, they want you to do a three-act demonstration and you'll need the next four days to get the whole thing together,' he said.

'What did Stan mean about bloody-mindedness?' Darina prevaricated.

'Only that the inspector and his sidekick appear to have decided already that Phil Burrell has thrown himself off the boat.'

They found a table in a pleasant bar. Realizing there was no one else within earshot, William launched into an account of the morning's proceedings. Darina listened to him with half an ear. Later she would regret her inattention but at the time nothing seemed to her as important as the news she had to tell him and she was impatient for him to finish.

A waitress appeared at their table.

'What will you have, darling? A white wine or something stronger?'

'Actually, something non-alcoholic,' Darina said.

'Good heavens! Your session with the chef is going to be serious stuff, then.'

'The chef!' With dismay, Darina recalled that she had an appointment with him that afternoon.

'Don't say you'd forgotten! What *has* happened?'

An impressive-looking pink drink in a sugar-encrusted goblet decorated with a parasol arrived together with beer for William. Darina took a deep breath and said, 'I think your great wish may be granted. Soon there could be the patter of tiny feet.'

He looked at her as though he hadn't heard.

'It isn't certain, of course,' Darina went on. 'But if Jim French manages to find a pregnancy test kit in Sandane, we should know quite soon.'

'Pregnant?' William croaked. 'You mean, you think you're going to have a baby?'

'It's what pregnant usually means. I know we said we were going to wait for a family . . .'

'You said *you* wanted to wait for a family,' William

said swiftly, his eyes very bright. 'You know I want us to have children as soon as possible.' He reached forward and grasped her hand with his. 'I think this is the best thing I've heard in a very, very long time.' He paused for a moment then added, 'I just hope *you're* pleased.'

Darina swallowed hard – and saw some of the delight fade from his face.

'You aren't pleased, are you? You don't want a family,' he said flatly.

'I do,' Darina assured him quickly. 'It's just, well, it's just rather a shock. I mean, we hadn't been planning to have a baby quite this soon.'

'You mean, you hadn't.'

Darina nodded, her eyes fixed on his. 'If you're happy, then I am,' she said robustly. 'I just need a little time to get used to the idea. At least,' she added, striving for a light-hearted note, 'at least if I am pregnant I'll know it wasn't seasickness making me feel so wretched.'

William didn't say anything. He remained grasping her hand very tightly and looking at her keenly. Finally, 'I think it's just wonderful,' he said softly.

Darina smiled at him and tried to stifle the last of her doubts. 'And so do I. Let's go down to the cabin and see if Jim has managed to find that kit yet. What with the tea Mary ordered for me and now this,' she indicated the pink drink, 'I should be well equipped to provide what I suppose will be necessary.'

Not only did they find the pregnancy kit in the cabin, but also a note from the chef regretting that he would be unable to keep their appointment that afternoon and making it for two days later.

153

'I can't say I'm sorry,' said Darina. 'Though I suspect it means he isn't at all keen on discussing Scandinavian food. Never mind, now we're both free. At least, I *suppose* you're free?'

William assured her that he was.

They had a moment's panic with the kit when they thought all the instructions were written in Norwegian, then they found an English translation, together with a German, a French, a Spanish, an Italian, Arabic and something that looked like Japanese. 'Goodness,' said William, 'Quite something imagining girls in all these countries trying to find out whether they are expecting or not.'

'I suppose we'd better get on with it,' said Darina nervously.

Was she pregnant or wasn't she? And if she was, what was it going to mean to their lives?

Chapter Sixteen

Enid Carter slipped on her medium-length black chiffon skirt and added a white polyester blouse that looked like silk if you didn't look too closely. Years of cruising had provided Enid with a wardrobe of standby items that carried her through whatever dress code the captain chose. Except it was probably Head Office rather than the captain, it seemed they regulated everything these days. Tonight had been designated 'informal' but that didn't mean 'casual'. No, informal called for a 'cocktail or day dress' for the ladies and suit and tie for the gentlemen.

Enid ran a comb through her corrugated curls and remembered that she hadn't yet made an appointment with the hairdressing salon. Perhaps she'd have them change the colour? Maybe a touch more pink? When you had a face like hers, you needed something different to make an effect.

She found the cameo brooch that George had given her shortly after they were married and pinned that at her neck. Then added her long diamond earrings. They were a present when little Jackie was born. As always when she slipped the long hooks into her ears, Enid remembered Jackie's gurgle and the way he'd wave his starfish hands at her. That short time before they'd realized what was wrong had been the happiest of her life. But even the rest of his time with them had been a joy. Sometimes she thought all delight in life had vanished with Jackie's death. It was as though her juices had dried up and left her hopelessly withered.

Enid looked at the cascade of diamonds hanging either side of her lined face. Withered was certainly the word for her now. Jackie had belonged to a different woman and a different life. Were he and George happy together in heaven now? According to Father Anthony they were.

When George died, Father Anthony had been very comforting. 'He and the little one,' he'd said – for Enid had told him all about Jackie when he'd first come to the church, 'he'll be teaching him cricket and football amongst the heavenly host.' That had been almost too much for Enid because George would never have been able to teach Jackie cricket even if he'd lived. Not the way Jackie was.

Enid had a moment's vision of George, taller than he had been in life, thundering up to the crease in Ian Botham style, bowling at a strong young figure with dark hair and a straight bat. Clouds were around their feet and an angel was keeping wicket. Such nonsense! She'd have to tell Father Anthony exactly what she thought of his whimsicalities one of these days. But people had an awkward habit of turning on Enid when she told them what she thought.

'You need to use tact,' George had told her once. Later he'd said that she lacked any political sense, she didn't know when to hold back or how to phrase what people didn't want to hear in such a way as to make it acceptable. George had been very good like that. Too

156

good! It was just as well he'd had her to stop him getting above himself. Just because he'd done so well in business didn't mean they should get fancy ideas. Too many people got fancy ideas.

In the end, she'd found out exactly what George meant by tact. At least, she supposed he would file his dalliances under some such label.

Enid dabbed powder on her nose, added a bright turquoise to her eyelids, and scarlet to her lips. Without checking the overall effect, she grabbed her evening bag of black velvet embroidered in gold (a memento of their cruise to the Indian Ocean) and carefully opened her cabin door.

Enid had an inside cabin, it was cheaper. Travelling alone was an expensive business, there were always single supplements and Enid had no intention of sharing with anyone. So relying on the steward to tell her what the weather was like outside instead of being able to judge for herself was a sensible choice. In exchange for a porthole she had space and comfort and, right from the start of the voyage, Enid had found the cabin across the corridor from her a perfect focus for her inveterate curiosity.

She'd seen Daphne Rawlings enter shortly after the first tea session. 'No better than she should be, I'll be bound,' had been her initial reaction on seeing the lottery winner's close friend. 'Far too attractive to be on the loose. Sexy, too.' Long years of practice had given Enid an ability to identify whatever quality it was that made women sexually attractive to men and with this woman it was quite obvious. Enid had soon engineered a conversation with her and introduced herself.

Enid peered into the corridor. Daphne's door was

shut. Enid slowly closed her door until a crack remained just wide enough for her to see across the corridor. She waited a few minutes. People passed on their way to drinks but nobody emerged from the other cabin.

Enid checked her watch. Twenty minutes to the start of the second sitting. Had she missed Daphne's departure? She reapplied her eye to the crack. A couple of minutes later, her patience was rewarded by the sight of Daphne emerging, dressed in a short bronze silk dress that showed off her slim legs. It had a boat-shaped neck that was ideal for showing off the heavy gold circlet she was wearing. The woman had a wonderful dress sense and some good jewellery. Enid wondered who had paid for it.

She noticed that Daphne didn't lock her cabin door. Enid remained with her eye fixed to the narrow opening and waited. After another couple of minutes, the lottery winner's husband emerged from Daphne's cabin into an empty corridor. He locked the door behind him and, whistling through his teeth, disappeared out of Enid's sightline. She opened her door wider and watched him saunter casually along the corridor.

Enid shut the door and sat down on one of the cabin's chairs. How stupid of them! If they'd come out together, it would have looked as though he could have just dropped by for a chat. Instead it was obvious what was going on. Men who cheated on their wives shouldn't be allowed to get away with it. She would have to do something. Enid looked at her watch again. It wouldn't do to be late for dinner, she'd think about a course of action as she made her way to the restaurant.

Enid reckoned she'd been placed on an interesting table. She liked the cookery girl and her husband, very friendly they were (though it had been a bit of a shock to discover the young man was a detective). Enid did hope Darina really was pregnant. Of course, it was more than possible Mary French was mistaken. Enid couldn't help remembering the number of times she had hoped and hoped, only to be disappointed in the end. No doubt they'd know this evening and Enid was sure that Darina would tell her the truth, whatever it was, even if they kept it a secret from the others.

What with that and the disappearance of that young Purser, this trip was really turning out to be very interesting. Enid wondered if Darina would pass on to her husband the titbit she had given her that afternoon. If not, she'd have to find some other way of making her suspicions more obvious. You never knew about people, did you?

As Enid made her way along the corridor, she turned her attention to the others on her table. Could there be anything interesting about any of them? The singer talked too much but he could tell a tale with verve and Enid admired that. She didn't think much of his girlfriend, not much upstairs and far too ambitious. Also, for a girl given a trip by an attractive man, Tara was paying too much attention to Julian. At the start, Enid had thought she would need to do something about that situation but it was clear that it didn't worry Mervyn. Why had he brought Tara with him? He must have had other choices. That was something for Enid to think about.

Beth Cartwright was interesting. She had nothing much to say for herself but Enid felt she was probably

159

one of the deep ones. She'd have to find out what made her tick.

The disappointment at the table was young Julian. All those looks and so little personality! But good looks could make things too easy for some people. They didn't have to develop character to make an impression. She wondered if he knew what his father was up to.

Enid reached the restaurant in a state of pleasurable anticipation. Now that William had managed to get the waiters to remove that odd place no one had come to sit at, they were quite a cosy group. She'd ask Julian about his parents and their friend, see what that brought forth.

At the table, though she was surprised to see that the vacant place was back. How stupid those waiters were! Never mind, William would deal with it. The perfect man to have beside you in a crisis.

William and Darina arrived at the table wreathed in smiles. 'It's not every day I learn I'm going to be a father,' he announced exuberantly, and he ordered two bottles of champagne. 'We want you all to celebrate with us,' he told the table.

Mervyn led the congratulations in his mellifluous voice. Darina smiled and explained what had happened. 'These kits are supposed to be very reliable these days,' William said. 'And the line was definitely blue.'

'Does that mean it's going to be a boy?' asked Tara. 'Well, blue is for a boy,' she said rather sulkily after the shouts of laughter had died down.

'I see we've got the ghost's place back with us,' Enid said. 'Can you get them to take the spare chair away?' she said to William.

'I think it's for me,' said a voice.

Enid looked up. Standing at the empty place was a very tall, very stylish young man with a shaved head and a wonderfully dark bloom to his skin.

William got to his feet. 'Luther, great to have you join us. This is Detective Sergeant Luther Conran,' he explained to the table. 'Joined us this morning to investigate the disappearance of Phil Burrell, the stores manager.'

The table appeared stunned. Enid certainly was.

'What's happened to Inspector Rider?' William asked the young man.

'The inspector doesn't approve of socializing,' Luther said as he sat down beside Enid. 'He's going to have something in his cabin but allowed me to contaminate my soul by joining one of the tables.'

'How lucky it was us that had the space,' William commented.

The champagne arrived.

'Have you decided if that poor man threw himself off the boat?' Tara exclaimed. Her body wriggled with excitement. Whether at the drink or the arrival of Luther Conran it was difficult to decide.

'I'm afraid I can't discuss the case,' Luther said pleasantly.

'No, of course you can't,' Mervyn said swiftly. 'I remember when . . .' and he was off recounting the tale of some case of theft and a police investigation during one of his tours. There was an almost audible sigh from around the table.

'Anyway,' said Beth, who was on Luther's other side, 'you've hardly had time to come to any conclusion.'

'That poor man,' said Tara with theatrical

161

emphasis. 'I can't bear to think of him casting himself
off the boat in despair.' She looked round the table but
no one would catch her eye.

'Much better to think of the new life we've just
heard about,' Enid said prosaically. 'Children are the
hope of the future.'

'Oh, yes!' breathed Tara. 'That's so very true. Babies
are wonderful.'

Enid doubted Tara had ever allowed herself near a
baby.

'Are you pleased?' Beth said straightforwardly to
Darina.

What a question, thought Enid, the sort that George
was always telling me I shouldn't ask. Then, as she saw
Darina turn a little pink and say that of course she was,
Enid decided that Beth was really quite astute. Blunt
but astute.

'Of course she's pleased,' Mervyn declared. 'Why on
earth wouldn't she be!'

'Not everyone wants babies,' Beth said quietly.

'Don't you?' asked Enid, abandoning everything
George had tried to instil in her over the years.

Beth looked down at her glass of champagne. 'When
I was first married, I thought I did but it's just as well it
didn't happen, I don't think I'd be a good parent, and
my own parents were so hopeless I really wouldn't
know how.'

'What happened to your husband?' asked William.

'I'm a widow,' said Beth in a brave voice.

'I am sorry,' he said. 'He must have died very
young.'

Beth nodded. 'But the marriage wasn't very successful, so it was just as well there weren't any children.'

Enid wasn't at all surprised to hear that. The girl wasn't nearly giving enough, no man could live with such a self-contained, inward-looking wife.

'I can't wait to be a father,' William asserted. 'We want children very much.'

'Lots of people want babies who can't have them,' Enid found herself saying. 'It's a tragedy for them. And I don't understand why it's so difficult to adopt these days.'

'It's the change in society's attitude that is at least partly responsible,' Luther put in pleasantly, looking up from his study of the menu.

'What do you mean, society?' Enid asked.

'I mean that these days there is no stain to being born outside marriage, so the supply of illegitimate babies up for adoption has declined.'

Luther Conran had a very pleasant voice, it had a deep timbre and an almost cultured accent, decided Enid. She felt quite strange sitting so close to a black man in such a social context.

I'm not racist, she told herself. She had nothing against coloured people, it was just that she'd never met any. Of course she came across them, in the supermarket, in the hospital when she went for the check-ups on her eyes, but in her part of Derbyshire there weren't all that many. If she'd found herself sitting next to a Russian, she would feel just as strange. But a Russian wouldn't have looked quite so obviously different. It was that difference that was so, well, interesting.

'But just as society progressed like that, so did science, enabling many couples who would have remained childless to conceive,' Luther continued.

163

'I'd never thought of it like that,' said Enid. 'And, of course, so much better to have your own child than have to adopt.'

'Why?' Tara asked abruptly, losing for once her air of studied charm.

Enid was taken aback. 'Well, it's a matter of genes, I suppose. Passing on your own instead of receiving somebody else's.'

'I'm adopted,' Tara said defiantly. 'And I've always thought of my parents as just that, my parents.'

Interesting, thought Enid. Perhaps that was why she was so pushy and touchy.

'Isn't it true that genes can cause trouble?' asked Darina. 'Isn't that what scientists such as your stepmother,' she said to Julian, 'are trying to do? Make sure that errant genes aren't handed down?'

'But Jools' stepmum is all for changing the genes in plants, not people,' said Tara shrilly. 'Didn't you tell me that she wants to produce these monster foods no one wants to eat?'

For a moment the table was silent. Then Darina said, 'Tara, there is a lot of debate on the safety of genetically modified foods, both on whether they provide risks to the environment and on whether they are safe to eat. What is needed is research to enable us to learn more about them.'

Tara stuck out her bottom lip in a sulky pout.

'And medical biotechnology,' added William, 'can be immensely helpful. I mean, Enid mentioned handing on one's genes, well, sometimes they can cause a great deal of trouble. Think of cystic fibrosis, for instance.'

Something began to pound in Enid's head. She

164

hadn't foreseen where this discussion was going to lead. No more brains than a scared rabbit, George used to say. Perhaps he'd been right.

'Wouldn't it be wonderful if such genes could be replaced so that babies were born without diseases like that?' finished William.

'Yeah, great,' Tara said mechanically.

'As I said this morning,' Beth contributed in her neat little voice, 'not all biotechnology is a bad thing.'

'Next thing you know, we'll be able to choose the colour we want to be,' Luther Conran said.

Enid couldn't bear it any longer. She put down her menu and clenched her fists together under the cover of the table. 'But it's all against the law,' she cried out, much louder than she'd intended. Everyone looked at her.

'Against the law?' repeated Luther. 'Not yet, I don't think, Mrs Carter.'

'It's against God's law,' Enid said passionately. She looked across at Darina. 'Would you want your or your husband's genes mucked about with? The Lord gives and the Lord takes away, blessed be the name of the Lord.'

'Amen,' said Luther gently. 'I'm really glad to meet someone who believes so strongly, Mrs Carter.'

Enid felt despair. She'd done it again, torn it, George would have told her. But such things had to be said.

'I'd like to see you up against my stepmother,' Julian said suddenly, leaning towards her from across the table. 'I reckon it'd be some battle.'

Enid said nothing but she came to a decision. This

scientist who was mucking around with God's work should know how her personal life was being mucked about. And she knew what she was going to do about it.

Chapter Seventeen

Darina was with the chef. 'It's cooking that makes the most of superb ingredients,' she said a trifle desperately. 'Simple but with style.'

Martin Ireland, the chef, was a big man with biceps that challenged Popeye. His tall chef's hat couldn't restrain the luxuriance of his dark hair, and his fleshy face and ample figure said here was someone who loved good food. He'd greeted her courteously but Darina could tell instantly that the galley was his kingdom and he didn't take kindly to any intrusion. To arrive with the blessing of Head Office had added suspicion to resentment.

'So nice to meet you, Chef,' she'd started, hoping for some way of making contact with him. 'I love the food you're serving, particularly the soups, they are really outstanding.'

This had not struck the right note. 'Really?' he said, with just a touch of incredulity. Oh dear, was he one of those who regarded soups as occupying a lowly rung on the haute cuisine ladder?

'The depth of flavour,' she continued. 'The stock you use is obviously superb and I love the subtlety of the seasonings! Of course the rest of the menu is exceptional but so often people overlook soups, don't you find? Think they can throw anything at them and as long as they can be eaten with a spoon, people will find them acceptable? Left over vegetables, bits and pieces of this and that, I think some kitchens regard them just as a recycling tool.'

'I tell my soup sous chef that a potage needs as much care and attention as a poussin.' Martin Ireland looked pleased at his little word play.

Breathing a sigh of relief that he had unbent slightly, Darina had got down to discussing the possibility of adding some Norwegian and other Scandinavian dishes to his menus. But very quickly she saw that Norwegian traditional cooking with its wonderfully simple casseroles and fish dishes did not appeal to someone dedicated to providing large numbers of people with the haute cuisine they looked for on a luxury liner.

'Quality ingredients. We deal with those every day,' Chef said a touch frostily. 'And we already use smoked fish in our menus.'

'Of course,' Darina murmured. She decided to change her approach. 'I think what Head Office were thinking of was perhaps a lunch menu or one of your incredible midnight buffets done in traditional style.' She produced the sheets of recipes and notes she had prepared.

Chef ignored them. 'I believe you are going to do a demonstration of open sandwiches?'

Darina nodded. 'Francis Sterling has suggested tomorrow afternoon. I understand we shall be at sea then.'

The purser had actually suggested the morning but Darina had said the afternoon would be better, then explained about her morning sickness. He'd congratulated her warmly, said the ship's doctor was excellent if she needed any medication or a check-up, then looked again at his charts. 'We've the Latin American dance class followed by Bingo in the Neptune Lounge; there's a classical music talk, "Beyond Vivaldi", in the theatre followed by a film. The Pearl Lounge has a talk on aromatherapy and then a class on making artificial flowers. Hey – that's a good one, roses from crêpe paper, you wouldn't believe how easy and effective they are.' Darina hoped she looked sufficiently enthusiastic about the prospect. Francis returned to his charts. 'I'm afraid the Coral Lounge is out too because it's needed for rehearsals for the evening show.'

'Heavens, what a busy life it is on board ship! It sounds a bit like the army, keep us occupied and keep us out of mischief.'

Francis twinkled at her. 'Better believe it! But where can we make space for what I am sure will be a much welcomed additional entertainment?' He studied his charts again, then smiled. 'I've got it. The bar on the Corniche Deck – that's the open one. The weather forecast is excellent and it should be ideal. Passengers can sit at tables and watch you perform, Chef can pre-prepare some of your sandwiches and we can serve them as you make them.'

'Open air?' Darina wasn't at all sure. 'Will anyone be able to hear me?'

'Sure, we'll give you a microphone. It's great up there.'

There didn't seem much option. Obviously every corner of the *Empress* was utilized in the never-ending task of providing entertainment for her passengers whilst at sea. With all the other options, would anyone want to come to her demonstration? Too late to duck out now, though, it was all arranged.

Today the *Empress* was at anchor in yet another wonderful fjord and Darina, feeling horribly nauseous, had forced herself to stagger on to the tender ashore to take a coach up into the mountains to a summer farm where the famous caramel-coloured Norwegian goat's cheese was made. Now she was feeling all right again and just as well. This encounter with the chef was a bit like a chess match. It shouldn't be like this, Darina thought as she asked Martin Ireland where it would be possible for her to prepare for the demonstration.

'No problem,' Chef said, dropping his guard. 'Give me your requirements and it will all be prepared for you.'

That was a bit better! Darina took a deep breath. 'I don't know if the purser has had a word with you but he suggested that maybe the galley could make up some of the sandwiches beforehand so they could be served to the audience towards the end of the demonstration.'

'No problem,' he said again. It was as though he wanted to prove that his department was capable of anything.

Thanking him profusely, Darina handed over her description of the sandwiches and a list of exactly what she needed. 'If there's anything you haven't got, let me know and I'll produce an alternative,' she said. 'The smoked eel, for instance, and the gravadlax?'

'We have plentiful supplies of both,' the chef assured her.

'Ah, do you marinate the salmon on board?' At last, Darina thought, they could have a discussion on methods and flavours and even, perhaps, compare preferences.

He shook his head. 'No time. It comes vacuum-packed, we have an excellent supplier.' He ran his eye down her list of ingredients. 'No trouble with any of this.' He picked up the sheets of her other recipes she had given him and flicked through them. 'Maybe an alternative lunch menu one day. And perhaps open sandwiches for a late-night snack would work.' He was now sounding positively cordial as he shuffled the recipes together. 'We'll see what we can do.'

Darina breathed a huge sigh of relief as she left the chef's office. It looked as though she'd fulfilled her commission. Now she only had the demonstration to give. She just hoped someone would turn up for it.

Emerging through the restaurant, Darina looked at her watch. William's deck tennis match would be over and he'd be enjoying the sun in some corner, if he hadn't chummed up with one of the other players. Either way, he'd be happy while she ironed her outfit for that evening.

The passengers' laundry, a useful room with washing and drying machines and a row of ironing boards, was at the other end of their cabin deck. When Darina arrived, two of the boards were already occupied and at one of them was Joyce Harwood. She looked up as Darina came in and her worried expression brightened. 'I've heard about the baby,' she said. 'Congratulations.'

'I think the whole ship knows by now. I've never known such a place for spreading news.'

'Regular gossips, cruisers are,' the other woman ironing said. 'There, that's done, the old man will be respectable this evening.' She carefully removed a dark blue striped shirt from the board and left the room.

Joyce was also ironing a man's shirt, attacking the white cotton with fierce concentration. 'Children are a wonderful thing,' she said as Darina adjusted the temperature on her iron.

Darina remembered Joyce's outpourings. 'I'm sure yours are a great source of comfort,' she said and wondered if the tiny foetus inside her would one day be a support to her. But a certain sorrow and an uncertain joy was what children were said to be.

'Is your husband managing to relax at all now?' Darina asked, testing her iron on an inside edge of her silk top.

Joyce's worried expression returned. 'I don't know what to do with him,' she burst out and pushed the iron fiercely down a sleeve. 'I've told him if he can't cheer up for himself, to do it for me. I've suffered just as much as he has but I want to try and enjoy this trip. It's cost the kids a fortune and the least we can do is forget about things for a bit. Is that so wrong?'

'It seems very sensible to me,' Darina said. 'But people respond to situations in very different ways. It sounds to me as though your husband needs some professional help.'

Joyce swished the shirt around on the board and started attacking the back. 'Try suggesting that to him!'

They ironed in silence for a couple of minutes. Then Darina became aware of Joyce sneaking little glances at her, as though there was something she wanted to say but wasn't sure how to begin.

'Nice and quiet in here, isn't it?' Darina said encouragingly.

'Look, do you mind if I ask you something?' Joyce said, pushing the iron with great force around the cotton. 'It's been worrying me ever since Michael told me. He doesn't want to say anything about it but I think he should and I don't know what to do.'

'Ask away, but I can't promise I can help.'

'Well, it's about the first night out, when that crew person disappeared,' Joyce said, her head down over her ironing.

Darina started smoothing out her top, the hairs on the back of her neck suddenly electric.

'Michael saw that chap. He says it isn't important, that it doesn't mean anything. I've tried to get him to talk to your husband, but he won't.' Joyce jerked her iron around the shirt front in exasperated movements.

'What did he see?'

'Oh, it wasn't anything much,' Joyce said hastily. 'If it had been really important, I'm sure he'd have come forward.'

Darina controlled herself with difficulty. 'I'm sure he would. You never know with these little things, though,' she said as casually as she could. 'Sometimes they're like a missing piece of a jigsaw. What was it he saw?'

Then it was as it had been in the museum café. Once started, Joyce poured everything out. Everything but exactly what had happened. 'That first evening Michael couldn't settle at all. We drank in one of the bars, then had a walk round the deck, then we went into the Oyster Bar – I noticed you and your husband in there – and had another drink. We saw the argument and that woman being knocked about and Michael said it served her right. She was obviously trying to play one

173

off against the other. I was quite surprised because
normally he doesn't notice anything like that. Well,
when it looked so nasty, I said I wanted to leave. So we
went down to our cabin.' Joyce moved the the iron in
short, sharp bursts while she talked. 'We had a bottle of
whisky there and Michael poured himself quite a large
one. He wouldn't undress, he just sat in a chair, looking
miserable. When I tried to cheer him up, he switched
on the television.' Joyce gave a harsh little laugh. 'He
didn't want to talk to me.' The hurt her husband had
dealt her was clear in her voice.

Darina finished her top and started on the trousers,
wielding the iron while trying the tricky business of
looking sympathetic at the same time.

'I said something about turning the sound down in
case it disturbed other people and he exploded,' Joyce
said unhappily. 'He ranted on about how I was just like
everybody else, then he grabbed his jacket, said he was
going for some air and off he went. I waited and waited
but he didn't come back and eventually I just fell
asleep, with the light on and the television playing.
Well, I was that tired, it had been such an effort trying
to kit us out for this trip and persuade Michael we
should come.'

Joyce stood gazing at the white bulkhead, fresh
paint covering but not concealing ancient chips in its
surface.

Darina still had no idea what it was Michael Harwood
had seen. 'When did he tell you what happened?' she
asked baldly. Polite approaches were obviously not
going to get her anywhere.

'What? Oh, yes, I'm sorry. My daughter, Maggie,
says it's useless asking me to tell anything, I never get

to the point.' Joyce put a finishing touch to the last piece of the shirt she was ironing and held it up to inspect her handiwork.

Darina could have shaken her. Instead she carefully arranged a leg of her silk trousers so she could press it without leaving a crease down the middle and waited.

Joyce hung the shirt on a wire hanger, suspended the hanger from a convenient bolt in the bulkhead and leant back against her ironing board. 'Michael was that grumpy the next morning I couldn't get anything out of him, so I just left it. But after we all heard about that young chap jumping overboard, well, I think he was so shocked that he told me what had happened before he knew what he was saying. I told him that he should tell someone. Especially when we heard from Enid that your husband was a detective and he was looking into the disappearance. I mean, he's such a nice chap, so easy to talk to, not snooty at all. But Michael wouldn't hear of it, said it couldn't be of any interest. He said if someone wanted to throw himself overboard, he should be allowed to do it.

'Do you know what I think?' she added suddenly. 'I think he doesn't want to have to tell anyone he didn't know what to do with himself at that time of night when he should have been tucked up in bed – with me,' she added almost as an afterthought.

'So what *did* he see?' Darina felt very near exasperation with the woman.

Joyce stared at her, 'Oh, isn't that me all over! Well . . .' She took a deep breath and finally related exactly what Michael had told her.

175

'I shall have to tell William,' Darina said when she'd finished.

Joyce nodded vigorously. 'That's why I've told you.'

'And he will have to talk to your husband.'

Worry lined Joyce's face. 'You mean, he'll have to know I've talked to you? He won't like that.'

Darina thought that the person who wasn't going to like this at all was Inspector Rider. From what William had said, it sounded as though the inspector had already decided what had happened to Phil Burrell. Now, with this evidence, it looked as though he was going to have to think again.

Chapter Eighteen

It was not easy for Luther and William to get Michael Harwood to confirm the story Joyce had told Darina but eventually they managed it.

He'd taken them to the flight of stairs that connected the open Corniche Deck to a small upper deck. 'I was coming across from the other side of the ship, round this bit here,' he said, indicating the bulkhead where the stairway to the upper deck started, 'and I ran straight into him.'

'You recognized him? In the dark?' William had asked sceptically, remembering it was the first night out, long before they reached the land of the midnight sun.

Michael had looked at him scornfully. 'There was a light,' he said. 'There it is.' He pointed at the bulkhead.

The light didn't seem very powerful but it would certainly have made identification possible. And if the Harwoods had been in the Oyster Bar at the time of the incident, the man would certainly have been able to recognize one of the participants.

'There were two officers involved in the argument that night,' Luther said, speaking slowly and clearly as if to a foreigner. 'Describe the one you saw here.'

'I'm not an idiot,' Michael said resentfully. 'I know which was which.'

'I'm sure you do. Nevertheless, indulge me.'

The farmer said enough to demonstrate that it was certainly Phil Burrell that he'd seen.

'Which direction was he coming from?' asked William.

Michael waved towards the stern, which was where the Oyster Bar was located.

'Did he say anything?'

Michael shook his head. 'He hardly seemed to notice me.' He sounded resentful, as though Burrell should have stopped and passed the time of night with him.

'And you saw him run up there?' Luther waved a hand at the stairway to the upper deck.

Michael nodded.

'And what did you do then?'

Michael looked puzzled.

'I mean,' said Luther as though he was talking to an idiot, 'did you stand looking at the sea? Did you look up the stairs at the man who had nearly knocked you down, or did you proceed along the deck and, if so, in which direction?'

Light slowly dawned on the man's face. 'Ah, I see. Well, I didn't do anything for a moment. I mean, he'd nearly knocked me down, I wasn't feeling all that steady,' he said resentfully.

William could just picture him, too much to drink, obsessed with his own problems, rocked back on his heels by his encounter with a man in a hurry. No, he wouldn't have moved immediately, he'd have waited for a moment to let everything settle back into place. 'Did you say anything to Mr Burrell?'

'Say anything?' Again that look of incomprehension.

178

'Such as, "Mind where you're going!" or just "Eugh!"?'
Michael shook his head. 'I don't think so.'

'OK. So, you're waiting just here,' Luther stood where Michael had indicated. 'What did you hear as he gained the upper deck?'

'I told you already!' Michael objected.

'So tell us again.'

'I just heard the man say, "God, I couldn't believe it," or something like that,' Michael said sulkily.

'You're quite sure?' William pressed him.

'No, I'm not. You've confused everything.' The farmer looked pugnacious and as though all his ills were their fault.

'What sort of tone did he say it in?' asked William.

'For God's sake, how would I know?'

'Think back, remember standing here, by this light, the man dashing up the stairs. Now hear him say that phrase again.' William waited hopefully.

Michael looked at him as though he was mad then, reluctantly, closed his eyes. He seemed to concentrate for a moment. William and Luther each held their breath.

'It was sort of surprised. Yes, surprised, that was it.' At last they seemed to have got some sort of co-operation from the man.

After the two policemen had dismissed the farmer, William said to Luther, 'If we can rely on his evidence, it appears that Phil Burrell, instead of throwing himself overboard, or drowning his sorrows in drink, *did* have a rendezvous with someone on that upper deck. Funny place to meet, it wasn't exactly a nice night.'

'But it's quite sheltered up there,' said Luther. 'Boat like this, there aren't many private places.'

'So maybe whoever wanted to meet him there is sharing a cabin? Or if alone didn't want Burrell seen near it,' mused William. 'And it *is* the deck we thought Phil Burrell might have fallen from.

'And whoever was waiting for him took the opportunity to tip him over the rails?' suggested Luther.

'It certainly seems a possibility. Look, let's go back a little. Francis Sterling, the purser, told Burrell to wait for him outside his office while he saw that Karen Geary was all right. Francis then dressed him down briefly and sent him off, saying they'd go into the matter further in the morning.

'Now, Sterling's office is on one of the main decks outside the Coral Lounge. Suppose while Burrell was waiting, someone came out of the lounge, saw him and wanted to chat. Burrell says he can't talk, he's waiting for someone. They arrange to meet on the upper deck.'

'Because it's private,' said Luther, thoughtfully. 'Suppose it was Summers? He'd have heard Sterling tell Burrell to wait for him there. We know he left the bar before Sterling and Geary. He could have invited Burrell to meet him to resolve matters. If they were going to fight, where better?' He looked down at his notebook. ' "God, I couldn't believe it." That could fit in. He couldn't believe Summers had made such a fuss.'

'It's certainly a possible scenario. We'd better have another word with Summers. But there's the Keep Fit Instructor, Lulu Prentice. If Burrell dumped her and she wanted to discuss something with him, he'd be surprised at that, too.'

'And if she was hoping to come on to him, she'd want to be somewhere private,' Luther agreed. 'She shares a cabin and is definitely athletic enough to have pitched him over the rails.'

'Of course, there's always the possibility that whoever he met up there wasn't responsible for killing him,' said William with a sigh. 'They could have come along after the meeting had ended.'

'In which case, why not come forward and say they'd met with Burrell and he was fine when they left him?'

'I'm being devil's advocate here. I don't believe that's what happened, any more than you do. I think the person who waited for Burrell on that piece of deck dumped him overboard.'

'Hmm,' said Luther. 'Inspector Rider is not going to like this one little bit. When he detailed me to see Harwood after I reported what we'd learned via your wife, I'm sure he thought it would be a simple matter of tidying a nuisance out of the way. He thinks he's more or less wrapped up the investigation and has now, according to the medic, succumbed to flu.'

'You mean, he didn't ask for me to sit in on the interview?'

Luther shook his head. 'That was my idea,' he confessed. 'Look, Rider's on the way out. He's got six weeks left to retirement. He can't wait. He's only on this job because the chap who should have come broke his leg falling over a mutt when chasing the mutt's owner for possession of a class A drug.' Luther's full lower lip curled out disdainfully. 'I don't have to tell you what he thinks about having to work with a black man! Or what he said when he found out there was a bright young detective chief inspector already on the crime scene.'

There was silence for a moment. Then Luther added, 'By the way, congratulations on your impending fatherhood. Not all the chaps I know would be so pleased.'

'You don't want children?' William had already learned that Luther wasn't married.

Again that pushing out of the lower lip. 'My girl-friend is white. My mother is beside herself. She thinks diluting the blood of her Jamaican ancestors is a crime next to murder.'

'What about your father?'

'Says it's up to me but to remember the children.' Luther let out a heavy sigh. 'Sometimes I think the faster all the genes get mixed up together and everyone is born the colour of putty, the better.'

'Things are better than they were,' offered William.

'Sure! My younger sister got offered a job the other day. On the telephone. She was told she had all the right qualifications and sounded as if she would be perfect. The actual interview was a formality, they said. Then she walked into the room, they saw the colour of her skin and suddenly the job was already filled and all they were offering was travel expenses.' Luther sounded very bitter.

'Tough!' William couldn't think of anything else to say.

'Anyway, your offspring will have no such diffi-culties. Come on, let's go and have lunch. You did say your wife was going to be busy preparing her dem-onstration, didn't you?'

Chapter Nineteen

Michael Harwood stood leaning over the deck railing. The flat, sparkling sea churned into a rich, creamy foam that streamed out astern as the ship steamed on to Tromsø, its next port of call. He watched the white wake spread out and it seemed to call to him.

Michael turned away and looked instead at the scene on board. The sun was shining. All around him passengers were emerging from lunch. They looked as though they were having a good time. There was a game of table tennis going on. People were spreading themselves on loungers, bringing out books and knitting. At the Corniche Bar, tables under blue and white striped umbrellas were filling up with people ordering coffee and beers. It all looked so cheerful. Nobody seemed to have a care in the world, they were enjoying being treated like kings. They behaved as though they actually liked travelling in this great floating hotel with people waiting on them, never having to lift a finger. For Michael it was purgatory. Everywhere he went there were people, there was nowhere he could go to be on his own.

Somewhere there Joyce would be, no doubt having enjoyed a hearty lunch.

Michael burned with rage. Joyce had betrayed him.

She'd told that tall, blonde girl, Darina, what had happened that first night. Darina had told her police-man husband and Michael had spent the morning with him and the black detective. Going over and over the same ground. What, exactly, had he seen? What, exactly, had he heard? How, exactly, had Phil Burrell behaved? And why, exactly, hadn't he told them before?

For a long time he'd refused to say anything. Slowly, persistently, they'd worked on him. The old Mutt-and-Jeff technique, the good guy and the bad guy. The good guy, of course, had been William Pigram, the blonde's husband.

Why had Joyce done it?

Because she'd had to, she'd said when she told him.

For once they'd actually had a row. He'd shouted at her, he'd hit her, his fist striking her ribs under the soft flesh with such force she'd collapsed on the bed and looked at him with terrified eyes, one hand going auto-matically to the place his fist had landed.

'I think it's broken,' she'd gasped. Her eyes were those of a puppy he'd had to hit to make it obey him.

He'd stormed out of the cabin, afraid that if he stayed he'd hit her again. The battle Michael fought every day was to contain his rage. He'd been angry for so long. It had built up gradually. When you were a farmer, you didn't expect everything to go your way. Nature was awkward. Just when the cows were pro-ducing record quantities of milk, mastitis struck. If you thought the harvest was going well, you could be certain rain would come. If the beef market was healthy, the animals weren't. Your porkers could fatten like a dream but the price they'd fetch would be ridiculous. There was always something to have to cope with.

Just one time, sometime in the eighties, everything had come right together and farming had been really profitable. For a little while it seemed as though life had been tamed. Then BSE had made itself felt and after that it had been one disaster after another.

Joyce had had the children. Michael might be their father – indeed, he was sure he was – but she looked on them as hers not theirs. After the house had gone, everyone said what a tragedy it was for her. It was she who got all the sympathy.

This cruise, now; it was for her the kids had clumped together enough to buy the tickets. It wasn't for him. Perhaps because when they were growing up he'd treated them like puppies, striking them when they got out of line; they feared him, respected him but didn't love him.

Love! What was that anyway? Michael was with Prince Charles on this one. Joyce said she loved him and there must be something that kept her with him. Or was it just a sense of duty? She had that all right. She'd made that clear last night. 'It's your duty, Michael,' she kept saying.

But, in the end, as always, it was his fault. If he hadn't told her what he had seen, there wouldn't have been anything for her to go to the police with. He must have been mad! The anger pressed behind Michael's eyeballs so that he viewed everything through a red haze.

Through that glare, Michael saw Shona Mallory with her friend, Daphne Rawlings, and her husband, Paul, on the deck below taking one of the tables with the striped umbrellas at the Corniche Bar.

Michael brought a fist down on the rail beside him with desperate force. If it wasn't for people like her, scientists, he wouldn't have been asked to plant that damned crop. Test trials indeed! It had been the work of the devil.

Michael had been brought up to believe in the devil. It was the devil that made him so wicked. It was the devil that had to be beaten out of him by a father who'd taken a whip to him every time he transgressed. That was when he'd learned to contain his anger, to push it down inside him, clamp it with iron chains while he worked off his rage on the fields, on machinery, on animals, shouting and cursing at them the way he wanted to shout and curse at the people who made life so difficult.

But he had no work to do on this ship and the only way he could get rid of his anger was by lashing out. Like last night. Like . . .

Now, he wanted to take that stupid scientist by the throat and show her what science had done to turn farming into a nightmare. Without proper thought, Michael found himself taking the stairs down to the Corniche Deck. But by the time he worked his way to the area with the tables and umbrellas, he realized that something was going on. That blonde girl, Darina, was standing behind a long, white cloth-covered table.

'Ladies and gentlemen,' she said through a microphone. 'Thank you for coming. Aren't we lucky with the weather? Now, I'm sure you've all heard of the famous Scandinavian open sandwiches. They are beautiful to look at, delicious to eat, and so useful. What I'm going to do this afternoon is to show you how easy they are to prepare.'

On another table behind her were plates of sliced chicken, ham and cheese and various smoked and preserved fish, glass bowls of scrambled and hard-boiled egg, chopped herbs, sliced potato and tomato, bowls of lettuce and other saladings and slices of various breads.

'Sit down,' said someone impatiently behind Michael.

Anger flooded through him again. He looked around but couldn't see where the Mallorys were sitting. Then a hand waved at him and he saw Joyce at another table.

He hadn't been able to face her that morning. Always an early riser, he'd dressed and left the cabin before she was awake. The bitterness of her betrayal and the frustration at his own foolishness meant he still couldn't bring himself to talk to her.

'Sit down, please!' urged the same voice from behind him.

Michael moved out of the way, ignoring Joyce's pleading wave of her hand, and looked again for the scientist.

Now Darina was buttering bread, explaining the different choices there were: white, wholemeal, rye, crispbread, how each should be chosen according to the topping and that a good layer of unsalted butter was essential both for flavour and to protect the bread from getting soggy.

Some remote area of Michael's brain applauded this – far too many people had decided butter should be replaced with some sort of low fat spread.

Darina made more enticing arrangements on slices of buttered bread: scrambled egg on rye with anchovy;

smoked salmon on brown bread with dill and lemon; three folded and overlapping slices of salami decorated with slivers of tomato; sliced breast of chicken with grilled red pepper and caramalized onions. She placed the finished concoctions on a large dish. 'These are ideal for a light lunch,' she said. 'Or for a supper. They are a wonderful way to entertain and sometimes you can even use up some leftovers.'

None of this registered with Michael, still trying to locate the table where the Mallorys were sitting.

Waiters were beginning to circulate with little plates bearing small versions of the sandwiches Darina was making. Michael found it hard to credit that these people, who must all have had a large lunch, were tucking in, while exclaiming at how attractive they were.

The fact that a thin slice of rare roast beef had been arranged in a wave on lettuce anointed with a horse-radish mayonnaise and then garnished with slices of new potato and gherkin passed him by.

'Some of you,' continued Darina, 'were in the party yesterday morning that went to the goat farm in its summer home in the mountains above Geiranger. What I'm using here is the rich, caramely traditional Norwegian cheese I bought there, perfectly comple-mented with very untraditional roasted aubergine. Weren't you all impressed with how lovely the scenery was and the natural way the goats were raised and cheese made?'

Michael paused in his survey of the tables. Yes, he'd been in the party and now he realized that some of his anger had been ignited by the sheer beauty of the mountains, the small lake, the graceful trees and the enchanting little goats skipping about the meadow backed by tiny wooden houses where the milkmaids stayed. He hungered anew for his own farm, but his farm as it had been in the old days, when the production of food had been difficult, labour intensive, fraught by unkind weather patterns but simpler and, in his memory, more satisfying. He remembered his ruined crops, his burned-out home and lost livelihood and he hated the beauty he saw all around him.

Suddenly he saw Shona Mallory.

'You!' he shouted at her.

People turned to look.

'It's your fault.' He strode towards her. Murmurings broke out. He reached the table where she sat with her husband and her friend. She looked at him. She was quite pale. 'It's because of your stinking hi-tech crops that I'm ruined. And I won't be the only one.' All the arguments of those punks who had destroyed his crop came back to him. 'You're destroying our heritage.'

Paul Mallory rose, grabbed his shoulder and said, 'Here, you can't talk like this.'

Michael shook him off. Nothing could stop him now. He thrust his face close to Shona Mallory's. 'You're poisoning our future. You should be locked up, you should. People like you shouldn't be allowed. GM crops are garbage!' He was shouting now.

Round him pandemonium had broken out. People were crying out, 'Hear, hear! It needs to be said.' Others were shouting at him not to ruin the demonstration. Above them all came Joyce's voice, faint but clear, desperate, crying his name. It meant nothing to him.

Daphne Rawlings shrank away, she looked terrified. But Shona Mallory sat very straight in her chair, contempt written over her face. 'You know nothing,' she said slowly and clearly. 'You are ignorant, a Luddite.'

Michael seized her shoulders and shook her. His rage consumed him. He wanted to destroy her and her sneering expression.

He was pulled away from the table by Paul Mallory and William Pigram. 'Come on, old chap,' William said. 'You're spoiling everyone's afternoon.'

Michael struggled but they were too strong for him. He was marched away from the bar area. Out of the sun, the lounge was cool and shadowed. Suddenly Michael felt his rage evaporate. He slumped between the two men and let out a half sob. 'Leave me,' he groaned. 'Leave me.'

'Oh no,' said William. 'You've ruined my wife's demonstration and frightened this man's wife practically to death. You'll tell us what it was all about.' He stood tall and stern and Michael collapsed into a chair.

Paul Mallory murmured something about leaving the matter to the police and left.

Police. The word echoed in Michael's mind. It was all going to start all over again.

Chapter Twenty

Darina had endured some tricky moments demonstrating but never anything like this! The place was in pandemonium. People were shouting, Michael Harwood was behaving like a madman and Shona Mallory was sitting there frozen.

Darina abandoned her open sandwiches and ran across to Shona's table. William and Paul had already hauled off the luckless farmer. 'I'm so sorry,' Darina said to her. 'All you all right?'

'Of course,' Shona said, very coldly. 'That man is deranged.'

Darina felt an instant's repulsion. Such self-possession was chilling. But the woman must be in shock. To have been so nearly attacked would be enough to unsettle anyone. The fact that Shona Mallory did not appear to be unsettled, far from it in fact, could merely mean that that was her defence in moments of drama.

Shona rose. 'So ignorant,' she said, 'so stupid.' For an instant her voice shook. That was the only sign she gave that the incident had in any way upset her. Then she walked steadily away from the little table with its striped umbrella. If she knew everyone sitting around the tables was following her with their eyes, she gave no sign.

Daphne hurried after her, calling for her to wait. Shona never slowed her pace.

'Huh!' said Enid, suddenly appearing at Darina's elbow. 'Fine friend she is.'

Darina hardly heard her. She was looking around. 'Can you see Joyce?' she asked Enid.

'She ran off when Michael started his rant,' said Enid. 'She was very upset. Pushed me away when I tried to say it didn't matter.'

Oh dear, thought Darina. Enid was hardly the best of people to have at one's side in this sort of situation.

Then she remembered that she hadn't finished. People were still sitting, eating the plates of small sandwiches that the waiters had handed round, others were getting up and milling about, talking excitedly. There seemed to be just the one topic of conversation and that was the unacceptability of genetically modified foods. 'Scientists and politicians have to be made to listen,' was a constantly reiterated comment.

She went back to her table. 'Ladies and gentlemen, I've got a few more things to show you, would you like me to continue?'

Those sitting at the front of the table area appeared keen but many others drifted away or sat talking together at the rear tables.

Darina did her best but she was heartily relieved to reach the last of her open sandwiches. She arranged parallel lines of prawns on wholemeal bread. 'The Danes call this one a traffic jam,' she said, garnishing the result with a butterflied slice of lemon and a sprig of parsley. She placed it with the other sandwiches and displayed the final colourful assembly. 'You can see how attractive even simple arrangements can be,' she said, raising her voice against the noise coming from those talking at the back. She abandoned any idea of showing how meatballs were made and said, 'I've given you recipe sheets with some other dishes that show exactly what the food of this beautiful country is about, using really good ingredients without fuss. There's a marvellously simple beef casserole, a wonderful lobster salad and, of course, the famous meatballs.'

'I bet the Norwegians won't be voting for genetically modified food,' someone called out from the back of the audience.

'Not something they want polluting their fields,' agreed someone else.

Through the enticing aromas coming from the open sandwiches, the only thing Darina could think of was how delicious it would be to chew on a lump of coal. She longed to be able to find a bunker and pick out a shiny black piece and crunch it between her teeth. Perhaps with a seasoning of raw onion. Bliss!

'That woman shouldn't be allowed to give so much money to genetic food research,' someone shouted out.

'Too right,' someone shouted back. 'Should be a law against it.'

Darina felt she knew how the storming of the Bastille had started. It was crowd pressure. Any moment now a movement would start to march on Shona's cabin.

'The genetic techniques have a lot to offer us,' she said firmly, more glad than ever to have a microphone. 'Crops are being developed that will provide us with fibres to revolutionize clothes. And in a few years other crops may be able to provide an economic, renewable

193

resource for petrol. Much more useful than tomatoes that don't rot so quickly.'

It was a mistake to take up the argument. People began to fling words at her, calling her a liar and suggesting she was under contract to one of the multi-national corporations responsible for GM development.

Darina gave up. 'I hope you've enjoyed watching and sampling some of the food. And that you'll try some of the dishes when you get home,' she said. 'If anyone hasn't got a copy of the recipes, there are some more on the table here.' She indicated a small pile of the sheets that the purser's office had run off from her master copies.

It was over! Darina felt her limbs trembling as reaction set in.

Francis Sterling came up. 'How are you doing?' he said. 'You were wonderful. I'm so sorry about the interruption. You never know what is going to happen with passengers.'

'Not often anything like that, I hope,' Darina said.

'Not often, no.'

A few people came up to compliment her on the demonstration and ask questions. Most, though, were leaving the deck area. The weather was getting cloudy and without the sun it was chilly.

'Looks good, that,' Enid said, poking at one of the sandwiches with a scarlet-painted fingertip. 'Come and have a drink before dinner in my cabin. See you at six thirty, right? Have to go now, it's Bingo.'

'Leave that,' Francis said as Darina started to pile the dishes she'd used together. Smiling waiters came up and removed them from her. 'Come and have a cup of tea and relax.' The purser took her arm and gently steered her in the direction of his office.

William came up. 'Darling, I'm so sorry about all that, how did it go after we took that wretched man away?'

'We got through,' Darina said briefly. 'How's Michael?'

'Feeling very sorry for himself. He's got an appointment with the captain and has gone off to find Joyce.'

'Enid says she was terribly upset. Oh, and Enid's asked us for a drink this evening in her cabin.'

Darina could see that William wasn't exactly delighted by this invitation. 'We'll have to miss Mervyn's concert,' she added slyly.

'I accept,' he said briskly. 'Now, I'm sorry, darling, but if you're sure you're all right, I should find Luther and see if he's managed to have a word with Inspector Rider regarding Michael Harwood's statement.'

'I'll look after her,' Francis assured him.

Watching William's tall figure swing away, Darina thought how ironic it was that William might complain about her work interfering with their life together but he seemed not at all reluctant to let his invade their holiday. Then she remembered that it wasn't exactly a holiday, after all she'd been working that very afternoon. She wished, though, he hadn't had to leave so quickly. She would like to have discussed the afternoon's events with him. She was sure Michael had not been responsible for all the disturbance. There had been someone at the back of the audience stirring up the feelings against GM foods.

Chapter Twenty-one

Enid's cabin door was already open when Darina arrived. 'You look wonderful,' she cried, welcoming her inside, then she peered into the corridor. 'No William?'

'He sends his apologies.' Darina said lightly. 'He's got some official business.'

'More detecting, I suppose? Gives him something to be occupied with, doesn't it? Leaving us to enjoy ourselves.' Enid had an air of suppressed excitement about her. Bangles on her wrist were set a-dance as she flung her arms around, the wide cream chiffon sleeves of her blouse fluttering and revealing the crêpy skin on the upper part of her arms. Her face worked itself into a variety of contortions, with winks for emphasis. Her laugh would have done credit to a hyena.

Already in the cabin were Beth and Tara, clutching glasses filled with a violently green mixture. 'My own invention,' Enid said proudly, holding up a cocktail shaker. 'I call it The Empress's Screw.' Again that slightly manic laugh and more winks. 'Crème de menthe, vodka and a little something extra.'

Darina didn't dare try to imagine what that little something extra might be. 'Enid, it sounds wonderful but in my condition I think it would be better to stick to tonic or mineral water.'

Enid looked disappointed. 'What a shame! The Screw really puts you in the mood for the evening. What do you say, girls?' She turned to where Tara and Beth were sitting on the bed.

'It's great!' Tara held out her glass for a refill.

'A long time since I've had anything like it,' said Beth. 'And the colour almost matches my dress.' She'd lost some of her usual prissiness, was it the effect of the alcohol, or the intimate surroundings? Her eyes were shining and she looked really attractive in a loose-fitting emerald-green caftan.

Tara was wearing a long black sheath that plunged at the back well below her waist and was held up by the thinnest of straps. It displayed a startling expanse of bare skin.

'How are you getting on with organizing a singing spot for yourself?' Darina asked her, sitting in one of the two chairs the cabin offered and feeling rather staid in her beige silk trouser two-piece. 'Have you spoken to the cruise director?'

Tara gave a little pout. 'She's useless. Every time I try to talk to her, she's chatting to just the most boring couples on the cruise. Finally I managed it but she said there just wasn't any time available, the official pro-gramme was full. There's even a pianist playing in the Ocean Lounge in the evenings so Julian and I can't do another of our impromptu concerts there – well, it would appear impromptu but of course we would rehearse it beforehand. I mean, if you can do a cookery demonstration, why can't I give a concert?'

Darina murmured something about it all having been arranged before coming on board. 'Not the exact time but the possibility had been discussed, so I came prepared.'

'I thought you coped very well with the fracas in the middle of your demonstration,' Beth said, swirling a finger in her glass and licking it. It was the sort of feline gesture that could have been expected from Tara; from the prim Beth it seemed incredibly sexy.

'You were there?' Darina said expectantly. 'Did you notice who whipped up the mood after Michael Harwood had sounded off at Shona Mallory?'

'Wasn't it spontaneous?'

'I don't think so, it seemed to start at the back, on the right as I was looking at the tables.'

'Why, that's where I was sitting,' Beth said, sounding surprised. 'I didn't notice anything. Except,' she paused for a moment, 'I remember thinking that one particular man seemed to be doing most of the shouting.'

'Really?' Enid exclaimed. 'I was a bit further towards the front from you and, yes, I remember thinking I heard the same voice being very vocal.'

'Do you know who it was?' Darina asked.

At that moment Mary and Jim French knocked at the already open door. 'Sorry we're late,' said Mary, 'I had to iron Jim's shirt and there was quite a queue at the laundry.'

'Naughty, naughty!' said Enid roguishly. 'You should be better organized. Take a seat on the bed and have a Screw.' She handed out more glasses of the green concoction.

Beth gave Darina a glance that seemed to say, 'Watch me,' shifted up the bed and patted the quilted cover. 'Come and sit here, Jim,' she offered. 'Didn't I see you at Darina's demonstration? And making quite a noise, I thought.' She gave Darina another glance. 'Didn't everyone make their feelings about GM foods felt?'

Jim gave her a roguish glance and plumped himself down on the bed, his eyes on Tara's bare back; his cummerbund was stretched tightly round his middle and his thighs seemed in danger of splitting his trousers. 'Don't know much about GM foods.'

'Darling, of course you do,' said Mary in surprise. 'Weren't you sounding off about them the other day? And didn't you say it was a crime for that woman to give all that money to GM research?' She turned to Darina. 'I had a front-row seat at your demonstration, but Jim, well, cooking isn't exactly his line, so he said he'd sit at the back. I really enjoyed it. I think I'll do some of those sandwiches for our next ladies' lunch.'

'Oh, good,' said Darina. 'It's always such a relief when someone actually wants to make something I've demonstrated.' Could it have been Jim French who'd encouraged the anti-GM reaction, she wondered?

'Those sandwiches are perfect for my bridge parties,' Enid cried, producing a glass of tonic water for Darina.

'I thought they'd be good for when I have someone round,' Beth said.

'Splendid! Do you do a lot of entertaining?' Darina realized that she knew almost nothing about the girl.

'Not really, my hours are so odd.'

'What do you do?' Enid shot the question at Beth as she added more of the sinister-looking green liquid to her glass, then topped up Tara's again.

'I work in a hotel, as a receptionist.' Beth was back in her prissy mode. 'It's shift work and non-hotel people never understand why I can't be available when they are.' Then Beth named one of the big hotels in Manchester as her workplace.

'Ah, so exciting!' breathed Tara. 'All those rich and famous people coming to stay or dine in the restaurant.'

Beth gave a short laugh. 'Far more very ordinary business people. Not much glamour about it.'

Enid clapped her hands together. 'Glamour is everywhere if you look for it. Look at us, aren't we glamorous? Not me, perhaps, my time was many years ago, but you girls look sensational.'

'Absolutely!' agreed Jim happily.

Both Tara and Beth looked pleased.

Enid leaned forward in her chair to look out of the open door down the corridor. 'Thought your husband might manage to join us after all,' she said to Darina.

'I should be surprised if he does,' Darina said drily. 'When he gets his teeth into a case, nothing else gets a look-in.'

'Anyway, Julian says the pianist in the Ocean Lounge has to have a break and he'll see if he can organize us to do a spot then,' Tara said, exactly as if nothing had interrupted her initial comments.

'It sounds as though you two are getting on famously,' said Beth.

Darina thought there was a faint tinge of envy in the quiet voice.

Tara's face lit up. 'Jools is fabulous. He doesn't seem very forceful on the surface but he knows what he wants and he intends to get it. And I'm part of it. With him behind me, I'm going to be a star!'

200

'I'm sure you will be,' Jim said, lust in his voice as he looked at her.

Mary French gave him a look that seemed to say he'd better watch it and Darina started to wonder about the state of their marriage. What was it Enid had said when Mary had gone to find Jim to ask him to get Darina the pregnancy testing kit?

'What of your friend Mervyn in all this?' Enid asked Tara eagerly in her excited voice. 'Isn't he going to object if you see so much of Julian?'

It seemed to Darina that Enid would enjoy the drama of a full-scale bust-up.

'Mervyn and I aren't an item!' Tara screamed with laughter. 'We're, well, we're just friends. He had this double cabin and no one to come with. I said a cruise sounded divine so here we are.' She sobered. 'Actually, he's got quite an eye for that Karen Geary, the cruise director. That's really why he won't speak to her about me. Doesn't want to push his luck. They've been on a cruise together before and he fancies his chances this time around.'

Did he, indeed? Darina squirrelled this bit of information away to tell William. Who knew how it would fit into the jigsaw of information he and Luther were building up? She wished she'd paid more attention to his account of the investigation instead of being so involved with how he would react when she told him they could be starting a family.

A group of passengers went by, laughing. Enid looked at them with keen interest. After they'd passed, she peered out again into the corridor. At home, Darina thought, she would be the neighbour who sat in her window and checked on all the activity in her road. The one who knew when marriages were breaking up before the participants did.

'Jools wants to get some money out of his stepmother to start up his company. Once he's done that, everything will take off – Milky Way, here I come!'

'I wouldn't rely on that,' Enid said. 'From everything I've heard, Shona Mallory is a pretty determined woman and I read that she intends to give the whole lot to set up a foundation.'

Beth nodded solemnly. 'Determined, that's what she is,' she said. She swirled the remainder of her cocktail around, watching the liquid climb up the edges of the glass. 'Good this,' she said. 'Don't usually drink this sort of thing. Cocktails aren't my style but I like this.' She was ever so slightly slurring her words. If she wasn't used to drinking spirits, two powerful cocktails of vodka and crème de menthe, plus whatever Enid's little secret was, were more than she should have attempted.

'Have some more,' Enid leapt up to refill her glass. Darina wished she could think of a tactful way to suggest Beth switched to tonic.

Tara shook her head when the shaker hovered over hers. 'I have to remain at least half sober,' she giggled.

Tara continued to favour them with Julian's plans for her and her ambitions. Beth was now lying against the headboard of the bed and had returned to dipping her finger in her glass and sucking it.

Then Darina noticed Enid's eyes brighten as she caught sight of something outside her door. Across the way stood Shona Mallory, dressed in a rather dreary full-length frock with white flowers on a dark background. She took a letter out of her little evening bag, glanced at it then slipped it back. She raised her arm to knock on the door of one of the outside cabins but hesitated, looked around, saw Enid's open door and came over.

'Would you mind if I used your telephone?' she said in a clipped voice. 'My friend may be in the shower.'

'Please,' said Enid, waving a hand towards the instrument.

Shona eased her way into the crowded cabin, picked up the receiver and punched in a cabin number.

Tara's eyes had widened as the lottery winner came into the cabin but she hardly hesitated in her listing of her aims. 'And I want a musical,' she said as Shona waited for her call to be answered. 'I'm as much an actress as a singer. Merve says so.'

Darina wondered if Mervyn was perhaps more interested than Tara realized.

Then she dismissed the thought. However skilful his interpretation of his operatic roles, there was nothing subtle about Mervyn's approach to life. Any more than there was in Tara's. But she was perfectly capable of playing more than one tune at the same time. After all, she was a musician, wasn't she?

'I'm sure you're a great actress,' Jim breathed in her ear. Once again Mary shot him a warning look.

Shona's fingers were drumming on the wall of the cabin as she waited, holding the receiver to her ear. 'She can't be in her cabin after all,' she murmured and Darina thought there was relief in her tone. Then, 'Oh, Daphne, I was just about to put the phone down. It's Shona. No, I decided not to go to the concert after all, I thought I'd come round for a drink with you. Be with you in five minutes, OK?' Without waiting for an answer, she put down the receiver.

Silence fell in the cabin as Tara finally appreciated that no one was listening to her.

Shona looked at them all. Two bright spots of red blazed on her cheekbones. 'I didn't mean to intrude,' she whispered. 'But I have to prove this one way or the other. I mean, she might just have refused to answer the door.'

They all looked at her questioningly.

'It's private but if it's true, then everyone will know anyway.' Shona gave a bitter sigh. 'And if it's true, they should have known better, a boat is like a glass house. Well, I can cast stones as well as anyone.' Her voice was tight and controlled, her shoulders tense. 'And if it is true, he's shared my bed for the last time.'

The door to Daphne Rawling's cabin opened. Shona straightened, a dangerous gleam in her eye.

Paul Mallory stepped out, buttoning up his shirt and hopping on one leg whilst he inserted a naked foot into a shoe. Daphne thrust his jacket at him. 'Go on,' she said urgently. 'She'll be along any minute.'

'She's here already,' Shona said and walked across Enid's cabin to face them. 'I think we should discuss this inside, don't you?' she added.

A moment later all three of them had gone into Daphne's cabin.

'Well,' said Enid gleefully. 'I said she was no better than she should be!'

'My word,' said Mary French. 'Who'd have thought it!'

Darina looked at the closed door across the corridor from Enid's cabin. From behind it could be heard the cold, steady tones of Shona Mallory telling her friend and husband exactly what she thought of them. She

204

remembered the piece of paper Shona had taken from her little handbag.

'You sent her a letter, didn't you?' Darina said, turning to Enid.

Enid didn't even try to deny it. 'Well, she should know what's been going on. I'm surprised she hadn't already guessed.'

'And you didn't sign it did you?' Darina said sternly. 'It could be classed as a poison-pen letter.'

'Ooh, you are a spoilsport,' Enid exclaimed petulantly.

'I think she was right,' Beth said unexpectedly, opening her half-shut eyes wide. 'It was Enid's bounded, I mean bounden, duty to let her know what was going on.' She got off the bed. 'I think I'd better leave now,' she said and weaved uncertainly out of the cabin.

Darina watched her. 'She doesn't look as though she's in any fit state to find her cabin,' she said.

'She's only one deck up,' Enid said cheerfully. 'She'll be OK.'

'I'll just check on her,' Darina said. 'I'd thank you for the drink but I have a nasty feeling everything has turned out exactly as you planned.'

Chapter Twenty-two

William and Luther were having another word with Harry Summers.

The first officer came off watch that day at four o'clock and he'd been asked to report to them at six. 'That gives him a couple of hours, long enough to worry about what we want and have a couple of drinks, not long enough to rest up before we close in,' Luther had said.

He'd raised an eyebrow when William arrived in his dinner jacket. 'Hoping we'll be finished by eight thirty, are you?' he said drily.

William shrugged his shoulders. 'Be prepared, as the Boy Scouts used to say.'

Harry Summers turned up on the dot of six, worry lines between his eyes and with the loss of some of his sangfroid. 'I thought we'd been through everything,' he said abruptly.

'We've got some new evidence,' Luther told him coldly.

There was the faintest flicker of unease in the first officer's eyes but he said nothing. He hadn't changed out of his uniform and William would have been ready to swear that he could sniff alcohol on his breath. But there was no hint he'd had enough to affect his judgement

His previous interview had shown him to be a cool customer. Even now only the tight fist he laid on the desk in a seemingly casual gesture betrayed tension.

Luther sat upright at the desk in Roger Coutts' office, William sprawled lazily in a chair by its side. 'Tell us again,' said Luther, pronouncing every word with crisp clarity, 'what you did after you left the Oyster Bar the first night out.'

'After the fight, you mean?'

'Yes, I mean after the fight,' Luther said.

The first officer crossed one leg over the other, tilted the toe of his beautifully polished shoe towards his gaze as though he needed to admire the quality of the leather, and said, 'I went to bed.'

It was a wearisome interview that got nowhere.

No, Harry Summers had not left the Oyster Bar by way of the purser's office. No, he had not seen the stores manager after the fight. No, he had not gone on deck. What he had done was to retire to his cabin. 'There's a lift just outside the Oyster Bar that goes straight down to my deck,' he said, 'and I took it.'

No, he hadn't seen anyone on his way to his cabin. No, there wasn't anyone who could vouch for him.

Finally they'd had to let him go.

For several minutes the two detectives sat without speaking. Then William said, 'He's hiding something, I'm sure of it. Did you see the little tic in his left eyelid?'

Luther nodded. 'We couldn't shake him, though. And we have absolutely no evidence against him.'

William thought for a moment. His position in this inquiry was nebulous, to say the least. He was quite without official standing. On the other hand, he out-ranked Luther considerably and the younger man had

207

shown every sign of respecting his judgement. 'Are we,' said William slowly, 'approaching this from the wrong end?'

Luther regarded him. 'You mean?'

'Why don't we order some sandwiches,' William said, looking at his watch. 'Much better to try and sort something out here than go down to dinner. What do you think?'

By way of answer, Luther reached for the telephone and requested whatever the kitchen could come up with for them. 'We deserve better than a couple of sarnies,' he said when he'd finished. 'Now, you were saying?'

'We're trying to find out who rather than why. Look,' William said, sitting up straight and drawing his chair nearer to Luther's, 'Stan and I tried to be objective in our report. We presented the facts as far as we had been able to ascertain them. Both of us had a gut feeling that Burrell didn't just jump into the ocean, that there was something more sinister at work. But we had no evidence and it wasn't for us to draw conclusions. Your Inspector Rider decided on the basis of our report before he and you ever set foot on this boat that it was a clear case of suicide. As far as I can see, nothing altered that opinion until Michael Harwood came clean on what he'd seen.'

'What he thought he'd seen,' interposed Luther.

'Quite. Now it looks as if Burrell met someone after the fight and the inference that has to be considered is that that someone tipped him overboard. Now, if we could discover *why* someone felt it necessary to dispose of Burrell, we would probably come up with *who*.'

'You mean that it was premeditated and not a sudden burst of anger? A fight that got out of hand?'

'Harry Summers's hands were unbroken when Stan and I interviewed him. He had no visible damage to his face either. If he'd been involved in a fight, he would have shown some sign of it. I'm sure of that.'

'So either he wasn't the person Burrell met or they didn't fight?'

'Exactly. What we have to ask is this: was Burrell involved in something or was he perhaps in possession of information that meant his removal was essential for someone?'

'You mean, was he a blackmailer?'

'Not necessarily. He might just have made it clear that he knew something. Or,' he added slowly, 'maybe he recognized a passenger.'

'What could he have known about them?' Luther asked dubiously.

'It might be worth asking the shipping company to identify those passengers who've sailed on their other ships at the same time as Phil Burrell.'

It took over an hour, including the time taken to eat two sizzling steaks with chips and salad followed by a sinfully rich chocolate pudding, before they'd scrutinized the last of the reports.

William said, 'I keep coming back to Geary's account of her relationship with Burrell and the first fight between Summers and Burrell after Burrell had met Karen Geary in that Lisbon bar. What was it she said?' He flicked through the papers until he found the right place. 'Here it is: "We met ashore in Athens and had a drink together. He was depressed, said he was afraid he was drifting into more of a relationship with Lulu Prentice than he wanted. That he'd had a disastrous marriage and didn't want to run the risk of

209

another liaison that would turn sour. So I tried to cheer him up, told him all the right things, you know: you're an attractive man, you'll soon find the right woman, all that. He was terribly sweet, helped me back with my shopping. We had the odd drink together after that. We hadn't arranged to meet in Lisbon, but he ran into me and it seemed only natural to pop into a bar. I don't know why Harry got so upset."' William shuffled the papers again. 'Here's Lulu Prentice in her interview. "We were getting along fine until Karen sticks her big oar in. I tell you, when it comes to collecting scalps, Buffalo Bill has nothing on that woman. It took long enough for me to rebuild Phil's confidence after his disastrous marriage, then she has to come along and ruin everything." '

'Do we know anything about this so-called disastrous marriage?' asked Luther, doodling on his pad.

'Only that his wife was a very large, very difficult woman. We've not only got the doctor's word for that, someone in the purser's office had a friend in the *Empress of China* who filled her in on some of the details when Burrell joined this ship.'

'Confusing, their both being called the Empress of something,' said Luther.

'Apparently they were almost identical. Burrell met his wife on board and after they were married she sailed with them a couple of times. Not a very popular soul apparently, according to our informant. The marriage didn't last long, by the time he joined this ship he was divorced.'

'Long enough to give him the heebie-jeebies about a relationship with Lulu Prentice,' said Luther.

'Not with Karen Geary, though,' commented

William. 'Though I suppose they hadn't had time to reach that stage.'

William thought how glad he was Darina wasn't a difficult woman. Oh, they had their little disagreements and there were times she went quite quiet on him but by and large she was an easy companion. At least they could talk when things went wrong. It didn't sound as though Phil Burrell had had much ability in the talking department. He looked again at Karen Geary's statement and something suddenly took on an unexpected significance. Something that could make sense of a number of unexplained details. 'Look at this,' he said. 'Both times, in Athens and Lisbon, Karen Geary came back to the ship loaded with shopping bags. Stan said that in Lisbon he saw Burrell helping her with them up the gang plank, with Summers looking on from an upper deck. Geary herself said that in Athens Burrell had helped with her shopping.'

'Shops till she drops, obviously,' Luther said derisively but it was plain he was thinking about the fact.

'Geary herself was very nervous when we interviewed her. How about when you saw her?'

'The Inspector didn't feel it was worth spending much time with her, he merely showed her the statement she'd made and asked if there was anything she wanted to add. There wasn't.'

William mentally cursed the way Rider had approached the whole case.

Luther dropped the statement he was holding back on the desk. 'So, what are you suggesting now? That it's nothing to do with the previous ship, that Summers and Geary have some little scam going that Burrell got hold of?'

211

'Just let's think about cruising,' William said slowly. 'Ships travel from port to port, all round the world but always coming back to the United Kingdom, often within a few weeks. They know exactly what their itineraries will be months, even a year or so in advance. The same ports come up again and again. I understand officers serve no more than some two years on the same ship before switching to another ship but that even after switching boats they will visit many of the same ports.'

'What are you saying?' asked Luther, sitting very still.

'I'm saying there is plenty of opportunity for making contacts of all sorts, not only in Europe but throughout the world and that ports have more than their fair share of criminal activity. The opportunity is particularly good if you are an ex-member of the Royal Navy and have an even wider experience of trouble spots plus a knowledge of a certain form of law enforcement.'

'Are you suggesting what I'm thinking?' asked Luther. 'Class-A drugs?'

'It would be interesting to know if our cruise director has ever asked a passenger to take a package ashore for her,' William said. 'Would they be so kind as to post something for her, on the basis that it was impossible to find a post office open on a Sunday, the one day the ship has in the home port. It would work even better when the cruise ended in a foreign port. Of course, she'd say, the office would do it for her but they tended to take a few days and it was something for a godson's birthday, or some such story. Look at the passengers we've got on this boat; there are any number of senior citizens who would swallow a story like that without any difficulty if she'd taken the trouble to join them for a few drinks, and flatter them with her attention.'

'And the package would contain drugs,' Luther sounded matter of fact.

William nodded. 'We all know it's much easier for them to arrive in mainland Europe than it is in the UK. I would be surprised if there's much check on the passengers leaving this ship or travelling home by air, but I'm pretty sure the crew has a very close eye kept on them. Frequency of travel, that's what usually exposes couriers.'

'Which is why mules are always being sought, one-timers who will bring in a consignment for the big boys.' Luther tapped his pen against his teeth. 'So what you're suggesting is that Harry Summers arranges for someone to meet Karen Geary in a cruise port and hand over a consignment of drugs in a bag switch over a drink in a bar. Only instead of an attaché case, it's a carrier from some smart shop?'

William said nothing and Luther thought about it for a little then said, 'It's a pretty theory, I grant you, but have we anything to back it up?'

'Only the suggestion that Harry Summers is living above his means and Karen Geary does an awful lot of shopping. And that Harry flipped when he saw those precious bags being carried aboard by Phil Burrell, combined with the fact that Karen seemed to be getting a good deal too close to him for Harry's comfort.'

Luther thought some more. 'What's this ship's itinerary? Is there anywhere on this cruise they could be thinking of pulling off that sort of switch?'

'Trondheim and Bergen are the only places with worthwhile shopping centres. There was no way, for instance, that she could come back from Sandane or Geiranger with large, glossy shopping bags.'

Luther made a note. 'Might be worth talking to Customs and Excise and getting the Norwegian authorities involved. They could arrange to have her watched in those places.'

'They'll be pretty anxious to get rid of anyone involved in drug running, I would have thought,' offered William, delighted his theory was being taken seriously. 'It would also be worth checking into Summers's naval background and exactly why he left the senior service for the commercial.' He couldn't believe that Rider hadn't done this already.

'Right,' Luther agreed. 'Now, can we think of any reason why someone else should want to knock off the stores manager?'

'Roger Coutts wants his job?' suggested William, straight-faced.

'Come on, I thought you wanted to help!' complained Luther. 'What about the Lulu girl? What a name,' he added, sorting out her statement again. 'If Burrell had just dumped her, she might be so peeved she'd want to get rid of him. And she'd have the skills for it. Pushing somebody overboard can't be the easiest of operations.'

'That's a good point,' mused William. 'Do you remember the statement given by Mrs Witchett of cabin A373? She said she thought something had fallen past her window and hit the water with a splash. She'd assumed it was a bag of rubbish, even though it seems she knew the ship didn't ditch rubbish overboard. But she didn't mention hearing any cry. If Burrell either jumped or was pushed, I'd put good money on him giving the most unearthly of cries as he fell.'

'So maybe Lulu hit him over the head with something.'

'Stan and I did consider whether she could have been angry enough to want to do away with him. The sort of woman who takes that sort of revenge, though, is quite rare and usually has a psychopathic personality that refuses to admit what they are doing is wrong. Unless she's keeping up a very, very good front, Lulu Prentice doesn't fit that profile.'

'What about other possible feuds or tensions amongst the crew?'

'Nothing out of the ordinary.'

Luther doodled on his pad for a moment then looked up. 'I would assume Stan Dobson is near retirement. How dedicated is he to getting his pension?'

William felt a jolt of alarm. 'What are you suggesting?'

'Call me cynical but working with an officer who will do anything to finish his time without making waves or having to work too hard, I suppose I'm more than usually suspicious of people who could be in the same position.'

William swallowed hard. 'I worked with Stan Dobson for a couple of years,' he said after a moment or two. 'He was an excellent police sergeant who never flinched from his duty however unpleasant it might be. He's also someone who could never hide his thoughts. Wouldn't have been much use in the CID!'

'Don't lose your rag, you have to admit that at the very least it's a possibility he's either concealing evidence or aiding and abetting Summers.'

William thought of the security on a ship like the *Empress*. He didn't know much about the measures that would be taken to detect any smuggling operation, but they would be there. With Stan Dobson in charge of them. Just how well did he know the ex-sergeant of police? It was a question to which he'd have to give careful consideration – but not now. He looked at his watch. 'Shall we call it a night? We might just catch coffee in the dining room with the others.'

They left the office, Luther locking the door. As they started along the corridor, they met a man coming in the other direction carrying two suitcases, followed by a woman with a load of clothes in her arms. William recognized the husband and friend of the lottery winner, Shona Mallory. Apparently one of them was moving cabin and from a look at what Daphne Rawlings was carrying, it appeared to be Paul Mallory.

Chapter Twenty-three

Darina did not find dinner easy. To start with there were three empty places at the table.

She had caught up with Beth just as she was trying to fit the key into her cabin door. After her third try, Darina took the key gently from her, opened the door and waited for her to enter.

'You wanted something?' Beth said haughtily and stood, swaying slightly, showing no inclination to go inside her cabin.

'I just wanted to see you were all right,' Darina said, feeling foolish and regretting her charitable impulse.

'I did not, did *not*,' Beth repeated with careful dignity, 'drink too much.' The statement would have carried more weight if her voice hadn't been slightly slurred. 'Just because I prefer to have a rest in my cabin rather than come to dinner, there is no need for you to think I couldn't if I wanted to.' She leaned against the door jamb with an owlish look.

'Well,' Darina said feebly, 'that's all right, then.' She held out the room key. Beth snatched it from her with a wild swipe of her hand.

'There,' she said, 'I'm home and you can go.' With this she swept into her cabin with a royal air and closed the door in Darina's face. It locked shut with a clunk of finality.

Darina went off to dinner feeling more than usually foolish.

Not only Beth's place at the table was empty, though, William's and Luther's also remained unoccupied. Looking at the captain's table, Darina could see three empty places there as well. The captain looked far from pleased when he realized they seemed likely to remain empty but no doubt he had faced worse crises at sea and would rise to the occasion.

She'd expected to find Mervyn also absent, conserving his singing energies between concerts, but he was there, saying he wouldn't eat but needed cheering up because his concert hadn't been well attended and he didn't feel he'd given of his best.

Tara was unusually solicitous of him, apologizing for not being at his concert and saying she was sure it had been great, then promising to come along to the second performance.

'Listen, girl, there's no need to act as though I was on the verge of senility,' he said irritably as she continued to try to cheer him up. Tara then sulked.

Julian was no help either. Darina wondered if he'd heard of his father's falling out with his stepmother but when she saw how he kept glancing at the captain's table with its depleted numbers, decided he couldn't have. She wondered how he would react to the situation. She had the impression there was little love between the boy and his father's second wife. Had he contributed to the failure of their relationship? Being a stepchild or a stepmother could be very tricky.

Enid, though, was full of chat. She gave them a full

account of a trip she'd taken up the Nile the previous year, including a description of what must have been every tomb she'd visited.

Darina missed William more and more. Not only for his company but because he could always be relied upon to keep conversation flowing in an interesting manner. She listened to Enid with only half an ear; she was wondering whether she and her husband were drifting apart at the very time they should be coming closer and closer together. Then, as Enid described with malicious delight how a crew-member had been caught stealing from passengers, Darina suddenly remembered what it was that she'd been trying to recapture from a previous monologue of Enid's.

And as she remembered, it seemed she might have identified a reason why someone might have wanted Phil Burrell out of the way. She was therefore doubly delighted to see her husband and Luther come into the restaurant as coffee was being served. William exuded the bonhomie of a man who has spent his evening well. He was expansive, telling Enid he was sorry not to have been able to join her for drinks, then drawing Mervyn into a discussion on the ridiculous story of *Il Trovatore*. 'I mean, how can you have a plot with half the action taking place before the first curtain-rise?' he said.

Enid gave a manic giggle at this. 'Don't you often find the really exciting things happen offstage, so to speak?' she said. 'But of course it's much more satisfactory to be in at the kill, as you might say.' She raised her eyebrows and gave Darina an arch look. 'I sometimes think I'd like to be the proverbial fly on the wall, seeing everything going on but not having to be part of the action.'

219

'I'd love to have a magic ring that would make me invisible,' Tara chipped in. 'Wouldn't that be great, Jools?'

'What?' Julian brought himself out of some reverie. 'I wouldn't want to be invisible,' he said with some force. 'I want people to know that I'm there.'

Poor Julian, didn't he realize he had to contribute to life if people were going to register his presence? That it wasn't enough just to be a pretty face?

'When I get my management company going, then everyone's going to sit up and take notice,' he added.

'Sure they will,' Tara said. She smiled and patted his hand. 'And I'll be your first and most famous client.'

'Think you can do it, boy?' asked Mervyn. 'Do you have the connections?'

Julian nodded with a rare show of animation. 'Yeah, like I said, I've done the gigs, been on the circuit, met the managers and everything. I got the whole thing planned out.'

'All he needs is proper backing,' Tara said to Mervyn. 'And he's going to get that from his mother.'

'Stepmother,' Julian corrected her.

'She going to back you?' Mervyn asked.

Julian nodded. 'Sure thing.'

'Not too sure, I wouldn't say.' Enid glowed with assurance. 'Not now she's split up with your father.'

Julian sat very still, it was impossible to gauge what he thought.

It was Mervyn who reacted. 'Are you serious?' he demanded.

Enid nodded. 'We were there,' she glanced towards Darina, 'there's no doubt, is there?'

Darina didn't like being applied to in this way, she

was angry with Enid for what she'd done. 'We were just onlookers,' she said. 'How can we know exactly what will happen?'

'What a pity Beth isn't here, she would agree with me,' declared Enid.

'What, exactly, *did* happen?' asked Luther, every inch the investigating policeman.

So Enid recounted the tale. The only detail she omitted was the fact that she had sent the letter to Shona.

'My God!' said Mervyn. 'I'd say that marriage is at an end.' He turned to Julian. 'I mean, is your step-mother the sort of woman to take that sort of behaviour lying down?'

He shook his head, his face stony. 'Absolutely not. My father's a bloody fool. Fancy bedding his tart under Shona's nose like that.'

'But perhaps she'll lend you the money anyway?' suggested Mervyn.

Julian seemed to shrivel and his handsome looks became blurred at the edges, like the picture of Dorian Gray starting to absorb all the evil actions of its subject. He shook his head violently. 'Not a hope now,' he said.

'Not a hope? Must be something you can do, boy?'

'If you can think of anything, let me know,' Julian said, almost viciously.

Mervyn didn't pursue the matter but Darina noticed that he seemed to scrutinize Julian and Tara unusually closely before getting up and saying that his first-sitting audience awaited him and he must go and give of his best.

'It'll go great, Merve,' Tara said, catching at his hand impulsively. 'I'll come along, just like I said.'

His face lit up. 'That'd be great.' Tara tucked her hand into the crook of his arm and they left the restaurant together.

'Well, look at them,' declared Enid as they left the table.

Julian stood up. 'Nothing wrong with that, you old witch,' he said. 'So don't you go spreading any more gossip.' Then he, too, left the restaurant.

For once Enid seemed deprived of speech.

William and Darina exchanged glances and stood up also.

'I know I've been an interfering old woman but I hope we can still be friends,' Enid said. 'It's not often I have the chance of meeting people as charming and intelligent as you two. Do say you forgive me?'

William looked at Darina enquiringly.

'They're cheating on that poor woman,' Enid continued. 'And when she's paid for everything! I couldn't let it continue.'

'I never think it's a good idea to interfere in what other people get up to,' Darina said, feeling unbearably sanctimonious. 'I'm sorry you sent that note, I can't pretend otherwise. No doubt you had to do what you thought was right but I think it's a pity you didn't sign it,' she ended firmly, then grabbed William's arm and made sure they left before Enid could reply.

On deck William and Darina stood and gazed at the sun. 'Quite a bit off midnight,' observed William, 'but isn't it light?'

Darina agreed. 'Daylight, clear enough for anything, you could even play cricket.'

'Think how long a one-day match would last in this

latitude. You could have seventy overs for each innings, or more.'

'Heavens, don't even think about it,' groaned Darina, who had been dragged to too many matches, where she spent the time reading through recipes whilst William reacted to the play with what seemed to her excessive disgust or delight.

He smiled but said nothing. Darina leant on the ship's rail and looked at the sun, its light hardly dimmed by the clouds scudding across its face. As she stood there, Darina heard a familiar voice coming from a small group of deckchairs further towards the bows. It was Michael Harwood.

'It's no use, Joyce . . . can't see any future . . . don't say that, Captain's put me on best behaviour . . . got to *do* something.'

'Darina, recovered from the upset this afternoon?' Francis Sterling appeared at her elbow. She reassured him he had nothing to worry about as far as she was concerned. 'And Michael Harwood appears to be contrite,' she said in a low voice, indicating where he and Joyce were sitting with a jerk of her head.

'Good, good. Too bad it had to happen, though,' he said. 'Can I ask you both to join me for a drink?'

Darina didn't need to look at William for him to know exactly what she felt. 'Sorry,' he said, 'I think we need something approaching an early night. We just wanted to catch the sun before going to bed.'

Safe in their cabin, William said, 'What was all that business with Enid and the Mallorys? It really got you going. Did she actually send Shona Mallory an anonymous letter?'

Darina nodded. 'Yup, her cabin is opposite Daphne

223

Rawlings' and, as far as I could make out, she wrote to
Shona Mallory suggesting that if Shona intended to go
to Mervyn's concert tonight, her husband would make
an excuse not to accompany her. Instead he would be
making love to her friend. Then Enid invited all of us
to get together in her cabin. She wanted Shona to catch
them *in flagrante delicto* in front of us all,' Darina said
indignantly, starting to undress. 'The woman's like an
unstable firework, you never know when she's going to
go off or in which direction. I should have known when
Shona came in to telephone her friend that something
was up, Enid was practically dancing with excitement.
I just thought she'd had too much to drink. Her face
when Daphne Rawlings' cabin door opened and Paul
Mallory emerged doing up his clothes was positively
gleeful.'

'Hmm,' said William, rolling up his bow tie neatly.
'The reaction that startled me was Mervyn's when he
heard that the Mallory marriage was breaking up. He
seemed really put out at the news. It was as though
he was kissing goodbye to getting Tara off his hands.'

'Funny that, as I'd have said that Tara wasn't on
them. She says she's just along for the ride, so to speak,
as Enid would say,' Darina giggled. 'But they went off to
Mervyn's concert like the warmest of friends, if not
something more. Maybe we're all wrong about her
getting off with Julian.' She took off her trousers and
top and found a hanger for them. 'Tell me how your
meeting went, I bet it was a success, you had the look
of a man who has come up with a winning accumulator
bet.'

'Ah, well, I've gone out on a bit of a limb,' said
William. 'Whether there's anything in it or not, we shall

224

have to see. I may be proved to be an utter fool.' He told her his theory about Harry Summers and Karen Geary and a drug ring.

'Hmm,' said Darina, taking off her make-up. 'I can see the captain going for that in a big way.'

'I'm not looking forward to suggesting to the staff captain that it's a possibility,' William said, moving into the bathroom.

'Poor man can't be enjoying this trip, what with the disappearance of his stores manager, you impugning the honesty of two of his officers, a passenger near to nervous breakdown and another who seems to enjoy stirring up trouble, not the trip of a lifetime.'

'A busy ship is a happy ship, isn't that the motto of the *Empress*?'

'There's something Enid told me a few days ago. It was when Joyce guessed I was pregnant, so I wasn't concentrating at the time, but it came back to me today.'

William stood in the bathroom door, cleaning his teeth. 'And what did the great mischief-maker tell you?'

'I know it'll sound pretty far-fetched coming from Enid, and I'd hate to think what she suggested is true, but you may think it's worth checking out.' Darina threw away the cotton wool she'd removed her make-up with. 'She says she and Mary and Jim French were all on a cruise on the *Empress of China* and Phil Burrell was working on it. Apparently there was a rumour that a paedophile was among the passengers and because Mary French said she didn't remember Enid, Enid thinks it means the paedophile was Jim French. And her implication, she never got near actually saying it but I'm sure it's what she meant, is that Jim killed Phil so that he wouldn't tell anybody who he actually was.'

'Some theory!' said William, disappearing back into the bathroom.

'As I said, it's not one I think stands up but I thought you'd want to know about it.'

'Uh huh?' came from the bathroom, followed by a noisy cleaning of his teeth.

Darina sighed. On their honeymoon, she and William had worked on an investigation together and for once she'd felt they were completely on the same wavelength. Too often before and since, though, he seemed to resent it when she appeared to encroach on his profession. Was it her fault that so often she became embroiled in investigations of one sort or another? How were they to manage if every time it happened William distanced himself from her? Was a child going to bring them together, or drive them apart?

She thought about the scene she'd witnessed earlier that evening between Shona Mallory, her husband and her new friend. There was a relationship in dire trouble. She swallowed hard. 'Do you think the Mallorys will leave the ship tomorrow, at Tromsø?' she asked, slipping into bed and folding back William's side of the bedclothes.

William emerged, vigorously drying his face with a towel. 'Mallorys leave? Is that what you said?'

Darina nodded. She picked up her bedside book and opened it, trying to banish both the vision of Shona's set face and her worries about her own marriage.

William sat on his side of the bed and yawned. 'Who knows! I should have thought it would be uncomfortable for them to remain. On the other hand, they've paid for the best accommodation and people are

226

sometimes determined to get everything they're entitled to. Especially people with money.'

'This isn't proving a happy cruise for Michael or Joyce Harwood either,' said Darina, wondering how long Joyce could keep her marriage going.

'Nor is it the holiday you promised me,' William said, picking up his library book.

If that wasn't the back end of enough! Darina gave up the conciliatory approach. 'Not my fault if you insist on being involved in detective work. You can't complain about me being too busy. I haven't touched my laptop since we got on board nor spent all my time in the kitchen, or even made a fuss about wanting to do some shopping.'

William turned and drew her to him. 'Darling, you can spend all day on your laptop if that's what you want. And as for working in the kitchen, when everything that comes out is so delicious, who am I to complain?'

Darina looked at him. 'Can I have this in writing?'

'Any time.' He drew back the bedclothes and ran his hand up her flat belly. 'I shan't even ask if you want to continue working after our child is born because I know that you will.' He pulled up her nightie and threw it on the floor then ran his hand over the soft skin round her navel. Darina said nothing.

'Is there really a baby in there?' he marvelled, bending to kiss the flat flesh. 'It's a miracle, isn't it?'

Darina cupped the back of his head in her hand, feeling the springiness of his dark hair. No more than William could she really believe in the new life Mary and science told her was even now growing in minute stages within her womb. 'You know what really worries

227

me about having a baby?' she murmured, feeling herself beginning to dissolve under the sweet, butterfly kisses William was giving her stomach. 'Being a parent is so important, what if I'm a complete failure?'

'You won't be,' William's arms tightened around her. 'Think how brilliantly you'll feed it! Love and good food, no better recipe for being a mother.'

'And I'll have you to help, won't I?' continued Darina as if he hadn't spoken.

'Of course. I can't wait to be a father. We'll be a family!' William marvelled.

'If you're there, perhaps I might manage,' Darina said sleepily.

'Of course you will. And I will be there. I promise.'

Darina felt him gather up her hair and hold it in one hand while he turned her face up with the other as he found her mouth with his.

Darina doubted that he would manage to find the time to be the father he so confidently had pledged himself to be. But maybe, somehow, they would muddle through.

Chapter Twenty-four

For two days Darina and William were able to enjoy their cruise as normal passengers, visiting Tromsø and Hammerfest. Inspector Derek Rider had recovered sufficiently to resume command of the investigation and he had both dispensed with William's services and refused to be convinced by Michael Harwood's statement to alter his view that Phil Burrell had committed suicide.

'He says Harwood may well have seen Burrell,' Luther reported to William over a drink in the Oyster Bar. 'But that doesn't mean Burrell had an assignation arranged with anyone but death. That could well have been what Burrell meant.' Luther looked into the depths of his beer glass, his expression gloomy. 'As for the fragment of speech Harwood says he heard, Rider claims it could easily have been said by someone else. He says Harwood is far from the most reliable of witnesses.'

'So there we are,' William said to Darina in their cabin later that night as the ship steamed from Tromsø to Hammerfest and they changed for dinner. 'A line is being drawn underneath the investigation.'

'Are you very upset about it?'

William shrugged his shoulders. 'What evidence is

there that it was anything but suicide? Burrell appears to have been something of a loner who developed a fixation on someone who was never going to be anything more to him than a friend. He had a failed marriage behind him, the relationship with Lulu Prentice had come to nothing, he might have felt that losing any chance with Karen was the last straw.'

'But you don't think so.' It was a statement rather than a question as Darina hunted out the waistcoat she felt would give a proper Western flavour to her trousers and check shirt for the Rodeo theme that was being followed for that night.

William sighed wearily. 'What does it matter what I think? At least Rider seems to be taking the drug-smuggling suggestion seriously. He's having talks with the Norwegian officials and Interpol, they hope to arrange to keep Karen Geary under surveillance whilst we are in the big ports. Do you think this will do?'

Darina looked at him. Jeans and a brushed cotton shirt were a good start for a Western look. She opened a drawer. 'I've got a small scarf somewhere that you could tie round your neck. Yes, here it is.' She took out a blue and white square and tied it for him. 'Just the right touch. Now, have you got a belt with a big buckle?'

'Now am I the sort who wears big buckles?'

Darina riffled through his clothes and found a couple of belts, neither of which had a buckle much bigger than the modest width of the leather. From her collection of costume jewellery she found a turquoise native Mexican brooch that she managed to fix on to one of the buckles. William fastened the belt round his waist, looked at himself in the mirror and a pleased look came over his face. 'Hey, that's great! All I need is a stetson and I could be taken on as an extra in any cowboy film.'

'I do not have a stetston,' Darina said firmly as his gaze seemed to wander towards her wardrobe. 'Come on, cowboy, you look great, let's go and forget all about poor Phil Burrell.'

'I like the ponytail,' William said, opening the door for her and flipping the long, straw-coloured fall of hair. 'Takes years off your age.' She aimed a punch at him as she went through, pulling back her fist at the last minute.

Days in harbour had a totally different rhythm from days at sea, Darina decided. It wasn't only the obvious – the fact that they weren't sailing – at sea the ship was full of activity; the passengers were offered an almost bewildering choice of pastimes, including sunbathing themselves in sheltered spots on deck in the almost constantly sunny weather. Then the ship became a little world on its own and after several days together, passengers had made friends, established routines, and formed favourites amongst the ship's company.

In port, attention switched back to the outside world. Ship activity wound down. As passengers vanished on shore excursions to enjoy the wild beauty of Norway's mountains, glaciers, waterfalls and rugged landscape, or wandered around the port on their own, clutching sheets of information provided by the company, the *Empress* had a pleasant air of relaxation. Many of those who chose not to go ashore relished the quiet and ignored the diversions that were still provided and instead enjoyed the uncrowded public rooms.

Whether on shore or aboard ship, no one seemed much occupied by the drama surrounding Paul Mallory's affair with Daphne Rawlings.

Word quickly spread that Shona Mallory had disembarked at Tromsø and flown home. Many people in fact put her departure down to the incident at Darina's demonstration and discussions raged over the possible hazards of GM foods. Nobody appeared to support Shona's idea of a foundation devoted to researching food biotechnology. 'Don't you think more research is needed?' Darina suggested when she found herself appealed to by total strangers who were sharing their luncheon table. 'After all, the technique isn't going to go away.' This did not go down well.

When the news spread that Shona Mallory had discovered her husband together with another woman, it caused a brief excitement. But interest in the matter quickly died as the *Empress* left Hammerfest and steamed towards the North Cape. The question now occupying most of the passengers was whether the weather would allow them to see the midnight sun. So far the evenings had been remarkably clear as the gap between the sun's disappearance below the horizon and re-emergence grew shorter and shorter. At the North Cape it would not set at all.

As the ship left Hammerfest, Francis Sterling came across Darina in the main reception hall. 'Hi,' he said. 'You'll be delighted to hear that Chef is doing a special Norwegian buffet at eleven tonight, so everyone can stoke up for the midnight sun.' He pointed to a notice above the day's menu on the reception counter. 'All thanks to you and your demonstration.'

'That's wonderful!' Darina was really delighted. 'Has he got everything he needs?'

Francis grinned. 'Chef reckons so. We were almost out of smoked fish but we picked up some more at Tromsø and our stores have been able to yield everything else. Incidentally, have you been shown round them yet?'

Darina shook her head. 'What with poor Phil Burrell's disappearance, I didn't really expect there to be an opportunity.'

Francis looked shocked. 'Good heavens, we're better organized than that! Come with me.'

He led the way to the stores manager's office. Roger Coutts was now back in possession and working on the computer. He looked up as the purser entered. 'Not a problem, is there, sir?'

'I'll say there's a problem. Here's our travelling cookery expert who hasn't had her promised tour of the stores area yet.'

Roger jumped up hurriedly and caught his leg in the chair. He clutched the desk for support. 'That's terrible! I didn't know she needed one.'

'Well, when can you fit her in?'

'I don't want to interfere with your schedule,' Darina said.

'I'd be delighted,' Roger assured her. 'Can you wait a few days until we reach Trondheim, when it will be nice and quiet? I'd have plenty of time to show you everything then.'

For a brief moment Darina hesitated. Trondheim, full of historical interest and third largest city in Norway, was one of the places she was really looking forward to seeing. But the ship would be there all day.

A look at the stores shouldn't take too long. 'Fine,' she said.

'Eleven o'clock all right?'

Darina nodded, 'It's very kind of you.'

'Right-ho, just knock on the door and I'll take you down.'

Darina found William. His face dropped when she told him what had been arranged. 'I thought we'd be able to explore Trondheim together,' he said despondently.

'What a pig you are! You spend all your time closeted with Luther over the Burrell investigation, then complain when something comes along for me!'

'Ah-hah, do I detect some asperity?'

'If you do, can you blame me?'

'Oh, very well, I suppose it's only fair for you to do something you want. But I hope it won't take long,' he added. 'There's a lot to see there.'

The buffet that night showed Chef at his best. Open sandwiches were only a small part of the feast that included Norwegian fish mousse with prawn sauce, spiced herrings, meatballs, a casserole of meat and potatoes known as Sailor's Stew, and red cabbage, liver pâté, gravadlax, a ham and pickled beetroot. He'd even produced a version of the wonderful Swedish dish Jansson's Temptation, with sinfully seductive anchovies, potatoes, onions and cream. 'Wonderful,' Mary French said with a pleased sigh, helping herself generously beside Darina. 'I can't believe it's only a couple of hours since we ate a five-course meal!'

What amazed Darina, though, was that the chef, after appearing to sniff at all the recipes she'd brought for him, had used every single one, including the Danish apple pudding known as Peasant Girl in a Veil. She confined herself to a little piece of the fish mousse and some prawn sauce. William, though, loaded his plate with what looked like something of everything. 'Just so I can check that the chef's followed your directions,' he told Darina.

Just before midnight, she and William went up on deck.

The ship was steaming very slowly not far off the coast. The sun, low in the sky, illuminated the scene with a pearly light that was very clear but had a mysterious quality that could never be confused with daylight.

On the port bow, the North Cape loomed round and dark. 'I think it's a shame they had to build an observation point,' said Jim French, appearing at Darina's right shoulder. 'Look, you can even see the coaches.'

Darina was slightly surprised that the staid Jim French should prove so sensitive. 'But, see, reindeer,' she cried. 'On the top of the hill.'

Just visible to the right of the Cape was a herd walking steadily along the ridge, outlined starkly against the mother-of-pearl sky.

While she watched, enchanted, the captain came on the ship's broadcasting system, and explained that they were now at the North Cape, that it was midnight and he'd stopped the ship.

William put his arm round Darina and held her close. 'Isn't it wonderful?' he breathed in her ear.

'Magic,' she agreed. At that moment, it was.

Chapter Twenty-five

Several days later the ship arrived at Trondheim. In his day cabin, Captain Walters was not a happy man. He rubbed his chin and contemplated the policeman standing in front of him.

Tall and lanky with a thin, cadaverous face, the captain had worked his way to the top of his profession by combining excellent seamanship with sensitive man-management. As far as the passengers were concerned, they found the essence of his charm in a wonderful smile that suggested each person he spoke to was the only one he wanted to be with at that particular moment.

No cruise since he'd become captain had had such a disastrous start. The disappearance of Phil Burrell, the stores manager, had been a bitter blow. But at least the official investigation had been conducted with a certain amount of sensitivity. Whilst the captain would have preferred a verdict of accidental death, at least suicide would be better than murder.

Since then, however, it had looked as though matters with the ship generally were improving. His staff captain, Alan Greenham, had reported that that day's regular meeting between himself, the purser and the doctor had gone extremely well. The ship was running smoothly and everyone had agreed that First Officer Harry Summers was now behaving impeccably, probably because he was facing an investigation by the shipping company over his behaviour in the Oyster Bar that first night of the cruise.

There was no more than the usual amount of trouble with the crew, you couldn't expect perfect behaviour when you had large numbers of men and women confined in a small space for long periods of time. Outbreaks of drunkenness, growth of tension that could show itself in arguments and fights over any number of minor causes, were all minimal on this cruise.

For a time, though, it had looked as though there was going to be difficulties with the passengers. The trouble during the cookery demonstration could have developed quite nastily. Steps had been taken to ensure the main miscreant, Michael Harwood, would not offend again but you never knew how something that obviously resonated through so many others on board would develop. The captain only hoped his staff captain would persuade the man to talk to the ship's doctor. He obviously needed help.

Another unfortunate circumstance was the discovery that the focus for the discontent, Shona Mallory, had caught her husband in a compromising situation. Still, all that seemed to have been sorted out by Mrs Mallory's departure from the ship at Tromsø.

At the end of the staff captain's report, however, Geoffrey Walters had felt a certain satisfaction. The weather continued fine, he'd been able to bring the ship to the North Cape on the stroke of midnight with the sun shining in all its glory – always a highly enjoyable experience. A short visit to the small port of Bodø had passed without incident, they'd had an equally peaceful day sailing down the Norwegian coast with the entertainment staff at full stretch, and the ship was now safely tied up at Trondheim.

Until Inspector Rider had appeared in his day cabin, the captain had had every reason to believe things were improving. As it was, he was now being asked to face a totally unacceptable proposition. 'Let me get this quite clear. You are accusing my first officer, Harry Summers, and Karen Geary, the cruise director, of systematically smuggling drugs?'

Inspector Derek Rider blew his nose noisily. 'Evidence seems to point to the possibility, sir. We can't say more than that at this stage. Sergeant Conran and I have spoken with the Norwegian officials. From now on surveillance will be carried out while the ship is in port and should Geary or Summers go ashore they will be followed. It's considered that Trondheim and Bergen are the most likely places for a handover to be undertaken.'

The captain regarded him coldly. He was not impressed with the inspector.

'You realize the passengers' baggage is regularly inspected by sniffer dogs before disembarkation?'

'Every cruise?' Rider asked doubtfully.

The captain straightened some papers on his desk. 'Not every cruise, no. But often enough. And every now and then there are spot checks on passengers as they leave the ship.'

'Spot checks.' Again that sceptical tone. 'Concentrating on the insignificant elderly? I would doubt it.'

'Customs and Excise know their business.' The

captain's irritation showed clearly. 'If any such operation as you suggest existed, I feel confident it would have been picked up before now. Have you discussed this suggestion with Detective Chief Inspector Pigram?' The younger man was officially a passenger but he'd shown intelligence and common sense since the disappearance of Phil Burrell. Which was more than could be said of this man.

'It was the chief inspector who initially formed the theory,' the inspector said quickly.

All too eager to offload responsibility for a course of action that was shown up as unviable, thought Geoffrey Walters.

'We've been investigating your first officer's background,' Rider continued. 'Confidential naval information suggests he was under suspicion at one stage of being involved in a drugs incident. There was insufficient evidence to bring a charge but he probably thought it unlikely he would progress very much further in the service and switched to the merchant navy.'

The captain turned and looked out of his day cabin at Trondheim. It was one of his favourite ports. Like most Norwegian towns, it had suffered down the ages from war and fire but it contained many picturesque areas and a wealth of late-eighteenth-century wooden houses. From the ship he could see the Gothic cathedral and part of the city wall. The sight brought him no comfort.

On the face of it, such a drugs operation as was being suggested should be impossible to carry on for any length of time. If it was true, had Harry Summers and Karen Geary had luck on their side or was there another explanation? Was a rotten apple infecting a whole barrel?

'What is Security Officer Dobson's opinion of all this?' he said finally.

'You are the only member of the ship's crew we are apprising of the situation,' Rider said stiffly.

The captain stared at him. He felt he'd aged several years since the man had entered his quarters. 'I suppose I should be grateful you've let me know,' he said bitterly. 'Keep me informed as to progress.'

'Of course, sir,' said Derek Rider.

After he'd left, the captain sat heavily in his swivel chair. This suggestion was appalling. Yet the more he considered what he'd been told, the more possible it seemed. Harry Summers was definitely living above his professional income. Initially it had been thought that his wife was the one with the money. The separation had appeared to contradict this for Harry had just bought a brand new Series 5 BMW, which had been waiting for him on the dock when they returned from the last cruise. And the Geary woman certainly over-indulged in the shopping at various ports.

Could any of the other officers be involved? The police hadn't seemed to think so but they didn't know the ship's personnel the way he did. Had anyone been turning a blind eye? Or been more deeply involved? Steepling his fingers, the captain thought deeply unpleasant thoughts. The ring of the telephone was a not unwelcome interruption.

Until he realized the nature of what he was being told.

Francis Sterling was drinking coffee in his day cabin. He, too, had his problems. The main ones had been aired at the meeting with his heads of department that he held after the executive meeting.

All had agreed that, apart from that terrible business with Phil, basically the cruise was proceeding smoothly. None of the various departments had any difficulties of note. Food and beverages had ample supplies; a malfunctioning washing machine in the laundry had been dealt with; one of the stewards had reported finding some wacky baccy in a passenger's cabin but had ditched it down the lavatory and didn't anticipate any further trouble; the sous chef who had injured a hand at the start of the cruise had recovered its full use and was working normally. It was all very satisfactory.

Such trouble as there was concerned the passengers. There was, for instance, the Mallory business. Francis would have liked to have been able to say goodbye to Mrs Mallory and express his regret over what had happened. But she had left the ship at Tromsø without giving notice and now Daphne Rawlings had moved into the suite with Paul Mallory. Well, it was only the purser's business as far as it affected the other passengers and so far it hadn't appeared to.

The main trouble, though, with the current cruise was that the passengers in general were underperforming. The bars, the casino, and the shop were not resounding to the chink of money. Head Office was not pleased.

'Well, my girls and boys are doing what they can,' Karen had said, smoothing down her short skirt in a satisfied manner, her expression complacent. 'The cruise programme throughout the day and evenings is very well attended and all the entertainments produce

happy audiences. I don't know what else I can do.'
There was a murmur of agreement from the others.

The concensus of opinion was that if you had a
passenger list whose average age was around seventy
and who had been attracted by the scenic but austere
pleasures of the Norwegian fjords, there wasn't a great
deal that could be done to loosen their pockets.

'They're certainly enjoying themselves,' Francis
Sterling had said finally, closing his notebook. 'We have
a large number of regular passengers and I'm confident
those who haven't sailed with us before will be doing so
again. Head Office will have to settle for that.'

Sitting in his office after the meeting had broken
up, however, Francis was not happy. The disappearance of Phil Burrell had been a terrible blow and the
police investigation thoroughly unsettling. The fact
that it appeared to have been decided that Phil had
thrown himself overboard was even worse. Surely he
hadn't been the suicidal type? But he acknowledged
that the alternative was even more unthinkable.

Worrying also was the mental condition of the
farmer, Michael Harwood. Who knew what someone
like that would do next? The man's anguished expression as he'd had his dressing-down by the captain
haunted Francis. This was a man under severe emo-
tional pressure. He'd offered him the opportunity of
discussing his troubles with either himself or the ship's
doctor, Ian Westlake. The man had reacted as though
he'd suggested a whipping in the fo'c'sle. Francis had
asked the Harwoods' steward to keep a close eye on
him. He didn't want another dive overboard at dead of
night.

Why was it whenever Enid Carter sailed with them,

there was trouble amongst the passengers? She was such a game old duck. Strong, too, for her age. Francis had seen her whip-corded arms manhandle a heavy case down the corridor as though it was a pillow.

As Francis tried to think what else could be done for Michael Harwood, his telephone rang. After the call all his previous worries seemed minute in comparison with the situation he now had to deal with.

William and Luther sat in a quiet spot in the Neptune Lounge wrangling over a cup of coffee as to whether they should go ashore or not. 'If Karen Geary catches sight of us, she might abort a possible handover,' said Luther. 'We've got to leave it to the Norwegian officials to follow her.'

'But there's so much to see,' complained William. 'We can steer clear of the shopping area, surely?' He was still annoyed that Darina had taken herself off for a tour of the food lockers. What on earth was the attraction of seeing how comestibles were stored?

'Oh well,' said Luther. 'We could take a quick look at the warehouse district, the port guide makes it sound worth a shufti, but if we catch sight of a redhead, we skedaddle back to the boat. All right?'

William nodded. He had no intention of jeopardizing the operation he had suggested.

'And no visits to pubs or bars,' Luther added.

'At this time of the morning? Have a heart.'

They went and collected jackets, there was a chill wind blowing. But just as they were about to walk down the gangway, a security officer at the top stopped them. 'Call just come through, sirs. You are to report to the Stores Deck. This officer will show you the way.' He indicated a member of the purser's department standing at the side of the video display unit.

William and Luther looked at each other. What had happened now?

Chapter Twenty-six

That morning Darina had been delighted to find that her sickness had greatly improved. She knocked on the door of the stores manager's office on the dot of eleven, feeling alert and alive.

Roger greeted her with a broad grin and took her along the corridor to an unobtrusive door. Behind it the wood panelling gave way to a world of riveted steel and green paint.

'We're now between decks,' he said, leading her down a metal stairway to the innards of the ship.

'You mean, a sort of mezzanine floor?'

'Yeah, that sort of thing. Every bit of space has to be used. Now, let me show you around. This is the meat-preparation area.'

In a stainless-steel room butchers were using band-saws to cut up large joints of frozen meat, the blades whirring at incredible speed through meat and bone. Others were chopping defrosted meat into pieces. 'This is for the crew's dinner,' Roger said.

'A curry?' asked Darina. One of the young butchers smiled and nodded his head. They all seemed interested in her.

She admired the cleanliness of the equipment and the butchery area. 'How do you deal with all the waste?'

she asked. 'I've heard that you don't throw it overboard any more. Which I think is a shame for the gulls and the fish.'

'Ah, too much danger of contamination,' said Roger. 'What happens is that we reduce all our waste to a sludge with special disinfectant. Come with me.'

Darina waved goodbye to the butchers as Roger took her into another room. 'Good heavens,' she said. 'That looks like the biggest mincing machine I've ever seen.'

Roger laughed. 'It can even take large bones. The sludge goes into a tank and then that is decanted, either into the ocean at specially designated areas where it can dissipate in deep water, or it's taken off the ship in port.' He picked up a large plastic jerrycan. 'This is the special stuff we mix in with the waste that prevents it getting smelly.'

'Heavens,' said Darina. 'I can't bear to think about it. Let's see where you keep all the stores. Do you buy from each port you call at?'

Roger shook his head. 'Not unless there's some sort of emergency such as an unexpected run on a particular ingredient. We need to control both quality and price. Now here's where we keep the fruit and vegetables.'

Roger led her to a large steel door, covered with what seemed endless coats of paint. 'Raj, can you open, please?'

A grinning crewman reached for a large padlock, unlocked and swung back the door. A fresh, earthy smell reached Darina's nostrils as a light was switched on to reveal an Aladdin's cave of fruit and vegetables.

'You should have seen it when we sailed,' said

Roger, taking her in and displaying the huge variety of boxes filled with produce. 'You could hardly move in here. They're all regularly inspected, of course.' He picked out a squashy tomato from one of the boxes.

'Is it all fresh? You don't use any frozen?'

'Hardly at all. Chef is very insistent that fresh is best.'

'I'm impressed. What about the meat?'

'Mostly frozen.' Roger led the way out and got a different crew-member to open another of the large steel doors.

A whirl of frozen air dropped out. Then Darina saw that inside were huge piles of vacuum-packed meat stacked on a series of deep shelves, the packets varying in size from a sack of potatoes to a catering size bag of flour. 'Good heavens,' she said faintly. Shivering, she stepped inside and peered at the labels. 'What a variety of different meats.' Anonymous in their envelopes of heavy duty plastic, each faintly rimed with frost, were rumps of beef, saddles of lamb, huge packets of stewing steak, venison, loins of pork and no doubt much else. Rather than being arranged by type, they were all jumbled up.

Roger followed her inside. 'They're arranged in order of use,' he said. 'That's odd,' he added, looking towards the back of the freezer. 'Somebody seems to have rearranged some of the meat.'

'How can you tell?' Darina looked at the neat piles; she would have been hard put to say what was what without close inspection. Near at hand the stacks of packets had been plundered but on the shelves further into the vast freezer they made solid walls, each one as anonymous as a brick unless you checked the label.

The stores manager appeared to be acquainted with his goods as intimately as the mother of quins with her identical offspring. 'Just a minute,' he said and stepped past her. He started to take down some of the packets of meat. 'You can tell by the way the frosting's been disturbed on the outside wrapper.'

Darina felt the cold bite into her and hoped he wouldn't be long.

Suddenly he stopped his work and peered behind the wall of frozen meat from which he'd removed the top packets. 'Oh, my God!' He stepped back and whirled around. 'Don't look,' he mumbled through a hand clamped to his mouth. He staggered out, his face as white as the frost edging the shelving.

Darina had a strong feeling she would do well this time to curb her inveterate curiosity. But curiosity triumphed and she stepped forward to see what it was he'd uncovered.

Immediately she regretted not following her instinct and her blood turned so cold it seemed to freeze in her veins.

Neatly lying behind the piles of wrapped meat was a body.

The short silver hair was matted with blood that had frozen into messy droplets. The eyes were horror-wide and the mouth open in an eternally silent scream.

Darina had no trouble in recognizing Shona Mallory. It took a little longer to realize that the body was naked. Her stunned gaze travelled down the slender form with its small, high breasts that were now so much frozen meat, past the small knot of her navel, down to the triangle of dark pubic hair silvered with frost, then, with heart-stopping incredulity, she saw that beyond that point there was nothing. Shona Mallory's legs had disappeared.

Darina forced herself to look more closely, unable to believe the limbs hadn't folded themselves away like a contortionist's. But all she could see was the cleanly amputated ends of Shona's hips.

Everything went black as she slid to the floor of the freezer in a dead faint.

When consciousness gradually returned, Darina found she was sitting on a chair on the deck outside the meat locker surrounded by anxious faces. The only one that registered was William's.

'Are you all right, darling?' he asked.

She put a hand to her head. 'I feel very strange,' she said and even her voice sounded remote. Holding William's hand hard, she recognized others. Francis Sterling, looking pale and shocked, was conferring with the staff captain, Alan Greenham. Luther was there as well, his dark face blending with the not quite so dark faces of the crew he was attempting to shoo away. From the still open meat locker fell frozen air, its pale swirl heightened by the flash of a photographer's bulb. Her head swam and she found it impossible to bring into focus what she had seen in the meat locker.

Then the doctor, Ian Westlake, arrived. He gave her a rapid examination and took her pulse. 'You should do,' he said cheerfully. His voice seemed the one normal note in the whole scene. 'But I think we'll take you along to the Sick Bay and give you a proper examination. Ah, there it is!' He turned and Darina saw one of his nurses arrive with a wheelchair.

'I do not need that,' she protested, trying to rise.

But her legs felt like cotton wool and she wasn't sorry to have Ian press her back into the chair. 'Trust me,' he said. 'Just lie back and let us take charge.'

'Yes, please be sensible,' William urged.

'I'm always sensible,' protested Darina, and forced herself to move without help from the chair she was sitting on to the wheelchair.

'Determined, aren't you?' said the amused voice of the doctor. 'No bad thing. All right, Nurse, you take her to the Sick Bay and I'll be along in a minute.'

Which meant, Darina supposed, that he was going to examine the body and pronounce poor Shona Mallory dead. As though she could be anything else!

Darina was wheeled along to a lift not far from the lockers. Obviously used for catering purposes, it was very different from the plush passenger lifts. When they emerged, it appeared they were on the Corniche Deck, next to the open-air restaurant area. 'A long way round, isn't it?' Darina murmured as she was wheeled along the deck, gathering curious glances from passengers who hadn't gone ashore.

'It's the easiest way,' the nurse said. 'Now we can get the proper lift down to the Sick Bay deck.'

A worried Mary French leapt up from where she was drinking coffee at one of the tables. Jim didn't appear to be with her. 'Are you all right, Darina?'

'Just had a little faint,' said the nurse promptly. 'We're going to give her a good check over.'

'Let me know if I can do anything,' Mary said as the nurse's strong hands pushed the chair along without pausing. Darina tried to smile and gave Mary a wave that she was horribly afraid looked as weak as it felt.

The nurse was skilled at manoeuvring the chair through the doors and into the corridor where the passenger lifts were and for once in her life Darina was happy to let someone else take command.

Down in the sick bay all was pristine clean and quiet. The nurse helped Darina on to a bed and told her to lie there quietly until the doctor came. Her movements were all deft and skilful. Her feet moved agilely, her rubber soles squeaking slightly on the polished floor.

Darina closed her eyes and tried to forget the legless body.

Instead, everything rushed back at her like a horrifying video, unrolling the ghastly reality of what she had seen.

The nurse was there with a stainless steel bowl for Darina to cough up her soul into. 'That's all right,' she said gently when Darina tried to apologize. 'Only to be expected. Just glad I didn't have to see what you did.' She produced a glass of water for Darina to rinse her mouth out and then sat quietly beside her waiting for the doctor.

'So, you think you're pregnant?' said Ian Westlake jovially as he came into the Sick Bay some quarter of an hour later.

By then Darina, though still surrounded by an air of unreality, had recovered some of her poise. She submitted to his examination and answered all his questions as though it was someone else describing symptoms.

'Well,' he said finally. 'Basically you appear to be in splendidly good health. We can't be one hundred

251

per cent certain without sending off your specimen to a laboratory for a pregnancy test, but from your symptoms and the results of the test you've carried out, I'd say you're probably three months along the road to having a splendid baby. Of either sex.' He cocked his head on one side, his dark eyes sparkling at her, his manner all gracious bonhomie. 'Do you mind which it is?'

Darina shook her head. 'Not in the least, but William says he'd like a boy.'

'Of course he does. What man doesn't want to hand on his genes to a son!'

'Have you got children?'

Ian spread out his hand on his desk and looked at the splayed fingers. 'Alas, no,' he said after a minute. 'Wish I had. I'm divorced now, though,' he added, cheering up. 'May meet a lovely lass on one of these cruises, then, who knows!'

Darina could just imagine what an attraction Ian Westlake was to single women on this ship.

'Now, you've had a very nasty shock, would you like a tranquillizer?'

'No!' Darina was positive. 'I don't want to take anything that could possibly affect the baby.' She hesitated for a moment, then said, 'Doctor, did you have a look at Shona Mallory's body in the meat freezer?'

His momentary jocularity vanished as he nodded. 'I did.'

'It wasn't my imagination that there weren't any legs, was it?'

'I'm afraid not.'

'Were they, were they taken off after her body was frozen?'

252

He bunched his fingers into a fist and studied the result. 'I'm no expert,' he said slowly, 'but I'd have said, without a doubt. You can see the marks of the saw on both the flesh and the bone.'

Darina didn't want to think about that. 'I thought she'd got off at Tromsø,' she said.

'So did we all. Fact remains that as far as I know, no one saw her do so. The point was raised only this morning at the executive meeting. Francis Sterling, the Purser, was saying how much he regretted not being able to say goodbye to her. Nasty business altogether.' He paused for a moment.

Darina waited.

'I saw her the night there was all the trouble with her husband,' he said slowly. 'Not that I'd heard about the trouble then.'

'You did? Where?'

'Up on the Corniche Deck. I'd had to visit a patient in one of the suites, thought she was dying but it was merely a bad case of indigestion.' He gave a slight smile that seemed to say this sort of thing was a hazard of his job. 'Thought I'd catch a glimpse of the midnight sun before turning in. She was leaning over the rail, looking at the view.'

Darina wondered if it was really true he'd been a bone specialist before joining the shipping company. Had it been the breakdown in his marriage that had caused him to change course so violently?

'Did you speak to her?'

'Only "good evening". We hadn't really met, though I knew who she was, we all did. It's not often you have a millionaire lottery winner on board.' He gave a wry smile. 'I don't think she even noticed I was there.'

Chapter Twenty-seven

William arrived at the surgery as Ian Westlake finished with Darina.

'How are you, darling?' he asked, concern in every note of his voice.

'She's fine,' the doctor said. 'But I think she should rest this afternoon.'

'Of course she will, I'll see to that,' William assured him.

The doctor rose. 'Now, I'll get the nurse to wheel her back to her cabin.'

'You're talking about me as though I'm some sort of idiot,' Darina said with a smile. 'As you said, I'm fine and I certainly don't need a wheelchair any more.'

The doctor surveyed her. She'd put flat shoes on for her tour of the food lockers and he had the advantage of an inch or so, which he made the most of. Darina got the impression that he could be a formidable opponent when he chose. But he merely said, with one of his charming smiles, 'I think you'll do.'

Back in the cabin, William said, 'What would you like to do now? A rest or a light lunch?'

Darina shuddered. 'Never, ever, mention food to me again. I'm not sure I will be able to eat anything for the rest of my life.'

'Something to drink? A glass of white wine couldn't hurt, surely?'

Darina shook her head. 'I think I'd just like to lie down for a little.' She took off her linen trousers and sand-colour sweatshirt and slipped underneath the quilted cover of the bed.

William hung up her clothes then stood beside the bed. 'Isn't there anything I can do for you?'

'I'd love it if you could stay and talk,' Darina said hopefully. 'But not if you have to get back to the . . .' she faltered for a moment, 'to the investigation that must be going on.'

He drew up one of the cabin's comfortable small chairs and sat beside her. 'Inspector Rider has declared me persona non grata as far as the case is concerned,' he said with a shrug of his shoulders.

'Oh, darling, I am sorry.' Darina put her hand over his. 'What an idiot that man must be not to want you as part of the team.'

William gave her a wry smile. 'Thank you, darling. But it's more important to be with you.'

She knew he meant it but, equally, Darina knew that if the phone rang at that moment with Inspector Rider asking him to come and help, he'd ask apologetically if she'd mind if he went – and would expect her to encourage him to go.

So she'd better make the most of him now!

'I'm really sorry you had to see that terrible sight,' he said, taking her hand in both of his and holding it tightly.

'Who could have done it?' Darina said, opening her eyes wide in order to prevent any tendency they might

255

have to close and so bring back the sight of poor Shona Mallory's mutilated body. 'Have you any idea?'

'The most obvious suspect, of course, is her husband. He stands to inherit several million pounds, unless, of course, it's already been tied up in that foundation that's been talked about. Rider will have to ascertain that as soon as possible.'

'But would Paul Mallory have known about the frozen meat locker? And where would he have got the key to it?' Then Darina gasped slightly as she understood exactly where whoever had killed Shona Mallory had obtained the key not only to the meat locker but to every other part of the food section.

William nodded. 'I'm afraid that could very well be why poor Phil Burrell was dumped overboard.'

'After his set of keys had been removed,' Darina said. 'But that, again, means that whoever killed him knew all about the ship. It suggests another member of the ship's company.'

'Or a regular passenger,' William added. 'And there are any number of those aboard.'

'But who could have had a motive for killing Shona Mallory?' Trying to make some sense of what had happened, Darina found, stopped her remembering the awful sight she'd faced in the meat locker.

'That brings us back to Paul Mallory,' said William, leaning back in the chair and stretching out his legs. 'Rider and Conran will have to check if he has sailed in the *Empress* before.'

Darina could see William was itching to be part of the investigation. 'I suppose I'll have to give a statement?'

'I'm afraid so. I'll see if Luther can take it.'

Later that afternoon, Luther came to the cabin and took Darina gently through her experience. When he'd finished, he said, 'I'll get this printed out and then you can sign it. It shouldn't take long.'

'How's the investigation going?' asked William, who'd sat quietly while the statement was being taken.

'As you might expect,' Luther said gloomily. 'All the correct steps being taken with very little result. The ship's photographer, poor sod, has taken a full set of shots. The doctor's pronounced Shona Mallory dead. The husband has identified the body. The only finger-prints we've been able to find on the packets of frozen meat have all belonged to ship's crew. The inspector wanted the locker sealed off as a scene of crime but the necessity of feeding over seven hundred passengers plus more than that number of crew persuaded him this wasn't possible. None of the meat that was packed around the body can be used, of course, though those thick plastic bags it's packed in would protect the contents from anything short of an explosion and the body froze long before it could start decomposing. However, there's enough meat on the other side of the freezer to keep passengers and crew from starving. Did you know the ship has a morgue?' he added.

'Good heavens!' said William. 'Yet, I suppose if you consider the number of geriatric passengers there must be on every cruise, it's a necessity.'

'Certainly come in very handy on this one,' Luther said drily. 'The inspector's trying to get a pathologist flown out to Bergen to carry out an autopsy.'

Darina swallowed hard and asked, 'What about the missing legs?'

'Ah, yes, the legs.' Luther cleared his throat then said

in his pleasant, deep voice, 'We're working on the theory that Mrs Mallory was killed the same night she chucked her husband out of her cabin. Her body would then have been put in the meat locker, well hidden behind the packets of frozen meat. It must have taken some forty-eight hours to freeze sufficiently for the blood not to spurt everywhere when the bandsaw was used.'

Darina flinched, it was a hard fact to face. 'You mean, her body was being sawn up and put through that huge mincer?'

Luther looked at her with respect. 'You worked that one out, did you?'

'Having seen all the equipment, it isn't difficult. But it does mean, doesn't it, that the killer not only knows exactly all about the stores area but is strong as well? I know Shona wasn't very big but a dead frozen body must be extremely tricky to haul around.

'There's a small trolley kept for moving the stores, which could have helped. We'll have to get it checked by Forensics when we get back.'

'More specialized knowledge,' said William. 'Do you know yet whether Paul Mallory has travelled on the *Empress* before?'

Luther shook his head. 'We're waiting for that information from Head Office.'

'And how does he explain the story that his wife left the ship at Tromsø?' asked Darina.

'Ah, that's a neat one, very neat. According to him, she rang him in his friend Daphne Rawlings' cabin after she'd found them together, and said that she was leaving the next day and told him to take her heavy luggage home with his when the ship docked at Southampton. He said that after we docked at Tromsø, he went along,

258

and found the cabin empty and the packed suitcases sitting in the middle of the floor. He assumed that she'd left, just as she said she would, and moved his lady friend into the suite with him.'

'Has the doctor told you he saw Shona Mallory on the Corniche Deck that evening?' asked Darina.

'Yes, he's not sure exactly when it was but thinks it was about eleven thirty.'

'Would that have been near the lift I was brought up in from the Stores Deck?'

'Yes. There are what could be splashes of blood on one of the walls and the floor. It looks as though that was how she was brought down to the Stores Deck.'

'This is someone remorseless, cunning and extremely resourceful,' said William. 'And good at covering his tracks.'

Darina thought about the tall, attractive figure of Paul Mallory. His face was intelligent and mobile but not, she would have said, particularly determined. Except, when someone is desperate, they can discover unexpected reserves. Had Paul Mallory been that desperate?

During the afternoon Darina remained in her cabin and William stayed with her. Much as she would like to have seen Trondheim, she knew she wasn't up to walking around. They snoozed and talked about their first child and watched an old romantic film being shown on the cabin television. By the time evening arrived and the ship sailed, Darina hadn't forgotten what she had seen that morning but some of the horror had faded.

Dinner that night was another black-tie affair.

William suggested that Darina might prefer them to eat in their cabin.

'It's very thoughtful of you, darling, but I'm feeling much better and I think we should go to the restaurant. Apart from anything else, I'm sure you'd like to see how the passengers are reacting. The news must have got around by now.'

William kissed her. 'What a helpmate you are, darling! You're quite right, of course, I do want to hear what people are saying.'

'I'm not looking forward to seeing Enid, though,' said Darina. 'I can't help feeling that if only she hadn't interfered, Shona Mallory would still be alive.'

'I don't excuse the old trout but I think this killer merely took advantage of the situation she created. Without it, some other opportunity would have been found,' William said, looking out a dress shirt.

When they arrived at their table, William impeccably dressed in dinner jacket and black tie, Darina in a black devoré velvet skirt and white silk shirt with a huge collar. Only Enid was at the table.

It was immediately obvious she knew something, she was full of excitement. 'Have you heard?' she exclaimed as William held out Darina's chair for her.

'Heard what?' asked William repressively.

'Why, that Mrs Mallory didn't get off at Tromsø at all. She was chucked overboard, just like that poor Mr Burrell.'

'I happen to know that that isn't true,' said William coldly.

She waited, looking at him with bright eyes. When he said nothing further, she added, 'Well, that's what's going all round the ship, anyway.'

'You shouldn't listen to gossip,' said William.

'Oh,' Enid looked a little deflated. 'Oh, well, I'm glad it isn't true, anyway,' she said defensively.

'Who told you?' asked Darina, picking up the menu.

'Oh, I don't know,' Enid said vaguely. 'It was just something I heard.'

'What did you hear?' asked Beth, coming to join them.

'Nothing, nothing at all,' snapped Enid.

Beth looked at her in surprise but didn't comment. She, too, picked up the menu.

Darina wondered why she bothered to consult it when her choice was always for plainly cooked fish or meat served with a salad.

Darina put her menu down. She didn't feel like food tonight. Then she picked it up again. She must eat for two now. Maybe she could manage a clear soup followed by fish.

Tara arrived with Mervyn. They were chatting happily together. Tara looked around as she took her place. 'No Jools yet? I wonder where he's got to. We've been practising a new set today, he says he's going to try and grab the piano later tonight. You had better all be in the Coral Lounge tonight so you can hear me,' she said importantly.

She was wearing an electric-blue dress with a tight-fitting strapless bodice and a full skirt that came no further than just above her knees. She seemed as charged with electricity as the colour of the dress.

Mervyn for once appeared happy to let her hold the limelight. 'I shall be there, sweetie,' he said cheerfully. 'Leading the applause. Know you'll do well.'

The waiter appeared to take their orders. Enid

261

looked at the chair where Luther had been sitting. 'No nice policeman with us tonight, then?' she asked William, her voice loaded with meaning. 'Perhaps the rumour wasn't so far wrong after all.'

He said nothing.

Darina looked around and saw that, once again, Paul Mallory and Daphne Rawlings were missing from the captain's table. But, then, so was the captain.

Julian appeared just as the soup course was cleared away. He was very pale but his eyes gleamed with excitement. The waiter was immediately at his side and after a moment's hesitation he ordered a steak and his usual beer. Then he looked round the table and said, 'Well, I suppose you all know?'

'Know what?' asked Beth in her precise voice.

'That my stepmother has met a very unpleasant end,' he said with a small gasp. For once he seemed to fizz with energy. 'I suppose I should be mourning her but we weren't even friends and I can't pretend what I don't feel.'

Enid leaned towards him. 'What are you saying? That she's dead?'

He nodded.

'I knew it, she fell overboard,' she said with a look of triumph at William.

For the first time Julian looked slightly flustered. 'No, no, that wasn't what happened at all. She was, well, she was hit on the head then pushed into the ship's fridge.'

'Oh, my God,' said Tara dramatically. 'You mean, she's been murdered?'

Julian nodded. 'That's what the police say. I've had to tell them everything I've been doing since she was last seen on the night, well, the night she found out about my father and Daphne.'

'Oh!' exclaimed Tara faintly. 'They can't suspect you, surely?'

Mervyn patted her hand. 'I'm sure they can't, sweetie,' he said with great conviction. He glanced at Julian a couple of times as though there was something he'd like to ask but couldn't decide whether to or not.

Tara didn't hesitate. 'Does this mean,' she said in a high, breathy voice, 'that your father will have all the money now?'

There was a sort of rustle around the table. It seemed to Darina as though they were all hanging on what Julian would say.

A waiter arrived with their main courses.

Some of Julian's excitement evaporated as a steak was slipped in front of him. 'I don't know,' he said miserably. 'My father doesn't know whether Shona set up the foundation before we came on this cruise or not. If she did, well . . .'

'You mean that then all the money will have gone? Vanished?' Tara cried out. 'She can't have done that.' She looked as downcast as a child told that Christmas had been cancelled.

'If a foundation is as complicated to set up as a contract is to write, I'm sure Julian's father will find that matters haven't been quite wrapped up yet,' Mervyn said with conviction. 'I wouldn't worry about things.' Again he gave that possessive little pat to Tara's hand. She clutched at his and took a couple of deep breaths.

263

'Of course, I think it's dreadful about your step-mother,' she said earnestly to Julian. 'I really am very, very sorry.'

'Yeah, well.' He put down his knife and fork, the steak hardly touched. 'I'd better go and see how my father is, he's pretty upset.' He got up from the table.

'What about our gig?' Tara said, clutching at his arm.

'Don't worry, I'll be in the Coral Lounge in good time,' Julian said, smiling down at her, almost as though nothing had happened. Then he was gone.

'Well!' said Enid excitedly.

'His father made quite a scene outside their suite that evening,' Beth said quietly.

Attention immediately switched to her.

'When was that?' asked Darina, remembering the state the girl had been in when she'd seen her back to her cabin.

'Oh, I'm not sure,' Beth said. 'I'd had a bit of a sleep then something woke me. My cabin is just down from their suite. I looked out and there he was, knocking on their door, begging her to let him in. He tried to open it but she must have locked it from the other side. He sounded very angry, called her a cold bitch and, well, all sorts of other things. I don't know why somebody else didn't hear it.' Beth looked round at the table. 'She seemed shocked at what she was saying. 'I suppose they were all eating or at one of the entertainments. Anyway, finally he banged the door with his hand and shouted at her that she'd be sorry, he'd see she was sorry. Then he went away and I went back to bed,' she ended lamely.

There was the ring of truth about her account thought Darina. It seemed all too likely that Paul Mallory would have lost his temper. He must have seen any chance of getting hold of some of the lottery millions disappearing for ever.

Chapter Twenty-eight

The old train rattled up the steep slope with Norway displaying her verdant splendours, birch trees sweeping down to green meadows and a brilliantly clear bustling stream racing over boulders and winding its busy way through the almost impossibly beautiful terrain. Yet again the sun was shining, its golden light dappled through nervously quivering leaves, the air fresh as a leaping salmon.

Darina turned to William. 'You just don't think of a modern, civilized country, as this unspoilt, do you?'

'What?' he said, turning away from the window and what had seemed a deep contemplation of the beauties of nature.

Darina sighed. She knew where his thoughts were. If the scenery had suddenly switched to industrial slums he would hardly have noticed. Back on the *Empress* she knew that Paul Mallory was being grilled by Inspector Rider and Luther Conran. That was where William wanted to be. Instead, she had dragged him on to this vintage railway ride up into the mountains from Åndalsnes where the ship now lay peacefully in yet another of the austerely beautiful fjords the *Empress* had threaded its majestic way through. 'You can't go back to England without having seen *something* of Norway,' Darina had said that morning.

He'd given her a shame-faced grin and said of course he'd go with her. Standing on the platform waiting for the steam engine to arrive, he'd noticed that Karen Geary was part of the tour group and he'd cheered up even more.

The train had old-fashioned carriages with a side corridor. Darina had been amused to see William had unobtrusively managed to choose a compartment next to the one chosen by the cruise director.

'Any chance of a cup of coffee, do you think?' William asked, bringing his attention back to the present.

'Tea!' Darina said sternly. 'You know coffee isn't good for you.'

William groaned. 'Well, tea then.'

The compartment door slid open and Mervyn Pryde stood there holding a clipboard. 'William and Darina Pigram all present and correct,' he said, ticking off their names with a flourish.

'Earning your passage, Pryde?' joked William.

'Just giving a helping hand,' Mervyn said smoothly, not at all put out. 'I hope you enjoyed Tara's little impromptu concert last night?' He leaned against the open sliding door, seemingly in no hurry.

After dinner, Tara had flitted around the Coral Lounge like a flea who couldn't decide who to bite next. She'd snapped at Mervyn, been rude to Enid, demanded drinks that remained untouched, leaned over the piano and flirted with the pianist, then abruptly left him and darted outside, only to return a moment later and have another go at Mervyn. Darina had to feel sorry for her. Here was a chance for her to show what she could do and it looked as though the person she was relying on to take her on to another level of the entertainment world, was going to let her down.

She had been amazed at Mervyn's patience. He must be genuinely fond of her. Then she thought that, as a professional singer himself, he must understand what she was going through.

Finally Julian had reappeared and the ship's pianist had taken a break, disappearing from the lounge to a polite scattering of applause.

And at last Tara was able to show what she could do.

It had been a memorable half-hour. Tara had sung a cunningly balanced programme of old favourites, current pop songs, a folk tune or two and even a couple of arias from light opera. It certainly showed off her considerable versatility, and Darina wondered how much had been Julian's choice and how much Tara's. At the end the lounge had been crowded with even the ship's pianist standing at the back and joining in the enthusiastic applause.

Tara had loved her reception. She'd bowed gracefully, waved a grateful hand towards Julian, her face alight with excitement.

Throughout her programme, though, Darina had noticed her eyes constantly seeking Mervyn's, almost as though she needed his reassurance. And it was he she looked at as she finished the last number. Only when he had led the applause did she appear to relax and give them all a brilliant smile.

Again Darina wondered exactly what the relationship was between them. Just close friendship between colleagues? Or was it something deeper?

And what of Julian? The way he kissed her hand at the end of the programme then stood with his arm around her, sharing in the acclamation quite definitely displayed more than a manager's appreciation of his protégé's performance. How far was Tara taking advantage of him? And how far would either of them go to ensure the funds were available to develop her career?

'Tara was splendid,' Darina told Mervyn now. 'She's got a lovely voice and knows how to use it.'

'She's good, isn't she?' he agreed simply. 'Been well trained, all she needs now are the right breaks. I'm working on Karen to offer her a place in the next troupe she's putting together. Pity I couldn't get her to hear her last night.'

'You couldn't?' asked William, who suddenly seemed to take an interest in the conversation.

'She said she was involved in the Pearl Lounge show,' said Mervyn. 'But I went through later and she was sitting in the audience, chatting with a couple of old dears. She could easily have slipped through for at least part of Tara's performance. Still, I suppose she has to do her job.'

'I didn't see Tara this morning, is she with us?' Darina asked.

Mervyn looked down at his clipboard. 'No, said she needed to give that youngster some comfort. Losing his mother like that – nasty shock, only right she should help if she can. Well, I must finish my passenger count and then return to charming dear Karen.' He gave them a cheerful grin and slid the compartment door shut again.

'Well, well,' said William slowly.

269

Darina waited for him to say more but the train drew into what looked like a wayside halt and stopped to take on water, a process which seemed to take some time.

There was no platform but passengers managed to climb down from the high carriages and wander along the line. They were up in the mountains now, and there was much to admire in the beauty of the rugged landscape with its rippling river and graceful trees.

Amongst the passengers standing around by the wooden hut that bore the name of the halt, Darina noticed Joyce and Michael Harwood. She watched Michael kick moodily at loose stones while Joyce talked gently to him. How long before she gave up on being treated like some inferior servant?

As time wore on, William became impatient. First he rattled the coins in his trouser pocket, whistling tunelessly through his teeth, then he rocked back and forth on his heels whilst exchanging comments with Darina on the scenery, his interest growing less and less with the passing minutes. Finally he stalked off to try and find out what was happening.

Darina was content to observe the scene around her. She recognized a number of the passengers now, there was a sense of community amongst them, conversation was general and there was a lot of laughter. Mervyn Pryde could be seen listening attentively to Karen Geary address several passengers with exclamatory gestures. For once he'd given up centre stage. Then she noticed a lonely looking figure hovering on the edge of the loosely grouped people. The elegant trousers and camel jacket with a pashmina scarf casually but effectively tied around her neck easily identified her, even at a distance, as Daphne Rawlings. 'Apparently we're waiting for a regular train to pass through,' William told Darina.

'Nothing to be done but enjoy the view, then,' said his wife cheerfully. She watched as Daphne started to stroll lifelessly away from the group, holding her upper arms as though she was cold, though the sun was shining and the wooded area was sheltered.

After another five minutes or so, a sleek, modern train thundered through the halt. It rushed up the slope and soon vanished.

Passengers started to climb aboard its ancient cousin, the high steps making it difficult for the less agile.

Suddenly there was a cry.

Joyce Harwood was lying on the track underneath the train, clutching at her hip, her face screwed up in agony. 'I think it's broken,' she gasped.

'I don't know what happened,' Michael said as William and Darina came up with other passengers.

'You were right behind her as she was trying to climb up,' one of the other passengers said suspiciously. 'It looked to me as though you were pulling at her trousers.'

'I was helping her,' he said resentfully. He looked down at his wife. 'Are you all right, Joyce?' he asked stiffly.

'Of course she isn't all right!' said Jim French, a dogged figure by the train's wheels, as he bent over the fallen woman.

'If everyone would move back,' Karen Geary said in a high, nervous voice.

William shouldered his way through and spread

out his arms, 'Move back, please,' he said with authority.

People allowed themselves to be shunted backwards until a space was cleared in front of the train where Joyce was lying.

'She fell as she was trying to get on to the train,' said someone. 'She seemed to sort of turn as she fell and ended up underneath.'

'I saw that man grab at her,' said someone else, indicating Michael. 'He had his hands on her hips. I don't think he was helping her at all, I think he was pulling her down.'

'How dare you!' shouted Michael. 'How dare you suggest I would harm my wife!'

'Please,' said Karen, pushing her hair away from her face. 'Let's get this poor woman out, we can investigate what happened later.' Beside her stood the train conductor, an elderly, tall and solid Norwegian. He had demonstrated the facilities of his train with pride earlier but now looked extremely unhappy at what had happened.

Mervyn Pryde thrust his clipboard and pen at William. 'You're official, you get the names of the witnesses,' he said. 'I'll see what I can do to help move her from underneath the train.'

William automatically took the clipboard and Mervyn joined Jim French where he was crouched beside Joyce. She moaned as one took hold of her shoulders and the other her legs, then shrieked as they tried to move her.

Michael leapt forward. 'What the hell are you doing to her?'

'Stop!' said William. 'Don't move her, you could be

making the damage worse. Haven't you got a telephone in the office, there?' he said to the conductor, nodding towards the hut. 'I can see a road behind those trees, access for an ambulance.'

Looking pleased to have something to do, the conductor hurried off.

Michael thrust Jim French out of the way and knelt beside his wife, crouching down awkwardly beside the railway line. 'Joyce, speak to me, please, Joyce!'

'She's fainted, man,' said Mervyn. 'She can't hear you. But at least she's not feeling any pain. Hold her hand gently, that will comfort her.' He crawled out from underneath the train and Jim French joined him. Michael took Joyce's limp hand in his in a way that suggested it wasn't an action he knew much about.

Karen Geary was all of a flutter. 'We'll have to find out exactly what happened,' she said to William. 'Statements always have to be taken if there's an incident. Can you help, please?'

In a moment William had the scene organized, separating those who said they had seen what had happened from those who hadn't. 'One at a time, inside the carriage,' he said and helped the first one up the train's steep steps.

Darina wondered exactly what had happened to Joyce. Michael had seemed as angry at his wife as at the rest of the world. Could he possibly have been overcome with fury and pulled her down the steps? Well, if anyone could find out the truth of the matter, it was William.

A few minutes later the conductor hurried back

from the halt station and said that an ambulance and paramedics were on their way.

The situation looked under control and Darina couldn't see there was anything she could do to help except remove herself from the still crowded scene.

She walked away, along the track, following the direction Daphne Rawlings had taken. If William was sorting out the truth of how Joyce Harwood had ended up underneath the train, perhaps she could learn something from the friend who'd stolen Shona Mallory's husband.

Chapter Twenty-nine

Darina caught up with Daphne several hundred yards from the halt.

'I'm afraid there's going to be another delay,' she said as she came level with her.

Daphne looked round, startled. 'Good heavens,' she said, turning round and seeing the distance she'd come. 'I had no idea I'd walked so far. I could have missed the train!' She hunched her shoulders. 'Not that it would have mattered.'

'I don't think Karen would have allowed the train to go without everyone on board,' Darina assured her. 'And of course it would have mattered. You don't want to be stranded out here.' She looked around them. 'I don't think it's somewhere trains stop regularly.'

Daphne clutched her arms more tightly across her chest. 'Oh, God,' she said in despair. 'Everything has gone so wrong! What am I going to do?' She seemed in genuine distress as she turned to Darina.

'Look, there's a bench over there,' said Darina. 'Why don't we go and sit in the sun and wait for the ambulance to come?'

'Ambulance?' Daphne cried. 'What's happened?'

Darina told her as she led the way to a simple

wooden seat that had a fine view down the valley to the stream far, far below them.

'I can't be surprised at anything now,' said Daphne. She looked towards the train, where Michael Harwood, no longer crowded by curious passengers, was still crouching by his wife.

'Isn't that the awful man who attacked poor Shona?' she said in astonishment.

'Yes, it is.'

'Good heavens! And I suppose he pushed her underneath the train,' Daphne said with surprising viciousness.

Darina said nothing. It wasn't a suggestion that should be encouraged. And what could be Michael's motive? She was very much afraid, though, that the farmer was one of those people who bottled rage inside him until it could no longer be contained, when it erupted with results that had nothing to do with reason.

'Mind you,' added Daphne, 'I can understand why he got so cross with Shona. It was ridiculous her setting up that stupid foundation. As though any of us want GM foods!'

It was not Darina's intention to defend the dead woman's actions but she couldn't help murmuring something about the need for more research into genetically modified crops. 'The technique might be able to bring enormous benefits.'

'That's what Shona kept on saying,' Daphne hunched her shoulders over and looked down at her very smart low-heeled shoes. 'I couldn't see it myself. And when I think of what the money could mean to Paul and Julian, well, I couldn't understand her!' She looked at Darina, baffled.

'Did you discuss it? You seemed very close.'

'Oh, God, yes! But it was no good. She was absolutely determined. Shona held that large sums of money ruined people, they had to earn it or it was no good. All right for her, she was very highly paid.'

'Did her husband go along with the idea of the foundation?'

Daphne looked at her without speaking for a moment. 'You were one of those people in the cabin opposite mine, when Shona caught Paul, weren't you?' She didn't sound resentful or angry, just very tired.

Darina nodded. 'I'm afraid so. I was very sorry for you all, it wasn't fair we should all have been an audience like that.'

Daphne said wearily, 'It was dreadful. We never meant to hurt Shona. She seemed so wrapped up in her professional life, she had no idea what Paul needed. If I could bring a little warmth and humour into his life without her suffering, what was the harm? The affair would have burned itself out in time without her being any the wiser, if we hadn't come on this damn cruise!'

'Whose idea was it?' Darina asked curiously.

'Oh, Shona's,' Daphne said quickly. 'She said she wanted to give us all a really good holiday before the money was all tied away.' She picked one of the tall grasses that grew by the bench and started stripping the feathery end from the stalk. 'I've got to talk to someone, I'm going out of my mind, why not you?' She didn't look at Darina. It was as though she hardly cared who she was.

But then she said, 'Shona seemed to be getting on with you so well when Paul and I found you at tea together. She didn't take to people easily, she could be very shy and awkward.' A pause then, abruptly, 'It was you that found her, wasn't it?'

Darina nodded. She couldn't bring herself to say anything about that.

'I was really very fond of her, you know? I like women and I have a lot of women friends. Usually I steer clear of affairs with their husbands. It, well, it can get awkward, as you saw the other night. When Paul and I first met we didn't even like each other, I suppose it was because subconsciously we realized what could happen. It was Shona who insisted we became friends.' She dropped the bare stalk and brushed the seeds from her beautifully tailored trousers.

Darina waited for her to say more. In her experience, people always said more.

'Paul and I met in the local one night by accident. Shona was working late so we had a drink then he suggested he bought me supper. Then one thing rather led to another.' She ran the fingers of her right hand down the crease of her trouser leg. 'Lovers are more exciting and less trouble than husbands and is it my fault if wives get complacent and stop trying to please? Get into bad habits and fail to see the warning signs?'

It was illuminating to get a glimpse of what predatory women on the prowl could see in people's marriages. The sun was shining directly on Daphne, revealing with cruel clarity the faint network of lines around her eyes, a puffiness below them and creases in her neck. Darina realized the woman was older than she seemed at first meeting, maybe even older than Paul Mallory.

'No, I'm not in the business of causing divorces,' Daphne continued, turning towards Darina in a confidential way. 'Particularly not between Shona and Paul.' She gave a short, rather ugly laugh. 'I expect you think I'm not a very nice woman but when you're on your own, life can be tough. I can't afford to make wrong decisions and Paul is definitely not the man for me.' She opened her eyes wide and paused but Darina said nothing. 'I need my men solvent, successful. Fond as I am of Paul, I have to admit that he has made a crashing failure of his business.'

'What sort of a business is it?'

'Oh, public relations. Paul's very good at the client end and he understands spin like no one else but as far as proper costings or working within a budget are concerned, he's hopeless.'

'Doesn't he have a good accountant?'

'Paul thinks he can handle what one might call the creative financial side himself.'

Darina wondered exactly what Daphne was including in that definition of 'creative finance'.

'I run my dress shop on a very tight budget. I control everything, stock, staff, expenses, discounts, I can't afford not to. If Paul let me, I could handle the financial side of his business brilliantly but he's in far too big a mess for me to help at this stage.' She made an impatient gesture. 'Those bloody policemen can't see that he needed Shona to keep him from bankruptcy!'

'You mean, he couldn't afford to be divorced?'

'No way! Any more than he can afford to find himself without a wife now. It was Shona's salary which allowed them to keep up their Surrey style, the house, the golf club, the big cars, the entertaining Paul found necessary.'

'But what about the millions Shona won on the lottery? Surely they are now all Paul's?'

'No!' Daphne banged her hand down in frustration. 'It all goes to that stupid foundation.'

'You mean, it's all been tied up already?'

'That's what Paul says and he should know.' Daphne took a deep breath. 'I'm not sure he'll even have the money Shona said she'd clear his debts with, who knows what calls there'll be upon her estate. I tell you, I need someone in Paul's position like a hole in the head,' she said grimly. Then gave another of her gruff, apologetic laughs. 'As I said, you must have a very poor opinion of me but Shona wasn't exactly a warm and cuddly person. I admired her mind and her principles but she could be a cold bitch.' In the circumstances, the word struck Darina as unduly harsh.

Daphne fiddled with the ends of her pashmina. 'Shona was going to clear up his debts but she refused to back his company. It was killing Paul to have to go to work for someone else after running his own show but she claimed there was no point in allowing him to fail again. Shona was very hard like that.'

'So I suppose she wasn't going to back Julian's either?' Darina thought of the boy's eagerness to set Tara on the road to fame and fortune, together with himself. A road that needed to be paved with a certain amount of gold if it was to lead anywhere.

Daphne shook her head, the blonde curls shimmering in the sun. Darina wondered how much she had to spend at the hairdressers. Daphne might run a strict budget but it must include a generous amount for her own adornment. Then she thought of the chic clothes Daphne had displayed on the cruise, she was about the best-dressed woman on the boat and even at wholesale prices, her designer wardrobe must represent a considerable expenditure.

'Shona said Julian needed much more experience. If she backed him at this stage, he'd only fail as well.' She cleared her throat. 'Shona said she'd seen how money could ruin a young man and she wanted Julian to make his own way. As I said, she could be very hard.'

'I suppose she was self-made?' Darina suggested.

Daphne nodded vigorously, 'She came from a very humble background but she was very clever. She told me once her father used to beat her regularly if she didn't attend to her schoolwork closely enough.' She paused and to Darina it seemed as though she was considering how much else she would tell her. When she started speaking again it was more slowly. 'She told me once that she knew someone at university who came from a very wealthy family and that had ruined him. Paul' – she looked at Darina for a moment – 'Paul says that Shona had an illegitimate child after she took her degree. He didn't know who the father was but I got it out of Shona just before, well, before she caught us. It was the rich boy she mentioned to me. I think she loved him very much. But by the time she realized she was pregnant, he had died and she said that if his family had known she was carrying his child, they would have taken it over and ruined it the way his father had been ruined. So she gave it up for adoption.'

'She didn't have an abortion?' Darina thought of the little life she was so sure was within her womb and wondered whether there were any circumstances that could bring her to destroy it.

Daphne shook her head again. 'I told you I thought

281

she was cold and you might think that would have been her natural reaction but she said she couldn't do away with it. Someone put her in touch with a couple who were desperate for a child and they adopted it.'

What a tragic story it sounded, Darina thought. No wonder Shona had found it difficult to show emotion. 'Did she keep in touch?'

'No, she said it was better the child knew nothing of its genes and started with its own identity. She did say it had tried to get in touch with her before she married Paul but she'd refused any contact.'

'It? Shona didn't say what sex it was?'

'No, she was quite careful about that. But, then, Shona was careful in every way. Look at how she caught Paul and me! I suppose we were mad to think we could get away with it. But there's something about life on board a ship; it's as though you're caught in an iridescent bubble that has nothing to do with the real world, you seem to have permission to behave exactly as you want, not as you should.' She gave a sudden shudder. 'I think it was one of the worst moments of my life when I opened the door and saw her standing there! Heavens, how she lit into us!' Daphne folded her hands tightly together, the knuckles white with pressure. 'We deserved it of course but that didn't make it any easier to take.

'And then she left. I thought Paul was going to have a nervous breakdown, he was so upset. He really cared for her, you know? I was just a diversion on the side because she left him alone so much.'

Daphne turned away and clasped her hands together again. 'I know it looks as though Paul murdered her but he couldn't have done.'

'Do you mean,' asked Darina slowly, 'that he spent the whole night with you?'

'Of course,' Daphne said eagerly. Too eagerly?

'He didn't go and try and talk to his wife?' Darina asked, remembering Beth's account of what she'd seen outside the Mallory suite.

'Well, yes, he did that,' Daphne acknowledged.

'With any success?'

'He said she wouldn't open the door.'

'So he wasn't away from you for long?' Darina suggested.

'No, and then he spent the night in my cabin,' Daphne said resolutely. She released her hands and ran them down her trouser legs as though wiping sweat from her palms.

Faintly at first and then more loudly, they heard the wail of an ambulance. A moment later it swept round the corner of the station.

'I'm sorry,' said Daphne, getting up. 'I didn't mean to bend your ear quite so much but it's been such a help being able to talk to someone. I've never felt so lonely in my life.'

As Darina followed her towards the train, she mulled over the fact that in giving her lover an alibi, Daphne gave herself one as well.

Chapter Thirty

Darina tried to talk to Daphne again but the woman seemed to avoid her. After Joyce had been taken off in the ambulance, accompanied by her husband, everybody got back on the train for the last little bit of the trip.

William had finished taking statements. 'Difficult to say exactly what happened,' he told Darina. 'Everyone's got a slightly different account. On the face of it, it was a straightforward accident but a couple of people say they saw Michael grab her hips and pull her off the train.' He frowned at his little stack of notes.

'He could equally well have been trying to push her up the steps,' said Darina with little conviction in her voice.

William nodded. 'We'll have to wait until Joyce regains consciousness. I just hope she hasn't broken anything.'

'She'll probably back her husband's story, she's the most loyal wife I've ever met.'

Then she gave William an account of Daphne's conversation with her. 'It's a bit like Joyce's accident. Not necessarily what it looks like on the surface. I mean, why be so definite that she didn't want to break up Shona's marriage when all the evidence shows that they were getting more and more careless? And by giving Paul an alibi, she provides herself with one as well.'

'And just how tied up *are* those lottery millions?' asked William.

'I think she wanted me on her side. I'm sure she told me all that because she knew I'd tell you.'

'And I'd fill in the official investigation,' William said. 'Quite neat.'

The passengers were put in coaches to return down the mountain to the ship. Daphne got the last seat on the first coach, leaving Darina and William to catch one of the others.

The scenery on the way back was even more spectacular than it had been on the railway trip. Jagged-edged mountains lowered darkly against a sky from which the sun had vanished, leaving it grey and threatening. The darker grey stone crags were studded with a few remaining pockets of snow. Darina was impressed but preferred the tamer mountains they'd seen earlier on their cruise, with their enchanting waterfalls that arranged themselves like bridal veils as they cascaded down into the depths of the fjords.

Back on the *Empress*, William said he had to prepare a report on Joyce's accident and took himself off to Stan Dobson's office to use his computer. Darina asked him to find out how Joyce was and to let her know.

Going through the main reception area, Darina ran into Mary French. Her face lit up as she saw Darina. 'How's Joyce Harwood? Have you heard?'

Darina shook her head. 'William is finding out.'

'Is she coming back to the boat? Or will she have to stay in hospital?' Mary was all concern.

'I really have no idea. Michael is with her.'

'That man!' Mary was all scorn. 'Oh, look, there's Enid Carter. I don't want to have to talk to her, let's go and have lunch.' Without waiting for an answer, Mary walked rapidly towards the stairs that led down to the restaurant.

Rather amused, Darina followed, hoping that with the number of people in the reception hall, Enid hadn't noticed their retreat.

'Where's Jim?' she asked as they went down the stairs.

Mary said nothing, just marched into the restaurant and found them a table for two. 'Such a blessing we don't have to sit at our dinner tables for lunch,' she said, waving at a waiter. 'Now, I want a stiff drink, how about you?'

Darina ordered a mineral water.

'Oh, of course, I forgot all about your happy news for a moment,' Mary confessed, her face softening.

'That's all right, I forget myself every now and then. Now, what's happened with Jim?'

'Last seen going off to have a drink with Daphne Rawlings,' said Mary. The waiter brought their drinks. Mary raised the large Scotch she'd ordered. 'Cheers,' she said defiantly.

Daphne Rawlings, eh? She hadn't lost much time.

'Why are men such idiots?' Mary asked, put down the drink and picked up the luncheon menu.

'I'm sure you don't have to worry about Jim,' Darina said diplomatically, deciding fish would be nice and light.

'I don't?' Mary said wryly. She ordered a curry dish. 'Jim has no more sense where women are concerned than a fledgling bird has about cats.' She started crumbling a roll, making no attempt to eat any of it. 'We were getting on so well this cruise, I thought that, for once, he wasn't going to make a fool of himself.' She sighed deeply. 'Remember Enid's little drinks party? Did you see his eyes when that woman opened her cabin door with her negligee hardly done up? Displaying most of what she had to offer?'

Darina confessed that this aspect of the scene had escaped her attention. 'I was just so cross with Enid as I realized what she had done.'

'Enid! That's another thing,' Mary burst out and downed some more of her Scotch. 'When she said she'd been on that *Empress of China* cruise in such a meaningful way, well, I knew she'd realized what Jim had been up to. I could have died!' More whisky disappeared. 'All I could think of to say was that we'd never met before. I knew she didn't believe me,' she added gloomily. 'And I bet she's been telling everyone all about it.'

'All she said to me was that there'd been a rumour a paedophile was on board,' Darina said, fairly confident now that, whatever Enid tried to suggest to the contrary, Jim was not an abuser of children. 'Wasn't that what she said to you, too?'

'Did she? I was that bothered at recognizing her, I hardly heard what she said.' Mary finished her whisky and waved at the waiter to bring another. 'Rumours, they fly round ships faster than Concorde. That's why I was so upset to see her. Because of all the nonsense with Jim and that tart.'

'I'm sure it couldn't have been anything serious,' Darina murmured.

'Of course it isn't ever anything *serious*,' Mary agreed, attacking her second drink. 'That's what he says to me every time. It doesn't help, though, not when I see him making such a fool of himself over these women who are only out for what they can get. They smell his money a mile off, it's as potent as French perfume. Hey, I've made a joke, French perfume!'

It took Darina a moment to remember their surname.

'Well, it certainly has an effect, however much I try and pretend we've hardly a bean to our names. It's Jim who insists on having a suite. We ran into that bitch Daphne as we came out one time. You could just see her eyes take in the situation. Jim calls me a surly cow for not letting him enjoy himself, but what am I to do?' More whisky disappeared.

Darina felt very sorry for her. 'How long have you been married?' she asked.

'Thirty-eight years. I was his secretary when he first started the business. He had the hots for me the moment I took off my coat that first day.' Mary unconsciously looked down at her front and Darina realized that beneath the ordinary blouse and plain jerkin was an extremely well-developed bosom. 'Of course I made him wait for marriage. That's what one did in those days. Eh, but he was fun then, we had such a time, until the children came along and I had to give up work and become a mother as well as a wife. Ever since then, well, it's been one bit of fluff after another but he swears it's me he loves and I suppose I have to accept it.'

'I wouldn't!' declared Darina roundly, wondering

how such a sensible soul as Mary seemed could put up with such behaviour.

'No, I don't suppose you would,' Mary agreed, beginning to eat her lunch. 'And if I were your age now, I wouldn't either. It's all different for today's girls. Not that that stops some of them behaving like old-fashioned tarts, though.'

'Is that what happened on the *Empress of China?*'

Mary nodded, her mouth filled with food. 'I could see she was trouble when I first saw our table.' She looked at her empty whisky glass. 'Better not,' she said. 'We'll have some wine instead, a glass of white won't hurt you.' Before Darina could object, she'd summoned the waiter and ordered a bottle of their best Chardonnay. 'Can't go wrong with that can you?'

Darina made a little gesture of acceptance. What else could she do?

'Anyway, there she sat, boobs out here, not more than twenty-five years old and all on her own. Said her mate had had to cry off at the last moment and that she hoped she'd be able to make friends with some people. Looking at Jim as though he was Santa Claus. Like I said, they just smell the money. For he's generous, you know? Always buys them expensive presents.'

Darina remembered that Daphne had said she liked her men successful and solvent.

'And of course she had a cabin to herself, her mate, as she claimed, having cancelled at the last minute. Whenever Jim wasn't around, she wasn't either. Didn't take long for people to catch on, I can tell you.'

'I don't think people notice nearly as much as you think,' Darina said, watching the waiter fill her wineglass. 'I'd never have guessed Jim was such a

289

Lothario. And Enid didn't either or we should have heard about it.'

Actually, suggesting Jim chased women was a good deal less harmful than that he was a paedophile but perhaps it was better not to point this out.

Mary looked unconvinced. 'Anyway,' she said finally, 'I was never so pleased as when we found we were on the other side of the restaurant at dinner. I couldn't have borne it if we'd been placed on your table. Not with Enid and that girl and her father. Not to mention the other girl of about the same age. Jim would have thought it was Christmas.'

'We haven't got a father and daughter,' Darina said, puzzled. Then, 'Oh, you mean Mervyn and Tara. They aren't related, he's one of the entertainers, and she's his friend. You haven't been to one of his concerts? He's singing opera and lieder.'

'Opera's not my scene,' asserted Mary.

'Tara's a singer as well. She's got a good voice but more pop than classical. I don't think there's much between them. Tara's got quite close to Julian, the Mallory boy.'

'Oh, that poor woman,' Mary said, her eyes filling with tears. 'Isn't that dreadful? And didn't you find her? You poor dear. What a tragic cruise this is.' She got out a handkerchief and wiped her eyes.

Darina cast desperately around for a topic that would cheer her up, then saw William enter the restaurant. She gave him a wave and he came over. 'Having a cosy girls' lunch?' he suggested with a smile. 'Leaving us men all on our own?'

'Something like that,' Darina said. 'What's the news on Joyce?'

'She dislocated her hip, that's why she was in such pain, poor thing. It's been reset but there isn't time to get her back to the ship before we sail from here so she and Michael will rejoin us tomorrow at Bergen.'

'Perhaps this will make Michael think about Joyce for once,' Darina said.

'Don't count on it,' said Mary, her words slurred. She rose from the table. 'I think perhaps I should go and lie down.' A little unsteadily, she left the restaurant.

'Good heavens,' said William. 'What have you done to her?'

'Oh, it's too long to go into, suffice to say that Jim is the original faithless husband and it looks as though he's now after Daphne Rawlings, or she's after him.'

'Good heavens,' said William again.

A waiter came up, cleared away Mary's unfinished lunch and took William's order for a curry.

Darina sat and looked at him. He looked back, his frank, grey eyes a little questioning. How dependable, intelligent and charming he seemed beside Jim French and Michael Harwood. She had a lot to be grateful for and it was up to her to encourage all his good points. Darina smiled at her husband.

'Just what are you cooking up now?' he asked suspiciously.

'A recipe for happy marriage,' she said sweetly. 'Have you had a chance to find out what's going on with the investigation?'

'I managed a quick word with Luther. The prime suspect is still Paul Mallory. They aren't placing much reliance on Daphne's statement that he spent the whole night with her. There's no record of Mallory having sailed in either of the Empress ships before but someone on the ship's staff has recognized Daphne from several years ago. She worked on the Empress of China, in the shop, on a round the world cruise.'

'Good lord!' Darina said.

Darina and William hadn't been in the Oyster Bar since they'd witnessed the incident between Phil Burrell and Harry Summers on their first night. That night they decided to try it again. And there was the first officer.

Sitting with him at the bar, clutching what looked like the remains of a dry martini, was Beth, dressed in a long, scarlet evening dress that clung to her thin body and revealed an amazing amount of flesh back and front. With them were Mervyn Pryde and Tara, wearing the least provocative dress Darina had seen her in so far, a full-skirted, off the shoulder number in emerald taffeta.

Mervyn saw the Pigrams and waved them over. 'Come and join us,' he said in his splendidly carrying voice.

William glanced at Darina. She gave a slight nod and they went across.

Darina found herself presented with Tara and Mervyn's profiles. Their noses were identical. She wondered that she hadn't noticed it before.

'Name your poison,' Mervyn said. 'I'm in the chair.'

Beth took the second martini he ordered for her and gave him a grateful smile. She was sitting on a tall stool, leaning against the polished wood of the bar counter, cheeks a little flushed. She took a generous sip of her drink and put a hand on Harry Summers's uniformed sleeve. 'Tell us some more about Trondheim,' she said in what might almost pass as a sultry voice.

He smiled down at her with a proprietorial air. 'It's considered to be the only one in Norway with a genuine air of the medieval about it.'

'That sounds just like Fodor,' said Mervyn jovially. 'Are you usually a walking travel guide?'

'Like a slot machine, I perform on payment,' Harry Summers said smoothly. 'The city is one of the oldest in Norway, it celebrated its millennium in 1997. In 1350 there was an outbreak of plague that killed most of the population and the appropriately named Great Fire of 1781 destroyed many of the old wooden buildings.'

'I love listening to you,' said Beth in a soft little voice.

Tara stared at her. 'Getting with the great big naughty world at last, are you?' she said.

Beth looked hurt. 'Not everyone is as in-your-face as some people,' she said sweetly.

Tara flushed. Mervyn put his arm around her. 'Julian coming to join us this evening, is he, my pet?'

She shrugged her shoulders. 'He's waiting for those awful policemen to finish interviewing his father.'

'Our cookery expert is looking very thoughtful,' said Harry Summers. 'What's occupying that pretty mind?'

It wasn't the sort of approach that cut much ice with Darina but she saw how she could use the opening. 'I'm wondering what sort of father William is going to be,' she said. She looked at the officer through downcast eyelashes. 'We've just discovered that I'm probably pregnant, you see. And it's so important that our baby has a father who will fulfil all his duties.' She'd better watch it, she was beginning to sound like Tara!

'Duties, eh?' Harry said with a nonchalant smile. 'What does our policeman think they should be?' There was an edge to his voice now. Darina thought he was probably preparing to extract some revenge for the interview he'd had with William and Stan Dobson.

'Playing cricket with the boys and telling the girls they mustn't stay out after eleven o'clock,' William said promptly. 'But let's see what the team thinks.' He looked down at Beth, 'What about you? What's your idea of the perfect dad?'

She coloured at the attention, then finished her drink in a quick gulp and said in a cold little voice, 'You shouldn't ask me about how fathers should behave, mine should have ended in prison. But then he was only a stepfather.'

There was a short silence broken, unexpectedly, by Tara, who said, 'That's dreadful! Mine was brilliant, really brilliant. He encouraged me with my singing and paid for lots of lessons. At least, I say it was my father but, as I told you that other time, I'm adopted. I suppose an adoptive father should behave in the same way as a real father?' She looked up at Mervyn as she said it.

'I'd say so,' he responded jovially.

'Have you ever tried to discover who your real parents are?' Darina asked her.

Mervyn was getting more drinks and before Tara could answer, one of them slipped through his hand and shattered on the floor. There was all the business of clearing up the broken glass. Afterwards Tara said, tossing her abundant hair, 'I haven't needed to contact my birth parents, not really. As I told you, I had a brilliant childhood. If you want my opinion, what a dad really needs is commitment, you know? Commitment to his child, like always being there for her – or him.'

There was the tiniest of pauses then William smiled at her. 'Well said, Tara, I think that about sums it up.'

'Everyone having a good time?' asked Karen Geary, suddenly joining the group.

'Oh yes,' said Tara quickly. 'It's all wonderful.'

The cruise director was dressed in one of her tightly waisted evening dresses. Pale pink satin tonight, strapless with a very short, draped skirt and trailing a fish tail behind. She made Darina feel her black velvet evening dress, which displayed quite an expanse of creamy flesh and came to just above her knees, was positively demure. 'We've got a splendid variety of things for you to enjoy tonight,' Karen said with vibrant enthusiasm. 'I do hope you've all checked your daily programmes.'

'Will you be giving us a test tomorrow?' Harry Summers asked challengingly.

'I'll deal with you later,' she said briskly. 'That is, if you haven't found other things to do,' she added, looking pointedly at Beth, who, nursing her latest martini, was now leaning against the first officer's arm.

He gently moved away. 'I shall be on duty any minute,' he said. 'Plain tonic is what I've been indulging in,' he added, as though anyone might be thinking differently. He looked at his watch, then whispered something in Beth's ear. She gave him a pussy cat smile.

'Well, I'm glad the ship is in safe hands,' Karen said tartly with a sideways glance at Beth.

At that moment Julian entered the bar. He was as white as the *Empress*'s paintwork and went straight to Tara. 'They've arrested Dad,' he said.

Chapter Thirty-one

Even as Tara grabbed at Julian's hand and tried to comfort him, the boy turned to William. 'There must be something you can do,' he blurted at him. 'He didn't kill her, I know he didn't.'

'Do you mean you've got evidence that proves he didn't?' William asked in a kindly way.

Julian stared at him. 'Evidence, what do you mean? Dad couldn't kill anyone.

'If he's innocent—' William started patiently.

'Of course he's innocent, I've just said so,' Julian insisted hysterically.

Tara took his arm. 'Jools, sweetie,' she said soothingly, 'he only means that as soon as the police find there isn't any evidence, they'll let your father go. And I'm sure they'll be considering other suspects as well, won't they?' she said to William.

'I'm sure they are doing so,' he said.

Darina thought he didn't sound totally convinced but Tara seemed happy enough. 'There you are! Why don't we sit down in the corner over there, Mervyn will bring you one of those beers you like and you can tell me everything that's been happening with your dad.'

Julian allowed himself to be led away.

'Good girl, that,' Mervyn said. He ordered a Becks, a white wine and a whisky then took them over to Tara and Julian.

'I've got to be off, duty calls,' said Harry Summers. He again whispered something in Beth's ear and she gave a very un-Beth-like giggle.

Karen looked round sharply. Her face darkened and her mouth tightened.

'Can I offer you a drink?' asked William politely.

'Oh, aren't you sweet,' she gushed. 'But duty calls me also. Hope to see you at the show tonight. It's Sondheim, just divine, the boys and girls are so clever!' She left the bar, high heels flashing, behind swaying.

'How about you?' William asked Beth.

She looked at him, her eyes larger than usual, her cheeks flushed. Her short curls were slightly longer now and suddenly she was a very attractive girl. 'Why not?' she said. 'I'm drinking dry martinis, straight up.'

'Right!' he said. 'What about you, darling?'

'I'll have a tonic water with a dash of Angostura bitters,' she said. 'I think this will be my tipple until the baby is born.'

'Poor you,' said Beth with a touch of her old awkwardness. 'I'd hate not to be able to drink alcohol.'

'I don't mind, I'm so pleased to be pregnant.' Darina suddenly knew that this was true. 'But you don't usually drink very much,' she added, thinking of the couple of glasses of wine Beth confined herself to at dinner.

'Every now and then I like to let go a little.' Beth popped the olive from her drink into her mouth and Darina was reminded of the way she'd dipped her finger into her drink in Enid's cabin. Beth could really be quite sexy when she lost some of her inhibitions.

'Are you going to visit Bergen tomorrow?' she asked.

Beth swallowed her olive and nodded vigorously. 'It's our last port of call. Hasn't the trip gone by quickly?'

To Darina it seemed as though an age had passed since they embarked at Southampton. So much had happened! 'Have you enjoyed the cruise?' she asked.

Beth nodded again. 'It's been even better than I expected.'

'In what way?' William asked.

'Oh, more diversions, more people I could relate to. I haven't been bored for a minute.'

Beth didn't seem to need much in the way of diversions, thought Darina, thinking how many times she'd seen her sitting on her own with a book for company.

'How is my patient?' asked Ian Westlake, joining their little group, looking very suave and debonair. 'I trust you are feeling more the thing now?'

Darina thanked him and assured him she had completely recovered. 'Nasty shock you had,' he said, then turned to look appreciately at Beth. 'Now, I don't think I've met this young lady.'

William performed the introductions. 'To think it's taken most of the trip before I catch up with you,' the doctor said banteringly. 'I shall have to make good one of the last few days.' Beth looked at her watch. 'Soon be dinner time,' she said, her voice once again precise and controlled. 'I must freshen up.' She slipped down from her stool, gave them all a small smile and escaped from the bar.

'Hmm,' said the doctor. 'Have I got bad breath or something?'

'She's a rather shy girl,' Darina said.

'You'll have to work on her,' William added with a grin. 'I think she needs a little male attention.'

'She's not that attractive,' Ian Westlake laughed. 'I'll reserve my charms for those who welcome them.' But he continued to look in the direction of where Beth had vanished. 'Something about her, though. Felt I'd met her before, know what I mean?' It was as though he had to justify his interest in her which he obviously felt had been rejected. Darina thought he probably wasn't used to passengers not being excited at his attention in them. Ian Westlake seemed to trade on his charm. She wondered if he missed his specialist status and Harley Street consulting rooms.

Just then Jim and Mary French entered the bar, Mary very excited. 'We've been asked to join the captain's table,' Mary told Darina. 'It seems some spare places have come up and the restaurant manager suggested we might like to move.'

'I think they must have arrested that Mallory chap for his wife's murder,' said Jim solemnly.

'Whether or not that's happened, he certainly isn't sitting with the captain any longer,' said the doctor drily. 'Nor is his lady friend.'

'Though I understand she's detaching herself from his side faster than an oyster slides down a gourmet's throat.'

Jim looked sideways at his wife, who said nothing.

'What does that suggest to you?' asked William.

'Oh, either that the man's definitely guilty or that none of those millions are coming his way. In which case he's probably innocent. Either way, I don't see the delightful Daphne hanging around. However, I'm sure she won't be short of male company for long, she's quite delightful.'

'Fancy chatting her up yourself, Doctor?' asked William.

'No, thanks!' Ian Westlake was quite definite. 'Piranha fish are household pets compared to that lady, I fancy.'

Mary said nothing.

When Darina and William went down to dinner, they found they were the first of their group.

'What an empty table,' said Enid, arriving just after them. 'Where is everybody?'

'I don't expect we'll see Luther,' said William, 'but I'm sure the others will be along soon.'

'I'm here,' said Beth, and slipped into her seat before William could hold it out for her. She'd quite lost her air of relaxation, and there was little sign of all the martinis she had drunk.

Mervyn arrived a few moments later. 'Tara's asked to be excused, she's holding Julian's hand; he's really very upset about his father,' he said. 'I've arranged for something to be served to them in the Mallory suite.'

He seemed somewhat abstracted, there were few tales of the operatic world for them tonight. Darina and William, aided by outrageous tales of previous cruises from Enid, did their best to keep the conversation going but it was hard work and they left before coffee was served.

'Let's go out on deck,' said Darina. 'It's quite a nice evening and I've got a wrap.' She slipped the cashmere and silk stole William had given her for Christmas around her shoulders and they made their way up to the Corniche Deck.

The ship had steamed well south of the Midnight sun now and the night was quite dark. But the sky was clear and the ship hardly moved as she creamed her way through the Norwegian seas and a thousand stars decorated the sky like tiny diamonds on dark blue silk. Darina took William's arm and enjoyed being so close to him. They appeared to have this part of the deck to themselves. 'What an interesting session that was in the bar tonight,' she said.

'Wasn't it just? Our little Tara isn't quite the airhead she makes out, is she?'

'And have you noticed just how like Mervyn she is?'

'Really?' William found them a couple of loungers in a sheltered spot and they made themselves comfortable. A light on the bulkhead behind them provided enough illumination for them to see each other without detracting from the starry heavens.

Darina told him about Mary French's comment at lunchtime. 'So that made me compare the two of them this evening. I keep telling myself it probably means nothing but they've both got this very slight bump in the middle of their noses. Have you noticed?'

'No,' William confessed. 'There's been so much else to think about. Are you suggesting they're related?'

'Oh, you are slow! Tara told us herself that she's adopted and when I asked her if she'd ever thought about getting in touch with her birth parents, Mervyn dropped his drink. It seems obvious to me.'

'You mean that he's her father?' William sounded surprised.

'I'm sure that's where she gets her singing talent from. She may not be an opera singer but she's got a really good voice.'

'So who's her mother?'

Darina shrugged. 'Your guess?'

'Wouldn't have an idea!'

She was silent for a moment, then she said, 'Has Paul Mallory really been arrested for Shona's murder?'

'I only know what Julian told us. He wasn't really very coherent so it may be nothing more than that Rider and Luther are continuing to question him.'

'You think they may have difficulty in coming up with enough evidence?'

William adjusted his position on the lounger. 'How would I know?'

Darina put out a hand to him. 'Poor darling, not being part of the investigation is really getting to you, isn't it? Do you think Paul's guilty?'

'Impossible to say.' William sounded irritable and frustrated. 'But I think I'm with the doc.'

'You mean, if the millions go to him, he did it, if they're already all tied up, he didn't?'

'Something like that. I know Luther's got enquiries going on in England, he may know the answer to that tomorrow.'

'I wonder, despite what she says, if Daphne doesn't believe Shona could have tied up all her lottery winnings before coming on this cruise,' Darina said thoughtfully. 'She's a very determined woman, out for the main chance, I would say, and keeps herself in very good shape.'

'You mean she wouldn't have difficulty man-handling a small corpse?'

'She must do a lot of humping of boxes in her shop. Though clothes aren't all that heavy.'

'Having lifted the cases you brought on this trip, I'd challenge that!' Then William grew thoughtful. 'She must know all about the layout of the ship and how the stores are kept.'

'You follow my drift, Holmes!'

'I think you're Sherlock tonight, I'm merely filling in as Watson.' He smiled at her through the dark.

'I was just thinking,' Darina confessed, 'that if Daphne ran into Phil Burrell the first night out and he recognized her, she might have had a reason beyond his keys for dumping him overboard.'

'You mean, he would have realized when Shona's body surfaced that it had to be someone with a good knowledge of the ship and remembered who she was?'

'Exactly.'

'Nah,' said William after a moment's thought. 'Whoever did the murder, they intended no one should find out until much, much later. If you hadn't been given that tour of the lockers, the body would have completely disappeared down that monstrous mincing machine into unidentifiable sludge. The whole ship thought Shona Mallory had left at Tromsø. She'd told her husband to take her luggage home with his.'

They sat quietly thinking about this.

'He could have been quite relieved not to find her at home when he got there,' Darina said after a little. 'It might have been some time before anyone realized she had disappeared.'

'Long enough for her movements to be untraceable.'

'What a diabolical plan! And to think it nearly

succeeded!' Then Darina thought of something. 'But, hang on a minute. If her body hadn't been found, Shona wouldn't be dead. Paul wouldn't have been able to get his hands on her millions! He'd have had to wait for, what is it, seven years before she could be pronounced dead? And from what Daphne said, he's on the verge of bankruptcy. He needs the money now.'

'Trust you to put your finger on the critical point,' said William, but he sounded happy about it. 'Look, I don't want to dampen your enthusiasm for discovering who murdered the person whose body you so unfortunately found but I can't share it. It's been made perfectly plain that I'm no part of the investigation and I'm quite happy to keep it that way.'

Darina doubted this. Much more likely that William was suffering extreme frustration, feeling hard done by not to mention rejected, and mulling the matter over with her wasn't helping.

However, she couldn't help adding, 'I bet Daphne's not the only passenger with a knowledge of the ship.'

'Have a heart,' said William. 'Here we are in the most romantic of circumstances, and all you want to do is discuss a most revolting murder.'

Darina was happy to allow him to forget his sense of rejection over the investigation but as he drew her closer she remembered exactly who it was who'd told her he'd been on other *Empress* cruises. Not only that, but this evening had revealed a possible motive for murdering Shona Mallory.

Chapter Thirty-two

The ship reached Bergen early the next morning.

'I take it you want to go ashore and explore?' said William over breakfast.

Delighting in the fact that her morning sickness appeared to have gone away, Darina said she did. 'Especially after having to miss Trondheim. Don't you want to, or will you be involved with Luther?'

'I think there's a pathologist flying in to conduct an autopsy, so both he and Rider will be tied up with that,' said William.

'Good,' said Darina. 'We can have a nice day out and forget all about murder.'

Darina and William's stroll through Bergen found them outside the leading hotel at lunchtime and Darina suggested they take a look at its famous cold table. 'Though there are hot dishes as well,' she added as she led the way in. 'Come on,' she said as William appeared to be hanging back.

He looked at his watch.

'It's a bit early, I know but when has that ever stopped you eating?' Without waiting for a response, she entered the hotel. The restaurant wasn't easy to find but eventually she was directed upstairs. Followed by a reluctant William, she finally tracked it down.

Already there were a few lunchtime guests. The head waiter came up and asked if they'd like a table for two. 'Perhaps you have booked?'

Darina explained they weren't sure they wanted to eat there but perhaps they could take a look at the famous smorgasbord? 'Of course,' she was told with a wave of the hand in the direction of the display. She had the distinct impression she hadn't made the most popular of moves but nothing was going to stop her viewing the food. It was the first opportunity she had had of seeing what the Norwegians could do in this direction.

Their efforts turned out to be considerable. Dishes were piled with arrangements of cold meats, fresh fish and smoked fish and shellfish, together with imaginative salads, all arranged on large serving plates in a refrigerated cabinet. Just as she was turning her attention to three huge containers of hot food over burners, William came up behind her. 'I'm sorry, but we've got to go,' he said in a low voice. 'Don't ask why, just follow me.' He grabbed her hand and pulled her, not in the direction of the exit, but through the swing doors into the kitchen.

'I never realized you were that interested in cooking,' Darina murmured as he guided her through the startled waiters and cooks.

'How about discussing marinating salmon with the chef?'

'I think there are better times,' gasped Darina, catching sight of a large figure, wielding a knife, bearing down on her.

It only took a few moments before they emerged on an access stairway that led down to the back of the hotel.

'What was all that about?' said Darina. 'Shall we ever be able to show our faces there again?'

'When I explain I'm a detective working with their officials, I'm sure we will.'

They found their way back to the front of the hotel where there was an open area with an elaborate memorial to Norway's famous composer, Edvard Grieg. A bronze statue of him playing the violin was perched halfway up a small mountain that grew out of a water feature, all underneath overhanging trees. 'Can we sit down for a moment so you can explain?' asked Darina, trying to move in the direction of a bench. 'Or are we in some sort of race?' she added as William put his arm through hers and walked her swiftly past the memorial, round the corner and into the wide street that led down to the harbour. Halfway down was a huge block of stone surrounded by bronze-formed seafaring folk. Darina liked the way the Norwegians decorated their towns with sculptures of all sorts but she was in no mood now to examine such features.

Once they were out of sight of the hotel, William slackened his pace. 'I'm sorry, but we might have ruined everything.'

'Everything? How dramatic! Come on, you've got to explain. Are we allowed to stop for a bite to eat or is there a prize if we get wherever it is first? And where on earth is it anyway?'

William squeezed her arm but continued to walk. 'Poor darling, I'm sorry, you've every right to complain. OK, this is what happened. While you were putting that restaurant's food under your expert's microscope – that waiter seemed to think you were going to stuff your pockets with his choice titbits, by the way – I was giving the tables the once over. Thank heavens the room was L-shaped so that I wasn't in full view.'

'Oh, quite,' agreed Darina. 'Perish the thought that I might have wanted you as a decorative asset for all to admire.'

William ignored her. 'Tucked away to one side was a table with a gentleman obviously waiting for someone to join him. On the floor were two large, glossy carrier bags.'

'Fascinating,' murmured Darina. 'The mad shopper of Bergen, do you think? Obviously not someone from the boat or you would have said. So why don't you tell me just why you were so interested?'

It was as though William hadn't heard a word she'd said. 'As soon as I saw him, I knew I should have stopped you going in but you were so mad keen and, after all, it might have been all right.'

Darina stopped in the middle of the street, ignoring the people who almost bumped into her. 'William, if you don't tell me exactly what all this is about, I'll – well I don't know what I'll do.'

He continued imperturbably. 'But sure enough, out of the corner of my eye, I caught sight of Karen Geary coming in, with two carrier bags identical to those by the table. Well, I knew I just had to grab you and get us out of there as quickly as I could.'

Darina sighed deeply. 'I see, Karen Geary, another of the mad shoppers! William, please, start at the beginning.'

So, still standing in the middle of the busy pavement, he did. As Darina gradually realized what he was telling her, her eyes grew wide. 'You mean you suspect her and Harry Summers of running drugs? Good heavens!' she said as they started to walk slowly on.

'I couldn't tell you before because, as you can appreciate, we've had to operate under the tightest security on a need-to-know basis. The only member of the ship's company who's been told is the captain.'

'You mean you think others might be involved?'

William shrugged his shoulders. 'We don't know. It could be. But once I'd put together all the bits and pieces, all of Summers's actions made a sort of sense.'

'You mean why he got so angry about Phil Burrell being involved in any sort of way with Karen?'

'Exactly! Otherwise, why be bothered about her having a drink with a not outstandingly attractive junior member of the company?'

'But if that drink was in a bar where she was supposed to have switched shopping bags for one loaded with cocaine or heroin or whatever? Yes, I can see that he might get upset. And then when he saw Phil actually carrying the bag up the gangplank, he lost his cool.'

'Cool is a word the first officer needs to be better acquainted with. He thinks he's the king of it but he can't keep his temper. That scene in the Oyster Bar could so easily have been avoided. All he had to do was join the two of them and make it quite plain to poor Phil who was in control. He outranked him on every front, it shouldn't have been difficult.'

'Instead of which, his behaviour then led to exposure now?'

'We certainly hope so. The Norwegian Customs and Excise are tailing Karen, they'll be lunching at a nearby table and watching every move she makes. If the

309

bags are switched, Karen will be arrested as she goes back on board.'

'What about the mad shopper in the restaurant?'

'He'll be put under surveillance to see if he can lead to bigger game.'

'And you expect Karen to cough up all she knows?'

'Can you see her letting her accomplice get away scot-free?'

Darina thought of the effervescent cruise director. No, if she was in trouble, Darina would bet her best olive oil that she'd drag in anyone else she could, and excuse herself by saying she was only obeying orders.

'Do you think she actually told Phil anything?' Darina asked. 'Or do you think he might have guessed? Might he have said something to Harry Summers that suggested he knew what was going on?'

'Until you found Shona Mallory's body, yes, that was what I thought. And I think Luther agreed with me. Incidentally, he suggested Stan Dobson might be involved.'

'That nice security officer you used to work with? Surely not!'

They were approaching the port again. In the distance she could see the *Empress*.

'Quite, that's what I told him,' William said repressively.

Darina knew he wouldn't take kindly to one of his colleagues being accused of criminal activities. Yet, surely, every eventuality had to be considered. She thought again about the disappearance of the stores manager. 'So, when Shona Mallory's body was discovered, you changed your mind and decided Phil had been chucked overboard in order for the murderer to get his keys?'

'Something like that. Look, would you mind if we went back to the boat? I want to let Luther know it looks as though he might have an imminent arrest to make.'

There was a great deal more of Bergen to see but Darina knew that she'd lost her husband as far as being a tourist was concerned. She could, of course, continue looking round on her own but rubber-necking had lost its appeal for her. So she agreed and William flagged down a passing taxi. 'I know it's not far but I daren't let you past all those shops again,' he joked.

On their way from the docks, they'd passed a whole string of wooden houses that must have been several centuries old. Once doubtless the home of fishermen, they had now been converted to attractive little shops selling souvenirs, Norwegian crafts and a great deal else. It was true that Darina had thought that she'd try to find a few presents to take home for her mother and other people on the way back but she could see that William was desperate to get back to the ship. And now she could see why he had seemed so uncharacteristically lukewarm about discussing the suspects in the Mallory case. All his energies were involved with possible drug smuggling by Karen Geary and Harry Summers. A case that Darina could tell he had had the major part in putting together. A triumphant conclusion to that operation would go a long way to smoothing his ruffled feathers at being ostracized from the murder inquiry. Yet Darina wished he was more inclined to discuss the details of Shona Mallory's killing because there were a number of features surrounding it that didn't seem to add up. Thinking about the odd little details that puzzled her occupied the short drive to the ship.

When they arrived at the bottom of the gangplank, William said, 'I rather pressganged you into coming back with me, would you like to take this taxi back into town again?'

'No, I think I'll go and try out the ship's indoor pool,' she said. 'A quiet swim is just what I need.'

At the top of the gangplank William asked Stan Dobson where the inspector and Luther Conran were, then, with a sketchy wave of his hand, he was off.

Darina was quite happy to be left on her own. She was sure that if she really thought about everything she'd learned during this trip she could sort out who had murdered Shona Mallory and, probably, Phil Burrell, though at that moment she was by no means sure they had both been killed by the same person. William had told her everything he knew or had learned from Luther Conran and Darina had an excellent memory, almost as good as his. Already certain aspects were coming together and the picture they were forming was quite different from the official one according to William.

Chapter Thirty-three

Darina found her bathing suit and a wrap in her cabin. She wound her long hair on to the top of her head and fastened it with a couple of combs, then found her way down to what seemed like the bowels of the ship. She had a sudden vision of the hull submerged in the vast ocean, all that water pressing on steel plates. It seemed strange to think of passengers floating inside a pool that was floating on so much more water.

The pool itself was in the gymnasium. Darina hadn't ventured here before. She looked around with interest. It was well equipped with exercise machines, a sauna, massage cubicles and a small shop offering sports equipment.

'Hi!' said a small girl dressed in a black tracksuit with an *Empress* logo on it. She stood bouncing up and down on her trainershod feet. 'Come down for a swim? Can I interest you in a fitness assessment? Or how about a foot and ankle massage? I'm Lulu, by the way, the Keep Fit Instructor. Nice to see someone else under the age of forty, you should have been doing the mile walk every morning.'

'You've had my husband a couple of times,' said Darina, giving her a smile, the girl's enthusiasm was infectious. 'Tall with dark hair.'

313

Lulu's face suddenly crumpled. 'Oh, God, you mean he's the police chap Stan got to help him try and find Phil? Jesus, and I never realized! Oh, I'm sorry, I'm such a chump but it's all been so awful, I don't know how I've kept going.' She drew her arm across her eyes. It was the action of an urchin rather than a grown woman. Then she took a deep breath. 'Look, let's forget about all that, shall we? Nothing's going to bring Phil back, I've faced that now. But it's hard. The last time I saw him was the evening he disappeared, you know? I wanted him to spend some time with me but he wouldn't.' Her voice grew darker, almost vicious. 'I knew who he was going to see all right. Much luck it would bring him! I could see he was upset by some-thing, probably to do with her. I told him he looked as though he'd seen a ghost and he said, I could say that. Well, I could have laid any number of ghosts for him but he would have nothing of it.'

'I expect you had to tell the police all this? It must have been very upsetting for you.'

Lulu nodded, her eyes luminous with unshed tears. 'I didn't mention the ghost bit, though. Sounds a little creepy, doesn't it? And he wasn't creepy, not my Phil.' Again her tracksuited arm was dragged across her eyes. Then she gave a wavery smile. 'Not much use that, now, is it? So, any way I can help you?'

'I hoped to have a little swim,' Darina said, holding up her bathing suit.

'Well, that's just fine. The water's lovely and warm, you enjoy it. I've got one of the walkers coming for a foot and ankle massage but otherwise I'll be here if you need me. You can change in that cubicle there.'

The pool was a giant tank let into the floor of the

gym. You had to step up and over the edge then down into the water, which was, indeed, at a most comfortable temperature. Two swift strokes, though, and Darina was at the other end. Olympic size it was not!

Still, after a little, she managed to work out a sort of paddle that took her backwards and forwards and then round and round the pool in a gentle exercise that was very relaxing.

As she swam, she reviewed the contradictions in the facts as William had more or less presented them.

Item one was the theory that Phil Burrell had been disposed of so that his keys could be obtained. Which suggested that Shona Mallory's death had been all worked out. But why such a complicated way of disposing of a body when there was an ocean available to swallow up someone who needed to be got rid of? It had worked with the stores manager, why not the scientist as well?

Awkward item two was the timing of the murder. It seemed the killer had taken advantage of the break-up between Shona and Paul. No one could have known that Shona was going to discover her husband and friend together. All right, Enid had stage-managed the actual revelation but she must surely be the most unlikely murderer ever! Tara, Beth, Jim and Mary French and herself had all witnessed the actual scene but news of the break-up had spread rapidly in the way of such things on board ship.

This in turn suggested that the killer's plan of campaign had in fact left a certain amount to chance. Did that tie in with disposing of Phil Burrell so that keys to the food lockers would be available?

Had the original plan been to tip Shona overboard and had something interfered with that plan?

Darina was becoming dizzy with her circuits of the little pool. She flipped over and started to swim in the other direction. Then she thought back to the night Shona must have disappeared. The ship had been north of Tromsø. Well within the Arctic Circle. Then it struck her. Of course, it would have been daylight! Was that the factor the killer hadn't taken into account?

Darina imagined a razor-sharp mind that was cool and calculating. Even the most careful of minds, though, could be tripped up by a detail. Usually it was by something very obvious, something that could hit them right between the eyes, like the midnight sun!

So there the killer was, up on the Corniche Deck, and there was Shona Mallory, and it was bright as day. Even though no one appeared to have noticed them at the time, there would have been the ever present danger that they could be seen. So why not abort the plan? Was it that it would be too dangerous to try for another opportunity? Or that the murderer knew Shona intended to leave the ship next day so it was now or never? Whatever, the plan had to be rapidly rethought. And that's where a knowledge of the ship entered the scene. The killer must have known about the lift and must have had Phil Burrell's keys on them. Whatever the original reason for acquiring those keys, they couldn't be left in the cabin where they could be found by an inquisitive steward.

Tired of circling the pool's confined space, Darina swam to the steps, anchored her toes under one of the treads and stretched back into the water, assembling more pieces of information, trying to fit them into a pattern.

What was it Michael Harwood had thought he'd heard Phil Burrell say as he ran up the steps to the upper deck? 'God, I couldn't believe it!' Suddenly Darina stopped floating and grabbed at the steps as she remembered Lulu saying that Phil thought he'd seen a ghost.

Maybe he had.

Darina climbed out of the pool and towelled herself off then changed into shorts and a T-shirt.

At the back of the gym Darina could see Lulu giving someone her foot and ankle massage, which seemed to include most of the lower leg. After a moment or two, Darina realized the lucky recipient was Beth. Lulu was giving her advice on keeping healthy. 'I hardly need to tell you about exercise, though, you're in great shape.'

The door into the gym behind Darina opened and she was surprised to see Daphne Rawlings come in dressed in a tracksuit. Then wondered why she should be surprised. Hadn't Shona Mallory told her she'd met Daphne in a health club?

'Hello,' Daphne said smoothly. 'Nice to see you again. Been swimming, I see,' she added, with a look at the wet ponytail hanging down Darina's back. 'Thought I'd have a workout on one of the cycles.'

'Just what I was going to do,' Darina said, though until that moment nothing had been farther from her thoughts.

Daphne went over to one of the machines with a lithe step and arranged herself astride. She fiddled with the controls. 'Have to set myself a bigger challenge each time, don't you find that?'

'Er, well, I don't think I am as experienced as you.'
Darina looked at the machine next to Daphne's. Lulu
saw her trying to work out what the various dials
meant. She came over. 'Exercise often, do you?'

'Not very,' Darina confessed.

'I'll make it easy for you, then,' the girl said cheerfully. 'There, you should find that a doddle.' She went
back to Beth, wrapped her in a towel and said, 'You stay
there and have a nice rest, do you good.'

Darina started to pedal away. Beside her Daphne
was cycling at a steady pace. She had slipped off her
sweatpants to reveal the sort of Lycra shorts professional cyclists wore. Her legs were slim but seemed
amazingly strong, they drove the pedals with efficient
energy.

'Have the police finished with Paul Mallory, do you
know?' asked Darina. 'William has been cut right out of
the investigation,' she added.

Daphne threw her a swift glance. 'As far as I know,
they're holding him for further questioning. I think . . .'
She hesitated then added, 'I think they're waiting to find
out whether Shona's money is tied up in her foundation.'

'I thought you said it was,' Darina said, remembering their conversation beside the railway line above
Åndalsnes.

Daphne never broke the rhythm of her cycling.
'That's what Paul told me,' she said. 'But maybe that's
just what he wanted me and the police to believe,' she
added in a sad little voice.

Darina wondered just how devious Daphne could
be. Had Paul really told her that? Or was she trying to
distance herself from him and his involvement in
murder? Or was it all a double bluff? Was she trying to

create the illusion of a man on the verge of bankruptcy and herself as a harpy who wanted an out from their relationship, while all the time she remained madly in love with him?

Daphne said nothing more; she appeared to prefer to concentrate on her cycling. Darina found she had to work hard to keep a steady pace herself. But all the time little details were clicking into place as she remembered other fragments of Daphne's conversation with her and just what had happened at her cookery demonstration.

Once again she saw Michael Harwood's furious face and Shona Mallory's impassive countenance and heard the cacophony of voices rising in hatred against the scientist.

Then she saw again the twin profiles of Mervyn and Tara in the bar the previous evening. 'I'm adopted,' Tara had said.

Beth flung off the towel and rose, stretching her arms. 'That was wonderful,' she said expansively. 'Now I'd better have a bit of a workout too.'

She took the third cycle, set the controls and started keeping pace with Daphne.

Darina watched Daphne eyeing her sideways, then saw her up the tempo of her cycling. She must work hard at the health club she went to in Surrey! But Beth had no trouble keeping up with her. Of course, she was younger and had only just started on her machine.

Now Daphne was beginning to puff. So was Darina. She slowed down then stopped. 'That's enough for me,' she said. 'I need to get into training.'

Beth's face was set and she crouched in a professional manner over her machine. 'You need to have one at home, then you can exercise regularly,' she said, her voice steady.

Darina leaned on the handlebars of her machine and watched the two of them. Beth was going to win whatever contest it was they were involved in easily. Her legs pounded powerfully at the pedals, her face bore an expression of peaceful concentration. Daphne, on the other hand, looked furious. All at once she took a look at the milometer of the machine, said, 'That's me for today,' and stopped cycling. There was sweat running down her forehead.

'Got the old pores opened then, I see,' said Lulu, reappearing in the gym. 'Come back tomorrow and I'll help you with your technique.'

'My technique does not need help,' snapped Daphne. Then she caught herself. 'But thanks, Lulu, that was great.' She put on her sweatpants and walked stiffly towards the door. 'See you later, I hope,' she called to Darina.

'My, what a little paddy,' said Lulu, collecting towels.

Darina changed back into her trousers then called on the purser.

'My dear Darina,' he said with a big smile as she knocked at his open door. 'Come in, you're the best thing I've seen all day. Sit down and have some tea.'

'I'd love some,' said Darina, realizing that she hadn't had any lunch.

Francis picked up his telephone and gave the order. 'Now, have you just come for a chat or is there something I can do for you?'

320

'If you've got a moment, there's some information I need.'

'Name it,' Francis said promptly.

'I take it you've got all the personal details of all the staff under you?'

He looked slightly taken aback. 'Ye-es,' he agreed cagily.

'You know William's been working on Phil Burrell's disappearance,' Darina said quickly. 'Well, he's got caught up in another investigation and I wondered if you could let me see Phil's details.' She opened her eyes wide and looked straight at the purser.

The tea appeared. For a few minutes Francis was involved in pouring out and handing over a cup. Darina was delighted to see a plate of patisserie and helped herself to a large chocolate eclair.

'I do wonder what you are up to,' he said slowly. 'But for some reason I trust you and that husband of yours and, anyway, Phil's gone so I can't see much harm in it.'

He turned to his computer and brought up a company record card complete with photograph. Darina felt a catch in her throat as she looked at the open face of the stores manager.

'What was it you wanted to see particularly?' asked Francis.

'The details of his wife, well, ex-wife,' explained Darina.

'I'm not sure we've got those, I think Phil's divorce had gone through before he joined us.' Francis scrolled down the record. 'Oh, no, here they are. The decree nisi seems to have gone through after his contract with this *Empress* started. Is that what you need?'

321

Darina checked the name and age. 'Did you ever meet her?' she asked.

Francis shook his head.

'Your doctor, Ian Westlake, did. He said she was very large and formidable.'

'I know Phil had a terrible time with her. I remember he said once that she was so charming when he met her. Sexy and fun was the way he put it. But that all changed once they were married. I got the impression that was when she'd put on a lot of weight.

'Weight can be lost,' said Darina.

He looked at her curiously. 'Like to tell me what all this is about?'

'Later,' she said. 'I need to talk to William first.'

The phone rang. Francis almost leapt to attention as he answered it. 'Yes, sir,' he said into the receiver. 'At once, sir.' He put the phone down as though it had burned his fingers. 'That was the captain. I've never heard him sound so angry,' he said. 'I wonder what can have happened?'

Chapter Thirty-four

It was over an hour before Darina was able to catch up with William. She stationed herself in the main reception hall, through which most people seemed to pass on their way to whatever part of the ship they wanted, and eventually her patience was rewarded.

He came down the stairs together with Luther Conran. Both of them looked exceedingly pleased with themselves. They saw Darina waiting on the circular seating in the centre of the hall and came up to her.

'Anyone can see that was a successful operation,' she said.

William's grin broadened. 'Karen arrived back with an impressively large consignment of crack. As soon as she realized we were on to her, she told us everything.'

'Exactly as we, or rather, your husband, thought,' Luther said in his slow, resonant voice. 'Stupid bitch was conned into it by Summers with the lure of easy money and his charms at her beck and call. Only it didn't quite work out like that. The money's been there all right but I gather Summers hasn't exactly been the light of her life she thought he was going to be and it's all been a great deal more hard work than she'd ever imagined.'

'She said if she had to chat up one more set of

old-age pensioners and then get them to post off the drugs when the ship docked, she'd go mental,' William added.

'So congratulations all round?' Darina suggested.

'Well, the Norwegian police are delighted but the captain is less than pleased,' acknowledged her husband.

'Told us it was just as well the cruise was nearly over,' said Luther. 'Seeing as how his first officer and his cruise director have both been arrested. We gather Summers was facing an inquiry into his behaviour on his return anyway, but now two replacements have to be waiting when the ship docks at Southampton in a couple of days' time. The inspector is cock a hoop, thinks that even if we haven't been able to pin murder on the Mallory man he'll still go into retirement flushed with glory.'

'Have you let Paul go, then?' Darina asked.

'Had to. As he told us right at the start, it appears that apart from a relatively small sum set aside to clear his debts all his wife's lottery winnings are tied up in a trust fund for the foundation she's created. There's no evidence to connect him to his wife's death and now there doesn't seem to be a motive either. We've got to start at the beginning again. The Inspector is not happy but, as I said, the drug bust has definitely improved his day.'

'What are you doing with Karen Geary and Harry Summers?'

'Normally we'd be escorting them straight back to the UK by air but with the murder inquiry still going on, and the ship being so near home, they're under lock and key. They'll be taken off at Southampton docks,' said Luther.

'So that's all very satisfactory,' Darina congratulated them.

'Have you had a nice afternoon, darling?' William asked her.

'Well,' she said, 'I think it may have been quite productive.'

He looked at her questioningly.

'I think I may have some suggestions to make about who killed Shona Mallory. Is there somewhere private we can go?'

Luther Conran looked at her askance. 'Is she serious?' he asked William.

'Better believe it,' he said with a wry smile. 'She has a knack of sorting out murder.'

The inspector was with the purser dealing with the drug-smuggling paperwork so they were able to use the office that had been put at police disposal.

When Darina had finished her explanations, the two men looked at her in silence.

'You see, it does make sense of everything,' Darina said earnestly. 'Why Phil Burrell had to be ditched and how the killer knew all the working parts of the ship, and it gives the reason for murdering Shona Mallory.'

'My God,' said Luther. 'But what a story! Can it possibly be true?'

'How much can be checked out?' asked William matter of factly.

'You could start with Paul Mallory. He knew about the baby, perhaps he knows the names of the adoptive parents. It mightn't prove anything but it would certainly be circumstantial.'

'There's one piece of evidence I bet we could find on board,' said William.

Luther looked at him questioningly.

'If Darina's right, the killer will have Burrell's keys on their person.'

Darina gazed at him approvingly. 'Of course, why didn't I think of that?'

William gave her an old-fashioned look.

'You don't think they'll have been chucked overboard?' asked Luther.

William shook his head. 'They open too many doors, hold too many possibilities, who knows when they might come in useful. As long as the killer feels safe, the keys will be kept.'

'Do you think we should check the cabin first?'

'We can, of course,' said William, 'but I doubt there will be much to find. Our murderer is not going to leave hostages to fortune for stewards to mull over.' He rose. 'We might as well check, though. If we are fortunate, our murderer will be there, if not, the steward can let us in.' He looked at Luther, 'How about Inspector Rider, should we involve him at this stage?'

'Do you want the whole operation to grind to a halt?' Luther asked. 'Let's work on a need-to-know basis. Inspector Rider does *not* need to know.'

'I only asked,' said William mildly.

They went down to the cabin.

There was no answer to their knock so Luther found the steward and got him to open the door for them. The cabin was neat to the point of non-occupancy. There were no books beside the double bed, no bits and pieces lying around. Nothing was on the surfaces in the small bathroom, everything was stowed away in the small drawers and cupboards so liberally provided. Luther began opening these and shuffling through their contents.

William started on the wardrobes. 'Look in the dressing table,' he instructed Darina.

Feeling like an intruder in someone's home, Darina pulled down the vanity unit. Instantly lit with the courtesy lamp, the contents were displayed. Again, everything was neatly placed with not a speck of dust to be seen. No keys either.

She closed the unit and looked at the shelf above it. In her and William's cabin, physically so like this one, papers lay untidily either side of the television set. Port guides, the ship's newspaper, each day's timetable, an invitation to a party by the purser, the card with the details of their table in the restaurant, together with odd culinary notes Darina had made. Here there was nothing. She wondered if all these pieces of information had been thrown out or carefully put away somewhere.

'No keys in the bathroom,' said Luther, emerging.

'So far nothing in the wardrobes,' said William. 'What about the drawers, darling?'

Darina came to with a start. 'I'm sorry, I haven't looked,' she apologized. She opened the first of the long drawers underneath the vanity unit. Here were all the ship's bulletins, piled together at one side, pants on the other, shirts in the middle, all beautifully folded. She resolved to tidy their cabin as soon as she had a moment.

The other drawers were similarly ordered.

No keys.

William moved on to another wardrobe. He removed

the life jacket and checked that before starting on the next batch of garments.

Luther opened the bedside tables and then crawled on the floor to unzip the cases under the bed.

Nothing.

Luther rose from the floor and carefully dusted his knees.

'Nearly finished here,' said William, going through the pockets of a pair of trousers. 'It looks as though we'll have to proceed to the next step.'

The cabin door opened.

The wardrobe door William had opened hid Darina and prevented her seeing who stood there. She heard a startled voice say, 'What are you doing in my cabin?'

Through a crack between the wardrobe door and its side, she saw a hand holding a door key. The hand was trembling very slightly.

Then she saw the trousers ripped out of William's hand.

'How dare you!' the voice screamed at him.

Darina silently moved the door and saw William make an involuntary movement backwards and Luther rush forward.

A moment later a judo kick at his private parts rendered him helpless as the trousers were whipped across his face. He fell to the floor, groaning. The trousers' owner advanced on William, hands held up in a judo pose, legs apart as thought the feet were performing bare. 'Don't you try anything with me.' The whisper after the previous hysteria was mesmerizingly sinister.

Darina looked wildly about the cabin. Luther was moaning in agony, rolling from one side to the other, clutching himself while he tried to absorb the pain. He was out of it for the moment. So far the newcomer hadn't noticed her, but she had no weapon. The killer's reactions were so swift and well trained that if she made a move it had to be effective. The boat was still in port, was there the possibility of an escape into Bergen?

Darina lunged forward in a rugger tackle. Caught by surprise, the killer fell forward and brought down William as well. The two of them were on the floor, one knee was on William's chest and punches were being aimed at his head while one leg lashed out backwards. It caught Darina in the chest as she tried to rise and she was pushed backwards, grunting. But not before she'd managed to grab the strap of the bag the attacker wore over one shoulder. The strap broke.

Darina staggered back, the heavy bag coming with her.

William managed to get an arm free. He aimed a blow at his attacker but with lightning reflexes the head swayed out of range. With lethal strength one hand grabbed his arm and the other gave him a knockout punch.

Someone emitted a bloodcurdling yell.

Darina raised the one weapon she had and wielded the bag. It connected with the killer's head and the figure swayed, dazed.

Luther clambered to his feet and powered in.

Darina realized that the person yelling was herself and that it had brought the steward. 'Get help,' she shouted at him. 'Call the captain, the inspector, Stan Dobson.'

The steward gave the scene one startled look and disappeared.

Darina scooped the cover off the bed and together she and Luther managed to wrap it round the still stunned figure. Immediately, though, the powerful arms began to thrash at the quilt. They were without effect. Shona Mallory's killer was as helpless as a turkey trussed for Christmas.

Then Darina dropped to her knees beside William. 'Are you all right, darling?'

He shook his head, blinking. 'My God,' he said groggily. 'That was a close call.'

'After two killings, there was no point in holding back,' said Darina, helping him to rise. 'Are you sure you're all right? That was a hell of a blow you received.'

'I'll live. You didn't do badly with that bag.'

Darina picked it up from the floor and opened it. 'No wonder it was so heavy,' she said, taking out a large bunch of keys. 'I think these have to be Phil Burrell's.' She looked at the bundled figure. 'It didn't take him long to recognize you, despite all the weight you'd lost, did it, Beth? Or should I call you Lizzie?'

Chapter Thirty-five

On his way to the interview with Beth Cartright, William, showered and changed, was stopped by Stan Dobson.

'Can it wait?' asked William, his fingers twitching with impatience. Rider wouldn't hang around before starting the interview.

'It'll only take a minute,' Stan said and took him into one of the service stations, abruptly telling the steward sorting out a tea tray to make himself scarce for five minutes. William looked at him more closely. The security officer's face was grim. 'I've just been put in the picture regarding Mr Summers and Miss Geary.'

'Ah,' said William.

'You might have warned me!'

'Look, you know the form, Stan, we couldn't possibly have said anything to you.'

The security officer dragged his hand down his face, pulling at the grey looking skin. 'I'll have to resign.'

'You'd have cottoned on to what was going on soon enough, Stan. We just struck lucky.'

'I should have put things together the way you did. I'm getting too old for the job, that's the trouble. Can't keep up the way I did.' He gave a tired rub to his eyes.

'Have you spoken to Summers?'

Stan nodded. 'Stupid sod. Said Bergen was supposed to be the last job. He'd made a pile, reckoned they'd been lucky to get away with things as long as they had and that it was time to get out. He was planning on a shore life with plenty of women.'

'So he wasn't too worried about the effect that fight with Burrell in full view of the passengers might have on his career?'

'No, I raised it with him and he said it was a relief to be able to give the bastard what he deserved. Possessive chap, Summers, can't stand his woman spending time with another man.' Stan looked round the service area and turned off a kettle that was coming to the boil. 'I shall miss this ship. But it's time to hand in my cards, I can't live with failure, you know that.'

He left abruptly and William followed him. It was a relief that Stan hadn't been involved with Summers and Geary but he felt for the man. Not a good way to sign off his career. Now the ripples of the first officer's actions spread out, affecting so many lives and managing to obscure the reasons for Phil Burrell's death. Not something he'd intended but it had happened nevertheless.

As William reached the stores manager's office, Rider came out. 'We can do without your services,' he said, running a finger round his collar.

William looked at him. 'I've been closely involved throughout the case and, together with Sergeant Conran, was responsible for arresting Beth Cartright. I am now part of the investigation team.' If necessary, he'd pull rank but he hoped this should do the trick.

Rider held his gaze for no more than a couple of

seconds before he dropped his eyes and shrugged his shoulders, then opened the door on Conran and the prisoner. A few moments later the three policemen faced the girl across the office table.

Beth was hardly recognizable as the prim girl who'd sat beside William at the dinner table. She'd made no effort to smooth her dishevelled hair. The jacket of her trouser suit was torn at the shoulder and the sleeve hung down, revealing a flash of her white blouse. It should have suggested vulnerability but instead conjured up shark's teeth. And her eyes! Her pupils, hugely dilated, flickered wildly, not like those of a cornered animal seeking escape, more like a hyped-up addict desperate to find some way of expressing his volatility.

Phil Burrell's computer had gone from the table, and in its place was a tape-recorder. Luther Conran recited Beth her rights. As he heard the phrases he knew as well as the Lord's Prayer, William watched their prisoner. She hardly seemed to take in what was being said. Her hands plucked ceaselessly at her trousers, ironing the crease, picking off fluff, both real and imagined. Her body was so tense it seemed she might leap up any moment or lunge across the table. Her mouth was pulled down in ugly lines.

'I'm not sorry,' she burst out when Luther had finished. 'She deserved to die!'

Well, that got rid of one problem. If Beth had insisted she'd found the bunch of keys and was going to hand it in, they'd have had very little evidence on which to charge her.

'You admit you murdered Shona Mallory?' Inspector Rider asked.

'Of course!' Beth looked across the table at the three of them with contempt. 'She was a cow. She condemned me to utter misery but I gave her a chance to make up for it. So what did she do? She rejected me a second time!'

'You mean, Shona Mallory was your mother?' William knew the answer but needed everything to be made clear for their case against her.

' "Mother" isn't the right word,' Beth said scornfully. 'She bore me, that's about as much as you can say. Then she abandoned me.'

'You mean, she gave you up for adoption,' Luther said, as though explaining matters to a child.

'She abandoned me,' Beth shot at him again.

'She was very young and I understand from Paul Mallory she felt she was giving you into a good home, a better one than she could provide,' William said quietly.

'She knew bugger all and cared less. She never checked up to see what was happening to me.'

'And what would she have discovered?' William asked. Having got Beth to confirm her guilt, the inspector appeared happy not to take part in the questioning. He'd put himself next to the wall and now sat running a finger backwards and forwards along the top of the tape-recorder as he listened to the proceedings.

'That my adoptive father was killed in a car crash when I was three. That Angela, my weak adoptive mother, remarried an animal who brought out all her worst characteristics. My stepfather abused both her and me and Angela turned out to be as bad as he was. They took turns in hitting me, Walter because it was the only way he could get satisfaction and she because she couldn't control me. Walter abused me sexually as well, of course.' Beth's scorn was dismissive.

It was a dreadful picture but William would be prepared to lay long odds on Beth giving as good as she got. He wasn't surprised to hear her mother couldn't control her.

'A sad history but hardly enough to justify murder,' William said, provocatively.

'No? You're wife's expecting a child, you try hitting it every time it fails to meet your expectations – or just because you feel like hitting something. Then start watching your back as it grows up.'

'Your mother, Shona, was very young when she had you,' Luther said.

'Old enough to know what is due to a child,' Beth came back with, her voice low and violent. 'And when I'd tracked her down and gave her a chance to do better, what did she do?'

'Perhaps you will tell us,' said William, sure that there was no way Beth could be stopped now.

'She wrote to me saying that it was better if we didn't meet!' Beth's lips drew back in a snarl. 'She rejected me a second time. I told Phil,' she stopped abruptly.

'You were married to Phil Burrell at the time?' Luther enquired matter-of-factly.

Beth nodded. 'What a repressed so-and-so he turned out to be! After the first few months a snowman could give more comfort than him. He told me to forget about it. Forget about it! Forget my own mother disowning me twice!' Her anger was incandescent, making her eyes burn with an unholy light. William could only imagine what living with Beth would be like but contrasting her detached, disciplined personality when they'd first met with her anger now, he thought being plunged into first a fiery furnace and then a freezer would come somewhere near it. Retreating into a world of his own must have seemed the best option to Phil Burrell. Yet she must have appeared more normal initially. Perhaps her schizophrenic personality only emerged after they'd got married.

'You didn't have a child of your own?' asked William. 'Someone you could give the love to you never had yourself?'

'Hand on my family genes? Are you crazy?' She forced her hands to stop their plucking and brought them together on the table before her. Her manic air suddenly disappeared and she was once again the prim Beth he'd first met. 'It was because I wanted a child I tracked down my real mother. Angela had just died of cancer. Walter had gone from cirrhosis of the liver a few years earlier, no loss to anyone, that, but it was too late for Angela to make any sort of life for herself or for me. Anyway, I found a letter with Shona's name and her college address amongst her papers. I reckoned the college would be able to forward a letter. I really hoped we could get together, that I could tell her how terrible my life had been so that she could make it up to me and I'd know my real mother had a heart.' Beth hunched over the table. 'Sometimes,' she mumbled, speaking as though to herself, 'sometimes I frightened myself with how I felt. But I told myself that was because of how I'd been treated. Once I found my proper mother, every-thing would be all right.' Her head came up, blazing eyes met theirs. 'What do I get from her? A cold note that says it's better we don't meet.' Suddenly the manic

Beth was back with them. 'And Phil said I should forget about it! I told him I could never forget what my mother had done to me and I'd kill her the first opportunity I had.'

'So when he recognized you that first night, you knew he had to go.' Luther made it a statement.

'He'd have ruined everything!' Beth erupted. 'As soon as I read that bit in the newspaper and realized she was going to be on this boat, I knew I could do it. It would be easy to get her alone on deck one night in the dark, reveal who I was so she'd know exactly what was happening, then a quick bash on the head and a push overboard. It was going to be so simple – but then I ran into Phil. Such a shock, it had never occurred to me that he could be serving on this ship.'

William didn't suppose she'd given her ex-husband a thought since the divorce. He remembered her telling him at the dining table that she was a widow. As she indeed had been by then. He marvelled at the control she'd displayed. So different from the unstable person facing him now.

'So you put your plan into operation, only it was Phil you lured to that upper deck. No doubt he was intrigued to meet you again and went without a suspicion. Did you hit him before you pushed him overboard?' he asked her.

Beth nodded. 'I'd brought a heavy hammer with me. I was going to chuck it overboard together with Shona. I didn't throw it away after pushing Phil over, though, because I needed it for my mother.' She explained it all to them as though she was proud of her foresight. 'I hit him behind the ear and he dropped like a stone. Then I removed his keys. I'd sailed on the sister ship to this so I knew exactly where everything was and how I could make his disappearance look like suicide. I heaved him overboard, it was like handling a sack of flour, and went down to his office, this office,' she added, looking around the room as though seeing it for the first time, 'and left a message on his computer. I'm sure you've all seen it.'

'Did you empty his half-full bottle of whisky, too?' Luther asked.

Beth nodded. 'There's a bathroom attached to this office, well, you'll know that too, of course, and I poured it down the basin. But I had a couple of drinks myself, I needed them by then,' she said with an hysterical giggle.

'So you'd got rid of your ex-husband, who could have either prevented you killing your mother or exposed you as her murderer. What happened then?' asked William. Inspector Rider appeared to have lost interest in the proceedings. He'd given up running his finger along the tape-recorder and sat slumped in his chair, his eyes half closed.

'I waited for the right opportunity. And it came, oh, how it came! That cold cow confronted with her husband's infidelity and her friend's treachery. I saw in a moment how I could make it work. It was easy to fake drunkenness and make everyone think I was incapable of coming to dinner, let alone murdering someone. Easy too to convince Shona I had more evidence of her husband's unfaithfulness. It took quite an effort to get her to come on deck. She wanted to meet in her stateroom but I said I wanted to be quite sure we wouldn't be interrupted. And since that booby, her husband, had already been battering on her door, she came.'

'And then you found it was practically daylight on deck,' interposed William.

Beth gave another hysterical giggle. 'I should have realized! It wasn't as though I hadn't been on deck for several nights before! But, somehow, I hadn't thought. I said I knew a quiet place we could talk and called the lift. Once we were inside, a quick bash with the hammer and it was all over.'

'She didn't notice you were carrying one?' the Inspector shot in sceptically.

Beth, lost in her story, was startled by his sudden intervention. She swung towards him, her eyes glittering. 'No, of course not, it was in my bag.'

'As were the keys,' said William, remembering the large handbag Darina had wielded with such force.

'And then you took her down to the Stores Deck, opened the freezer and arranged her body behind the packs of frozen meat?' suggested Luther.

'Oh, it was so cold,' Beth complained. 'I thought I would get chilblains. But I had to be sure no one would notice her body.'

'Was she in fact dead?' asked William.

'Oh, yes,' Beth said blithely. 'Quite dead. I'm very good with a hammer.'

William shuddered. The woman was completely mad and getting madder by the moment. He wanted to get away from her and her savage, corrosive anger. But there were still a few loose ends to tie up. 'Why did you strip the body?'

She gave him the look a school teacher gives a very slow pupil. 'Because her clothes would have caught in the bandsaw. I knew if I could get her cut up and put down the mincer there was no way anyone would know

339

how she'd disappeared. People would think she'd thrown herself overboard, like Phil. I did consider leaving another note but a note that was exposed as a forgery would be worse than none at all. So I didn't. After all, there were all sorts of other people who wanted her dead. If her body was found, everyone would remember what a fuss there was about her genetic engineering nonsense during that sandwich demonstration on deck.'

'It was you who incited that, was it?' demanded William, remembering with disgust how upset Darina had been.

Beth looked smug. 'It only needed a shout or two after that farmer got going.'

'And no one saw you down on the Stores Deck?' asked Luther, getting back to the main investigation. 'I understand work goes on there at various times through the night.'

'There are long gaps for refreshment and things,' Beth said happily. 'The worst thing was the weight of the body and the way it was so stiff. But it had to be frozen so that the blood didn't spatter everywhere when the bandsaw got going. And it was difficult getting what was left of her back behind the frozen meat but that trolley helped a lot. The legs were quite easy, really, and another couple of nights and the whole body would have gone. All turned into sludge to be dumped into a suitable part of the ocean. She wasn't genetically modified so it shouldn't have hurt the fish and other denizens of the deep.'

Even with all his police experience, William felt quite sick. There was one question, though, he had to ask. 'Did Mrs Mallory know who you were before you killed her?'

340

Beth looked him full in the face. 'Oh, yes,' she said quietly. 'Once the lift doors closed, I told her.'

So the poor woman had known that what she'd tried to do for the best had proved her death warrant.

'What did you do with the hammer?' asked the inspector prosaically. He now seemed to be quite interested in the proceedings.

Beth was back to plucking at her trousers. 'Gone! Thrown overboard in a plastic bag with Shona's clothes. So you won't find it. I didn't need it any more, you see.' She grew thoughtful again. 'It was nearly the perfect murder, wasn't it? Not in the way I'd originally planned but just as effective. I took advantage of everything, the fight in the bar, Shona falling out with her husband, even the midnight sun. Everything played into my hands, everything but your wretched wife,' she said to William. She grew vituperative again. 'What right had she to be rummaging around the frozen meat locker? If it hadn't been for her, I'd have got away with it all.'

Chapter Thirty-six

Much later, when Beth, Karen Geary and Harry Summers were all under lock and key, Darina and William went for a drink in the Oyster Bar before dinner.

'I thought you'd be interviewing with the inspector and Luther for the whole evening,' said Darina, 'and I'd watch the last of our fjords disappear on my own.' For the ship had left Bergen already and was steaming out to the open sea, rugged mountains still holding pockets of snow falling away behind them. 'It was a delightful surprise to meet you outside the cabin and have you suggest we came along here.'

'I'm hoping we can have a quiet drink on our own without odd policemen, crooks, geriatric passengers or self-absorbed entertainers interrupting us.'

Darina squeezed his arm. 'My feelings exactly. I want to know exactly what happened with Beth.'

William gave as sober an account as he could of the interview. 'I've left Rider and Conran dealing with all the paperwork and organizing her reception when we reach Southampton,' he said finally.

Darina was silent. Then, 'What a dreadful story,' she said at last.

'Not a redeeming feature to it,' William agreed. 'But,

look, I think it's only fair if you tell me what put you on to prim little Beth as the Lethal Weapon before you give your statement to Rider. He's reserving you for tomorrow. I don't think he's looking forward to the experience of having you tell him what we all missed.'

Darina adjusted the set of her leopard-print scarf on her knitted silk cream two-piece and thought back. 'There were two things, really. First, I was sure that Phil had met someone from his past. Lulu said he looked as though he'd seen a ghost. Michael Harwood overhead him say, "God, I couldn't believe it." To me that meant he'd met someone he not only hadn't expected but who'd given him a great shock. And that it was someone who he would know was responsible when Shona Mallory disappeared.'

'You placed much more reliance on Michael Harwood's story than we did,' William said a little stiffly. 'Nor had we heard the ghost bit from the keep fit girl.'

'I've been in a privileged position,' Darina admitted. 'You kept me in touch with the police investigation and I've been able to pick up all sorts of other bits and pieces.'

The drinks arrived and Darina paused and took a reviving sip of her white wine.

'Beth was a puzzle from the moment she appeared at our table but I didn't really suspect her of being involved at all until yesterday evening when I watched her drink several powerful dry martinis and remain apparently sober. Yet at Enid's drinks party she had seemed so overcome by alcohol that she was unable to join us for dinner.'

'I should have picked up on that,' said William gloomily.

'Of course, neither you nor Luther was at Enid's party,' Darina said gently. 'Then Beth obviously had a deep grudge against her parents, especially her stepfather. I could see her hate the way Tara said her childhood as an adopted daughter was brilliant. Once I learned from Daphne that Shona had had an illegitimate child that she'd given up privately for adoption, it didn't take much imagination to work out that if the child had been Beth, she would have resented bitterly the mother who had been responsible for her unhappy childhood. No wonder she grew up such a repressed and warped character.

'I think the worst thing as far as Beth was concerned was Shona Mallory's rejection of her after she tried to get in touch. The resentment that built up during her unfortunate childhood, turned to bitter hatred.'

'Was that when she got so fat?' asked Darina.

'How did you guess? She said food was her only comfort and she put on three stone in two years. Reading between the lines, I don't think the marriage would ever have been a great success, Beth was too controlling, Phil unable to cope with her. I should think her adoptive mother must have felt equally helpless. Beth hasn't suggested Phil hit her, though. I think he retired into his shell instead.

'Another thing that made me think was her abrupt departure from the bar when Ian Westlake started flirting with her. When he checked me over after the fight, I filled him in on Beth and he was flabbergasted. He said he'd never have recognized her, she was very fat when he was first introduced to her, with long, dark hair. But she was scared he would know who she was.'

344

'He did say he had the impression they'd met before,' murmured William.

'Phil, of course, met her before she'd gained all that weight, no trouble for him to recognize her even with a change of hair colour. It must have been a shock for her to find he was on this ship.'

William nodded. 'She's always been a loner, never made friends. She reckoned even if she did meet someone she'd served with, it had been so long ago and she looked so different, they wouldn't give her a second glance.'

'Did she say she wanted some of the lottery money?'

William shook his head. 'No, Beth says she has no need of material things, she only wanted to make Shona pay for the misery she had condemned her to.'

'What about her father?'

'Says she wasn't interested to find out who he was. It was her mother who had given her away, it was she who was responsible for Beth's ruined life. But what made you so sure she was Phil Burrell's ex-wife?'

'I got Francis, the purser, to show me his records. There was the name, Elizabeth. Apparently when she was married to Phil, she was known as Lizzie.'

'Sorry to interrupt you,' said a voice, 'but I want to thank you for proving my innocence.' Paul Mallory stood beside Darina.

He looked thinner and older than when she'd last seen him.

William got up. 'Can I get you a drink?'

'Thanks, I'll join you in a beer,' he said, sitting down heavily and giving a deep sigh. 'This has been the most terrible few days of my life. I still can hardly believe that Shona's dead. And then to have been accused of her murder like that,' he shook his head incredulously. 'Was it really Shona's daughter who killed her?'

'I'm afraid it was,' Darina said. 'Daphne said you knew about her illegitimate child.'

'Shona told me before we were married. Nothing about the father but I gathered he had died.' William returned with the beer. Paul thanked him and drank some. 'Shona was very reticent, always. It – well, it made communication with her difficult at times.'

'It must be in the genes,' said Darina quietly.

'But Shona could never have been capable of the vileness that was in the letter the girl sent her.' Paul looked down at his hands, turning them over as though they belonged to someone else. 'She didn't show the letter to me, I found it when she asked me to fetch her passport from her desk just before we were married. I don't normally read other people's correspondence but it was below the passport and a couple of words caught my eye. They weren't the sort of words you could ignore. So I couldn't stop myself. It threatened Shona with terrible things and was the most horrible letter you could imagine. She came in just as I finished reading it, she thought I couldn't find the passport. She saw immediately what had happened and told me everything. Apparently the girl had got in touch out of the blue and Shona had refused to see her. She didn't think any purpose would be served.' He shook his head. 'Shona was amazing like that. She found it very difficult to see things from anybody else's point of view. The fact that the girl had been desperate to contact her real mother quite escaped her.' He sighed heavily. 'Anyway, Shona asked me what she should do about this second letter. It was the only time I ever saw her in doubt about any action of hers. At that stage, having read the letter, it seemed crystal-clear to me. I told her not to reply and certainly not to tell the girl she was getting married. With a new name and a new address, she should be safe from any further harassment. As far as I knew, that was the end of the matter.' He sighed bitterly. 'If only Shona hadn't won that damn lottery money!'

There was silence for a moment then Darina asked, 'What will you do now?'

Paul's face cleared. 'I shall be all right. Shona made me a director of the foundation, with a proper salary, and gave me a public relations contract. I'd got her to see there was a big job to be done there, as important in its way as the research she wanted to ensure was carried through. She said we need to know much, much more about the effect of genetic modifications to plants and I said that the public needs to rebuild trust in scientific research and to learn not to be afraid of new technology.' Paul spoke quietly but his phrases were well honed. The job was obviously going to be one he was well suited to.

'Will Julian be able to get his agency started?' asked William.

Paul gave a slight smile. 'Not in the way he wants, no. But I think Shona was right that it wouldn't help him to have the sort of financial backing he imagines he needs. I'm sure I can find a few thousand from somewhere though, enough for him to get Tara launched.' He leaned back in his chair, expansive, in control. 'He's been lucky there, she's got talent and if he can't make her a success he shouldn't be in the business.'

'And what about Daphne?' asked Darina, determined to get to the bottom of his relationship with her.

'What about Daphne?' said Daphne's voice.

Paul looked up and his face broke into a warm
smile. He rose. 'Come and sit down, darling. I've just
been catching up with this dreadful business of Shona's
murderer.'

'Ah, yes,' said Daphne with a sweet little smile, 'it
was her daughter, wasn't it?'

Darina wondered if there was anyone on the ship
who didn't know what had happened yet.

Daphne sat elegantly in the chair Paul produced,
William waved at a waitress and a dry martini was
ordered.

Paul smiled again and put out a hand to Daphne.
She caught and held it in her own. He looked at Darina.
'Daphne has been my rock through all this. She never
doubted me.'

Darina glanced at Daphne and received a long, cool
look in return. Would she ever know the truth about
the woman?

'I hated deceiving Shona but the fact was, she
should never have married. She could never understand about sharing someone else's life. She was far too
wrapped up in her work, too undeviating in her principles. What I need is someone warm, who understands
me and what I need out of life. Daphne, in fact!'

Darina thought that was what most people needed
and wondered whether Daphne would continue to
supply the love and understanding. She gave William's
thigh a small caress and enjoyed the immediate feel of
his hand on hers.

'I thought,' said Paul, leaning forward and altering

completely the tone of his voice. 'I thought that I'd ask that farmer who made all the fuss at your demonstration, Darina, if he'd agree to act as a consultant to the foundation. Make a terrific story, doubter taken on board as adviser, show how open-minded we are and how determined the foundation is to take protesters seriously. Do you think he'd agree?'

'Why don't you ask him,' suggested Daphne. 'He's just coming in.'

Darina looked up and saw Joyce Harwood enter the bar, hobbling on two crutches. Behind her was Michael with the nearest to concern she'd so far seen on his face. Joyce caught Darina's eye and paused to give her a small wave, then sat down at a table near the door, wincing as she did so. Her husband hovered over her until she was settled, then stumped over to the bar and gave them an order.

'I'll go and have a word now,' said Paul. He got up and went over.

They all watched him as he spoke first to Joyce, quite clearly asking how she was, then rose as Michael returned to his wife. He shook his hand, Michael looking too startled to protest. A moment later they were both seated with Paul talking earnestly to the farmer.

'Pound to a penny he doesn't accept,' said William.

'Paul can be very persuasive,' said Daphne.

They saw Michael's face darken and him spitting angry words at Paul.

'I think your money's safe,' Darina told William.

But Paul held up his hands in a brief gesture of surrender and talked some more.

Daphne stroked the skirt of her short peacock-blue

crêpe de Chine dress that draped itself lovingly round her well-toned figure. She said nothing, but her small smile deepened. She lit a cigarette. As the first puff of smoke curled from out her mouth she said, 'For once I shan't be sorry to see the back of a holiday. It can't have been an easy time for you two, either.'

Darina and William agreed that there had been definite difficult patches.

'But no doubt you've enjoyed being together.'

Again they both agreed that that was so.

'And do I understand you are pregnant?'

'I have to have an official test done but, yes, I think I am.' Darina laughed suddenly. 'I knew it before but this cruise has made me very aware how important it is to be a good parent.'

'Good Lord, you're so right!' Daphne agreed.

Paul was suddenly back. 'No go as an adviser, I'm afraid,' he said with a rueful grin. 'But I've agreed that the foundation will buy their farm to use for growing experimental crops under strictly controlled conditions. We'll pay a good price, enable them to make a new start.' He looked very satisfied with himself. 'Now, darling, shall we have that stroll we promised ourselves and see the last of Norway?'

Daphne rose immediately. 'Thanks for the drink,' she said to William. 'See you around, no doubt,' she added to Darina.

As the two of them left the bar, Jim and Mary French entered. Mary's mouth tightened as she saw Daphne.

Daphne gave both of them a beaming smile and swept out with Paul.

Jim French followed them with his eyes, then

slipped his arm through his wife's and took her into a corner of the bar, making much of her.

'Another little thread tied up,' Darina said as Enid entered.

'I've been looking everywhere for you,' she cried, coming straight up to them, her manner agitated and her cardigan slipping off her back. 'Is it true what I hear?'

'What do you hear, Enid?' asked William with a sigh.

'That Beth Cartwright, the Beth Cartwright who sits on our table, killed that officer who disappeared and the lottery winner.'

'Yes, I'm afraid it is,' said William, then stood up with a look of relief as Stan Dobson appeared in the doorway to the bar and waved at him. 'Excuse me, I think I'm wanted,' he said. 'I'll be back in a minute.'

Darina watched him leave with a sinking feeling. Nothing else could happen on this cruise, surely?

Enid sat down heavily, her leathered face had the look of a collapsed rugby ball, all the breath knocked out of her. 'Oh, my,' she said. 'And she seemed such a nice girl. Quiet. Such an odd diet but very soft spoken and polite. Not at all like so many young people today.'

Darina had a quick image of quiet Beth taking on three people and very nearly managing to come out on top. 'I think she only showed one side of herself at dinner,' she said gently.

'This cruise hasn't been like any other I've taken,' mourned Enid. She'd lost all her bounce and vigour. 'I don't know what George would have said.'

Darina waved at a waitress then ordered a vodka martini for Enid. 'That will make you feel more cheerful,' she said firmly. 'And just think, you'll have enough stories from this cruise to entertain everyone on trips for years to come.'

'If I can bring myself to book any more.'

'Of course you can. After all, think of the number you've been on already without anything like this happening.'

'That's true,' Enid said, beginning to recover her spirits.

Her drink arrived and she attacked it with enthusiasm. 'That's better,' she said, sitting back in the chair and looking around the bar. 'Oh, there are Joyce and Michael Harwood!' She leant forward and said in a piercing whisper to Darina, 'I met them at tea, they'd just come back from the hospital. He went off to fetch her a book from the cabin and I asked Joyce exactly what happened to her on that train.'

Darina couldn't resist asking back in another whisper, 'And what had?'

'Joyce said she'd used the handle on the door to the carriage to help pull herself up, you remember there wasn't a platform and you know how steep those steps are on Continental trains. Well, apparently the door moved, she slipped and before she knew it she was on the track with her hip hurting like anything.'

Darina felt an enormous sense of relief. She really hadn't thought Michael Harwood had tried to pull his wife off the step, it would have been such a silly thing to do, but it was good to have confirmation. 'And Michael actually went and fetched her book for her?'

Enid grinned, looking much more like her old self. 'Amazing, isn't it? Sometimes takes a shock like that to bring a man to his senses. Thought too much of his own worries, not enough of her, that was the trouble.'

More of the vodka martini disappeared.

'Enid,' said Darina after a moment.

'Yes, dear?'

'Do you mind if I ask you something personal?'

'If I do, I won't answer, so ask away.'

'What happened to your child?'

Darina was dismayed to see Enid wilt, like a plant deprived of water. Her colour vanished and all her cheerfulness disappeared. She put out a hand. 'I'm sorry, I shouldn't have asked, forget I said anything.'

Enid rallied. 'No, dear, it's all right. It was so long ago.' She sighed heavily. 'Yet it seems only a few years as well. What is it about time that it can do that to you?' Darina said nothing. 'Well, anyway,' continued Enid, 'it was Duchenne's disease.'

Darina looked blank.

'It's a form of muscular dystrophy. We found out when Jackie was two and a half. That was such a dreadful day. I'd been so worried about him because he didn't seem to be as ahead as other boys his age and he walked in such a funny way, it was a sort of waddle.' Enid passed a finger under each eye in a swift action then said fiercely. 'The doctor said he'd inherited it from me. The female is the carrier and only boys are affected. The doctors said he'd never get better, only worse. Poor Jackie never grew very bright, he was in a wheelchair by the time he was ten and he died of a heart attack a year later. When we found out about it all, George said we shouldn't have any more children but I said the good Lord would make sure the next one didn't suffer in that way and the doctor said usually only fifty per cent of boys in a family had the disease. But I didn't get pregnant again.' She paused for a moment. 'Perhaps that was the Lord's way of making sure I didn't pass on my genes. Because if we'd had a girl, she might have had a child like Jackie.'

Darina couldn't help thinking of the way Enid had so roundly condemned the technology that might be able to ensure no future child was born with such a genetic disease. What faith she had! 'I'm really sorry,' Darina said. 'It must have been the most dreadful experience.'

'It was wonderful,' Enid said fiercely. 'I loved every minute of Jackie, even with all his troubles. He was a gorgeous child and never seemed to mind that he couldn't do everything other boys could. The day we found out about his disease wasn't nearly so awful as the day he died. I adored him just as you'll adore that child you're carrying.'

Without conscious thought, Darina put her hand on her stomach. Was there really a baby in there? She prayed it would be healthy and normal. Then wondered what normal really was. Beth, surely, wasn't. Yet to the outward eye, she appeared healthy and attractive.

William came back. 'I'm sorry, I'm going to take my wife away,' he said to Enid. 'Will you forgive us?'

'What's happened?' asked Darina as soon as they were outside the bar.

'Nothing. I just wanted you to myself for a little.'

'You mean they haven't discovered another dead body?'

'No,' he looked amused.

'Nor drug smugglers?'

'No.'

'Nor rats leaving the ship?'

'Nothing has happened.' He took her arm and started walking her towards the dusk outside – the midnight sun was far behind them now. 'Stan has just been with the captain and wanted to give us an invitation from him for lunch in his day cabin tomorrow.'

'What an honour!' Darina was amazed; the captain, genial though he had been at his cocktail party, had seemed to her godlike, separate from both passengers and crew.

'Better believe it. And Stan tells me that Roger Coutts has found some lobsters in the fish freezer so we shall have a feast.'

'I'm glad it won't be steak!'

'I wondered if you'd like me to organize dinner for us in our cabin rather than have to join the others. It's been a hell of a day and I'd like my wife to myself for a little. If I let you loose amongst the passengers, you'll be finding out if Mervyn really is Tara's father and who knows where that will lead!'

Darina laughed. 'No, I promise not to.'

'Even so, we haven't got much time left to be just us together before the sprog arrives.'

'You're going to love it, you know you are.' Darina smiled at him. 'And I shall too. I love being with you, you know I do, but isn't the cabin a bit confined for eating a meal in? We could always go to bed early after dinner.'

William kissed her tenderly. 'As long as we're together, I don't mind sharing you with the rest of the table.'

'Good,' said Francis Sterling, coming up alongside, 'because I want you to join me for a drink after dinner.

I must hear all about this ghastly business with Phil's ex-wife.'

William and Darina looked at each other and broke into laughter.

'You win,' said William to Francis. 'We'll be delighted to join you. But, please, anywhere but the Oyster Bar.'